Received on:

tarnish

tarnish

Katherine Longshore

VIKING

An Imprint of Penguin Group (USA) Inc.

VIKING
Published by the Penguin Group
Penguin Group (USA) Inc.
375 Hudson Street
New York, New York 10014, U.S.A.

USA / Canada / UK / Ireland / Australia / New Zealand / India / South Africa / China
Penguin Books Ltd, Registered Offices: 80 Strand, London WC2R 0RL, England

For more information about the Penguin Group visit www.penguin.com

First published in the United States of America by Viking, an imprint of Penguin Group (USA) Inc., 2013

LIBRARY OF CONGRESS CATALOGING-IN-PUBLICATION DATA
Longshore, Katherine.
Tarnish / by Katherine Longshore.
p. cm.
Summary: "At the English court, King Henry VIII's interest in Anne Boleyn could give her an opportunity to make a real impact in a world with few choices for women, but when poet Thomas Wyatt reveals he's fallen for her, Anne must choose between true love and the chance to make history"—Provided by publisher.
ISBN 978-0-670-01400-2 (hardcover)
1. Anne Boleyn, Queen, consort of Henry VIII, King of England, 1507–1536—Juvenile fiction. 2. Great Britain—History—Henry VIII, 1509–1547—Juvenile fiction. [1. Anne Boleyn, Queen, consort of Henry VIII, King of England, 1507–1536—Fiction. 2. Great Britain—History—Henry VIII, 1509–1547—Fiction. 3. Kings, queens, rulers, etc.—Fiction. 4. Sex role—Fiction. 5. Love—Fiction.] I. Title.
PZ7.L864Tar 2013 [Fic]—dc23 2012032988

Printed in U.S.A.

1   3   5   7   9   10   8   6   4   2

Set in Legacy Serif ITC Std   Designed by Kate Renner

To my sister, Martha, because the Longshores stick together.
Thank you for being the one to pick up the phone.

Greenwich Palace
1523

1

A DEEP BREATH IS ALL IT TAKES TO ENTER A ROOM.

Or to scream.

Or both.

I stand against a wall, five strides from the great oak door of the queen's apartments. The guard watches me sideways, pretending he's not. Pretending he's focused on the stairwell. The pretense fails to deceive me.

I haven't asked to enter. Nor can I turn and walk away. Before reentering the queen's service, I must solicit her welcome. And he knows it. I know he's looking at my risqué French hood. At the black hair it exposes. At my misshapen little finger. I shake my sleeve to cover it.

I know he's thinking about my family. My sister.

We stand like effigies, pretending not to stare at each other.

The walls loom, gray as the rain outside. Like the sky of England itself. Everything seems colorless and humbled, despite the layers of velvets and tapestries, the peacock plumage of courtiers and ladies. Greenwich Palace feels like my father's disappointment made tangible.

I take another deep breath and straighten my shoulders, just as Father taught me when he marched me into the presence of Margaret of Austria, the Duchess of Savoy. I was seven years old and terrified to be left in her care. Father offered only one piece of advice before abandoning me and returning to England. "When you're afraid," he said then, "you need to put an iron rod in your spine. Look your enemy in the eye. Take a deep breath and perform."

The prodigal daughter, he calls me now. Or he would if he were here.

I wipe the sweat from my palms on my skirt and approach the guard, who leers as if he knows all about me and opens the door. I blow him a kiss as I pass by, accompanied by a rude gesture. He pretends not to notice, and again fails to deceive me.

There is something of the dragon's lair in the royal chambers of a palace. And Queen Katherine's chambers don't shatter that illusion. Smoke from the candles congeals at the ceiling in a swirling, palpable mass. And the place swarms with courtiers ready to eviscerate you socially and politically.

Another breath, and I step into the presence of the queen. I have a feeling she won't be happy to see me return. My first duty is to kneel before her until she acknowledges me, and thank her. I worry that she will ignore me—more punishment for my indiscretions. And my sister's.

The room quiets as I enter. I bow my head and approach the queen. She is sewing tiny stitches around the cuffs of a shirt, embroidering a pomegranate motif of white on white. I watch her hands from beneath my lowered brow. They don't pause.

I kneel. She doesn't speak.

But behind me, I hear the whispers.

"Who is that?"

"What's she wearing?"

"She's one of *them*."

"That's the sister? They don't even look related."

"Perhaps they're not."

I struggle not to turn around and give the speaker the sharp edge of my tongue. Protocol demands that I not even look up until the queen acknowledges me.

Then I hear a giggle. Followed by another. And another. Like ripples on a pond.

I'm the stone that caused them and I'm sinking.

I curl my hands into fists under the folds of my sleeves. I know why they belittle me. They see me as the daughter of one of the king's minions—as the youngest of a family of parvenu graspers. They saw me return from France a year ago, only to leave three months later, dressed in humility and veiled in disrepute. Exiled by my expansively critical father. And now returned, supposedly reformed, though yet to be redeemed in Father's eyes.

"Mistress Boleyn."

I look up at the queen. The year has not been kind to her. Her face has fallen into soft folds, like a discarded piece of velvet. Still rich and soft, but a touch careworn. She's five years older than the king and she wears those years like eons. Her eyes reveal nothing to me—not malice, not kindness, not curiosity, not forgiveness. Queen Katherine has lived a lifetime at court and has mastered the art of giving nothing away. Her hands go still.

"I welcome you."

I hear a *tut* and a titter, as if one of her ladies questions the sincerity of that statement. The queen presses her lips together, but before anyone can speak, the door bangs open behind me, followed by a roomful of gasps and a trill of hysterical laughter.

I turn before the queen can grant me permission and see, there in the doorway, five men dressed in silks and scimitars, each with a turban wrapped around his head. Their eyes are white and wild.

Ottoman corsairs.

In England?

I steal a glance at the queen. She stifles a yawn behind a look of artful surprise.

King Henry is famous for his disguisings. For bursting into the queen's rooms in all manner of dress and disarray. For fooling no one, but delighting everyone. Except, it seems, the queen.

"We have come from Gallipoli and the coasts of Spain, searching for plunder." The voice—despite its rolling, guttural accent—starts a hum in my mind, a buzz of recognition at the top of my head.

"And women," another man mutters, his Kentish lilt completely at odds with his appearance.

The others laugh.

I risk a glance at the corsairs. The shorter man by the door is somewhat disheveled, and would be familiar to me even if he actually had traveled from the other side of the world. My brother. Next to him is the Kentishman, his blond hair curling from beneath his turban. He carries himself with the effort-

less ease of a dancer, and his eyes are the exact color blue that makes me wish he'd look at me.

But it's the man nearest me whose attention I'd do anything to have. He is tall and broad, his hand ridged with rings. His face—a little long, losing its narrowness, a hint of a cleft to his chin, and a mouth with a smile like a kiss—is so etched in my memory, I hardly know if he's real or a fevered imagining. The hum in my head increases, as if my entire body is tuned to his presence.

I remember the first time I saw him, gilded like a church icon, fashioned for worship. And the last time I saw him, shock transfiguring his face. I lower my eyes and stare at his broad-toed velvet shoes, decorated in pearls and gold embroidery. Breathe.

He walks boldly to the queen. He doesn't bow or acknowledge her rank and gentility. A moment unfurls between them during which no one moves or speaks. No one is allowed into the presence of the queen without obeisance. Except the king. He turns, his movements swift and decisive.

"Which one shall we take?" His voice is surprisingly high for a man so large, a presence so Herculean. The others reply with a roar and rattle of scimitars.

The feet turn again, toes pointed directly at my skirts.

"What about this one?"

He's dropped the accent. His words are full of tones round and rich like butter.

He reaches for my hand, his touch like a blinding jolt of sunlight. The fingers feel rougher than I expected, hardened

by hunting and jousting and wielding a sword and lance. They carry the scent of orange flowers, cloves, and leather. I do not require his hand to lift me up. I could fly.

I do not look at him, but stare at my hand in his. He twists the ring on my index finger, the single pearl disappearing into my palm. I will my heart—my tongue—not to make a fool of me. Again.

The queen puts a hand on my shoulder, her grip like a tenterhook, fastening me to the spot. I'm stretched between the two of them.

"I cannot permit you to spirit away my maids of honor, Master Turk," the queen says, with no hint of humoring the corsair. And perhaps a touch of disdain. "It is an affront to Spain and an affront to God, what you do."

Her soft voice with its strong Spanish lilt hisses across the room, and four of the men nod their heads in shame. The real corsairs have been raiding the Spanish coast. Stealing women. Some say the king does the same thing from the queen's chambers.

"This one belongs to me." The queen pats my shoulder once.

He drops my hand. I watch his eyes, fixed on the queen. There is a spark of anger there. And a deep burn of petulance.

I want to reach out. To take back his hand. To tell him, *I will be anything you want! I'll play your game!*

I tilt my chin to see the queen. She smiles at me benignly. Motherly.

"On the contrary, Your Majesty," I blurt. "I am not a possession and belong to no one."

The hush that follows mantles the room like deafness after cannon fire. The queen swells, and I'm sure the shock on her face is no match for the shock on mine. I fall into a curtsy, ready to grovel an apology, but I'm cut off by a laugh like wine in a fountain—singular and intoxicating.

Followed by the laughter of every person in the room—except the queen.

I risk looking up to see her hard-edged gaze returned to the man before her.

"Possession or not, I will not take her from you, my lady," he says, sweeping a bow over her hand and kissing it. "Because my heart belongs to you."

He removes his turban, revealing sun-bright auburn hair. The ladies gasp in false astonishment and curtsy low before him.

The queen just smiles tightly.

"My dear husband."

The other men remove their ridiculous headgear, revealing the king's companions. Henry Norris, his black hair brushed back from his wide forehead, mouth twisted in an ironic grin. My brother, George, his hair mussed as if he's just risen from his bed, eyes lighting on every girl in the room. My cousin Francis Bryan, with eyes like a fox and a grin like a badger. And the man by the door, all golden-blond curls and startling blue eyes.

The king flicks a single finger, and the musicians in the corner begin to play a volta. The queen sits back down on her cushioned chair, the motion as overt a signal as her husband's. She will not be dancing.

The king bends at the waist to speak to me, still on my knees before the queen. He exudes cedar, velvet, and élan. The hum traverses to my fingers and toes, followed by a frisson of terror that my incontinent speech will get me flogged or pilloried. Or worse, exiled from court. Again.

"Mistress Boleyn."

I bow my head further, unable to look at him. Unable to utter another word.

"Welcome back."

2

THE DUCHESS OF SUFFOLK AIMS A LAYERED LOOK AT ME FROM beneath her gabled hood as she steps between me and the king. One side of her mouth twists upward, the other down. Then she turns her back on me. She is the king's younger sister, and despite the death of Louis XII eight years ago, still styles herself Queen of France. In a court ruled by tradition as much as royalty, she has precedence of rank over everyone but Queen Katherine herself, so the king will dance with her first.

My own brother is lounging against the doorframe, mouth open in a laugh, but his face is bitter. The blond man next to him echoes the laugh, but not the bitterness, and it sparks a flicker of memory. It's like a glimpse of something caught at the corner of the eye: a golden boy reaching for the sun against the shadowed gray stone of what used to be my home. The image slides away, taking any hint of the man's name with it. He nudges George, nods his head at me.

My brother's eyes are the same color as mine—dark. So dark that sometimes you can't tell if they have a color at all. His face quickly loses any trace of mirth, but I can see the hesitation in his frame.

Our childhood friendship has been lost in the depths of the

English Channel and in the mire of the years I spent in France, growing up and away from him. But he is the closest thing I have to an anchor here in the English court, so I smile, and his hesitation breaks, propelling him forward. Toward me.

I notice little Jane Parker in the corner, watching George. She twists her knuckles into her teeth, her expression screaming her every emotion. She's besotted.

"Welcome back, Anne."

George leads me into the improvisational dance steps we used to practice in the apple orchards of our childhood, back when he would drop me accidentally on purpose and collapse on top of me, shouting that I'd broken his back with my weight, and then giggling uncontrollably.

Now he holds me firmly. And doesn't laugh.

As we circle the room in the precisely measured steps of the dance, I see faces turn away from me. The ladies study their hands or the windows or the other dancers. The men don't even pretend. They just don't look.

"Why do they hate me, George?" I ask. I keep my voice quiet, so he can pretend not to hear me.

"They don't hate you, Anne. Not yet. They just choose to ignore you. And your indiscretions. You're like the green castle in the middle of the room that nobody wants to see." His lips twitch as he tries not to smile at his own joke.

"*The Château Vert* was a year ago, George."

"Yes, and everyone remembers it as a triumph and a gorgeous display. The castle! The costumes! The pageant!" George twirls me once, out of step, causing me to stumble.

"The dancing." He catches me and holds me tightly, his grip as hard as his voice, fingers pinching the tender skin over the bone.

My dance with the king. One stupid mistake. One mindless, improvident action based on a ridiculous infatuation. It got me exiled.

"Am I never going to be allowed to forget it?"

"Certainly not if you controvert the queen. Or throw yourself at the feet of the king, though it certainly saved your skin today."

I say nothing. Just as he wishes.

"You are here to be useful. Not a hindrance. Your only purpose is to advance our family. If you can't do that, you might as well have stayed at home."

"Home?"

Home for George is Hever, where I was born. The place from which I've just escaped exile. Home for me is France, where I grew up. I would love to be sent home. Away from England. Away from the eyes that stare but don't look at me.

"Or been married off to James Butler and both of you sent to Ireland with the uncivilized ruffians. You'll fit right in."

"That betrothal hasn't been agreed upon." I don't react to his criticism.

"Close enough," George mutters.

"James Butler is like a bear, only less sophisticated."

This teases a smile from George, and I want more. I want to feel closer to him, as though, somehow, the time and distance between us can be breached.

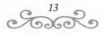

"I'd marry a bear to get my birthright." The smile disappears. "And you're set to steal it from me."

"I'm not stealing it, George! The earldom of Ormond is Father's. It's yours."

"Father would happily give it to your fiancé if it means pleasing Cardinal Wolsey."

"James Butler isn't my fiancé. It's not my fault Wolsey wants to appease the Irish lords by giving Grandmother's inheritance to the Butlers. I don't want your birthright."

"You don't want to be a countess?"

"Not if it means marrying James Butler."

"You should take what you can get, Anne. The only way a woman can advance in this world is through marriage. And the only way anyone can get ahead in this court is through peerage. Without a titled husband, you are nothing."

"Like Mother?" I slather those two words with all my bitterness.

As we begin a turn, I catch a glimpse of pain on his countenance, but it is gone when he faces me again.

"Mother is a Howard. Descended from dukes."

"That hasn't secured her a place in their hearts." I fling out a hand, indicating the queen, the Duchess of Suffolk, the king. Mother is no longer at court. Not exiled, just not invited.

"You don't need a place in their hearts, Anne. You need a place in their circle." He pauses. "Unlike Mother."

"And how am I to accomplish that?"

"Marry well."

"And until then?"

"Stop saying whatever comes into your head."

I laugh hollowly. "You know me too well to think—"

"Then at least make an effort to look the same as everyone else," he says, exasperated. "Any circle is broken by an odd piece."

"Is that how you see me?" My tone is teasing, but I extract the words like splinters from my throat. "As an odd piece?"

George takes my question seriously.

"You have to be more like the others if you want to be accepted at court. Your sleeves are too long and your bodice too square. Your hood and your accent are too French. You are too different."

"I'll take that as a compliment."

"It wasn't intended as one."

"Different isn't synonymous with defective," I tell him. Though George has managed to make me feel that way.

"But conformity is synonymous with success."

"Baa-a-a," I bleat.

We separate in the dance and I turn to the room, confronted by quickly averted suspicious glances. I've just been caught making barnyard noises in the queen's chambers. I lower my eyes and come back to George, who laughs at me.

"Just like sheep," he says. "Act like the others. Join in the conversations. Fit in. This isn't France, you know."

"Yes, I know that all too well."

"They are our enemies now." He lowers his voice.

I don't. "Not mine."

"Don't say that too loudly, Anne."

"Friendship is not dictated by the whims of kings and Parliament, George, but by the heart. I spent seven years of my life in France. I know nothing else."

I turn away, rubbing my hands against my skirts, ready to leave the room. But George takes my wrist, spins me back into the dance.

"You are English. You are a Boleyn. Act like one."

"You can't tell me what to do." I cringe at my childish rejoinder.

"But Father can."

Yes. Father can tell all of us what to do. And we will do it.

"Father isn't here."

"And I must take his place."

I can't help but laugh. "You'd make a great father figure, George, with your gambling and your unsavory activities."

"I keep my activities discreet." He has the grace to look affronted. But I see past the mask and catch the hint of a smile, the one he used to have when we spent hours compiling inventive insults until we struggled to breathe through our laughter.

"No, George, you just run with a flock of black sheep."

"Yes. And the king finds us charming. But what is charming in a man is despicable in a lady, so don't go getting any ideas."

There is real warmth in his voice now, the hint of a tease. I look into his face, the sharp features and steeply arched eyebrows. We are so much alike.

"Your point is taken, Brother."

The music ends and he snaps a quick bow. He reaches to tuck a stray hair back beneath my hood, his fingers soft. I want

to lean into his hand, feel the comfort of it. Feel the welcome of family.

He sighs and looks at me keenly.

"You know, if you tried harder, you would almost be pretty."

I arrange my features to mask how deeply the wound cuts, right along the rift of our broken friendship.

"High praise, indeed."

And I walk away, cradling the pain like deadweight in my arms.

3

I keenly feel my difference after my dance with George. I settle into my duties to the queen. Try to remember to hold my tongue. But I feel uncomfortable in my own skin. In my clothes.

After the travesty of *The Château Vert*, that bilious green castle, I spent the days of my incarceration at Hever elaborating all of my gowns. I adapted the French off-the-shoulder look of the sleeves, and turned the oversleeves up to my elbows, showing off the tightly cuffed undersleeves, a dramatic effect. King François had been in ecstasies over the look when his mistress wore it. I modified the tight-fitting bodice, curving the square neckline up over the bust to disguise the insignificance of my breasts. I edged everything in dark velvet and the embroidery of my favorite emblems.

I made my clothing more French, a link to my chosen homeland. Everyone knows the English courtiers have no style of their own and so copy that of France with a passion close to mania. I wanted to set the fashion. Be admired for my innovation.

But the new war with France has changed attitudes. Changed sensibilities. Changed allegiances.

So all I get is laughter. Or worse, pity.

From a few, I sense undiluted animosity. Apparently, English opposition to the French is not limited to political rivalry.

I am a failure. George is right. I am too different. Perhaps it is time to reinvent my appearance.

I study the Duchess of Suffolk, the standard around which all the ladies rally. She wears her clothes like someone expecting to be watched, to be copied. And everyone does, because if they don't, they suffer a slow social death.

The ladies of the court are like a flock of sheep led by a wolf.

The duchess's entire ensemble falls like water in drapes and curves, from the slight peak of her hood—showing a discreet and modest shock of coppery hair—to the twice-fitted sleeves with draping cuffs, to the long cascade of train behind her.

I know what I look like, standing isolated in the center of the queen's watching chamber. My French hood sits so smoothly and so far back off my forehead that it has to be held by pins to my black hair. My skirts are bunched over my flat hips with copious organ pleats. The duchess does not need them.

No wonder they all laugh at me.

I leave the queen's apartments without permission, though I doubt my absence is noticed. Or regretted. I go to the maids' dormitory and dig through my cedar chest tucked behind the bed I share with Jane Parker. We face the wall farthest from the door. Farthest from the center of the court.

I pick up a bodice of gray silk trimmed in blue velvet that was made just before I left France. It is my least favorite color and getting too tight in the bust. It doesn't matter if I ruin it.

I take it to the only one of the ladies of the court I know will help me.

My sister.

Mary sleeps in a single room in the lodgings of the inner court. Theoretically, it is assigned to her husband, a gentleman of the king's Privy Chamber, but he generally makes himself scarce.

I'm glad to find her alone.

"Nan!" Mary looks up from her sewing when I knock and enter her little room. Her voice is round and delicate, though tuneless.

But Mary is beautiful.

Her skin is naturally pale with just a touch of pink. She has wide eyes, smooth hair the color of freshly cut oak, both of which she got from our mother. I once heard my father remark that I must be a changeling child, as all the beauty on both sides bypassed me.

Jealousy rises in me like a twist of smoke from a snuffed candle.

"So nice of you to visit."

Mary reaches to embrace me, but I thrust the bodice at her before she makes contact. I don't need my big sister to mother me.

"I need to change," I blurt. "This. I need to change this. Everyone is laughing at me."

Mary's gabled hood makes her face appear even rounder, like a moon, pale and glowing. The only thing not pale about Mary is her eyes, deep brown and kind, but often strangely vacant,

as if she has left her body and wanders different landscapes.

Right now, she's looking at me as if she's never met me before.

She turns her gaze and runs her hand along the stitching at the neckline.

"Lilies," she murmurs.

I almost snatch the bodice back from her. I spent days on those stitches. Weeks. Each one took me farther from Hever, reminding me of the lilies around Fontainebleau. Of fleurs-de-lis. Of France.

"Lilies symbolize chastity and virtue." Mary lifts her eyes to mine and gives a wicked smile. "A bit prim, don't you think?"

I shake my head. That wasn't my intention.

"We could alter the shape." She studies the curve of silk and buckram. "Display your assets."

"What assets?" I reach for the garment, but Mary pulls it away from me, holding it aloft in her right hand.

"I've changed my mind." I reach again, but her body is in my way. "I don't want to change." Not for Mary. Not for George.

Mary giggles and dances away from me.

"Give me a minute to work some Boleyn magic on your bust. You'll be impressed." She grins. "So will James Butler."

I scowl. Mary understands nothing.

"Go play your lute." She waves me dismissively away.

Go play your lute. Go change your clothes. Go become a sycophant and a sheep.

I cannot wreak my words on Mary. She doesn't deserve it. So I pick up my instrument, to lose myself in the music.

I keep my lute in her room because she has more privacy. Stuffed amongst the maids in our dormitory, I never know who's riffling through my things or listening to my music or reading over my shoulder. Yet Mary's quiet and nearly empty room is the place I go so I won't feel so alone. Two outcasts together.

The room is little more than a closet, with poky windows and an inadequate fire. An aging tapestry lines the wall, threads fraying loose and the left half bleached by the sun. But the bed is draped in new velvet, with a feather mattress and real pillows.

Occasionally the lesser ladies of the court visit her. Never the duchess and her confederacy. No, the room is kept quiet for the visits from the king—thus the attention paid to the bed trappings.

I keep my lute in the corner farthest from the window. I like knowing I can find it there. A friend. A reminder. A refuge.

I take my time to tune each course of strings, two to a course. They grow taut, twanging. The body of the lute feels like a belly pressed against me. The wood is smooth beneath my fingers, the strings almost sticky. I pluck them individually, like a conversation.

I love the lute for the dual tone of its strings, for the echo of its notes along my limbs. I love the delicate knots carved into the soundboard and the whiskery feel of the frayed frets beneath my fingers.

I pull the music into my mind. I can feel the vibration of the strings like breathing, like a heartbeat. It's a song I heard the king perform two nights ago, during one of his impromptu

entertainments, trying out new material on the girls of the queen's household. His voice rich and his eyes roaming.

They never landed on me.

Mary hums along, and I grit my teeth to keep from telling her to stop.

The tune breaks and stutters in my mind and I have to go back, close my eyes, concentrate. I'm getting two notes wrong. The highest ones. Either the lute is out of tune, or I am. I bear down a little harder, my anxiety growing to get just this one thing right.

"The king used your lute to play that song to me last night."

With a *spang* the chanterelle, the highest-pitched string, snaps and whips out, clattering in the quiet.

"Shit."

I sit in a pinprick of silence. The music is still in me, in my fingers, but I can no longer let it out.

"Nan. Watch your tongue."

She's not my mother. And George is not Father.

"Not you, too!"

There she sits, all placid by the fireplace, enjoying her un-demanding life of leisure and prestige. All the queen's ladies treat her as an abomination, but she has all she needs, all any-one would need. She has the king. And all of Father's praise.

She looks at me with her big, brown doe eyes, and I suddenly want to pluck them out.

"First George and now you, Mary? Reminding me how much I humiliate the rest of the family. How mortifying to have a sister who doesn't fit in!"

"It's not you, Nan, it's your choice of words."

"My choice of words. To whom I choose to speak them. The way in which I string them together. The timing. No, Mary, it's not that. It's you and George wanting me to fade into nothingness because no one at the court wants to befriend me or hear what I say, and you find that embarrassing."

"You're hardly embarrassing, Nan." Mary speaks almost absently. For her, the argument is forgotten before it has even begun. But I'm not ready to let it go. I want to take it all out on someone. The pain and the loneliness. The humiliation. The desperation.

"Stop calling me Nan. I'm not a baby."

"Then don't act like one."

Mary is so easy. I clench the pleats of my skirts in my hands.

"At least I don't play the whore."

I watch her face. Watch the hurt first dawn in her eyes and then drain the color from her cheeks. I expect to feel triumphant. Powerful.

But I have never felt so worthless.

Silently, she hands me the bodice, the seam at the neckline half unpicked. And silently I leave.

4

Little slivers of rain work their way in through the chinks in the withdrawing-room window, like the little slivers of gossip that work their way under the skin. The room is wet and suffocating with it. Everyone is crowded and close, avoiding the weather.

I wear the gray bodice, which I have unbecomingly refashioned to a more English style, the lilies covered with appliqués meant to be the Boleyn bull, but looking more like marauding boar. I intended to show solidarity: the Boleyns sticking together. But Father is in Spain; Mother, silent and invisible in the country—endlessly visiting Howard relatives.

Mary won't speak to me. Not that I blame her.

George says only a good marriage will help me get ahead. The entrée to the circle of nobility, or perhaps the circle of patronage. They are not necessarily the same. George's friend Henry Norris has no title, yet he's one of the men the king trusts most. And influential friends of the king often are gifted with titles of their own—like Charles Brandon. He was once just the son of the old king's standard-bearer, but now he's married to a princess of the blood and carries the title Duke of Suffolk.

His duchess—the king's trendsetting sister—now sits in the center of the room. She holds her own court, glowing in golden attention, as if she is queen, not Katherine. I study her face, her gray eyes so like the king's, but harder. Her waterfall of tastefully pink skirts flows around her.

The duchess looks up and catches me staring. Her gaze slides rapidly from my hood to my hem. Her lip curls, her eyebrow raises, and she opens her mouth to speak. I am unable to move, dreading what she has to say. I dread even more what I might reply. But before she can say a word, a voice behind me cuts across the room.

"Well, if it isn't George's little sister."

The duchess jerks her gaze to find the speaker at the table of gamblers who have been slapping down cards and groats and boasts and bets at the far end of the room. And I whisper a blessing before I turn as well.

George looks how I feel, surprise glimmering for an instant on his face and then vanishing behind welcome. His hair is expertly tousled, his inky velvet doublet smooth and clean, his soft hands no indication of the dirt he gets into. He sits with Henry Norris, who appears to be paying more attention to my bustline than to the conversation around him. James Butler, my future spouse, is next to him, glowering, his hair thick and coarse over his beetling eyebrows. And at the far end of the table sits the speaker, dressed in green like a modern-day Robin Hood, his gold curls sporting a hint of red at the temples—the Kentishman from the king's disguising.

He leaps from behind the table to approach me, moving

with the hidden strength and lissome grace of a cat. I get the feeling this man will always land on his feet.

"Haven't seen you since I broke my toe climbing the courtyard wall at Hever."

I swallow a knot of vanity, and it sticks in my throat. Because he has seen me. At the disguising. He just doesn't remember.

Or perhaps I just made no impression.

He stops and crosses his arms. Leans back and appraises me with his devastatingly blue eyes. He is still several strides from me, so we face each other like players on a stage, our audience all around us.

I glance at my brother, who expects my silence, and then back at this Robin Hood, who expects my response. He expects me to know him.

"Forgive me, sir. But I do not recognize you."

He laughs.

"Thomas Wyatt."

I do know him, or of him. His exploits are infamous in the maids' chambers. Word is, he's incomparable in bed. And he's shared many. He's a poet. An athlete. A miscreant.

"Your neighbor, from your days in Kent? We used to play naked in the fountain at my father's castle at Allington. Without our parents' knowledge, of course."

He winks at me.

The other men laugh, and I hear a rustle of skirts and whispers from the duchess's confederacy. I twitch a glance at George, who is glaring at me as if this man's innuendos are somehow my fault. Wyatt smiles like a gambler who has laid

down a hand full of hearts. I can't let him get the better of me. I can't let this man win.

"It's no wonder that I don't remember you, Master Wyatt, for we must have been much smaller." I pause, blink once, and then open my eyes into blank innocence. "Though for all I know, some things might still be quite small."

The table roars with laughter. The corner of Wyatt's mouth twitches, but his gaze never wavers from my own. When he speaks, his voice is silvery with seduction and wickedness.

"That is a matter which one day you might take in hand to establish the truth."

The devil I will. The men draw out one long, rising murmur and turn to me expectantly. Like they are watching a tennis match.

"Then I shall have to weigh this great matter very carefully," I say, before I can even think, "extracting from it only that truth which I can swallow."

Wyatt's eyes widen. I realize what I've just offered and bite my lip to stifle a retraction. Norris is pounding on the table with glee, and Butler looks as if he's swallowed a toad.

George jumps to his feet, unbalancing a wine goblet with his elbow. He grabs for it and catches it just before it topples, sweeping it up into a gesture to honor me, baptizing me with tiny drops of claret.

"My clever sister," he declares.

George's friends tip their drinks to me, and I flounce a little curtsy.

"Clever?" The coldness in James Butler's voice creates an

awed hush at the gaming table as he lumbers around it and out into the room.

Butler stands half a hand shorter than Thomas Wyatt, but must outweigh him by several stone, his chest and shoulders hard and bulky beneath the velvet of his doublet. He looks like a bear ready to take on a fox.

"Yes, clever," Wyatt says to him. "It means ingenious. Witty. Showing intelligence and skill."

It's only a repetition of George's comment, but the reflection of praise warms me.

"I know what it means, Wyatt. And wouldn't use it here."

A titter behind me indicates that the duchess and her confederacy are still listening. Why should they not be? Not only am I tarnishing my own reputation, but the men are about to come to fisticuffs. Fighting is not allowed within the confines of the court, making it doubly entertaining when it happens.

"You are a man of few words, Butler, and limited speech. Pray tell, what word would you use?"

Wyatt seems completely unconcerned by the palpable menace coming off the man my father intends me to marry. In fact, he seems determined to incite more. Butler turns and stares at me, his face emotionless, his eyes like stone.

"Wanton."

Butler drops the word into the quiet room, ready to combust.

"How dare you?" My hands ball into fists. I might flout the laws of the court myself.

George makes a move as if to shield me. Or perhaps to shield Butler. George and I used to fight as children, and I usually got the best of him. But we are cut short by a laugh. A low, rolling burble that douses the smoldering tempers.

Wyatt claps Butler on his shoulder. Butler doesn't seem to feel a thing.

"Ah, my dear James, you have spent too much time in Cardinal Wolsey's household with the likes of Henry Percy. The game of courtly love and the sometimes . . . ribald banter that accompanies it always catches the witless and sanctimonious unawares. It is nothing but *talk*, my friend, and talk is meaningless at court. Meaningless and soporific."

He says this with such ease and cordiality that Butler doesn't realize he's being insulted. He seems entirely under Wyatt's spell.

I wish I could do that. Turn tragedy to comedy in a moment. Cover indiscretions with poetry. Be accepted despite being unacceptable.

I could learn a thing or two from Thomas Wyatt.

"Witless?" The gray light of understanding begins to dawn on Butler's face. He is not as stupid as he appears.

"As meaningless a word as *wanton*, I am sure," I say. Again all eyes turn to me. Again all ears listen. I apply what I've gleaned so far from Thomas Wyatt's demonstration of his abilities. Say what you want to say, as well as what the listener wants to hear. "For the future Earl of Ormond could never be witless. Nor would he ever marry a wanton." My father contends that the earldom truly belongs to the Boleyns. And I will never marry James Butler.

If I can help it.

Butler narrows his eyes, but Wyatt proffers a devastating grin.

"Nor would he ever call his lady so," he says. "For earls are gentlemen and accord their ladies naught but the tenderest of words and devotion of heart, soul, and body."

For an instant, he holds me in his gaze, and I am as trapped as an insect in amber, the corner of my mouth pitched in admiration at his finesse. Then George throws an arm around my shoulders, as if to claim me. So I take the goblet from his other hand, raise it in salute to Wyatt, and drain it in a single motion.

Then I turn on my heel and leave the room before I say something I may later regret.

5

THICK, WET ENGLISH AIR GREETS ME AS I PUSH THROUGH THE outer doors into the base court. At least it's not raining. I breathe in deeply, the water chasing the smoke from my lungs and the heat from my face. My senses fizz with exhilaration at what I just experienced. A war of words. At the very least a battle. Words to which people *listened*. I glance around the courtyard, eager for more, but the clusters of courtiers just ignore me. The door behind me bangs, and I turn to face Thomas Wyatt once more.

"Headed to the mews?" he asks. Such a casual, unimaginative question.

"And why would I do that?"

"You go every day. To visit your little falcon."

"Have you been watching me?" The compulsion to spar is eclipsed by curiosity.

"I watch all the queen's ladies. Especially the new ones."

Of course.

"The ones you haven't slept with."

A flash of a wicked half smile.

"Yet."

He knows he's appealing, but I will not let him charm

me. I learned early on that my virginity is the only treasure I carry in a royal court. Everything else about me is worthless. Or belongs to my father.

"Watch all you want, Wyatt, but you're not getting anywhere near my bed. I saw in France what happens to girls who fall for men like you." I saw what happened to my sister there.

"I am a respectably married man."

"It doesn't seem your respectability prevents you from extramarital amusements. I know the people with whom you choose to associate."

He takes another step toward me, too close by far.

"Watch what you say, Anne; your brother is one of them."

"That's how I know." I turn and walk toward the mews, uncomfortably pleased when he falls into step beside me. "All you do is play games—jousting and cards, hunting and women. You build a reputation for seduction and pretty words, but show little discrimination."

"Ah," he says, leaning so close to me that I smell sugared almonds on his breath. "Have you been watching me?"

Really. The man is insufferable, and doesn't deserve a response. But I can't help myself.

"I suppose you're here with an offer I can't refuse."

Again the quirky uptick, creating a dimple to the right side of his mouth. Just one.

"Perhaps I'm here to take you up on yours."

I turn at the door of the mews to look him in the eye. Perhaps George is right. Perhaps my incontinent speech will get me into trouble one day. Just not today.

"I had thought you more perceptive than to take me seriously," I say. "But then, the game of courtly love always catches the witless unawares."

Wyatt throws back his head and laughs, a great burbling roar that draws the attention of the courtiers clustered against the walls.

His breath tickles the hair that has escaped my hood at the temple as he leans ever closer.

"I always take such offers seriously."

"Well, you can sing for it, Thomas Wyatt." I'm tired of his drivel and innuendos. "I saw what happened to my sister when she was my age. She succumbed to King François and the other golden boys of the French court. To their sweet words, their grins and dimples. They laughed at her behind her back. They talked about her like she was chattel. A mare to be ridden and passed on. She was forcibly removed from France by my father and married in shame."

"She came to our court and enchanted our king."

That is unlikely to happen twice in one family.

"You think you know everything, don't you?"

"And you know nothing."

I square up and itch to strike the look of amusement off his face.

"For your information, I can speak French better than anyone in this court. I know Latin and some Greek. I have read the works of Erasmus and the poetry of Clément Marot. I've met Leonardo da Vinci!"

My words tumble over one another and I sound breathless. I pause to collect myself.

"But you don't know anything about how to get along in the English court."

"I know perfectly well how to get along in this court."

"So you choose to be segregated. A pariah. The one person in the room with whom no one will speak or even make eye contact."

No, I didn't. It was chosen for me. By the court. By my clothes. By my tongue. The pain of having this pointed out to me by a stranger settles hard into my chest. Maybe life would be easier if I just fit in.

"A loss for words." He smiles. "I'm sure that doesn't happen very often."

"Why are you speaking to me?"

"Because I want to help you."

I gaze at Thomas Wyatt without reaction, the courtier's smile on my lips but not reaching my eyes. I can't trust him—a man for whom words are playthings and women little better.

"And what do you get out of this?" I ask. "You offer your assistance, but it's nothing that will line your pockets."

"Perhaps I only wish to promote the advancement of a former neighbor."

Even I can see that Thomas Wyatt would run down his neighbor with a rabid horse without a second thought. I make a noise halfway between disbelief and laughter.

"Would you believe I seek to further my own reputation?"

I am instantly wary.

"And tarnish mine."

"But yours is already tarnished, Anne. Perhaps it needs a little poetic shine."

"What do you know about it?"

"I heard a rumor about the Shrovetide pageant last year."

I hesitate. He wasn't there. Yet the gossip chases me.

"Oh?" I affect nonchalance. "What do you hear?"

"That you had too much to drink. That you stumbled out of the Château Vert and threw yourself at the king."

"I *danced* with him." Or tried to.

"But he didn't dance with *you*. It embarrassed your entire family. Humiliated your sister."

My sister wasn't the only one humiliated. A sharp jab of guilt in the back of my throat prevents me from swallowing. No matter what I do, no matter what my intention, I'm always hurting Mary, who least deserves it.

Wyatt doesn't know what it was like. The candles. The richness. The wine.

The king. The king was dressed in gold and crimson, like a god, with the emblem "Amorous" embroidered across his chest. We were masked. I was new at court, and everything seemed possible. For a single, glittering instant, I dreamed he could be mine.

How was I to know that he'd already slept with Mary?

"I'm trying to forget," I mumble.

"Everyone else already has." Wyatt reaches for my chin and

won't let go when I try to twitch out of his grasp. "It's time to give them something to remember.

"What do I get out of this? I get the admiration of every man here. At this very moment, I'm with a lovely girl who is melting at my touch after a little tiff. It only furthers my reputation."

"But that's not what happened." I fight the urge to see if anyone is watching. "And I'm not melting."

But I don't shake him off.

"Ah, but Anne, in this court, it doesn't matter what really happens. What matters is how it's perceived."

"So you get a little boost to your own self-worth," I prompt. "And you're not looking for anything else?"

"I'm always looking for something else, my dear," he says, his voice rolling low into an octave of seduction. "And you have offered a challenge I can't bear to pass up."

"And what is that?"

"You say I won't get anywhere near your bed. But I challenge you back, Anne Boleyn. I say that if I help you—that if the two of us gain your acceptance to this most unaccepting of courts—before long in this pretty, showy dance, you will want me in your bed."

I laugh right in his face. "Would you like to place a wager on that outcome?"

A glimmer of shock crosses his face—quick, like a sun shadow.

"I never pass up a bet."

"And if you lose—which you undoubtedly will—you will not press me further?"

"As long as if I win, you follow through."

We stand, motionless, the flow of barbs and banter stanched by his proposition.

Wyatt's smile vanishes. I feel something constrict beneath my lungs—something like fear.

"My maidenhead survived the French court intact, Wyatt." I somehow keep my voice even. "I think it can survive you."

His expression changes—a flash of understanding—and I realize I've just told him I'm still a virgin. Something unexpected in a French courtier. Or a Boleyn girl.

"You present me with high stakes," I say to cover up my discomfort. "And yet you forfeit nothing to me if you lose."

"If I lose, I will trouble you no more. I pledge to leave you to your happy life amongst the social elite and always mourn the conquest that never was. I will swear there was nothing between us but courtly banter, and bear the burden of the mocking laughter of my peers."

"You speak in riddles."

"I speak in poetry.

> *"If it be yea, I shall be fain;*
> *If it be nay, friends as before;*
> *Ye shall another man obtain,*
> *And I mine own and yours no more."*

I hold his gaze so that I don't roll my eyes at his doggerel. But one word strikes a reverberating chord in my mind—*friends*. I could use a friend here. Even one like Thomas Wyatt.

"If I lose"—Wyatt holds a hand to his heart—"I will write a poem about you that will be passed down through the ages as a masterpiece of all time. And I will always remain your humble servant."

He bows to me with a flourish, and I am able to affix a mask of nonchalance before he rises. I can't let him see that he's already charmed me. I can't let him see how much I need him.

"So what is your strategy?" I ask.

"I will pursue you. And you will encourage it."

"And what will that gain me?"

"The attention of all the other men at court. At least the ones that count."

"Like Henry Norris? No thank you."

"Norris can get you places. He's a favorite of the king."

"So is my sister."

Wyatt looks at me as one would an idiot child.

"But women don't matter at this court, Anne. In our world, women have no influence, carry no interest."

Have no voice. Have no lives of our own.

"It's the men that matter," he continues. "And most men are too stupid to see what's right in front of their faces. The only time they want something is when they can't have it, a jewel in someone else's bonnet. They take notice of something when it flashes a signal—like the white tail of a deer. The signal for pursuit."

"So you intend to be the flag on my ass?"

His grin broadens to double dimples.

"I intend to hold you up so that you catch the light."

A jewel. The image delights me. Wyatt cocks an eyebrow as if he's scored a point, and I start to turn away.

"Thank you for your offer," I say coldly.

"Thank you for your promise."

I pause. Look back. Narrow my eyes at him.

"It was a bet, Wyatt, not a promise. And I intend to win."

"Shall we kiss on that to seal the deal?"

He steps forward, and my partially turned shoulder brushes his chest, the fabric of his cloak sweeping against my skirts. I can see the stitches in his doublet and feel the heat of his breath on my forehead.

I look up into his face. He is so much taller than I am that I have to tilt my chin to see his eyes, which are focused not on mine but on my lips.

I take a step back.

"I have not yet agreed."

"And what will it take for you to agree?" Wyatt doesn't seem at all put off by my rebuff. Rather, he crosses his arms and leans back lazily, his body completely absent of tension, like a purring cat.

"Time."

"Don't take too much, Anne, or you may find yourself supplanted in my affections."

"Don't follow too closely, Wyatt, or you may be caught in the hunter's net yourself."

Richmond Palace
1523

6

I AM ALONE. AGAIN. THE SETTING HAS CHANGED, BUT THE REALITY has not. The court moved to Richmond because Greenwich was desperately lacking in air, but the crowded conditions grow even more stifling. I share a bed with Jane and two other girls, sleeping in rotation, the linens always damp and smelling of sleep and perfume. And once, I swear, the acrid sweat of a man.

Which makes me think of Wyatt's proposition. I admit, I'm a little afraid he might win our bet. He's charming and handsome and . . . persuasive. But I refuse to let that happen. Virginity is my trump card.

I can't help looking for him in the crowds at court. I tell myself it has nothing to do with his voice or his casual grace or his eyes.

No, it's his words that draw me to him. And the fact that he listens to mine.

But the burgeoning crowds of Richmond conspire to isolate me. To make matters worse, we are now less than an hour by barge from London, which means Cardinal Wolsey and his entourage of hangers-on fill the rooms by day more often than his regular Sunday visit.

The cardinal is the king's lord chancellor and most trusted

adviser, and his arrival always causes a bit of an uproar. I stand in a window of the queen's watching chamber and monitor his progress. The barge, decorated in gold and silk and tinsel and landing at the water bridge, becomes the focal point of anyone wishing access to the king. Men kneel before Wolsey, kiss his ring, whisper in his ear.

One wouldn't think to look at him that Wolsey wields the kingdom's power. He comes from nowhere, a family of merchants and butchers. *He* didn't need to marry well to join the circle. He just used his brains and spoke accordingly. The droopy skin of his cheeks reminds me of a loose-skinned dog, and his chin recedes into the folds of his cassock. But his eyes—shrewd and calculating—tell a different story.

I watch as he moves through the throng. He appears serene, despite the press of bodies and clamor of requests and complaints. His face is serene, but his eyes—shaded by his brow—are triumphant. They are those of a man who can change lives with a single, well-placed word. A man to whom people listen.

Wolsey is followed from the barge by a trail of courtiers. His own. For he holds court at least as well as the king. He collects his courtiers from the best families in the country—young men keen for position but perhaps not vibrant enough to engage the king. And others—like James Butler—are virtual prisoners, hostages to the political machinations that keep their fathers in line. There are no women in Wolsey's household. The boys come to the king's court to learn the rules of flirtation while their master changes the rules that govern us all.

The cavalcade disappears from view, but I continue to watch

the place just vacated. So much power in a butcher's son. The rain returns, and the flat, cloudy light hammers the river into pewter and erases the shadows from the wall. It is as if Wolsey's very passing has caused the sun to cease shining.

The door rattles, and I turn to see the duchess and her confederacy enter. She carries herself imperially, looking left and right to make sure that everyone is watching—and that everyone is bowing.

"Little Boleyn." The duchess's voice resonates high in her mouth, giving it a nasal quality. An ever-present sharpness.

"Your Grace." I keep my eyes on my hands. Deferential. Sheepish.

"Like a little sparrow, aren't you?" she asks. "Drab. And rather . . . disheveled."

Her confederacy titters, the sound rippling away into the room.

I bite my lip and think of George's words: *Be quiet. Be the same. Be accepted.*

I look up. The duchess's head is tipped to one side, her expression one of schooled amusement.

"Many creatures are not as they first appear, Your Grace." I cannot stop the words. "A falcon at rest may be drab and disheveled. And a cuckoo hides its ignobility by insinuating its offspring into a superior bird's nest."

As insults go, mine is thinly veiled, casting aspersions on the duchess's children—the cuckoos in the royal nest, placed there by Charles Brandon, whose ancestry is even more questionable than my own.

Her expression freezes. She turns without speaking, followed by a tide of skirts and gabled hoods. Jane Parker glances back at me—the last girl to follow—but quickly scuttles after.

I've done it again. I stand alone in the center of the room, wrap my misshapen finger in a pleat of my skirt, and twist the pearl ring with my thumb. The duchess and all her followers whisper together. The room begins to feel like one gigantic eye—staring, but not seeing. They will never accept me. I need to get out.

I move to the door just as it opens again.

"We have come to entertain the ladies," Henry Norris says as he enters. His gaze slides across my brow and finds the duchess and her confederacy behind me. He is followed by George, who studiously ignores my existence, and Wolsey's men, who crowd up behind him, eager and wriggling like puppies.

I stand to one side, barely observed and highly invisible, as more seductive prey is spotted within the room.

Finally, I can no longer stand it and push my way through the door, running nose first into a russet doublet. I look up into the face of a boy my age. His eyes are strange. Like chalcedony—more blue than gray but almost colorless. His hair is the color of fox fur, and just as thick, a swatch at the back of his head giving the impression of a feather in a cap. His face is cut at angles like stone, creating broad planes, sharp edges, and deep shadows. But when he smiles, the shadows melt away and I feel something warm and delicate rising within me.

He's looking at me. He sees me.

The man behind him gives him a push, and he stumbles forward into the room, breaking our gaze, but my eyes follow him. Until someone grabs my hand and yanks me from the room.

"You flirt with Henry Percy?" James Butler's voice is all rough edges like uncut granite.

"I'm doing no such thing." I wrench my hand from his and turn, but he's whip quick and his grip bites into my elbow.

"Good. His fate is decided. Like ours."

He manages to hide all but a hint of brogue by clipping his sentences and swallowing words. But he can't disguise his coarseness. His shirt is rumpled and his hair cropped roughly, as though trimmed with a scythe.

"Our fates are not decided, James Butler. There is no marriage until it is written and signed."

"And sealed," he leers, exposing the gap of a missing tooth next to an overly sharp canine. I suppress a shudder at the thought of his suggestion. Consummation.

"That will never happen."

"Wolsey and the king want this. It will happen."

The thought that the king is part of the execution of this contract makes me ill.

I allow Butler to walk me through Richmond's crowded rooms and to the covered gallery around the garden. Weak spring sunshine slants over the walls, igniting the gold flame of the cockerels that top the donjon's cupolas. They point north, into the wind, and for a moment I'm reminded of the Louvre,

the striped towers swept clean by rain. And I ache to go back. To be anywhere but here.

I'm shaken by my desperation to get out of this predicament. To get my arm out of his grasp. To unlink my life from his.

I stop. Square my shoulders. Take a deep breath.

"The marriage rests on the settlement of the earldom of Ormond," I say evenly. "That is yet to be decided."

I know George wants the earldom. So does Father. I am nothing but a bargaining chip, a sacrifice to the pretense of capitulation. They'll fight Butler. Won't they?

"The earl had only one son. My father." Butler's smile is mocking.

"His illegitimate son."

Butler scowls, but I continue.

"My grandmother was named as coheiress in the earl's will."

"Women," Butler says in a voice most people reserve for the stupid and the Irish, "cannot inherit. They don't know money. Don't know rules. They squander every groat on baubles."

He flicks the *A* pendant that hangs from a ribbon around my neck.

"Women," I counter, grabbing his hand and squeezing it to make a point, "are in every way men's intellectual equals."

He laughs, showing off his teeth.

"We can grasp languages and texts as easily," I continue. "Women translate Latin, compose music, even orchestrate war, as Queen Katherine did in Scotland when the king was away playing games in France."

"A fluke. Desperation. Look at her now. She can't produce an heir."

"She has a daughter."

"Just my point."

I could strangle him.

"Mary will be queen!" I cry. "As the king's only legitimate child, it's her birthright. I'm sure she'll do better than most men, who have lost entire peerages to depravity and gluttony."

"And to the wantonness of women."

"Wars are waged and death unleashed by men who follow without thought their own ambition and misplaced loyalty," I pursue.

"Like your grandfather."

My mother's father, the second Duke of Norfolk, was attainted after fighting on the wrong side of the battle of Bosworth that knocked the crown from Richard III's head and rolled it to Henry Tudor. The Howards have been weaseling their way back into Tudor court life ever since.

I'm embarrassed to be related to them.

"Traitors and pretenders," Butler growls. "I'm doing you a favor."

"How romantic," I say, wrenching my hand from his.

"Romance is only in books and music," he says. "You won't find any of that in Ireland."

I feel myself grow pale. I can't face a future with no music. All we hear of Ireland are stories of barbaric lords and fiefdoms, as if they continue to live in the Dark Ages. No music. No poetry. No court.

"Are you threatening me?" I demand, my voice stronger than my heart.

Butler's face lights up with wicked mirth and he laughs. I smell the meat on his breath.

"Yes. With me, you'll be a countess. Without me, you are nothing."

He snaps a smart bow and turns away before I can even curtsy back. Not that I plan to.

The walls of Richmond press in around me. Ladies whisper as I pass. I keep my face still and pleasant. I don't rush. I don't fly through the rooms as my limbs are desperate to do.

I move slowly, almost regally, to a quiet, disused antechamber at the far end of the palace, just beyond my sister's ill-attended room. It is musty and dirty, with a single, cracked window and no tapestries, and I believe everyone has forgotten about it.

It is the perfect place to cry.

And when the tears are spent, it is the perfect place to plan.

7

"WHAT DO I NEED TO DO?" I ASK WYATT WHEN I FIND HIM IN the long gallery.

". . . is exactly the right thing to say."

I struggle not to roll my eyes. It's hard to take the man seriously when he says things like that. But if I'm going to rid myself of James Butler, I need to attract the attention of someone else. Someone better. Wyatt just might be able to help me with that. So I will suffer his foolishness.

I turn to the maps that line the walls of the gallery. England. The Channel. The Low Countries. France. I run my fingers along the shadowy outline of what they call the New World.

"I wish I could go there."

He takes my hand in his and says, "Why would you want to leave England when everything you need is right here?"

He presses my palm to his heart, and I bite back a laugh.

"A little overdone, don't you think?"

"I've been pining for days." He leans in close, and I can see the rim of black around the blue of his eye. A tiny dark speckle, like a grain of onyx, glints in the right one. "It took you long enough to come and find me."

"You were supposed to be pursuing me." I feel his heartbeat beneath my fingers. His breath on my lips.

"You said you needed time. I do little pursuing unless I'm going to get something out of it."

"Your seduction techniques are not going to work on me, Wyatt."

"Do you want to bet on that?" The laughter in his voice is evident—a musical bass note that makes me want to laugh, too.

"I shall choose to ignore them, then," I say lightly. And repeat myself. "What do I need to do?"

"Flirt with me."

"Now?" I glance quickly around the room. It's full of maps and tapestries and quiet conversation. Courtiers plotting advancement. Ladies making assignations. Henry Percy. Norris. George.

Wyatt brushes a stray hair from my cheek to draw my eyes back to his.

"Constantly."

"Wouldn't that be a little obvious?"

"I believe I've said before that most people at this court can't see what's in front of them until you beat them with it. So, yes. It has to be obvious."

"And nothing else?"

"Nothing until you want it, Anne."

His gaze moves from my eyes to my mouth and back. Almost without my wanting to, I look at his mouth, the full lower lip and the hint of reddish stubble on the upper one.

"If you do as I say," he continues so quietly that I find myself

unable to stop watching his mouth, "I can guarantee the entire court will fall swooning at your feet."

I force myself to look back into his eyes.

"Think a lot of yourself, don't you?"

"I have to. Or no one else will."

"So what do we do first?"

"First we get their attention."

"And how do we do that?"

"It's already done. We have the entire room watching our intimate little scene."

I realize how we must look to all the others. Standing so close, gazing intently into each other's eyes. Like lovers.

"We have their attention. Now we need to capture their imaginations. Display your assets."

"That's what my sister says." I pull away and cross my arms over my chest. "I don't want lechery."

This isn't why I came to him.

"I meant your eyes. Dark. Mysterious. Alluring. And your face. So haughty, but such promises in those lips."

"My lips have promised you nothing."

"But the point is to look as if they might. You look like someone who has something to say. Something important."

"I do." I take his hand in mine again, hoping he's really listening. "I have ideas. I'm more than breasts and eyes and lips, Thomas Wyatt."

I pause for breath. I've said too much. But I can't stop.

"I deserve to be heard."

He studies me as one would a new species. We are separated

by space and silence, no longer the portrait of young love. This will never work.

"You're right," he says quietly. "You do."

He closes the gap between us, bends over me to whisper directly into my ear.

"Let's make sure you're heard. If you do as I say, if we work together on this, the most important ears at court will listen."

I snap my eyes up to his. *The king?* Our lips are inches apart.

"Good. Now, you must follow my directions exactly. Lower your gaze."

I continue to keep my eyes on his face. To show him that he cannot order me like a servant. Or a wife.

"They all see us. The men will watch your every move."

I hesitate. If he's right, my life at court could turn completely. Perhaps even the king himself will notice. Will hear.

I follow Wyatt's instructions and look to the floor at the center of the room. To the cluster of leather shoes pointed just slightly in our direction. I do not bow my head. I merely lower my gaze.

"Perfect."

The praise is like a strand of melody in my heart.

"Think in terms of music," Wyatt whispers, as if listening to the same tune, "of poetry. Because flirtation is a dance. Count the time in your head."

He taps it out along the pulse at my wrist.

"Now wait for a count of four. Count it in your mind. Then raise your eyes. Tilt your head. And smile. Just a half smile.

Don't look away. Another count of four. Then turn. And walk away."

I picture it, as if I am the one watching. The measured way it operates, like a crescendo, or an unfinished chord, leaving the listener breathless for completion. If he keeps his eyes on me no matter what I do, I will look as if I've captured him. As if I have the power.

"But wait," he says, just before I lift my eyes, his words like a caress on my cheek. "And this is the most important part."

He pauses. And then he does trace the line of my jaw, almost, but not quite, touching my lips.

"When you walk away—and every time you walk away from me   *don't look back.*"

Like Orpheus. Like Lot's wife. Looking back would break the spell.

He strokes one finger down the center of my upper lip, as if asking me to hush, then releases me.

"Now go."

I do exactly as he says. The look. The smile. The turn.

I feel him watching me. I feel everyone watching me. I consider emulating Queen Katherine, fingers pressed around each other like a gift, head bent in humble piety. But I am not a queen. Never will be.

So I straighten my spine, elongate my neck. I look down and to the left, not back at Thomas Wyatt. Showing just a hint of my face—an enigmatic glimpse—before I straighten again and walk through the door to the gallery and out of their view.

I hear a rising tide behind me, as if the room has released a collectively held breath.

A sense of power swirls through me like a draft of potent wine, and I have to steady myself, one hand on the cool stone wall. I long to lay my forehead against it but hear the returning murmur behind me and walk away.

8

For four days, nothing happens. Then, at Wolsey's next visit, Henry Percy smiles at me again. One of the king's men asks me to dance. And I hear, in the ripple of whispers around the duchess's confederacy, "What do men *see* in her, anyway?"

It's not much, but it's something.

I try to carry on my normal routine. Serving the queen. Avoiding Mary because I still do not know what to say to her. Practicing my music on strange lutes because I left mine in her room, at the mercy of the king. When I need to escape the castle walls, I visit my falcon.

The mews at Richmond is smaller and more cramped than the one at Greenwich. But I believe the falcons are treated better here, because Simnel, a falconer from the Royal Mews at Charing Cross, has come to care for them.

I carry sugar comfits in my pocket, stolen from the kitchen, nod a good morning to Simnel. Make my way to the dark corner of the back of the mews.

My merlin, Fortune, is smaller than an average female, but persistent. And tenacious. Once she gets hold of something, she will not let it go. This makes her a less than ideal hunting companion, but I find her character faults appealing.

Fortune emits a piercing cry when I run out of comfits.

"Shhh, little one." She dives at my empty hand. Her sharp beak pinches the skin of my finger, raising a welt. I shake my hand and laugh at her.

"What's the matter, little one, don't you love me anymore?"

"Actually, falcons are incapable of love."

I turn to see Henry Norris haloed by the light around the door. Everyone knows Norris. He tilts in the lists and wins accolades in every tournament. He is a gentleman of the bed-chamber, and therefore assists the king in his most private moments. Helps him dress.

Every time I see Norris, I think of the king's bare back.

"Sir Henry," I stutter as I dip a little curtsy. "You startled me."

Fortune pipes her agreement.

"That certainly wasn't my intention," Norris says smoothly, and moves over as if to examine Fortune. This is the closest he's ever been to me. And the most he's ever said to me.

Even in the dim light of the mews, I can see the wear of weather on Norris's skin. Days spent hunting have tanned his cheeks and chin and chiseled creases around his eyes. He is the same age as the king but appears older. And he is not nearly as alluring, though he would like to think he is. I can feel his presence, and his intention, in the way he breathes, the manner of his stance. Too close. Too encompassing.

I fight the urge to step away. This is what I wanted. The attention. Someone important who might—just might—listen. Norris is married. And libidinous. But powerful.

I turn my head to look at Fortune, who ruffles a bit. Nervous.

"I wonder, sometimes," I say, stretching my words as if searching for them, "if the court isn't a bit like a mews."

When I look back, Norris appears a little perplexed.

I finish my thought looking him directly in the eye. "Full of separately caged individuals incapable of love."

"Incapable?" His expression is one of mock offense. "All of us? By what reasoning do you come to this conclusion?"

I think of King François in France. Of the words he spoke to Mary that she shared with me, the eight-year-old confidante of a fifteen-year-old naïf. How he loved her. Worshipped her. Adored her. How Mary believed him. Believed in love.

How François passed her on to his friends when he was done with her. And each one took a piece of her until finally she was sent away and I was left alone in a foreign land. Again.

"Evidence of the opposite has yet to present itself to me," I answer.

"Wyatt seems . . . suitably passionate."

So it's working. "Oh?" I ask, wanting to know more. "What makes you say this?"

Norris's eyes drift down my face to my lips. And lower, to my bodice. Mentally, I shake off my revulsion.

"I've seen the way he looks at you," Norris answers. "And at cards last night, he . . . mentioned it."

Now Wyatt is talking about me?

"What did he say?"

Norris grins. "That the passion isn't one-sided."

I narrow my eyes. This wasn't part of the plan.

"Passion and love are not the same thing."

"Too true," says a voice behind us.

We both turn to see George stride in, twirling an empty goblet.

"Passion is easy to show," he says, "love, sometimes impossible."

I wipe my hands on my skirt to keep them from shaking.

"Though some of us could try a little harder," George finishes.

Norris takes a step backward, eyes twitching between my brother and me. George doesn't look at him.

Fortune cries, the tension too much for her. Or perhaps she is just looking for more comfits.

"Sir Henry, I would speak to my sister alone."

Norris doesn't move, stunned, perhaps, by George's bluntness and lack of courtly protocol. The Boleyns are like that. It remains to be seen if we are forgiven for it. Norris tips a bow to me and stalks out.

"Jesus, George," I hiss, "what do you think you're doing?"

"I just thought you should know that Father's going to be recalled. He's coming back." George heaves himself up from the doorframe as if his melancholy has weighted him down.

I feel as if the earth has shifted beneath my feet. We eye each other warily, the rustle of wings around us. Fortune flaps awkwardly on her post. Tethered to it.

Then George turns and walks stiffly through the door and into the wide, open courtyard beyond. I follow, leaving Fortune behind.

"When?" I call, trying to catch up to him, stumbling over the cobblestones.

"Soon. Summer." George waves a hand bleakly, as if trying to brush me away.

"He's coming here?"

George spins. "Of course he's coming here. Or Windsor. Or wherever the court happens to be located. To wherever he can keep me under his eye. And his thumb."

His *r*'s and *s*'s are overlong. His articulation is blurry, the music of his voice down tempo.

"Not just you." I offer an ironic smile that feels more like a grimace. "There's room beneath that thumb for both of us. Because we stick together, George, remember?"

My voice is from my childhood. The one where silence reigned at the dinner table, Father's palpable disappointment an unwanted guest. A childhood where George could creep into my room at night and I would pretend not to notice when the pillow was wet in the morning. A childhood where we could escape to the orchards and climb the trees and make a pact: that we would always stick together. We would always be friends.

A pact Father broke by sending me to the Low Countries and then to France. By turning George into a stranger.

"Do we, Anne?" George looks at me, his eyes dark with agony or anger—I can't tell behind the red-rimmed haze of the wine.

"We're Boleyns. Boleyns always stick together." I reach for him, but he twists away from me.

"We just present a united front. Unless it suits us otherwise."

"No, George," I tell him, wanting desperately to believe it myself.

"You are set to steal my inheritance from under my nose. Wolsey and our Howard uncle are pushing for a resolution of the Ormond inheritance. Their problems will be solved, and Father can't complain if Boleyn blood inherits the earldom eventually. So they want to give it to Butler—to you." He spits. "And you flaunt your unworthiness by throwing yourself at every married man at court." He flings his arm in the direction Norris traveled.

"I don't *want* your inheritance, George! I want nothing to do with James Butler or the earldom of Ormond."

"Well, Father will make sure you have it," George snarls. "To keep it in the family one way or another. Whether or not he finds you in Henry Norris's bed."

I bristle. "I'm not—"

"Or Thomas Wyatt's." George actually leers at me. "So I suppose you had better enjoy him while you can. I hear his tastes run a little . . . wild."

"I don't think I know you anymore, George Boleyn." I struggle to keep my voice from shaking. Rage and humiliation burn in my throat.

George sags and lifts the empty goblet—turning it entirely upside down—and peers into the void, trying to catch a drop. Then he levels his gaze at me, unswaying, and when he speaks, his words are unslurred.

"When Father returns, Anne, you will be the one who disappoints him. You will be the one who suffers his displeasure. Not

me, this time." His face twists into a horrific smile that doesn't meet his eyes. "Not me. You're the one with the court chasing your tail. You're the one everyone's talking about. You're the one who called Mary a whore, Anne. To her face."

I step back—slapped by my own words.

"One day"—George pursues me and whispers closely, his breath reeking of wine and malice—"someone will call you the same thing, and you'll know how it feels."

"I think I already do, George. Because I think you just did."

"Clever girl."

George lifts his goblet in an empty toast and walks away.

9

I GO STRAIGHT TO WYATT. I'VE LOST MY FAMILY. I HAVE NO friends. I don't know where else to go.

I find him in the gardens, amongst the lions and dragons, the knots and heraldic emblems.

"Can't stay away from me?"

Wyatt slips an arm around my waist and kisses me quickly. It's so English. So foreign. And far too intimate. My lips taste like sugared almonds when he pulls away.

"What's wrong?" he asks.

"What have you been saying about me?" I ask. "What have you been telling everyone about . . . about this?" I wave my hands through the little space left between us, fingers brushing the velvet on his chest.

He grabs my wrists and lowers my hands.

"You are shrill and agitated," he says tightly. "And this is not part of our plan." He grins. "We cannot have a lovers' quarrel until we are lovers."

"And we are not lovers!" I hiss at him. "So why is Henry Norris talking to me about passion?"

"Henry Norris will talk passion to any girl who listens."

"Why did it sound as if he'd heard about my passion from you?"

Wyatt pauses.

"Did you tell him something?"

"I may have . . . implied."

I set my jaw and ball my fists, tendons flexing against Wyatt's grip.

"You will not talk about me that way," I say, my voice low and dangerous. "I will flirt and pretend with you all you like, but I will not be the subject of lies."

"The small-minded interpret what they see and hear only as they wish to."

I scowl at him. "You are the one who told me the court is filled with small-minded people. Am I to assume everyone will interpret things this way? That they will think as my brother does—that I'm your whore?"

A look of shock crosses Wyatt's face, but he chases it with a wry smile.

"You're scowling," he says, and releases me to brush the strain at my brow.

"There's no one around! No one can see!" I slap his hand away. The man doesn't even argue properly.

"Makes no difference. You have to practice your art in private as well as public venues, my dear. You cannot let down your mask for anyone. Court is a game played in every corner and at every moment. Even while you sleep."

"Even when I'm married?"

"Especially with your spouse." Wyatt's face darkens, and I feel a distinct cooling in the air between us.

"It sounds exhausting." I feel exhausted. "Having to wear the mask for everyone. Even family."

Wyatt lets go of my other wrist, and we stand in the wan April sunlight, arms at our sides, unmoving.

"You and George were always close," he says quietly. "Always together as children. He told me once you slept in the same bed."

I glance up at him. Is he jealous?

"A closeness forged in the iron of my father's will."

"Your father doted on you."

I manage to suppress a snort.

"When I was six."

"No more doting?"

I have to look away from the sympathy in his eyes.

"When I was six, I was his clever little girl," I say, studying the light on the topiary leaves, concentrating hard to keep the pain from my voice. "But I grew up away from him. I came home from France thin and unnoticed, certainly unbeautiful, surpassed in my father's affections by my pretty, easy sister and her capacity to earn him accolades."

"Your voice is sweet, but your words are bitter."

"My words. Everyone tells me my words are wrong. Aren't you really saying it's me?"

He tilts my chin back to face him and gazes at me unspeaking, his narrow features serious.

"It is just something I think you should mind, Anne," he says softly. "Your words will be your downfall."

I take a deep breath, straighten my spine, and brush my hands on my skirt.

"Well, thank you for taking the time to make that assessment."

I turn to go, but he grabs my hand to stop me.

"You came to me for a reason, Anne."

My heart lurches. George. Father. Mary. Why did I think Wyatt could help?

Because he said he would be my friend. In a foolish poem. But even a pretend friend is better than no friend at all.

"My father's coming home."

Wyatt hesitates. "With his iron will."

I nod. I don't want to need him. But I do.

"He'll force my marriage to James Butler."

"And you want to prevent that."

"I want to find an alternative."

If I think I see a flash of sadness in those blue eyes, it vanishes quickly into skepticism.

"You don't have much time."

"Then you'll have to work your magic quickly." I try to keep my voice light, and offer a weak smile. But truly, Wyatt is my only hope. If he can do what he claims.

He slips an arm around my waist and, in what I'm sure he thinks is a seductive way, whispers, "You could succumb to my potent and innumerable charms and become my mistress."

"And tarnish myself so much that not even James Butler will want me? I don't think so."

Wyatt laughs. "I could spirit you away to the country, and no one would ever find you. Not even your father."

I manage not to pull a face.

"The country? That might be a fate worse than Butler. Try again."

"Then we'll have to find you someone with more influence. Norris?"

I turn to him full on. He needs to understand this.

"I will not be a mistress. I've seen what it did to my sister and her reputation. She may be a favorite of the king, but I've seen how mistresses are treated by everyone else. I know how they are vilified. I never want to be called a concubine." Or a whore.

"Ah." Wyatt guides me by the elbow along the path. He pulls a leaf from a shrub trimmed into the shape of a stag and twirls it. Speaks quietly from the corner of his mouth. "We have to keep moving. We are being watched." He nods toward the donjon—the palace's central tower—where the windows stare like blank faces from its façade.

"Being a mistress can be a noble pursuit," he says. "Your sister has done well."

"I would not wish for a life like my sister's, or any mistress's. Hidden away in poky rooms or country houses. Disguised as serving women. Even Bessie Blount, mother of the king's son, is not at court. All mistresses are confined to prisons because the men who 'love' them cannot allow them to be seen. Not a noble pursuit at all."

Then again, if King Henry asked, I might find it hard to say no.

"I'll take that as a refusal," Wyatt says, laughter in his voice. "So what you want is a husband."

I consider this for a moment, and Wyatt is silent. The only sound is the scratch of gravel beneath our feet. A marriage would save me from James Butler. It would nullify the influence of my father, placate my brother, put me on equal footing with my sister. Of course, it would also make me subject to the whims and words of yet another man's will. Someone else to silence me.

If only I could find a place where my own whims and words matter.

Ridiculous notion.

"Marriage seems my only option."

Wyatt stops and studies me. Unlike the king, who always seems to be in motion, Wyatt holds his stillness within him, as if it is an integral part of his being.

"There are always choices."

I shake my head. "Not in this case. I need to be rid of Butler before my father arrives. So I need a proposal. A betrothal. Something." I close my eyes and try desperately to think of someone who might listen to me, but the image that presents itself is of Thomas Wyatt, so I open my eyes to the real thing. "Preferably from someone *not* pursuing the earldom that rightfully belongs to my father. Someone at court."

We walk again, side by side beneath the gaze of the donjon.

"Then we shall have to get you into the center of attention— the attention of the royal circle—using much more . . . dramatic means."

"Dramatic?"

"A masque, my dear. An interlude. We'll stage a little play, with you as the focus. We'll invite the king and Wolsey and pretend it's just a little nothing, the whim of a poet. But you will be seen and admired by everyone of influence."

I will be seen by the king. Wyatt is wearing a smirk of supreme self-satisfaction.

"And so will you," I prompt. He has obviously already thought this through.

"My motives are never entirely unselfish."

I have a flashing memory of *The Château Vert*. I tremble at the thought that others will remember, too.

"But won't it take months to prepare? The costumes? The set?"

"It will be simple," he says. "No elaborate costumes. No enormous sets created to give the appearance of false castles. No gilded chariots. As if it's the spur of the moment. Improvisational. And starring whomever I please."

I'm quiet for a moment.

"Not to your liking?" There's an edge to Wyatt's voice.

"It's a wonderful idea."

"But?"

I glance at him. His knuckle brushes mine. It looks accidental, but I think I know Wyatt well enough now to believe it's contrived. It calls attention to our close proximity to each other.

I know him. But can I trust him?

I take a deep breath.

"Will this . . . interlude . . . not merely call attention to my former transgressions?"

Wyatt raises an eyebrow.

"You mean *The Château Vert*?"

I nod.

"No one remembers it, Anne."

"Yes, they do." My heart warps at the thought that the king remembers. That he thinks me a fool. If that's the case, I don't wish to remind him.

"No." Wyatt stops. "They don't. No one remarked on it. No one remembers it. No one cares."

"You knew about it, and you weren't even there!"

"Because your brother told me. No one remembers but the Boleyns."

"It got me sent away. Exiled to the country."

Wyatt sighs. Rubs his forehead. And continues up the path.

"The king's interest in your sister was just beginning then, wasn't it?"

I nod miserably.

I'd been at court for just a few weeks. I was homesick for France, mourning the escalating hostilities. Lonely. Father got me a position in the queen's household, a part in the Shrovetide pageant—a chance to shine. I wondered secretly at the time if the part of "Perseverance" was mine by design. More fool me.

Mary played "Kindness" and positively glowed in the white gown and gold bonnet. I stood beside her, flushed in the sunlight of the king's smile. When the dancing started, I leaped into the king's arms when he held out his hand. To her.

I can still picture the shock and astonishment on the king's face. The bewilderment on Mary's. Until he sidestepped me neatly and swept her away, leaving me alone in the center of the room, rigid with humiliation.

No one challenged Father's decision to exile me to the country. Not George. Certainly not Mary.

"The court doesn't care, Anne," Wyatt says. "Just your family."

A weight lifts from me. If the court doesn't care—if the king doesn't—perhaps there's hope for me yet.

"So what will be the theme of this masque?"

"Why, love, of course, my dear. Nothing but love."

"Sounds inspiring," I tease. "Tell me what I need to do."

". . . is exactly the right thing to say."

I laugh and squeeze his arm, his elbow brushing against my breast. The shadows from the slanting sunlight flicker like a frown across his face, then his dimple reappears in full sun.

"First, we must invite our cast to join us."

My footsteps slow of their own accord. I have no friends.

"Who did you have in mind?"

"Norris. Bryan. Your brother."

I start to interrupt—to argue—but he carries on.

"Your sister."

"She'll never agree."

"And Jane Parker."

I think of the look in Jane's eyes as she gazed at George. "A matchmaker now, are you?"

"Jane's infatuation is obvious to everyone. I'm just creating opportunity. She might be a good influence on him."

I think of George's red-rimmed eyes and empty wine goblet, and I certainly hope so.

"Unlike you."

"Balance in everything, Anne." He leaps onto the ground-trailing branch of an ancient yew tree and runs along it—arms outstretched—and turns without wobbling. "As for your sister, she will agree to it."

"How do you know?"

Wyatt walks back along the branch and returns to earth without a sound.

"Because you are going to go and ask her."

"And apologize." It's been so long, will Mary accept it? Will she even see me?

"Anne," he says, and takes me by the shoulders. He stares hard into my eyes and won't let me look away. "Listen to me. Are you listening?"

His intensity is frightening, as are his fingers, pressing firmly into my flesh.

"Yes."

"Never apologize. It doesn't suit you."

I look at him for a long moment, to decipher the meaning behind his words, and realize he means them exactly as spoken. "Never?"

I try to imagine a life like that. And can't.

"I speak too quickly," I explain. "Let my temper take the lead. Even the queen apologizes."

"Only to God or her confessor."

"She never speaks out of turn, or says anything hurtful."

Wyatt chuckles, a deep rumble in his chest accompanied by his voice's tenor overtone.

"It doesn't mean you'll never have anything to apologize for. It just means you'll never do it."

"People will call me a bitch."

"Who cares? They'll think you're better than they are. More important. Worth more."

I ponder that. I think about the women of the French court. Queen Claude, the woman who should have had the most power, the most respect, received instead the most pity. Not because she was lame. Not because she was always ill with one pregnancy or another. Not because her husband slept more vigorously and more passionately with other women.

But because she was meek.

And Françoise de Foix, the French king's mistress, who roamed the halls of Amboise with a voice like a barking dog, who demanded the high table and shunned the queen's maids, had all the courtiers on their knees in worshipful awe.

Françoise never apologized. I had hated her.

"But—"

"There will be no *buts* in this instruction. You either take my advice or you make your own way. I promise to pursue you. To put you in the path of as many influential courtiers as there are codpieces at court. To do my best to free you from the clutches of James Butler."

"And I appreciate that."

"So never say you're sorry. Do exactly as I ask, and within the month, everyone will want you."

He steps back like a painter admiring his own masterpiece.

"No one will be able to stem the tide of Anne Boleyn."

10

I DON'T SEE HOW I CAN SPEAK TO MARY WITHOUT ASKING FOR forgiveness. Because I want it desperately. I want to erase the entire episode and be a family again, the Boleyns united.

Until Father arrives.

I drag myself to Mary's door, take a deep breath, straighten my spine, and knock.

There is no sound from the other side, and I begin to wonder if Mary has gone out. But then the door swings open, and she stands staring at me, her eyes registering surprise and fear.

My heart breaks a little.

"Nan." Her voice is a whisper. She glances into the empty gallery behind me.

She doesn't want me here. She doesn't want to be seen with me. My entire body tenses with remorse, and I open my mouth to break Wyatt's rule, when Mary grabs my arm, pulls me into the room, and wraps me in a tight hug.

"Nan, I'm so glad you're here."

The corners of my eyes sting, and my apology rises to the back of my throat. The Boleyns do stick together.

"Did you come to play? Your lute is ready." She points to where it lies on a stool by the fire.

My fingers itch to pick it up, to slide right back into how we were before. But I can't yet.

"I came to ask if you'd be in a masque with me."

Mary hesitates. "Like *The Château Vert*?"

"Nothing so grand. An interlude. A little frivolity written by Thomas Wyatt."

"Wyatt?" Mary doesn't smile. "He's a married man."

"And you know what that implies." I bite my tongue at the bitterness of my retort and rush on to cover it. To prevent an apology. "He's a poet. He's asked me to take part. And . . . and I'd like you to join me."

"You're not entangled with him in any way."

"He seems . . . interested." I think of how Wyatt looks at me when pretending to be smitten, and almost laugh. "But I'm not."

"Well, anyone can be interested. It's whom you encourage that matters."

"Thank you for the sisterly advice, Mary."

The hurt look returns, so I reach for her hand.

"I appreciate your concern, truly. And your advice."

She smiles weakly.

"I hope you take it."

She sits on the empty stool by the fire. I stare hungrily at my lute. Mary follows my gaze and laughs.

"Come and play."

I carefully tune the strings of the lute, wondering if the king has played it lately. I imagine his fingers on the strings, the back of the lute pressed tight to his body, his heartbeat in the vibration of the deep voice of the bass strings.

When I first saw him, I was thirteen years old. A maid in the household of Queen Claude, freshly promoted from the nursery and freshly initiated into the court by an unpalatably deep kiss from King François.

François and Henry had agreed to meet in the Field of Cloth of Gold, just beyond the English Pale of Calais. And it truly became a valley swathed in gold, the countless tents radiant with it and glittering with jewels. King Henry had a temporary palace built of wood and canvas with real glazed windows that reflected the sun. A gilt fountain ran with two kinds of wine, at which courtiers from both countries drowned their sorrows at being bankrupted by the expense of clothing themselves.

Carefully, I pick out a French tune on the lute. One written to describe the extravagance and pageantry. As the music flows from my fingers, it carries with it the detritus of memory.

I stayed in Ardres, on the French side, with Queen Claude and her ladies. The two kings met on the field on the first day, like armies, it was said, to the boom of cannon. Three days later, François rode out to Guînes to meet (and probably grope) the English queen and ladies. And King Henry came to visit Queen Claude.

The red of his hair shone against his black velvet cap, echoed in a more subdued shade by his beard. He was dressed all in crimson and cloth of gold, with jewels at his throat and crossing his chest, on his cap and encrusting his fingers.

But it wasn't the gold that dazzled me. And it wasn't the jewels.

It was the way he wore them. The way they fit the body

beneath. Broad chest. Narrow waist. The hard edge of the muscles in his leg beneath the stockings. And he towered above us, especially the lame and stocky Claude, who glowed round and sweet like a gilded pudding.

My limbs weakened at the sight of him, trembling with the hum I felt in his presence.

And then he spoke. Smooth. Delicate. Rich. As though his voice could melt in your mouth.

I should like to create a sound like that.

I reach for the middle strings, the little finger on my left hand, misshapen from a childhood accident, unable to stretch as far as the others. I feel the vibration of the tenor strings as I strum the rhythmic music of the king's speech.

I'm just getting the fingering right—just finding the balance between the tenor and the bright, high notes of the glitter of gold in the June sunlight—when I'm interrupted.

"Mistress Carey."

The voice—rich, smooth, and sweet—sends me immediately to my knees. It's as if I have conjured his presence with the notes themselves. The vibration in the lute continues long after I stop playing.

I hear the king stride into the room, each footstep like the beat of a drum, the rhythm at a slightly higher pace than the rest of us live by. And though my face is lowered, I envision him, dressed head to foot in red and gold, his fingers gilded in rings that he rotates with his thumb, one after the other, when he is thinking.

"Your Majesty." Mary's voice sounds like tin by comparison.

I bury my judgment in my skirts. Mary doesn't deserve it. Or my jealousy.

"Your Majesty, my sister, Nan—Anne—is here."

"Of course." His briskness betrays no discomposure at finding me there when he assumed he had a private audience with my sister. "You are well met, Mistress Boleyn."

I rise from my curtsy, but keep my head down. My face feels hot. Hotter than the rest of me.

"The lute!" he cries, and arrives in front of me in two beats. "Is this one yours?"

"Yes, Your Majesty." I still can't look at him. I may never look at him again. He must have heard me playing. Did he recognize himself in the notes?

"I played it last night. It is a fine instrument. You play well."

"Moderately, Your Majesty."

"Well, you must play better than your sister." There is a rise of laughter in his voice. "For she is completely useless on the strings."

But not in other things. I manage to hold my tongue. George would be proud.

"Anne plays exquisitely, Your Majesty," Mary interjects. "And sings."

"A girl after my own heart."

He raises his hand. I can see it, beringed and bedazzling. His fingers touch my chin and lift delicately. He forces me to look him in the eye.

He is wondrous. His hair blazes and his gray eyes are like

sun behind a cloud, the animated features almost seeming to blur because nothing about him is ever still.

"I greet you like a sister," he says. But there is a hint of mischief in his half smile.

He keeps his fingers on my chin and lowers his mouth to mine. When our lips touch, it is like the alignment of stars. The hint of stubble on his upper lip tickles mine, and I realize, hysterically, that my mouth is bigger than his. The scents of cloves and orange water fill me to drowning, and for one incomparable, darting instant, I taste the sweetness of his tongue.

He laughs and breaks away and I am left breathless, dropping to another curtsy as he turns to my sister.

Mary's laughter echoes his, the sound high above me, thin and wispy like clouds on a summer day. I feel my blood surge within my skull, drowning out their voices with rush and roar. Blindly, my senses reach for him, the scent of cloves and the caress of gold.

I look up from my curtsy, sure that he will be watching me. As moved by our contact as I was.

But he stands with Mary, a full head taller, his neck bent at an angle to kiss her, his hair reflecting the flames in the hearth. She is almost completely hidden, engulfed by his embrace.

I stagger to my feet, my joints barely able to take my weight, my fingers and lips suddenly devoid of all feeling, jealousy tangling my skirts, and elation still racing in my blood.

Because etiquette demands that no courtier turn away from the king, I get to see his every move as I shuffle to the door. He

removes Mary's hood, smooths her hair away from his lips as he trails kisses down her jaw and neck.

I manage to slip through the door before his lips drift lower. And I sink backward against it, resting one hand above my heart.

Wishing. Imagining it's me dissolving beneath his touch.

11

I KNOW IT MEANS NOTHING. A JOKE. A TEASE. *I GREET YOU LIKE A sister.* But I touch one finger to my lips, almost able to feel his again.

I stumble through the outer court and into the darkness of the tower gate, across the moat and up the stairs to the queen's rooms.

Where reality hits me. I kissed the queen's husband. Coveted my sister's lover. Ridiculously pictured myself in the arms of the king.

The watching chamber ripples with gossip as I enter. Wyatt says they don't remember *The Château Vert.* I should stop assuming that gossip is all about me.

I avoid the queen's eye as I curtsy before her. I'm sure she can somehow discern what I've done. And how much I liked it.

I search for a place to settle, and Jane Parker smiles at me, then covers her mouth with her hand. Her cuticles are ragged. She glances over to where George is ensconced with the gamblers, his wine close by his hand. Tentatively, she pats the window seat beside her.

"Jane." I sit cautiously.

"Mistress Boleyn."

"Oh, please, call me Anne." I'm irritated by her formality. She may be of the duchess's confederacy, but we sleep in the same bed, for pity's sake. She lifts her hand to bite the cuticles, but I put out my own to stop it.

"Has Wyatt spoken to you?" I ask.

Jane's hand freezes beneath mine, and she looks at me like a startled rabbit.

"No." She casts a glance around the room to see who's watching, who's listening. Frowns. "Why would Thomas Wyatt want to speak to me?" Her upper lip twitches at the corner, and she peeks at me from beneath her lashes. "Not that I'm not delighted at the thought, of course. He's rather gorgeous. And highly beddable."

I fight back the irritation that continues to grow.

"I don't think that was going to be his topic of conversation." Though it might have been, knowing Wyatt. The irritation threatens to ignite and engulf me.

"Oh!" Jane's other hand flies to her mouth, and I can barely understand the words around it. "I'm sorry. Truly. I meant no offense. And no presumption. I forgot, I mean, I didn't think . . . I'm sorry."

She bites the curve of her knuckle and I wince because she doesn't.

"Nothing to be sorry for," I say, thinking of Wyatt's rule. *Never apologize.* Especially when you have nothing to apologize for. And I add, "Stop doing that. You'll hurt yourself."

"It doesn't really hurt anymore." But she puts her hand in her lap and covers it with the other.

"Well, it will make your hands ugly."

"That's what the duchess says."

"Probably the only time we'll ever be in agreement."

Jane laughs out loud and then ducks her head, her hands bouncing in her lap as she struggles not to move them.

"However, the reason I asked if Wyatt has talked to you is because he's planning a masque. An interlude. An entertainment for the king."

"And he wants me to join?" She sounds surprised.

"You were in *The Château Vert*." I manage to say the name without cringing. "It's not like you're no one here. Your father is Lord Morley, a gentleman of the chamber."

"But no one ever notices me."

"That's because you never speak."

"I'm sorry." Jane shrugs.

Again the unneeded apology. I had never thought about the useless, ineffectual habit of offering an expression of regret. Like bandaging a healed wound.

"But we're going to change that," I whisper to her. "Wyatt is penning his own script. For you and me and Mary."

Jane's expression is one of delighted awe. "Me and the Boleyn girls."

I save the best for last. "And George."

Jane's smile completely consumes her, and I hope her joy can make a difference in George's life. Perhaps with Lord Morley's influence, he can get out from beneath Father's thumb.

"When do we start?" Jane leans forward—childlike in her eagerness—and I feel a flutter of jealousy.

"I'll let you know."

Jane tilts her head at me.

"Are you his muse?"

"Whose?" My mind is full of the king. Of how I would feel if he were participating in—and not just viewing—the performance.

"Thomas Wyatt's."

My laugh carries an edge of embarrassment. Jane must think I can't follow a conversation. I contemplate Wyatt's inspirations, and his promised poem about me. One that will be passed down through the ages, he said.

But only if I win the bet.

"Hardly," I tell Jane. "I think women in general are his muse, so he doesn't need a lot of prompting."

"Oh." Jane appears to ponder this. "Well, he certainly seems . . . interested."

"As I said, Wyatt is interested in anything in a skirt. And I know where my boundaries are."

"You must admit it though. He is delicious."

Her face is lit with mischief. But her expression alters in an instant as she spies something over my shoulder. I have to force myself not to look.

"Mind you, that one is striking as well."

I turn. Henry Percy. His stillness is the complete opposite of Wyatt's and seems to emanate from a deep discomfort. But Jane is right. Definitely striking. I look away before I can be accused of staring.

"The duchess says that he's supposed to marry the Earl of

Shrewsbury's daughter," Jane whispers. "But they hate each other."

"Poor boy," I mutter. The court is full of such stories. My own included.

"Hardly," Jane scoffs. "He'll be the Earl of Northumberland soon and will run the Scottish borders and half the country."

I glance up again at Henry Percy—destined to be one of the most powerful nobles in the country. Destined from birth to be a member of the royal circle. A captive in Cardinal Wolsey's household. So free, and yet still tethered.

He is an enigma.

And he's watching me.

12

I ALMOST ASK WYATT TO INVITE PERCY TO PARTICIPATE IN HIS poetic interlude. But then I look at Wyatt's profile, head bent over parchment and ink. The set of his jaw, the intensity of his eyes. And somehow, I can't.

So instead, I stake everything on one night. On the hope that someone watching will see me and save me from my fate, like in a romantic ballad. Because I can't think of another way to save myself.

The interlude is a lovely little joke of a play based on the myth of Atalanta. No set. Simple Greek-inspired costumes wrapped over pale gowns and doublets. We will be the only entertainment of the evening. Except for the dancing.

Wyatt casts me as Atalanta and Jane as my companion. Mary is Aphrodite. I can't complain, because Mary does nothing but stand on a dais and look beautiful. I get to lead the chase.

Wyatt will play Hippomenes—the man who catches Atalanta through cunning rather than fleetness of foot. He dresses in golden sandals and a sky-blue tunic that reflects the periwinkle of my gown, giving the appearance that we are meant to be together. George, Norris, and my cousin Bryan round out the cast of men who lust after Atalanta enough to risk death for a chance at her. I find it a bit perverse that George plays a potential lover, but say not a word. This is Wyatt's show, and I'm following instructions.

I'm grateful for the distraction, because the king has decided to call Parliament to raise funds for the war against France. The galleries and gardens of Richmond are full of the news. Full of men bloated on the thought of war. There is more tension in the court. More rivalry. Less chivalry. And the endless clamor of backslapping and chest-thumping.

The afternoon before the performance, I go to the orchards to smell the blossoms and avoid the heady musk of martial fervor. Unfortunately, the Duchess of Suffolk has had the same idea. I see her gown of deep lake blue, the red of her hair beneath her gable, and realize we are on an intersecting course that I cannot avoid.

She is followed by her confederacy. I'm disappointed to see Jane among them.

"Mistress Boleyn." The duchess's voice carries the same tenor as her brother's.

"Your Grace." She rarely speaks to me. It is rumored that her husband will lead the English troops into France in the summer, and I can't help thinking of it as she slips her arm through mine and turns me to walk with her.

People shuffle and bow out of her way. It is as if she has a giant bubble around her, one that cannot be punctured. One that I, miraculously, find myself inhabiting with her. It's a nice place to be. Watched, but protected.

I pretend I don't hear the whispers and titters behind me as the other ladies follow. I do glance back once. Only Jane looks at me and flashes an almost-smile.

"I must ask you," the duchess says, the corner of her hood's gable preventing truly confidential whispers, "are the women in France very beautiful?"

"Do you not remember, Your Grace? You were the most beautiful woman in the court when you were there." Flattery will surely get me somewhere with the sister of the king.

The duchess caused a fuss in both countries when she married the aging King Louis. After a year in the Low Countries, I was uprooted and sent to serve her. Until she caused an international incident when Louis died suddenly and she ran away with the up-and-coming and entirely unsuitable Charles Brandon. Despite his title, he had no royal blood and no connections and the match brought the king's wrath down on them both.

I had to admire her for marrying for love—and against the king's wishes. But the Brandons were both soon welcomed back to his circle and have been there ever since. We can all pretend the discord never happened.

"I have certainly not forgotten the kindness of a little girl I knew there," the duchess says sweetly. "I spoke French so poorly, and Louis had just dismissed my great friend and translator Lady Guildford. I was eighteen and terrified. And heartbroken."

"Yes, Your Grace," I say. Though she hadn't cared a whit when she left behind almost her entire entourage. Including a

lonely eight-year-old girl and her dangerously pretty older sister.

"You are all grown up now, though," she continues. "And looking for a husband of your own."

"Yes, Your Grace."

"And not that spiteful savage James Butler."

I jerk to stare at her, startled.

"No, Your Grace."

I can't see her entire face, hidden as it is by her hood, but I think I see her smile.

"I understand being forced into an unsavory marriage, Mistress Boleyn. And I haven't forgotten your kindness. I'll keep my eye out for a lovely young man for you."

"Thank you, Your Grace."

Why is she being so nice?

I hear a ripple behind me. I try to catch the ladies giggling, but their faces are impassive. Jane won't look at me at all, her eyes only on the ragged skin around her fingers.

"In the meantime," the duchess continues, entering the donjon through a door that opens without her even having to touch it, and flicking a wrist at the usher behind it, "you might consider some other forms of assistance."

We enter her private rooms, and the duchess picks up a little gilded pot of Venetian ceruse, a paint used by some to lighten their skin. She, of course, doesn't need it. She's so pale I can see the blue blood at her temple. She's offering the ceruse to me.

I hesitate. It's said that wearing ceruse can cause teeth to fall out and hair to thin to near baldness. It's said it can kill. Slowly.

"It will make you look less . . ." The duchess turns a pretty pink.

"Swarthy."

I hear the word, sniped from behind me, but the duchess pretends not to.

"Pale skin against your dark hair will make you look more dramatic," she says. "It will accentuate the blackness of your eyes. It will be like a siren's call to the eligible men of the court."

My eyes are not *black*.

But tentatively, I stick a finger in the paste. It smells of beeswax and feels like clay on my fingers.

"Let me help."

The duchess delicately smooths some across my cheeks, over my brow, right up to my hairline. She rubs it across the skin of my neck and where my jaw meets my ear. She even covers my lips and dabs it around the thin skin of my eyelids. A prickling burn in the corners of my eyes makes me squint and blink.

"There."

The duchess stands back to scrutinize me.

"Now you need red."

She finds another paste and daubs my lips and smears my cheeks. My skin feels cold and heavy.

It's like a death mask, the white lead burrowing into my face and freezing my smile.

"Beautiful."

One of her ladies holds up a little mirror of Venetian glass so we can see ourselves, side by side. I see a girl, her face as pale

as white linen, her lips red as blood, her eyes wide and dark and starting to spiderweb with reddened irritation, next to a clear-skinned, gray-eyed beauty, unmarred and unpainted.

"How do I get it off?" I ask.

The duchess freezes, staring at my reflection. Her eyes harden and narrow slightly.

"Don't you like it?"

I glance at Jane Parker, who meets my eye briefly, terrified. But then she looks down again, picking at the ragged cuticles of her left hand.

"Of course I do," I say, gagging back the truth. "I mean for later."

"You don't take it off," the duchess says. "You just apply more."

She waves the mirror away.

"You're beautiful, little Boleyn."

I want to believe her. No one has ever called me beautiful before. Different. But never beautiful.

She presses the pot into my hand. "Use it. And everyone else will think so, too."

Not only has the duchess given me a gift, she's also given me a sentence: to wear this death mask until I need a real one. Which, if the physicians are to be believed, will be all the sooner because of it.

A finger pokes me in the ribs.

I sink into a curtsy, barely able to frame my face into a smile.

"Thank you, Your Grace."

"Enjoy it," the duchess says dismissively. "You may go."

Again the rustle of suppressed giggles. A jostling of sleeves and gowns around me, and I am shuffled to the back of the group. Propelled out the door. And deposited outside, like refuse.

A peal of laughter rings through the door before it closes.

13

"WHAT THE HELL HAVE YOU DONE TO YOURSELF?"

I've never seen Wyatt angry before. I touch my face. I can hardly feel my fingers through the mask.

"You look like a fool."

He grabs my chin in his hand, fingers digging in. I try to pull away, but find I can't move. We are in the pages' chamber, where our costumes and properties are stored. No one else is around to see, but the great watching chamber is just the other side of the door, full of people.

"Aren't you the one who tells me we should always be making eyes at each other?" I ask him, setting my jaw and looking at him directly. "Even in private? What happened to your grand façade, Thomas Wyatt?"

He throws his hand from my chin and stumbles away.

"Perhaps it's time for a lovers' quarrel," he says to the wall beyond. His voice is tight, the set of his shoulders rigid.

"We can't have one if we're not lovers."

My eyes, already burning from the ceruse, feel pinched with the onset of tears, and my throat constricts. I can't lose my only friend. My only almost-friend.

"That's good, because I wouldn't want a painted doll in my bed. All show and no substance."

I don't understand why he's so furious. Or why it shatters me.

"The duchess said I was beautiful."

I hate the sound of my voice. Like a child begging for sufferance. I press my palms on my skirts to still them.

Wyatt turns like a cat on the prowl.

"The Duchess of Suffolk?" He stalks back to me, and I flinch. At the sight of it, the predation in him melts away.

"Watch out for her, Anne. She will not be a true friend."

"But she is part of the royal circle—that inner sanctum of status and nobility. Shouldn't I be cultivating that?"

"Not with her. Not with them. No one in that family can be trusted. I advise you to stay away."

It is well known that Wyatt and the Duke of Suffolk don't get along. Some long-standing dispute. The stories make them both sound like infatuated girls, jealous over the king's attention.

"They can only bring you misery."

I'm suddenly tired of instruction. Tired of always getting it wrong, always seeking improvement and never seeming to achieve it.

"Your point is taken, sir."

I rub my hands on my skirts and turn to walk away.

"Don't do that."

More?

"Don't do what, Wyatt?" I don't even turn to look at him.

I can no longer muster the energy to keep up the pretense.

"That."

He takes my left hand—turning me to face him—and flattens it to his. It requires every bit of my resolve not to pull away, my crooked little finger awkward in his palm. He doesn't seem to notice—at least, he doesn't react. Someone must be watching.

"Rubbing your skirts. It's a habit, Anne. And a nasty one at that. It's as bad as Jane Parker biting the skin at her fingernails. But at least that brings attention to her face. Your compulsion makes your face invisible."

"You don't even like my face at the moment," I mutter. Like a sullen toddler.

"Try this." He reaches out to stroke a strand of hair loose from my hood. He winds it along the length of his finger, slowly. "You want to attract the eye." His hand releases mine and drops to my skirts.

"Not here." He draws the backs of his fingers slowly upward, like a man's gaze. "But here. To your breasts, your neck, your hair."

I feel a shiver of heat and hold my breath.

"Your eyes."

His own eyes find mine, and there is something in them I've never seen before. He rests his palm on the side of my face. I smell the ink, metallic on his fingers. I tilt my head slightly, his hand taking a little of the weight from my shoulders.

I want to rub my hands on something, but one is caught up against the velvet of his chest. And the other I find covering the hand that cradles my face.

I swallow, and his gaze trails the action at my throat and comes to rest on my lips.

"We're putting on quite a show," I murmur, and his eyes snap back to meet mine.

"You're learning well." A compliment. But his smile is tight. So after all his criticism, I'm not sure he means it.

"Let's hope it pays off tonight," I say.

Wyatt takes a step back, dropping my right hand from his chest and pulling my left to his lips in a showy, chivalric kiss. But he continues to hold it tightly.

"Absolutely." He nods. "Now go and get ready."

But he doesn't let me. He holds on. And I want him to.

"One more thing, Anne. Before you leave."

I suddenly wonder if he'll ask me to kiss him. I wonder if maybe I'll say yes.

"Yes?"

"Take that rubbish off your face before I see you again."

He bows, drops my hand, and walks past me to the watching chamber. I take a deep breath, avoid touching my skirts, and turn around to leave, assuming I'll meet the half-averted gaze of an inveterate gossipmonger.

No one is there.

14

I SCRUB MY FACE, THE PASTE LEAVING WHITE STREAKS OVER RED skin. The rough linen and cold water scour and burn. The cloth drags at my eyelids and plucks at the lashes. My eyes are as red as my lips—inflamed—my entire face mottled and puffy.

Not exactly the image I had in mind for my bid to conquer the court.

Mary and Jane say nothing when we meet to dress for the play. My face feels raw and my eyes ache. Even without a mirror, I know I look a fright. Jane won't look at me, and Mary just purses her lips together. I dawdle while they dress, helping Mary with her stays while she helps Jane with her skirts. They are beautiful, their faces unmarred.

I'm still in my chemise and bodice, my gown thrown across a cedar chest. Mary shakes out my sleeves before coming to me to lace them on.

"Stop," I say, and she freezes, a sleeve held out before her like a peace offering. "I can't. I can't face them. The crowd. The chorus. The cardinal." The king. "Not like this."

Mary lowers her arms, looks at me sternly.

"Yes, you can."

"Look at me! They will hate me. For my face. My dress.

Because I'm a Boleyn. No matter what Wyatt says, they will hate me. The duchess hates me."

"The duchess hates everyone, Anne."

"You can take over my role, Mary."

"No, I can't. I'm Aphrodite."

"Then Jane . . ."

But Jane is no longer in the room. Mary drops the sleeves and takes my face in both of her hands. Gently. Like a mother.

"Nan, you can't let a little animosity stop you. If I had, I would be pulverized by now. Don't you think I feel this every day?"

"You have the king."

"Yes. And that's part of the problem. I'm the king's mistress." Mary pauses. "But for how long?"

Before I have a chance to respond, the door bangs open and Wyatt strides into the room, fierce and feline. Jane pauses behind him, closing the door with her foot.

"What does Jane mean, you're not going on?"

Wyatt grabs me by the shoulders, then realizes he's touched bare skin at the neck of my chemise. He leaps away, shaking his fingers as if he's been scalded.

I'm so ugly even Thomas Wyatt can't bear to touch me.

I take a deep breath. Hold my hands still. "I can't go on like this."

He studies my face, and his tone softens.

"Good God, what has she done to you?"

Somehow this hurts more than his anger when he called me a fool.

"It will go away," Mary says quickly. "It already looks better."

When Wyatt reaches out to touch my face, I duck and step aside.

"Right," I say. "Let's just put it off for a couple of hours. It's only the king and the cardinal waiting."

Wyatt coughs a laugh, and while his back is turned, I grab a cloak to cover myself, then tie my hair into a knot.

"Actually," he says, "I already have a solution. One that won't require our notoriously impatient monarch to wait."

He turns to Jane, who brings her hands out from behind her back, and with them, three decorative masks. All in white, trimmed in gold. One simple, trimmed with braid. One plumed in peacock feathers—Aphrodite. And one edged around the eyes with black and gold, wings of gold-dusted feathers at the temples. Mine.

I look at Wyatt.

"When did you plan this?"

"When I decided the whole production would be more fun as a masque. Lends an air of mystery."

"And allows the men to choose their dancing partners," I add. He's thought of everything. If only the roles were reversed and I could be the one to make a choice.

Wyatt's dimple disappears when he catches a glimpse of my chemise beneath the open cloak.

"Get dressed." He turns back to the door. Pauses. Looks back. "You'll be wonderful. A jewel held to the light."

He disappears, and I find myself wondering what it would be like to dance with him.

Mary and Jane each fasten a sleeve, and we tuck my hair into the gold caul of my cap before tying on the mask. I feel hidden. Mysterious. Sheltered.

Beautiful.

I silently thank Thomas Wyatt for that.

15

THE GREAT WATCHING CHAMBER IS LIT WITH TORCHES AND candles, their dragon's breath swirling in the rafters along the gilded battens and Tudor roses. The walls are covered in tapestries shining with pigment and gold thread. But even they are unmatched by the riot of color presented by the audience. Mary, Jane, and I stand together in the pages' chamber, peering out at the assembled masses.

Wolsey is a beacon in his cardinal red—a great, round hump of velvet and fur, beaming with self-satisfaction. Behind him run layers of courtiers and sycophants, ladies with faces etched in envy. Percy is near the door, a pillar around which a tide of courtiers flows, bringing with them James Butler, ursine and unruly.

The queen sits on a dais, dressed in lustrous gray that tinges her skin green, and a Spanish hood that cloaks her face in shadow, the soft folds veiled and saddened.

The musicians in the minstrels' gallery start up a galliard, and a group of finely dressed ladies dance with the king's men. I see several of the duchess's confederacy amongst them. A well-cast prologue. Wyatt is quite a diplomat.

The dance is athletic and breathless, and the audience shouts and applauds when the dancers are done.

The person I wish to see most, however, is not here. When he enters a room, he infuses it with light like the moon and the sun all at once—drawing the eye to him, then searing the vision. But he isn't here.

The king isn't coming.

A sharp whistle from the audience wakes me, and I hear Wyatt, already narrating. Mary puts a hand on my shoulder.

"Remember, you're better than they are, Nan." She gives me a little push. "You're a Boleyn."

I adjust my mask and step into the chamber. The light from the torches blinds me. The colors of the doublets and gowns and the brilliance of the jewels and gold dazzle me.

"Smile."

Mary's disembodied voice comes from the shadows at my elbow.

I smile.

Mary moves past me, circling the great hall past all the courtiers, the brush of her skirts sighing over the floorboards and rushes.

I hear a muffled yelp as she passes the duchess.

"Excuse me, Your Grace." A carrying whisper.

I smile and look up. Wyatt is watching me. I imagine he has been the entire time, acting the part of the besotted lover.

"Atalanta," he says, raising a cheer from the men in the audience. "The most beautiful girl in Athens."

He turns to include the audience.

"But also the swiftest, my friends. She is quick as a doe and loath to be caught. Only one man will suit her: the only man who can catch her."

A boom of cannon sounds from outside, and the doors at the end of the chamber burst open. Four men enter, dressed in white and silver and cloth of gold, burning like flame and carrying with them the odors of night and saltpeter.

Four?

They, too, are masked, but easily recognized. Norris with his ink-black hair. Bryan, his dark-red tunic pulled tight around his wiry frame. George, his shambling gait giving him away.

And the fourth . . .

The fourth is the king.

He looks to me, his gray eyes clear and hot and knowing. A prickle at my neck quickly becomes a hum at the top of my head. I hardly know what to do with myself. I glare at Wyatt, who offers a minute shrug as if to say, *How could I refuse the king when he asked?* And then I feel a rush of warmth through me and turn back to the king. He must have asked to join in. I raise a hand to my lips, remembering the press of his there.

The king winks at me.

Wyatt stumbles over a couplet rhyme, and I glance at him in shock. Thomas Wyatt never drops a rhyme. He ignores me.

When I look back at the king, he has turned to Aphrodite, and my stomach roils with an unpalatable mix of jealousy, self-recrimination, and shame.

Fortunately, the play is a carefully choreographed dance and I know the steps well. Pursuit and escape. I can't actually

run about the room—it would look ridiculous. But the dance allows me to skip ahead of the men. Always in front. Always pursued. Never caught.

Mary sets up the final race, giving Wyatt the golden apples one by one. He rolls the gilded fruit before me to slow me down. Part of me wants to ignore them. To win the race. Lead the pack. But that isn't how the story goes.

So I pick them up as he races past me, toss them to the audience. All eyes are on me, faces upturned.

Wyatt, victorious, takes me as his prize, and Mary blesses the union to the applause of the audience. But just as we are about to move into the final dance, he stops us with an upraised hand. The court quiets.

"We come to you disguised, my lords and ladies. Is this who we are? Or merely who we wish to be? Beautiful." He indicates Mary.

"Loyal." He bows to Jane.

"And unobtainable." He turns toward me and hesitates.

His eyes are unquiet. The room falls into silence.

"Unmask!" a voice shouts from the audience.

"Let us be the judges!"

"Dance." Butler's growl is unmistakable.

"Let me set you a riddle." Wyatt turns from me to face the audience. "Solve it, and you tell me who is our Atalanta."

All eyes are on us as he approaches me with the measured steps of the verse.

> *"What word is that, that changeth not*
> *Though it be turned and made in twain?"*

I struggle to follow the riddle myself. A-N and N-A. It doesn't change, however it is turned. Unlike me.

> *"It is mine answer, God it wot,*
> *And eke the causer of my pain—"*

Wyatt cannot see my eyebrow raised behind my mask. He's laying it on a little thick.

> *"A love rewardeth with disdain*
> *Yet it is loved. What would ye more?*
> *It is my health, eke and my sore."*

Loved?

He stops in front of me, catches my hands before I rub them on my skirts, and holds them both to his heart. I take a step forward, wanting to taste the almonds on his breath, but his grip tightens and I stop. I study his face, but his true intention is hidden behind mask and make-believe.

"What word is it?" The voice is to my left. A mellifluous tenor. "Why, dear troubadour, the answer is simple."

Wyatt lets go of me and steps back, leaving me impoverished. So I turn to the speaker. The king is facing me, his hand extended, his gray eyes shining behind his mask.

"Anna."

16

Because he is still masked, I can dance with the king.

Because he asks.

I dance with the king.

The eyes of the entire room are on me. Still. Me. Anne Boleyn. I am nobody. And yet I am everything. I will not waste this chance. This time, my dance with the king will propel me forward, not send me home.

The top of my hood barely reaches his chin. I find myself facing the elaborately embroidered doublet—layered and appliquéd in damask and satin, blue, gold, yellow, and bronze. And the heat coming from it is intense.

Or perhaps that heat is coming from me.

This is my moment. This is my chance. I can be what I am. Only better. I know I can dance. In France, I was praised for the lightness of my feet, for the effortlessness of my movements. For the way I seem to feel the music in my limbs.

I feel the same rhythm in his.

The king lifts me with what seems to be so little effort, I feel like I am flying. Floating. His hands at the base of my ribs are like a tether to the sky. His touch sets my sinews vibrating like lute strings, all playing the same note.

My entire world is nothing but silk and velvet, fur and damask and the scent of cloves.

Until the dance ends.

He bows to me and turns, without a backward glance, to the audience, and we all unmask to gasps of practiced astonishment and wild applause. I manage a curtsy, though the note thrumming through my body conspires to unbalance me.

When the dancing continues, the king partners the duchess. It's only fair, because she is the lady of greatest precedence after the queen, who again refuses to dance. Norris—looking delighted—partners Mary, who gracefully adjusts his roaming hands. Jane looks at George, who turns on his heel and strides to the far end of the room, plucking up a wine goblet on his way.

"You didn't look out into the audience."

Wyatt steps me into a turn and I lose sight of Jane, who seems about to cry. The players are all supposed to dance together. I quell a stab of anger at my brother, but Wyatt doesn't miss it.

"Smile. You're supposed to be enjoying this."

I think of the one thing that can restore my good humor.

"Did you see, Wyatt? The king danced with me."

"It's all part of the performance, Anne. He answered the riddle."

Defeated, I search for Jane as we come out of the turn. She is in the arms of Henry Percy, who is smiling. But not at her.

"Was everyone watching?" I ask Wyatt, wanting to taste once more the heady excitement of being part of the most intimate layer of the royal circle. I look up at him. "Did you see?"

"Everyone was watching, Anne. And yes, I saw. You could have shown more deference to your sister."

"But he asked me, Wyatt!"

We execute a turn, and I spin away from him.

"During the play. She was Aphrodite. A goddess. And you treated her like . . . your sister."

"She is my sister, Wyatt."

"Still, deference is due."

We chassé four steps, only our fingertips touching.

"And you missed a line at the beginning."

"Because the king had joined us and I was a little bit surprised! Jesus, Wyatt, can I do nothing right?"

The dance brings us together again. Close. Pressed against each other, my hands in his.

"You dance rather well."

"A compliment."

I give him a hard stare until the dance requires me to move away from him, walking in a broad circle, before returning.

"You do," he says. "You flow with the music. It's very . . . sensual."

The word runs like water down my spine. But then I remind myself who it is I'm speaking to.

"You're still not winning the bet, Wyatt."

He looks away. I follow his gaze to George, who stands leaning against an embroidered silk wall hanging. George raises his goblet to us. We turn, and I don't see him drink. But I see Jane, watching his every move.

"Young Lord Percy can't take his eyes off you."

I meet Percy's gaze, his oddly colored eyes. Jane says something to him, and he answers. But his eyes never leave mine.

"You know"—Wyatt's voice is a little strained, but when I turn to look at him, his face is placid—"Percy could be the entrée into that circle of nobility whose acceptance you so desperately seek. Heir to the earldom of Northumberland. One of the highest—and oldest—noble families in the land."

There is no mistaking the sardonic edge to his voice.

"That's why we're doing this, right?"

He looks at me sharply. "So you can marry Henry Percy?"

"So I can gain acceptance. So I don't have to marry James Butler."

"You could always become my mistress."

The laughter is back in his voice.

"That would only solve one of my problems."

"Oh, I'm sure James Butler wouldn't consider marrying a poet's tarnished mistress."

"I would be the court darling, and the duchess would invite me to be her most trusted friend." I lace my words with sarcasm.

"I said before, Anne, she's not a friend you want to have."

"I think I've figured that out, Wyatt. But you know what I mean."

"Yes," he says quietly. "Yes, I do."

The dance ends and Wyatt takes me by the hand.

"Let's go see what the night will bring."

He leads me to Jane and Percy, who are standing silently, as if completely unsure of how to part.

"Mistress Parker," Wyatt says smoothly. "I hope to have the pleasure of your company in a dance."

Jane's face lights up, and I think about her words that first

day we really talked. How she described Wyatt as "beddable." I shoot him a look that's meant to say, *Don't try anything with her.* He flickers a frown back at me.

"Mistress Boleyn," he says, snapping a quick bow. "Lord Percy."

Percy inclines his head as I curtsy. As the son of an earl, he doesn't need to offer much deference to the daughter of a nobody.

"Dance?" Uttering one word brings a flush of color to Percy's face, and I am instantly charmed by his self-consciousness.

But when the music begins, he promptly steps on my white satin slipper.

He doesn't apologize.

And I wonder if Wyatt has been training him, too.

Percy's gaze intensifies as he follows the rhythms of the music. His eyes—a blue so pale they're like sunlight—keep flicking from my face to his feet to the other dancers and back again. Perhaps he's just nervous.

Of dancing? Or of being with me?

We execute a turn and when we face each other again, he clears his throat.

"The masque was very . . . entertaining."

His voice is musical. Like the bass notes of a lute. Thrumming. Resonant.

"Thomas Wyatt is quite a poet." I try to sound noncommittal, but it is obviously the wrong thing to say. Percy's face falls into craggy shadows and he glances over to where Wyatt is making Jane laugh so hard she can't find the steps. I miss one, too, but Percy catches me.

He clears his throat again. A judgment. He thinks I've complimented Wyatt because of an attachment.

"You dance very well," I tell him. Men need flattery. Especially noblemen.

"Thank you." He turns. Frowns at me. "So do you."

No comments on my sensuality from Henry Percy.

I watch him from the corner of my eye as we promenade away from each other. He is watching Wyatt's catlike grace. Comparatively, Percy is a bit stiff. A bit unsure of the steps. I find his insecurity appealing, a nice change from Wyatt's relentless self-confidence.

"I hear that you play the lute," Percy says when he returns to me, all of his attention focused through that penetrating gaze.

"I enjoy music."

"And I hear around the court that your voice could rival Orpheus. That it charms all the animals of the forest and entices the birds to dance."

I laugh. "You shouldn't believe everything you hear at court."

"There is much loose talk," he replies, and narrows his eyes once more at Wyatt.

He's trying to make sense of what he has heard. And I hope he is not one of the small-minded people who believe Wyatt's hints and implications.

"The court is full of stories told by perjurers and poets," I say a little more loudly than I had intended. As we turn again, I take a deep breath and when I come back to him, I murmur warmly. "And one can only believe the things experienced in the flesh."

My timing is just right. As I say the word "*flesh*," his hand is at my waist. I feel a squeeze of pressure before the flush starts at his ears and floods his face and throat.

Wyatt will be delighted. I risk a glance at him, expecting a nod or a wink or a single dimple at the very least. But his back is turned.

"Then I should like to hear you sing one day," Percy croaks, and I look up into his face. Vulnerability softens his features.

I lower my gaze, the steps of flirtation taught to me by Thomas Wyatt as measured as the steps of the dance as it comes to an end. Just as I begin to sense Percy's concern at offending me, I look up and smile.

"One day I will," I tell him. "For I would like to see what it entices you to do."

17

"You certainly made a spectacle of yourself last night."

George enters the maids' chamber at Richmond as if he's been here a hundred times before. He probably has. I shudder at the thought that he could have been the man I smelled on my bedclothes.

"You certainly made yourself scarce," I reply. I'm all alone—for once—looking for the little pot of ceruse. Wanting to give it back to the duchess. I find it and twist it in my hands as I sit down on the bed.

George sits next to me with a flourish and then lies down, his head in my lap, looking up into my eyes. Like a lover. He grins.

"The best girl was already taken by the king."

I stroke his hair, trying to tame it.

"Hardly," I say, the glow from last night still lodged in my chest. And the glow of George's praise.

When we were children Father sneeringly called George a girl when he cried. So we played a betting game to soothe the sting. *Who's the best girl?* The winner got all three desserts at dinner. Mary peed herself laughing the day George came into our room dressed in bodice and skirts, singing a love song in falsetto and salting it liberally with profanity and counterfeit flatulence.

He got all our sweets for a week for that stunt. Made himself sick on them.

"You deny the fact that our sister was the prettiest girl there?"

I sigh and drop my hand to the bed. Of course George wasn't complimenting me. Or renewing our childhood friendship. I surreptitiously wipe my hand on my skirts—George's hair is a little greasy.

"No need to be jealous. Mary's success benefits us all."

"What good has it done me?" I snap. I'm sick of George. Sick of his backhanded compliments and sly criticisms. I want so badly for him to sit here with me, reveling in our success. Not cutting it to pieces.

"It brought you to court, my dear. And won the king's support of your marriage to my legacy."

"I don't want your bloody legacy!"

"Well, you should, you know. If not for yourself, then for the family. A title is the only way ahead. Money. Influence." He looks up at me, his eyes savage. "Having a sister to sell. It's the only thing you're useful for, after all."

I push him off my lap, and he lands in the rushes with a thump and a laugh.

"Get out."

I kick at him and he grabs my ankle and pulls. I cling to the counterpane, but it does nothing to slow my descent and raises a cloud of dust as it falls to cover us.

George laughs again, an almost childish giggle, and I can't help but feel my anger diminish. We are tented beneath the counterpane. Just the two of us. Like it used to be.

"Girls are good for more than that, you know." I prepare to give him the same speech I gave James Butler.

"They certainly are, dear sister." George waggles his eyebrows. "Though I don't expect you to understand."

"Don't be disgusting."

I scramble with the counterpane to pull it off. Before it suffocates me.

"Don't make yourself more than you are." George stands and brushes his doublet. Checks his fingernails. "As a woman, you have no choice. You have to do what your father says. And eventually what your husband says. You can use your feminine wiles to encourage certain outcomes, but at the end of the day, their will is the only will that matters."

I think of Queen Claude: lame, pious, meek. She should have been a queen in her own right. As the daughter of a king she should have ruled. But French Salic law prevented it, so her debauched and warlike husband, François, rules instead.

Even royalty can be rendered impotent.

"I'll just have to put my feminine wiles to work then."

"You already are, dear sister. You have half the men at court panting after you. Just make sure you sell to a higher bidder than Thomas Wyatt."

"I'm not selling anything to Wyatt." I stand and put my bed back together. "Our friendship is strictly that: friendship."

"Anne." George's voice is full of pity, as if I've just admitted

to believing in true love. "Men and women cannot be friends. It's impossible. It's like the lion and the lamb. Oil and water. Grain and grape."

I turn to face him. "And why is that?"

"There are far too many reasons to count. Incompatibility. Dissimilarity." He leans toward me. "Sex."

I step back. "That's not an issue."

"Of course it isn't, dear sister. Wyatt has much better taste."

George raises a smirking eyebrow, but I refuse to rise to the bait.

"The real reason that men and women cannot be friends," George continues, "is that women don't know how to have fun."

I stare at him.

"That is wrong on so many levels, George."

"All you do is sit around and sew. Gossip. Maybe play a few boring tunes on the lute."

"Friendship is not based on fun."

"It is in my book."

"If we were given the chance to go out to London and roam the streets and attend a bearbaiting, we might do more than sew."

"You would drink in the taverns and get in a brawl and maybe go whoring afterward?" George laughs.

I scowl at him.

"There," he says, and pats my cheek gently. "See? No fun at all."

He kisses me sloppily.

"Be not afeard, my darling. Friendship has no place between a man and a woman. But fun?" He smiles a sly smile. "Fun cer-

tainly does—especially when it comes to sex. And occasionally serves a purpose, as well."

He walks to the door, creaking it open.

"Fun for whom, George? And to what purpose?"

He turns back to look at me. "Why, fun for the man of course. And for the woman, it serves all kinds of purposes, from hooking the man to providing him an heir."

"But no fun for the woman?"

"You just have to learn how to have fun with it, Anne. And you will, with the right guidance. I suppose Wyatt would serve you well in that capacity."

I make a rude gesture that he doesn't see because he has already turned and walked away. I can hear him whistling.

"Bastard," I mutter under my breath. I feel my hair to make sure it's tucked under the edge of my hood, straighten my sleeves, and follow George's footsteps through the doorway, clenching the pot of ceruse in my hand. I might as well have another confrontation. It seems to be the day for it.

But when I round the corner and see James Butler at the end of the gallery, I slow my steps until he disappears into the warren of rooms.

Better not to have more confrontations than absolutely necessary.

18

I navigate the chaos of Richmond to the room reserved for the Duchess of Suffolk. I take a deep breath, knock, and am allowed entrance. Her confederacy is there, fussing and bootlicking, except for Jane Parker, who sits in the corner, silent and unobserved.

"Your Grace," I say by way of announcement, and curtsy deeply. It doesn't hurt to soften a slight with deference.

"Mistress Boleyn."

I hear the coldness in her voice. And I believe Wyatt is right. She never really meant to be my friend, just wanted to use me as a doll for a day.

"I have come to return this, Your Grace."

I cup the little pot in my upturned hand and raise my gaze.

My eyes take in Mary Brandon, Duchess of Suffolk, sister to the king, with her perfect skin and silky auburn hair. Her damask sleeves are the color of a weathered rose, her bodice covered in pearls and gold. She doesn't need the ceruse. I should have just thrown it away.

I meet her gray eyes. They hold none of the merriment that the king's do. Still, the similarity stuns me.

"You have no use for it?"

Silence. Jane's hands twist in her lap, and I can see the effort it takes for her not to bite her nails. She catches my eye briefly, and I think I see her shake her head.

"No, Your Grace."

"You have no use for a token of friendship."

It's a statement. Not a question. She is equating her friendship with the ceruse. If I refuse it, if I refuse to wear it, I refuse her.

I think of Wyatt. The ripple of his laughter when I make a joke. The way he actually listens to me when I speak.

"No, Your Grace."

She draws herself up to her full height. She is tall, like the king. She looks down on me, eyes trailing the cut of my hood. My gown.

"You think because you inspire the lust of the men of the court that you have become someone. Someone risen. But you are nothing. And will always be nothing. No matter whom you dance with.

"You will never be one of the inner circle of nobility, Anne Boleyn. A Stafford. A Talbot. A Percy. No matter how many masques you do. Or heads you turn. You should accept the hand of friendship when it is offered."

"I am a Howard."

"I'm afraid often that is more of a hindrance than a help."

Someone in the room titters, but I don't look away from those gray Tudor eyes.

"One piece more of advice, little Boleyn," the duchess adds, affecting a generous smile. "You should stay away from that ras-

cal poet, Thomas Wyatt. He has no honor. He can't be trusted."

I think about the laughter I heard follow me from the room after she slathered me in ceruse. The way that muck felt when I scrubbed it off. The way she looks at me now as if I'm something she found stuck to the bottom of her slipper.

"That is interesting, Your Grace," I say, "because he says the same thing about you."

I know I will regret these words later, but they taste like sugared almonds and I savor them.

Bridewell Palace
1523

19

THE MEN OF THE COURT ARE ITCHING FOR WAR. FOR BLOOD AND pain and death and victory. They are like animals, caged. We move to Bridewell, hemmed in by the City, and tensions rise. Trapped between rivers and walls, squeezed by monasteries on either side, the men's restiveness only partially assuaged by flirtation, cards, and the talk of war.

It doesn't help that Bridewell was built for beauty and not for strength, with elaborately stacked brick that creates a winding effect up the façade and chimneys. The entire building is striped with windows to rooms two stories high. This palace isn't a place to attack or defend. It's a place to see and be seen.

A covered gallery reaches all the way to the monastery of Blackfriars beyond the wall, over the Fleet, slow and sluggish, more of a ditch than a river. Wyatt walks me across on the way to the queen's rooms, and we stop on the bank of the river to watch the noisome water meandering around a knot of grass and a downed tree.

"Not exactly the Loire," I say.

Wyatt chuckles. "Nothing lives up to France with you, does it?"

I sigh and look around me.

"Well. Bridewell has its charms. But Greenwich has poky

rooms. And Westminster is in desperate need of repair. And Richmond just feels . . . choked. None of them is like Wolsey's palaces. York Place. Or Hampton Court. And truly, not even those match King François's plans for Fontainebleau. With frescoes in the galleries!"

"Yes, but what about King Henry's tapestries?"

I scowl a little, which only seems to provoke mirth in him.

"I suppose they're beautiful." I pretend to pout.

"Well, I, for one, don't believe there's a place more magnificent than England. The rolling hills. The South Downs. The chalk cliffs of Dover. The forests that cover half of Kent. The river Medway as it flows past Allington. I can't imagine anything better, or ever wanting to leave it."

"But you have never seen France."

"I don't think I want to. Leaving the land of my birth would be exile. Even to see the beauties of François's frescoes."

"Well, you don't know what you're missing, Wyatt, sequestering yourself here, when you have all of Europe to explore."

I find myself staring blankly at Fleet ditch, thinking of all the places I've yet to see. Queen Claude, on the nights she would weep after the birth of her annual baby, would claim she wanted to take me—and all her own children—back to her home country of Brittany. She made it sound wild, magical. When I met Leonardo da Vinci, he claimed Florence was the only city a cultured young woman should ever aspire to visit.

I want to see it all. But my life is limited by more than rivers and walls and monasteries. These men have no idea what being

trapped really feels like. Only my words can set me free, and only when the right person hears them.

We continue through the gate and outer court. The royal apartments are accessed by a grand processional stair, facing the courtyard like a dancer ready to perform. There is no hall; instead the stair opens immediately into the watching chamber, and from there we curve to the right to the queen's northside rooms. The ceilings soar above us, but the structure still feels subdued by the king's rooms above. As if the men are pressing down on us.

Perhaps it is just my imagination.

Their restlessness is catching. I sense it as soon as I enter the room. Even Jane has laid down her needlework and is twisting her hands in her lap. It feels like the court is a pot near the boil.

I think about George's comment that girls are no fun. That we don't know how to do anything. I sneak a look at the men by the door, sitting at the gaming table. The betting is tense and furious.

They're playing primero, a game Father taught us all to play as children. George and I regularly challenged each other, claiming the loser was the "girl." From the look on his face now, he's winning.

Momentarily, I consider not going over. Not intruding. Letting George win alone.

But I want to show him that girls are smarter than he thinks they are.

More than that, I want to do something that makes me feel less powerless.

I walk to the table. George is hunched over his cards, his back curved like a bent bow—taut and ready to spring. Butler sits opposite him, his cards bending in the tension of his grip while he glowers at our approach.

Henry Percy tries to rise, causing the entire table to look up at me.

"Don't bestir yourselves, gentlemen." I wave an airy hand. "I'm just here to watch. Card games are beyond my ken."

I ignore George's snort of blatant suspicion.

"Would you like to learn, Mistress Boleyn?" Henry Percy's eyes are eager.

"Mistress Boleyn has a habit of making ill-advised wagers." Wyatt takes an empty seat next to George.

"So do you, Wyatt." George doesn't look at him.

"Not a game for ladies," Butler growls.

"Then it's a good thing you don't find me very ladylike," I tell him, and cordially thank Percy, who gets me a stool and seats me next to him.

I flash Wyatt a smile, but he doesn't catch it.

"Do you know the game, Mistress Boleyn?" Percy's words tickle my ear. He's sitting very close. His clothes smell of cedar, sharp and sneezy.

"I've played before," I say.

Men like girls to be helpless, I remind myself, noticing the disappointment on his face. They want to instruct. To advise. *To own.*

"But it's been a long time," I add. "I may need assistance."

I bite back my impatience as Percy tells me the point value

of each card, how the hands and combinations are ranked.

"Jesus wept, Percy, are you in or not?"

Wyatt's hiss cuts through the room. The tension in his shoulders has increased. I widen my eyes at him, but he still won't look at me.

"I'll join in the next round."

Percy leans closer, one arm encircling my shoulders so he can use the fingers of that hand to indicate the cards I hold. If I leaned just a little to the right, my cheek would brush his. I settle slightly, my back pressing into the curve of his arm. He drops it abruptly, his face pink.

Too much. Too soon.

I look at Wyatt again, hoping for some instruction. But his face is blank. Unreadable. He's playing his own game. Not mine.

Butler kicks the table leg, startling me so I look at him. He shows his teeth.

"Let's play," he says.

I know the game inside and out, but I am a little rusty. I make a couple of ill-advised moves. Percy corrects me. Gently. I murmur praise at him and he blushes again. Really, he is too easy.

"Sharing secrets?" Butler growls. "Perhaps you should sit next to me. I won't give special treatment."

The edge to his voice is shocking. Like a dousing with cold water.

"I like where I am, thank you," I reply. "Where I can see you."

Wyatt smothers a laugh.

And for a while, we simply play the game. I get lost in the heady feeling of gambling away my savings. Taking risks. Having fun.

When I raise the stakes again, I look at George. And for once, I see that he remembers, too. Remembers our childhood. Remembers that when we played against each other then, it didn't matter who won. What mattered was who made the biggest bet.

"You're as quick as a man," Wyatt says when I throw my next card down.

"There are some women who know how to play," I say, looking between him and George. "We're not only good for sewing and family services."

Norris whistles when I wager again. "You play like the king."

I vibrate with a warm memory of the king's hand on my waist.

"Except that when the stakes are high, she doesn't lose," Wyatt mutters.

"You should be careful what you wager," Percy says quietly, dismay sprawled across his expression. "And not call attention to it. Play only within your means. And your teaching."

"Have I surpassed your instruction?" I ask innocently. "Is there not more you can teach me?" I raise an eyebrow suggestively, giddy from all the attention.

Color deepens the shadows on his face. I'm beginning to enjoy making Henry Percy blush.

"You do need teaching," Butler says. "Maybe a caning will keep you in your place."

The table goes silent. Not one of them looks up from his cards. Not Percy, who has gone so still beside me, it's like he's trying to render himself invisible. Not George, who studiously runs his fingers along the coins in front of him on the table. Not even Wyatt.

Fear and anger well within me, pressing me tight against the stays of my bodice. Do they agree with Butler? That a woman should be seen and not heard? Should sit back and let others win?

Then Wyatt steals a glance at me. Slants his eyes sideways at Butler.

"I say, James"—the quiet humor in his voice freezes the men around us even more—"to whom will go that pleasure?"

George snorts and Norris brays, the lecherous light returning to his eyes when he looks at me. Percy's cards flutter in his hands like a fan.

Butler overturns his stool in his haste to withdraw, and he pushes roughly past Wyatt on his way to the door.

The entire table turns to me. Expectantly.

"I may not know my place . . ." I say quietly. I stand and lay my cards down, face up—a chorus of kings.

The men look from the cards to me.

"But I believe I know when I've won."

I pocket the coins and leave the room.

20

I CROSS THE YARD, HEADING TO THE GARDENS, THE ONLY PATCH of green in this pile of stone and mud. But it is all in shadow, and as the sun goes down, the air turns bitterly cold. English springtime.

I tuck my hands inside my sleeves. The duchess may say what she likes about the awkward length of them, but at least my sleeves keep me warm. Or warmish.

"I don't know what to do," I say when I hear footsteps approach. Without even looking, I know it's Wyatt. I knew he'd come. "He gets more proprietary every day." Every day that brings my father's footsteps closer to court.

"You could poison him."

"What?" I turn.

"It's the only way to remove the possibility permanently. It also sets your father up nicely to claim the earldom of Ormond unchallenged. I'm sure he'd support the scheme."

I wouldn't put anything past my father.

"There is no way I will resort to something so evil, so brutal. . . ."

I see little puffs of breath coming from Wyatt's nostrils as he tries not to laugh out loud.

"Well, if you're not going to take my problems seriously . . ."
I turn away and suppress a giggle of my own. Me, a poisoner.
Ridiculous.

"No, my dear, I absolutely take your problems seriously.
Without you here, my life will be nothing but desolation."

"You're wasting your poetry, Wyatt."

"Oh, but it brings me neatly to my next proposition. The
one that is sure to save you."

The intensity of his gaze matches the wintry sky behind
him. His sudden seriousness halts my breath.

"It may not be your only choice, Anne. But it may well be
your best."

I wait, chin tilted so I can see his face, the shape of his jaw. I
suddenly want to stroke it.

He clears his throat.

"You could become my mistress."

I feel as if a weight has landed on my shoulders, as if the
English sky itself is trying to force me to my knees. I turn and
stride back to the palace.

"I don't know why I bother asking you," I shout back over
my shoulder. "All you do is joke and offer no assistance whatsoever. I thought you were my friend."

It takes him only a moment to catch up with me—his legs
are so much longer. He lays a hand on my shoulder and I spin
left to shrug it off and keep walking. He stops, and I leave him
behind.

"I am your friend!" he calls. "Which is why I didn't want to
suggest . . ."

I stop and wait, but do not face him. I notice he doesn't apologize.

"Well?" I clench my jaw.

"You could marry Percy."

There it is. The idea that has been in the back of my mind. Spoken aloud. I allow myself a vision of a possible future. Me with precedence, a place at court, a name. A position in which someone might come to me for advice. Seek my favor. Ask my opinion. Listen.

The man who might bring me these things is just a shadow in the background.

I turn back to Wyatt, but I can't see his expression in the gathering dark.

"And why didn't you want to suggest this?" I ask, stepping closer to him. I want to *see* what he thinks as much as hear it.

"I don't like him. He's not the sort of man who can love someone like you." His face is a complete blank.

I shrug off his doubt—and my own.

"What's love? I'm not even sure it exists. And if it does, it certainly has no place in my world. The only thing a girl is good for is to give away or sell to the highest bidder. That's what George says. And I'm ready to sell."

Wyatt looks pained. "I think you could do better."

"Better than the Earl of Northumberland? Wyatt, my father is one of the 'new men.' Cardinal Wolsey calls him a *minion*. I am related in the interminably dark and murky past to Edward I, but I have no heritage, no title, no status, despite my sister's position in the king's bed. The Boleyns may be steadfastly

loyal, but they don't really engender love and friendship in any-one. Status and preferment mean more to them anyway. And in that light, I hardly think I can do better."

In the silence that follows, I hear the rustle of a thrush in the bushes, and the distant call of boatmen on the Thames.

"Is that really what you care about, Anne? Status and prefer-ment and ambition?"

"That's what I've been taught!" I want to tear his expression of pity straight off his face. "Isn't that why you brought me under your wing? You took me on as a business proposition."

"Well, now I consider you more than that."

"Really, Wyatt? And what do you consider me? What do you want from me?" I want him to say it. Without a joke. Without a tease.

"I want what's best for you." Wyatt looks down at his hands. They are not still. "As my business proposition."

So much for friendship. "You want me to believe that what's best for me is for everyone to continue to think I spend my spare time in your bed."

"No," Wyatt says, his voice a razor edge of controlled calm. "I just don't want you to tarnish your chances."

"You just want to keep me where I am. Because you've got me right where you want me."

"Oh, no, Anne, my dear," he says, the laughter in his voice ringing false. "You're not where I want you yet."

"And where is that?"

"On top, Mistress Boleyn."

My irritation finally burns through me. "Will you just stop with your innuendos, Wyatt!"

He roars his great burbling laugh, throwing me off-balance and bringing me to earth all at once. "Innuendo is all down to the interpretation, Anne." He sweeps me into the air as if we are dancing the volta. "I mean you are destined for great things! You're destined for the greatest gambles. For the kind of legendary love you only hear about in ballads."

He sets me down and turns me like a spinning top. I can't help laughing. The weight has been removed from my shoulders. But an ache is still lodged in my heart.

"Those love affairs end badly, Wyatt," I say seriously. "I think I had rather be well housed and well connected than alone and miserable after losing the love of my life."

"But they don't *all* end badly, Anne."

His left hand is still at my waist. My shoulder presses into his chest. I smell ink and earth and almonds. I have to pull away.

"Oh, really?" I ask, pretending I don't see the hurt in his eyes. "Name me one that didn't."

He strikes a pose of intense concentration. Frowns. He searches the horizon as if it will give him the answers he seeks. Shakes his head.

"No. You're right. They all end badly. You're doomed."

I swipe playfully at his shoulder. He catches my hand, swiftly as a hawk diving for prey.

"I mean it, Anne." His hand tightens. As does his expression. He will not let me go.

"You mean I'm doomed?" I tease.

"I mean you're destined for something better than Henry Percy."

I pull my hand from his.

"I don't want you to limit yourself too soon." He reaches for me again, but I step backward. Away from him.

"It can't happen soon enough, Wyatt. My father is on his way home. If I don't make my own choice and make it swiftly, I really will be doomed. I cannot wait for better things, no matter how much you beg it of me. I don't have time."

21

But time all too often comes screeching to a halt at court. The king and his councillors go to London to open Parliament, leaving the ladies alone with the old, the young, and the reckless. Leaving a void where once there was a constant intoxicating hum.

Because Wolsey is with the king, his men have no reason to visit. I'm grateful to be out from under Butler's resentful glare. But Henry Percy's absence lays waste to all my plans.

The remaining men at Bridewell roam ever more restlessly. Near-fights and arguments break out in the gardens and long galleries. Rumors explode into accusations. Men practice archery and swordplay in the yard, but this doesn't release the lust for blood and war. There is no room for jousts and no park for hunting. Just the quiet regulation of the monasteries that surround us.

George complains of boredom to everyone within hearing distance.

"I feel as if I've been conscripted into holy orders myself," George mumbles after a particularly dull morning spent on backgammon and prayer.

I have to agree with him. With only the queen's influence—

all needlework and hair shirts—we are suffocating on the tarnished piety of an incarcerated court.

My fear is that my time is slipping away and my father slipping nearer. I imagine him on horseback, heading for the Spanish coast. Or already on a boat bound for England.

It finally affects me so deeply, I go in search of George late one afternoon—unsure if Wyatt in his determination to make me "wait" will help.

I corner my brother just outside the queen's chambers. He is dressed in blue velvet, a gaudy, jeweled cap riding on his undisciplined hair, his boots cleaned and coins jingling in the pocket at his waist. He is far too smartly dressed for an evening playing cards. I forget my purpose in seeking him out as my suspicion overwhelms me.

"Where are you going?" I ask.

"When the cat's away . . . " he says.

I just stare at him. Force him to finish his thought.

"Bridewell is practically at the very heart of London. We've got to take advantage."

"We?" I ask.

"The usual crowd. Bryan. Norris. Wyatt. And I think we're going to corrupt young Henry Percy from the cardinal's household as well."

"Percy? He's here?"

"Yes. Wyatt invited him along. God knows why. The boy stalks the galleries of York Place like he's got a pike stuck up his arse."

I hardly listen to George's assessment. Wyatt invited Percy. *Here.* He is helping me. I could kiss him.

"So, what do you plan to do?"

"Wouldn't you like to know, dear sister?"

He begins to move past me, heading for the door. For the water gate.

"Will you take me with you?" The words come out before I can evaluate them. I hate asking George for anything. But surely this is what Wyatt intended.

He stares at me for a long, drawn-out moment. "To London?"

"Why not?"

"Because you're a girl." George ticks off his reasons on his fingers. "Because you're in the queen's household. Because it's London. And because it's a boys' night. We're going to see if we can lose Percy's virginity. Not something you want to be around for."

George doesn't know that's the very thing I need to be around for. Only after we're married. I can't believe Wyatt intends to take Percy to the brothels. George must have it wrong. George and his limited vision.

I think quickly, forming a plan. "When else can you have the opportunity to show two ladies of the queen's household the entertainments of the town?"

"Two?" George cries. "Now what are you cooking up?"

"Well, of course Jane would come, too. I can't go alone with a group of men. It wouldn't be seemly."

"It won't be seemly no matter how you look at it, Anne. And Jane Parker won't change that."

"But George, you said yourself how boring it is here."

"You're a girl. You're used to it."

"I'm from France. I'm not." I feel the frustration welling up in my throat. My very breath obstructed by the limitations imposed on me by society, by my sex, by George.

We are still standing there, trying to stare each other down, when Wyatt bursts in, talking away, Percy trailing at a cautious distance.

"There you are." Wyatt strides across the empty room, loose-limbed and confident, the complete opposite of the man who follows him. I smile at Percy, trying to shut out the thought of George's description of him, then remember Wyatt's instruction and turn away. Men only want what they think they can't have. So I turn to my instructor. My savior.

"You came looking for me?" I ask Wyatt. I spy a coiled thread of gold hair on the midnight-blue velvet of his doublet. The sight twists something hot and toothy inside me. I pluck the hair up between my thumb and forefinger and hold it out to him.

He pulls it delicately away, kisses it, and blows it toward the windows and the falling night beyond them.

"Mine," he says solemnly.

My laughter sounds a little too relieved, even to my own ears. "You do love yourself then, don't you?"

"More than anyone else," he says, laying a loud, wet kiss on the corner of my mouth. He turns to my brother. "Let's go, George."

"I'll only be a minute," I say. "I'll join you at the water gate."

Wyatt laughs. George doesn't.

"Tell her," he says. "Tell her she can't come. Tell her men and women can't be friends."

Wyatt's eyes don't waver from mine, but he shifts his weight from one foot to the other. His easy posture suddenly seems fabricated.

"He's right."

I feel like I've been struck. Wyatt turns his gaze to the darkened windows and they reflect the gold of his hair back to me. But not his face.

"London is no place for a girl, Anne," he says blandly, as if he hasn't just shattered me.

"Especially not where we're going." George grins. "Just a certain type of girl, eh, Percy?"

Percy's face flames, and George punches him in the shoulder.

Wyatt won't look at me. "Norris and the ferryman are waiting. Time to go."

George turns and walks away, but pauses at the door.

Percy hesitates, as if faced with a dilemma.

What will he choose? The brothels of London? Or me?

I can feel the sticky wetness of Wyatt's kiss on my cheek. I wipe it away and rub it on my skirt. I see Wyatt's eyes linger on my hands, so I clasp both of them together to keep them still. Even silent, he criticizes.

"Surely the court provides better pastime," Percy says.

I meet his eye. Shyly. I will watch only him. I will not turn my gaze to gauge Wyatt's reaction.

"The court provides me nothing." I can hear the contempt dripping from Wyatt's words like blood. "And any chance I have to get away, I do. The question is, Percy, what about you? Are there such enticements at your castle in Northumberland as there are here? And can anything compare to the City?"

"Alnwick has nothing as compared to here," Percy says, keeping his eyes steady on my face. "Nor, I imagine, does the City."

I feel a surge of victory. Take a step closer to him. Look away. Counting the beats in my head—the music of flirtation.

"Then stay," Wyatt growls. "You waste my time with your courtly drivel."

He turns on his heel and leaves without another word. And I finally allow my gaze to follow him.

I watch the tension of Wyatt's shoulders, the quickness of his step. The easy stride and lackadaisical effortlessness are missing, replaced by a ferocity I've never seen before.

When he's gone, he leaves a hollow space behind

And I'm alone with Henry Percy

22

HENRY PERCY. SOON TO BE EARL OF NORTHUMBERLAND. Warden of the east marches, charged with defending the Scottish Borders against the Duke of Albany and the barbarians of the north. Doomed to become a battle-scarred army rat like his father. Like the Earl of Surrey, my uncle.

The trouble is, Percy doesn't look cut out for all that. He looks like a musician. Like a cleric. His features are stark and shadowed in the candlelight, his face so full of feeling, his hands large and strong, but smooth, as if they've never held anything more solid than a quill in his lifetime.

"How do you like court, Mistress Boleyn?"

He presses his lips together. Not the thin lips of a cleric. Full lips. Soft. I return my eyes to his.

"At the moment, it's frightfully boring."

He looks shocked.

Oh, God. I can't believe I just said that. I'm supposed to be using my feminine wiles.

"With the king away," I amend.

Neither does that sound right. As if I look to the king for all my entertainment. Which I can't. But he is the king. Divine. Divinely anointed.

Our conversation stutters to a halt. Stillborn.

"I mean, everyone seems at a loss. Without the usual entertainments. Seeking escape."

I look over Percy's shoulder to the doorway through which Wyatt just exited, trying not to think about where he went.

"Thomas Wyatt is not the most faithful of men." Percy looks as cross as I feel.

"I think he and his wife loathe each other. And from what I hear, she isn't necessarily a paragon of virtue."

"It doesn't give him the right to . . ." Percy blushes. And I realize what his original statement meant.

"You think he should be faithful to me?" My heart clenches.

"I heard . . ." Percy cannot finish that thought. "And he kissed you."

I wipe the spot again.

"After a fashion." I shake my head. "Thomas Wyatt is not my lover."

"Oh."

So much meaning in one small sound.

"He claims we've known each other since I was two and we played in the fountains naked," I add, and immediately want to bite my tongue off. Because Percy blushes so hard his fingertips turn red.

"I mean we're like . . ." We are *not* like brother and sister. Not like George and me. "There is nothing between us." Something about the words sends a shard of ice through me.

"You're engaged to James Butler," he says with strained casualness.

"I am not! Who told you that?"

"All the court."

"Well, all the court is wrong."

"I suppose I shouldn't believe everything I hear at court." He throws my own words back to me.

"Certainly stories have a way of being told." I lace my words with a lightness I don't entirely feel. "Or worse, believed."

He nods, and we lapse into silence.

"For instance," I say to break it, "I hear you've been engaged to the Earl of Shrewsbury's daughter since infancy."

"Mary Talbot is a sour-faced harpy. Full of nothing but complaints and demons. Like her father and her brother and the whole of the English north."

"My Lord Percy," I say, touching his arm lightly with my fingertips. "I do believe that is the most unkind thing I have ever heard you say."

He has the grace to blush again.

"But you haven't denied my statement." I pretend to pout, feeling ridiculous. Pouting isn't my style. More like the duchess's.

"It is my father's choice, not mine. And I have not agreed."

"Fathers," I say knowingly. "Family pride. Alliances."

"You understand," he says, his face brightening. I'm starting to like the look of him when he smiles. The boy takes over, negating the angry young man.

"My father doesn't care that I have no wish to marry James Butler."

"James isn't so bad. He just doesn't know how to interact with people."

"Doesn't bode well for a marriage, does it?"

The seriousness returns.

"Has it been solemnized?" He presses his lips together. "Signed? Your betrothal?"

He looks away suddenly, as if the question was more than he intended to ask.

"Not yet." I plan my pause carefully. "But my father returns from Spain soon. And I think he'll apply himself to the business of alliances when he does."

"I should like more control of my life," Percy says, and I see his fists clenching at his sides. "To do as I see fit."

"You already did tonight," I say, and grasp his hand in mine. He shudders at my touch. Or trembles.

"Tonight?"

"Wyatt and my brother can be quite adamant. And yet you didn't go with them. Why not?"

I can't look away from his eyes.

"Because I'd rather be here with you."

Christ. At least he's direct.

"Well, you know, sir, you won't get the same from me as you would get from the companions my brother would search out for you in London."

He reacts with such shock and horror, one would think I'd handed him a serpent.

"I-I would never ask," he stutters.

He leaves me with an opportunity. One that I can't pass up.

"I hope someday you will."

His eyes widen. The black centers expand to encompass the

whole of the iris. I turn before the surprise leaves his face and lead him back to the queen's apartments. Safety in numbers. I have to move quickly and keep raising the stakes. But I have to play carefully.

Because if I do—if I win—I could be somebody, somewhere. Instead of nobody, noplace.

Greenwich Palace
1523

23

Now that war has been decided upon by Parliament, the entire court is out for blood. Mercifully, taxes and armies must be raised, so the inevitable still seems far away. The men must seek satiety at Greenwich, with its expansive deer park and its state-of-the-art tiltyard.

The king rides out every day, leaving before dawn and returning hours later. Wyatt rides with him. The men discuss the hunt far into the night. So singular of purpose. So exclusive.

But then a more general entertainment is planned—with a picnic—and I find myself invited. Not Mary. Me. I'm sure I have Wyatt to thank, though he hasn't spoken to me since that night at Bridewell. And Jane is coming, too.

I rise early that morning and dress in green and brown, my skirts the same color as the forest floor. I include a cap copied from one of the duchess's, but set it farther back from my face. She may be a bitch, but she does have style.

Jane ties my sleeves on securely and I help her tighten the stays of her rust-colored bodice. She can't stop fidgeting, knowing that George will accompany us.

"You should find another occupation for your hands," I tell her. "Or you will tear your fingers ragged."

She nods mutely. She looks as if she is about to be sick.

We make our way to the yards, creeping through the still-sleeping rooms. The palace has been aired and sweetened, fresh rushes laid down and tapestries shaken out. All is muted and shadowed, the subdued domain of the queen.

By contrast, the stable courtyard of the palace is a blaze of color, flickering with laughter and rocking with energy. I stand for a moment, just inside the gate, and take it all in. Courtiers slapping backs and placing bets. Everyone eager to be seen, to be heard. They are drunk on the exhilaration of it, or perhaps merely still drunk from the night before.

My brother, Wyatt, and Norris crowd a corner with the other young men, their chests puffed out like that of the rooster watching them from the wall above. They are falling all over each other with laughter.

"Come." I reach for Jane's hand. "Let us join them. They look as if they could use some maidenly influence."

Jane doesn't move.

"Watch," she says. "I think they've had enough maidenly influence."

Norris is holding up a hand in front of him as if it were a looking glass, shaping his eyebrows and examining the pores of his skin. Then he sticks out his lower lip in a quick pout. George whispers something inaudible, and they fall apart again, slapping Norris on the back and cheering.

"Did he just pretend to be the Duchess of Suffolk?" I ask.

Jane nods. "They already did Mistress Carew and Lady Kildare."

I push a breath through my nostrils. "Children."

I move to march over to then, when George steps forward. He widens his eyes to unseeing roundness, puts a hand up to his mouth, and sets to gnawing at it as if it's a leg of mutton.

Jane sucks in her breath. I turn back to her as the men laugh again. Her face is stricken.

"Jane."

She shakes her head rapidly, as if to dislodge the sight, and points a shaking finger.

"Look."

Wyatt is smoothing his hair as if tucking it into the band of a French hood. Then he elongates his neck and taps Norris playfully on the shoulder. Quickly wipes his hands on his breeches. George guffaws, and my brittle self-image snaps. Wyatt's eyes rise to meet mine and reveal an instant of panicked remorse that is swiftly replaced with a stare of belligerent defiance.

"We'll show them," I say to Jane, squeezing her hand hard enough to make her whimper. "We'll run their asses off."

The king strides into the center of the yard, suddenly the focus of attention. As always, he's like the hub of a wheel around which all other activity turns. The old hum strikes up in my chest when he spies me holding Jane's hand and smiles. He hasn't even noticed me since the masque, yet suddenly I feel I'm the only object of his regard.

"Mistress Boleyn!" he calls. "And Mistress Parker! Mount up, ladies, and get ready for the ride of your life!"

The men bellow, and Jane turns bright as a berry. I see color creeping up the king's face as well, and realize he didn't intend

the double meaning. He turns quickly to mount his horse, Governatore. And we are no longer at the center of the wheel.

"Allow me to assist you, ladies."

Wyatt has approached us, dressed in green, the yellow of his hair reflected by a golden feather in his cap. He grins at Jane, who starts to simper. Despite her love for George, Jane unaccountably loses all sense of decorum around Wyatt.

Beddable, I remember her saying, and fury rises in me like a tide, threatening to flood.

"Your assistance is not required, Master Wyatt." I will my voice to remain uncharged. And cold.

"Ah." Wyatt turns the fully dimpled grin on me. "But *required* and *desired* are two different things."

Jane giggles. I want to smack them both.

"The honey of seduction will go nowhere toward catching me, sir," I snap. "We only *desire* assistance from our friends."

Wyatt doesn't move. Doesn't falter. "I am your friend."

I can feel Jane's stillness behind me, the tension in it.

"My friends do not mock me."

"I wasn't mocking you, my dear. I was calling attention to you."

I hear Jane cough behind me. She doesn't believe him any more than I do.

"Calling attention to my . . . habits and affectations is not something I wish a friend to do."

"Perhaps it will convince you to cease them."

We stand glaring at each other like the still leaves at the center of a whirlwind.

I know he will not apologize.

"My friends don't criticize everything I do," I say. "My friends take my side in an argument."

"If you're referring to the London adventure, it definitely wasn't appropriate. Besides"—he finally looks away, and the clamor of the stable yard returns—"it seems to have worked out for you in the end."

"You sound like a jealous lover."

"It was a joke," Wyatt spits. "One you would have recognized as such a few weeks ago. Before you started to think so much of yourself."

"I hardly recognize you anymore, Thomas Wyatt. Much less your jokes."

"Do you know what I think, Anne Boleyn?"

"No. And I don't care, either."

"I think you're angry because I don't support your most recent power play. Your grasp for status. Kick the poet when the aristocracy comes calling. Assuage your doubts by negating all other opinions."

"Don't turn this around."

"Because you need to be angry with me? Is that it? I have a right to be angry with you, too."

"I am not the one in the wrong here!"

"Are you not?" he asks quietly.

Silence balls like a fist between us.

"Mount up!" Nicholas Carew, the Master of the Horse, cries. The stable yard explodes into activity, and the dogs bay from beyond the gate.

"Master Wyatt," Jane says evenly. She has heard it all. "Since you are the only man left unmounted, perhaps we do require your assistance."

Without speaking, Wyatt moves to place his hand beneath Jane's foot. On the back of her bay mare, she is graceful and more at ease. She thanks Wyatt quietly.

"Mistress Boleyn." Wyatt goes to one knee on the cobbles before me.

"Why are you acting this way?" I ask him. "Why are you doing this?"

"Why, Anne"—he looks up at me—"all men want what they can't have. I am only here for the chase."

The expression on his face—one of longing and wickedness and ambition—makes my heart stop and then start again with a bang. Pounding. The rhythm of the hunted.

He looks again at his hands, the fingers entwined. I raise my foot and place it there. His grip is steady and I feel the heat through the leather of my boot. I look at the feather in his cap, the curl of hair at his collar, the stretch of fabric across his shoulders.

The muscles tense to lift me, and I lose my balance. Fall into him, my bust practically pressed against his forehead. We both gasp, and I push away. I steady myself with one hand on the saddle. My horse shuffles nervously.

Wyatt stares at my boot, shoulders tense.

"Ready?" he asks.

I nod. Realize he can't see me. Clear my throat.

"Yes."

In one fluid motion, I am in the saddle, the roan mare shifting beneath me. His hand stays on my foot a moment too long. When he leans forward to speak again, his hair kindles gold in a shaft of dawn.

"I am here for the chase," he repeats. "But not all pleasure is in pursuit, my dear. And there is little pleasure in letting someone else win."

24

THE HUNT BEGINS IN A RUSH OF COLOR AND LIGHT THAT PLUNGES quickly into the darkness of the forest. The shouts of men mingle with the frantic baying of the dogs, the pounding of the hooves, and the crack and blast of twigs and branches breaking. Riding fast takes skill and concentration. I will myself not to think about Wyatt's words. About the look on his face.

Far ahead, I see the flash of white. The tail of the roe deer. With a roar, the company spurs the horses to a froth and we plunge from shadow to light and back again. Horses dodge through the trees, leap fallen branches, vault over streambeds clattering from the spring rain and ditches stagnant with frogs and water.

Does he want me? Or does he just want to win our bet?

We are not bow hunting today, but chasing the deer toward the toils—nets strung yesterday at the other end of the park. This hunt is more of a race.

Wyatt is ahead of me. I can't let him win.

I lean forward over the neck of my horse, her mane flapping against my cheek, ducking branches that come quick-fire at me.

We pass into a blinding splash of morning as the trees thin, and suddenly the king is beside me.

"You ride well, mistress," he says. He is not even winded. Man and horse are like a single creature—a centaur, one rhythm, one heartbeat—beautiful.

"I was taught well, Your Majesty," I reply, trying to suppress the gasp of breath as I suck it in.

"There is nothing like pursuit." The king flashes a grin at me, and we dive back into darkness and suddenly he is gone. Off to the right, dodging another tree. Leaping a ditch. Maneuvering his horse expertly, always with his eye on the quarry.

I turn my horse, her hind foot skidding in a fall of leaves, but she rights herself quickly, shakes her head as if to free herself of the rein, and charges ahead.

We break out into the heathland, and I find myself in the midst of the pack, surrounded on all sides. The king is ahead of me, flashes of gold and red in the spots of new sun, Norris on one side of me, Wyatt on the other. I think I hear George laughing.

I look from one man to the other. Check George. They are watching me. The gorse snags at my skirts, washing me with the stinging scent of sunlit resin. Norris spurs his horse forward, then reins it back again. Keeping pace.

I narrow my eyes at him. "A race?"

He grins and kicks ahead, his wild laugh scaring a raven from its perch high in the trees.

I lean over the neck of my horse and laugh, too. Lost in the motion. In the pace. In the race. Forgetting, for the moment, all the confusion.

When Wyatt pulls ahead, I can't keep up. I spur my horse,

but she stumbles, and I fall a length behind. Norris looks back once, laughs again, and dodges into the trees just ahead of Wyatt. George's horse clears a ditch and he tips his cap as he passes me by.

Wyatt disappears out of sight to the left. Never looks back. Lost in the trees.

"Ha!" Norris shouts again, and they are gone.

Jane catches up to me. Her face is flushed, her cap torn back from it, streamers of chestnut hair following her like a wake upon the river. We slow to a less reckless pace.

"You ride like a man," she says, and I can hear the admiration in her voice.

Ride like a man. Play cards like a man. I seem to fit better in the men's circle than the women's. Of course, the men's circle is wider. More encompassing. With fewer limitations.

"I'll take that as a compliment." We slow to a walk. A girl's pace.

"Oh!" Jane's face gets even rosier. "I meant it as such!"

She shakes her head and glances at her hands. She can't let go of the reins. She presses her lips together.

"I always say the wrong thing. It's the reason I never speak," she says.

"Perhaps I should take lessons from you."

We find the rest of the court surrounding the toils, a clutch of deer lathered and anxious in the nets. One doe keeps breaking away from the others, spinning out into the enclosure, only to stumble back again when faced with the men of the court, who have dismounted, ready for bloodshed.

Norris tips his cap to me and I nod in response. George approaches him, and they clasp hands. George doesn't smile. Norris must have won. George doesn't like to be bested.

Wyatt is nowhere to be seen.

A shout and a cheer herald the arrival of the king. One of the men beside him carries the weapons that will be used for the kill. The doe goes down first in a wash of blood, the courtiers mad with it, and I have to turn away.

Jane turns with me.

"It breaks my heart," Jane says.

"It does feed the court," I manage. Though the sight of all that blood makes me shudder. Death by sword. Why do men seek it out in war? In this respect, I am not like them at all.

"Join us for a feast!" the king cries, and I look at him, blood still on his hands, the blade dripping with it. "I find pursuit whets the appetite."

We follow him to a nearby clearing, a bower of silks and banners already set up, trestle tables laden with food and drink: wine and cheese and strawberries preserved in honey. Strawberries are my favorite, but today, they look too much like clots of blood to be palatable.

The king wanders the knots of courtiers, urging more food and wine and ale on them. He is lit by the sun that is now high and hot over the treetops. It erupts around him like a starburst when he approaches me, and I flatten my hands against my skirts to keep them still.

"And have you enjoyed the pursuit, mistress?" he asks.

"It was certainly invigorating."

He raises an eyebrow at my tone. "You don't like to hunt?"

I wonder at his ability to read me. As if we have known each other all our lives. I feel I can speak the truth to him.

"I prefer hawking." I lower my eyes. I can still feel his gaze upon me.

"Thank you for the excellent entertainment," Jane says.

I'd forgotten she was beside me. I'd forgotten everyone. I felt as though the king and I were the only two present.

I follow her into a curtsy.

"Perhaps we shall go hawking next time," the king says, still watching me. Just me. The bread goes dry in my mouth, and I have to take a sip of wine after curtsying my thanks.

There is a sudden noise from the other side of the meadow. Wyatt finally wanders in on his horse. His cap is gone, his hair tangled with little sticks and leaves.

"Wyatt!" the king calls, and walks away from me. "Someone has led you on a merry chase!"

"Yes, Your Majesty," Wyatt says with a grin, swinging down from his horse and handing over the reins to a servant. I can hardly look at him. He acts as if I don't exist.

"You look utterly weary, my friend."

Wyatt leans heavily with both hands on the trestle table, and nods slowly.

"It can't be the hunt that has exhausted you," the king says. "For I have known you to ride with me for hours and never tire."

"Yes, Your Majesty." Wyatt hangs his head. "It is the hunt. The hunt for hind, the hunt for heart." He scans the group until he finds me.

I want to groan at his overwrought melodrama.

The king raises an eyebrow. "Tell us."

Wyatt strikes a pose. Always ready to share his poetic prowess.

> *"What means this? When I lie alone*
> *I toss, I turn, I sigh, I groan.*
> *My bed me seems as hard as stone.*
> *What means this?"*

Jane squeezes my hand.

"A bad night then, my friend?" the king asks Wyatt.

"Any night alone is a bad one," Norris says.

Someone lets out a low whistle. And suddenly all eyes are upon me. Because of course I am the reason Wyatt lies alone. I feel the heat rise to my face, but I keep my eyes on him. He will not best me.

> *"In slumbers oft for fear I quake.*
> *For heat and cold I burn and shake.*
> *For lack of sleep my head doth ache.*
> *What means this?"*

He leaves the table and walks to the middle of the meadow, the sun on his hair like a torch. His voice is clear and carrying in the morning air. He shines. Even the king, in shadows behind him, is diminished.

> *"And if perchance by me there pass*
> *She unto whom I sue for grace,*
> *The cold blood forsaketh my face.*
> *What means this?"*

"It means you're smitten, friend!" Norris calls.

Wyatt turns to me, the sun on his face washing the shadows from it. His gaze perforates my heart, and I have to remind myself it's all a show. A game. A bet. And I don't want it to be more than that. It can't be more than that. He paces toward me, his voice so low the entire assembly has to lean forward to hear him.

> *"But if I sit near her by"*—

Wyatt falls dramatically to the empty bench beside me.

> *"With loud voice my heart doth cry,*
> *And yet my mouth is numb and dry:*
> *What means this?"*

He falls back against the table, right hand above his heart, the left over his brow with the palm facing outward, the very picture of unrequited love.

The table erupts into cheers and pounding. The women sigh.

Jane looks at me with tears in her eyes and mouths, *"Adorable."*

I wait for the applause to die down, delicately clear my throat.

"It means you need a glass of wine," I say in the driest voice I can muster, and give him my goblet.

My hand doesn't shake at all.

Norris cheers while the others laugh. George turns away. Wyatt raises the goblet to me in a mute toast, apology in his eyes. And something else. Something that sends my heart into a rhythm not my own.

"To friends," he says, so only I can hear.

And something inside me plummets.

25

My dreams are haunted by green and gold. But my days are haunted by other men.

The palace is full to bursting because Christian II, king of Denmark, is coming to visit. Deposed, he is wandering Europe like a minstrel, singing his song of woe, despite having repressed his subjects to the point of riot.

Jousts and banquets and dances are planned. Everyone forgets Thomas Wyatt's silvered poetry in the forest. Except me.

He disappears in the tumult, leaving me to navigate the new court demands on my own. Leaving me to Henry Percy.

Wolsey arrives at Greenwich, perched atop a donkey caparisoned with cloth of gold. The gaudiness of the trappings subverts the impression of the unpretentious cleric the donkey is meant to convey, but Wolsey doesn't acknowledge the irony.

His men come to the queen's rooms. Percy, straight and studied. Butler, unruly and explosive. And the king's men, too, savoring the cover of chaos for illicit flirtation. Norris, especially.

He sits beside me. A little too close. But not close enough for comment.

Butler, obvious in his awkwardness, brays at the card table.

"Mistress Boleyn," Norris says, "I hear you are to marry our friend Butler over there. The match made in York Place."

"Certainly not *in* heaven."

Norris laughs and allows himself to edge a little closer to me.

"And what about Thomas Wyatt?"

"What about him?"

"Rumor has it that you're his latest conquest."

I look at him archly.

"The term *conquest* suggests submission, Sir Henry."

Norris smiles craftily. "I wonder on which side," he purrs.

"And pray tell what justifies your interest in such a thing?"

"My dear, if anything bad should happen to him, I would look to have you."

He holds my gaze for a long moment, daring me to respond. But I retaliate.

"I would undo you if you tried."

Norris laughs.

"I'm sure you would, Mistress Boleyn."

He stands and walks away, his movements calculated. Exaggerated. He looks once over his shoulder, and grins.

Percy watches him go and moves to take his place. I sneak a sideways glance at him. Percy's clothes are almost camouflaged against the background of the courtiers who swarm the ladies of the queen's chambers like flies on butter. He wears little to distinguish himself—the opposite of Wolsey. Percy doesn't want to be seen or heard but merely exist, unremarked.

Wyatt's words come back to me: *You were meant for some-*

thing better. I shake them away. There is nothing better. There is only worse. Sold to James Butler in Ireland. Lodged beneath my father's shadow. Wasting away as the flirtatious—but unmarriageable—sister of the king's whore. Or the perceived mistress of the court's most notorious philanderer. No, my only escape is this man beside me. Bland, perhaps. But grand, as well.

I glance up to see the duchess studying me. Her gray eyes flick to Percy and back to me. I raise an eyebrow. She glares, and I imagine her face when I join the circle of nobility. So I compose my features and nod my head in deference. Let her think I submit to her superiority. For now.

"Are you friends with the duchess?" Percy asks.

His baritone rumbles through me and settles somewhere south of my heart. I'm used to him being silent.

"Actually, I think she wishes me dead."

"I'm sure you're witty, Mistress Boleyn. But sometimes you speak and act unwisely."

"One of my greatest faults."

"Most faults can be overcome."

"Do you have any faults, Lord Percy?" I tease.

"I am not as brave nor as adamant as my father." He has taken my question seriously.

"I'm sure even our fathers can be overcome." I lay a hand on his.

He twitches it away and I pull mine back into my lap.

"I sincerely hope so," he says. He turns to me, and for an instant I see something spirited in his gaze. But it disappears quickly.

"I need to tread carefully with my father. Someone so"—he looks to the door through which Norris exited—"flamboyant as yourself might make him draw the wrong conclusions."

I wonder what conclusions Percy himself has drawn.

"Are you saying you don't want to be seen with a girl like me?"

"I'm saying I need to ensure my name is not connected to scandal."

The Château Vert. Mary's affair with the king. George's increasingly visible drunkenness. My own flirtatiousness.

"*Your* name."

He nods, not hearing or comprehending the coldness of my voice. "The Percys have been nobility for centuries. We are related to the king."

And have managed to regain lands and titles despite sitting immobile on the wrong side of the battle of Bosworth. The Percys certainly know when to act. And when not to.

"In these days when the king appoints new men to ancient titles," Percy continues, "the old names must persevere. Unblemished."

"And yet here you sit. Next to the daughter of a new man."

Percy suddenly seems to realize my existence.

"Don't get me wrong, Mistress Boleyn," he says, and I see the fervency in his eyes once more. "You are related to Norfolk. To the ancient lines. You are . . ."

He stutters to a halt. Looks at my lips, then down at his hands, clasped in his lap. He exudes the scent of old paper.

". . . extraordinary."

A bubble rises within me, warm and fine and fragile. I spread my fingers on my skirts.

"I don't want my father's choice," Percy says with a cough. As if he feels he's said too much. "I want mine." He looks again into my eyes. "Which is why we must be careful."

The bubble expands at the sound of the word *we*. He looks away. I turn, too, and study the smoke climbing the walls up to the ceiling.

"There can be no indication of a relationship here until it is . . ." Another cough. "Consummated."

I catch his eye just before he looks away again. It is as if we are in the steps of a complicated dance.

"No one can know. Not your brother. Not your sister. Certainly not Thomas Wyatt."

Wyatt already knows. A little. He doesn't approve. He would never set himself up to be a spurned lover. He won't speak of it.

"Not your father."

I finally find my voice. "But when my father returns, he will push my marriage to Butler."

Percy sits so still and so silent, I'm not sure he heard me. The little noises of the room fill the vacant space: the whispers of the duchess and her confederacy in the corner, the soft slip of silk beneath the queen's fingers, the rattle of dice on the table by the door.

Percy turns and looks at me directly. "Then we must find a way to engender a more desirable result."

26

THE UPROAR OVER THE DANISH VISIT REACHES AN INTOLERABLE pitch. The prospect of a tournament makes the men insatiable in the practice of their war games, as evidenced by the constant clangor of metal and shatter of wood from the practice grounds. The women buzz and twaddle over gowns and silks and gossip—the nonessential commodities of court life relegated to the female realm.

The court becomes oppressive, and I begin to reconsider the appeal of Wyatt's teasing offer to hide me away in the country. I laugh at the idea as I slip down the stairs of the donjon and across the inner courtyard, hoping for a moment alone. The conduit burbles, but I still hear the knock of boots on stone behind me.

At the little gallery that leads to the middle courtyard I stop and turn. James Butler is practically on top of me.

"What are you doing?" The brutality in his voice is evident, but I refuse to back down and I won't step away from him.

"Exactly as I please."

My voice wobbles much less than my legs.

"You flirt with the whole damned court." His voice is roupy, ratcheting out of his throat.

"Not with you."

"That's what I mean!" he shouts. I take a step back and glance quickly through the gallery to the empty courtyard beyond. No one else is in sight. "You should not be flirting with anyone. For soon you will be engaged to me. You will be my wife."

"But we are not engaged." Nor will we be. If I can help it.

"Letters crossed Wolsey's desk this morning. Your father will be here any day. The Irish lords are pressing for my return. We will be married by the end of summer."

My fingers grow cold and I rub them hard against my skirts to warm them. Summers in England are short.

"You speak as though you already know the outcome of your life." I clear my throat to steady my voice. "But don't we rely upon God and the king to bring these things about?"

"Wolsey knows the fates of men better than the king."

It's true. Wolsey is a puppet master, pulling all of our strings.

"It *will* happen," Butler says, and I feel his presence as surely as I feel my breath. "And you will change your ways. If you don't, even I won't want to marry you."

"So I should hide myself away like a nun in a convent because your father may agree to this marriage? Or maybe I should just wait until I grow old and undesirable and then truly join a convent."

"You'll never be a nun."

"At least we agree on something."

Butler grabs me by the shoulders. "I will not hear that you are Wyatt's doxy. Or find your brother in your bed!"

I see a flash of memory: Butler outside the maids' room.

"Bedchamber," I correct him. "Don't be disgusting."

Butler shakes me so hard my neck hurts.

"You are nothing without me," he shouts, frustration straining his voice into the higher registers. "Nothing!"

I open my mouth to speak, to argue, to contradict, but I'm cut off by a rising shriek that echoes across the cobbles.

"How dare you!"

A tiny ball of deep-blue fury flings itself past me and straight at Butler's chest. Jane Parker beats at his arms with pale furs. Her hood is askew, strands of hair flying like witches' wings.

"How dare you?" she howls again, sounding like a madwoman.

Butler covers his face with crossed arms, releasing me from his grip. I take a step back. Jane looks like a weasel attacking a bear, leaping and stretching, the big beast reduced to terror at the surprise of her onslaught.

It would be laughable under other circumstances.

But fighting in court is forbidden and can cost the instigator a hand—or a head—so I grab Jane from behind, avoiding her flailing elbows, and pull. She steps hard on my slipper, the heel of hers digging into my instep, and I stumble.

The two of us fall backward, a tangle of skirts and pearls, to the damp cobbles of the walkway. She lands on me, heavier than she looks.

My chest collapses and a stopper is put into the bottle of my lungs. Everything tightens. My face strains with the effort to squeeze a tiny bit of air back into my body. Helplessness makes me rigid.

Jane rolls off me and turns, panting. When she sees my face, hers goes pale.

"Butler?" she cries. "What's wrong with her?"

James Butler has disappeared. He left us when we fell. Probably ashamed to be terrorized by a mere girl.

"Anne!" Jane kneels beside me, cradling my head in her hands.

I gasp, a long, low, whining sound. My chest heaves, my stomach with it. I might vomit. I turn to the cobbles, retching.

"I'm so sorry." Jane strokes my hair away from my face. "I didn't mean to hurt you."

I wonder manically if Wyatt would rebuke me for apologizing in a similar situation.

I struggle to draw another breath, and discover that this time, it is a little bit easier. This gives me courage, and I nod faintly at Jane to let her know I understand that she meant only to protect me.

Little, mousy Jane Parker rushing to my rescue.

My third breath gives me enough air to wheeze out a laugh.

"Oh! You're breathing!" She starts to cry.

I push myself into a sitting position and find myself patting her back. Comforting my comforter. The air comes more easily into my lungs and I feel the blood return to my face. Delicately, I touch my ribs, hoping nothing is broken. But the rigidity of my bodice seems to have protected me.

"He just made me so angry!" Jane sobs.

"He has that effect," I croak. "You knocked the breath out of me. I think I'll live."

She wipes her eyes with the heels of her hands.

"I can't believe you have to marry him."

"I won't if I can help it." I reach out to adjust her hood. A French one. "I'll marry someone else."

"Someone you choose?" Jane asks. "A love match?"

I think of Percy and wonder if love enters the equation.

"I would like to have a choice. Or at least some control."

"And your family will honor that?" The hope in Jane's voice is heartbreaking.

"My father only wishes to use me for leverage," I tell her, "and thinks my only goal should be to better my family."

"So . . ." Jane pauses and bites her nail. "What makes you think you can make a difference?"

I think of how a few months before, I had no friends. I was an outcast sitting on the fringes of the court. Now I may not be on top, as Wyatt wants, but I am certainly somewhere in the middle. Closer to the royal circle. I have made a difference already—escaped some of the restraints that bound me—with Wyatt's help.

"I hope we have more control than we are led to believe." I stand up shakily. "Perhaps I can circumvent my father's wishes. Use my own leverage."

I demonstrate by leaning back to pull her up.

"I have to believe that what I want matters, Jane," I tell her. "And what I think."

"And whom you love." Jane's voice is thick with thought. Then she brightens.

"Anne, are you my friend?"

I stare at her. The directness of her question startles me,

because it had never occurred to me to question our friendship. Not like Wyatt's.

"Never mind." Jane shakes her head. "It's ridiculous. I'm too quiet. I never speak. I just watch. That makes people nervous. They can't stand to be watched. It makes them feel judged. Anyone who has done anything remotely wrong always feels judged badly."

"That covers just about everybody at court."

"I know! Which is why no one likes me."

"I like you," I say, giving her arm a squeeze. "Of course we're friends."

She smiles weakly. "I'm nothing like you and George."

"That can be a good thing. We both tend to speak before we think. Not always an ideal quality."

"But you're both so vivacious. And elegant. Everyone follows you. George is the most talked-about man at court. And everyone is madly trying to copy your French hoods." She touches her fingers to the exposed hair at the edge of her own.

"What about the Duchess of Suffolk?"

Jane pulls her mouth down.

"The Duchess of Suffolk is more of an enemy than a friend. She only pretends to be nice to someone if she can laugh at her afterward and then speak against her. They're all like that. That entire crowd."

"At least I know you'll never speak against me."

"How is that?"

"Because, by your own admission, you never speak."

27

Jane's affirmation of our friendship makes me feel lighter. Lessens the burden of my worries. My father is only days away, Henry Percy is nowhere near making his decision, and James Butler is doggedly pressing claims—valid or not. Yet I still feel hope.

Greenwich is tucked into the bottom of a curve of the river Thames, facing water and a wide expanse of marsh on the other side. Behind it is a single, knoblike hill. At the hill's peak is Duke Humphrey's Tower, a pretty little place where King Henry has been said to hide his mistresses.

From the southeast flank of the hill, I can see for miles—all the way to St. Paul's, its spire like a beckoning finger. So I take Fortune up there for a taste of freedom.

I want to roll down the hill like I used to at Hever with George. Mary would stand over us, mothering, until we convinced her to join us by tickling her so hard she couldn't breathe. Then we all rolled together, George and I racing to see who could get dizziest fastest.

Fortune shuffles and cocks her head. She can sense the wind blowing in off the river, carrying odors of the court and the Isle of Dogs beyond it and the rattle and cry of men in the tiltyard.

She flutters again, lets out a high, trilling shriek.

I loosen her hood, untie the jesses, and unblind her. She blinks, squints, flaps, and becomes still.

That is when I release her.

I watch as she glides out over the slope, her cry coming back to me, pitched more like a song.

I lie down in the grass, its scents rising around me like steam. But I don't roll; I sing, my face tilted to the sun. I sing a silly little frottola in Italian by Josquin des Prez about a cricket who needs a drink. A cricket who sings in the sunshine for no other reason than love of the song.

There on the empty hill, I can sing whatever I want, however I want. No one listening. No one watching. On this hill, I am unobserved. Unjudged. I am free.

"*El grillo è buon cantore*, Mistress Boleyn."

I know that voice far too well. The buttery tones. The high-domed warmth. I'm surprised I didn't feel the vibration of his presence before I heard his voice.

I scramble to my feet, the breeze chilling my back where the dew soaked into my bodice and sleeves. I curtsy while surreptitiously trying to brush seeds and stems from my skirts.

"Your Majesty."

"The cricket is a good singer," he translates, obviously delighted to be able to associate me with the song. "And yet I rarely hear you sing."

His eyes meet mine as I stand. Those clear, intense gray eyes that appear to look at me and into the future at the same time. As though anything he sees, he can make happen.

"I prefer to play the lute."

He nods as if understanding me perfectly. "The tenor of the strings speaks to me somehow. And the diversity of tones available."

It hits me: *I'm having a conversation with the king. King Henry of England. Alone.*

"I agree!" I cry, and have to stop myself from reaching for him to emphasize how close he's come to speaking my own mind. "The lute is like a chorus! A single voice cannot compete."

"Yours can," he says. And the connection breaks. He's flattering me.

"A king should only speak the truth, Your Majesty."

"You certainly say what you think, Mistress Boleyn." His tone is even, his face immobile. Regret clutches at my throat. I have just called the king a liar. To his face.

Suddenly, he laughs—a fountain of mirth.

"I like that in a woman," he says.

"Others would list it as the most heinous of my many faults."

"I find it difficult to believe you have any faults."

Is the king flirting with me?

"I was taught to hide most of them by King François's sister."

"Marguerite." The king nods. "She was once put forward as a possible bride for me."

I try to imagine the fiery, opinionated Marguerite of Alençon in the place of complacent and pious Queen Katherine.

I fail.

"You are lucky to have known her well," he says.

"She gave me this when I left."

I touch the little gold *A* that rests below the notch at the base of my throat. And then swallow when he looks at it—at the teardrop pearl that hangs from it, resting just above my negligible cleavage.

"Beautiful."

"She is," I say weakly. Pretending he doesn't mean the necklace. Or anything to do with me.

"But she is a dangerous woman. Heretical. She supports her brother in a foolish bid to retain English lands in France."

Despite his assertion that he likes a woman who speaks her mind, I doubt he will countenance my disagreement. Or my opinion that King Henry's own dubious claim to the French throne does not justify his bid to beat France into submission—nor the chaos and death such an action is sure to generate.

No king wants to hear that. Especially from a woman.

"I can see you don't agree."

I look up at him. His face is a guarded question. I don't know how to respond. If it were Wyatt it would be easy. But the king?

"My brother would tell you that agreeableness is not integral to my character."

"Actually, your brother told me you're a very clever girl. Perhaps that's more important."

I stare at him, awestruck. My mouth must be hanging open, thus negating the image painted by George. And the king stares back until my emotions spin from incredulity at George's praise to tingling anticipation of what might happen next.

The king breaks the tension and speaks first.

"You must be wondering why I'm here."

"I was, actually." I find my voice. "It seems unusual for you to be . . . without occupation."

He laughs again. "I'm that transparent, am I? That I am always in need of some pursuit? Music, theology, building projects. If it's not statesmanship, it's hunting. If it's not jousting, it's war."

"You have many interests."

"You are a diplomat like your father. But the truth is, I do have an occupation." He moves closer to me. The braid on his doublet catches on the silk of my sleeve, and I feel the tug like a heartstring.

I wonder wildly if he followed me. If he intends to have two sisters at once. I wonder if Mary is waiting in the tower. I look up again into his mesmerizing gray eyes, knowing that I couldn't say no.

Except I'd rather Mary wasn't there.

"I have come to ponder my responsibilities," he says quietly into my ear, tickling my hair. "It is not easy to send fourteen thousand men to war. Including my best friend."

With a flash like gunpowder, my cheeks begin to burn. He doesn't pursue me.

I turn my head again to look him in the face. He is so close. I can see the stubble of his red beard at his temples, the flecks of gold and umber in his gray eyes.

He does confide in me.

"I believe that the right will win," he says quietly. "But it is not easy."

"How do you know you are right?"

"It is God's will."

"It seems more like a gamble. And a waste."

He steps back and a flash of anger crosses his face. My tongue has taken me too far again.

"You were in France too long. It affects your mind. Your loyalty."

"Not my loyalty, Your Majesty," I say with a deep curtsy, afraid to look him in the eyes again. "I am loyal to you. But my concern is for my friends still in France."

He towers over me, lucent with energy, more like the string of a longbow than of a lute. I feel his gaze rake me up and down, scanning my skirts, bodice, and finally my hood. I am unable to move.

"Your manner is French, madam. And your dress. Even your speech."

"But I am not French, Your Majesty," I say hastily. I try to lengthen my vowels, harden the *j* in *Majesty*. Be English for the first time in my life. I wish I had gabled my hood just a little bit more.

"If, as the Moors say, the enemy of my enemy is my friend," he says, his words barely able to escape his clenched jaw, "then the reverse must also be true."

The friend of my enemy is my enemy.

"You must decide where your true loyalties lie," he declares. "And who your friends are."

He turns quickly and walks away like a storm, blowing the grass into whirlwinds behind him. I watch as he approaches the palace, a great gleaming gold beacon, calling the courtiers to him without sound. And they run to catch up with him like a mass of multicolored ants.

Fortune returns to me silently, and I tether her back to my arm. Back to the earth.

28

THE KING PROBABLY THINKS I'M A SPY. IT'S THE PERFECT disguise—the daughter of a diplomat. He must think I have a network of contacts between here and Paris, all ferreting away information fed to me by my family. By my sister. My father will kill me when he gets back, if the king doesn't do it first. Or George.

I will get us all thrown from court. The Boleyns, exiled back to Hever. Together. A nightmare if there ever was one.

I run straight to Mary's room, and George's presence there, for once, makes me happy. I don't hesitate to tell them the entire devastating tale.

"Nan," Mary says, a ripple of concern on her forehead, "the king doesn't like to be contradicted."

"I know, Mary! Everyone knows that!"

"I can try to smooth things over for you," Mary says uncertainly. "But you have to stop doing this sort of thing. Acting on impulses. Speaking without thinking. It doesn't work here."

She moves toward me, ready to put her arm around me. Comfort me. Be motherly.

I twitch out of her grasp just as George slams his fist down on the table.

"What the *hell* did you think you were doing?" George grabs my arm roughly. "Telling the king you're loyal to France?"

"I didn't say I was loyal to France! I said I was loyal to him!"

"Well, that's not how he heard it."

"I said my friends were in France," I whisper, my anger gone. The choking emotion of it replaced by stifled tears.

"Oh, Nan," Mary sighs. "Don't you see that's just as bad?"

"I do now! But at the time, I thought . . . I thought . . ." I thought I was talking to someone who would listen. I thought, because we shared a love of music, because he understood and spoke exactly what I felt about the lute, that maybe he understood *me*. I thought that maybe—just maybe—the attraction I felt was mutual.

"You didn't think at all, stupid."

It's exactly what Father used to call George when he got his lessons wrong. George lets go of me and stomps over to the little tray by Mary's fire. Pours himself a goblet of wine and drinks most of it in one gulp.

"That's not fair."

"It's completely fair, Mary! Our little sister has been at court for less than a year and she's already jeopardized our position here numerous times! She's an unpredictable hazard. We need to marry her off to Butler and get her out of England as soon as possible if we want to save this family's reputation."

"Status at court isn't everything, George," my sister soothes.

"Yes it is! It is everything and it is the only thing."

"You're talking as if I'm not even here!" I cry.

"It would be better if you weren't," George growls, then

slams his fist down again. "God damn it, Anne! Father will be here in days. Days! You couldn't wait until he was here?"

"What difference would that make?"

"In his absence, he can blame me for your indiscretions. For your stupid mouth."

"That's ridiculous."

"Is it?" He comes close enough to me that I can feel his breath on my face, vinegar-yeasty from the wine. "Is it *ridiculous*, Anne? Do you remember when you ran down to the river and ruined your new frock? Or when you told Father to kiss your ass in French? Or when you broke your finger falling out of the apple tree? All. My. Fault."

The darkness in his eyes threatens to swallow me whole. I curl my misshapen finger into the pleats of my skirt.

"But you weren't even there when I fell out of the tree."

George had said girls couldn't climb trees. So I climbed as high as I could. Just to spite him. I climbed higher than he ever had. I knew it—and he knew it—because I picked the apple he'd coveted the day before and couldn't reach.

"That's why he blamed me." George's gaze is now flat with menace. He turns away from me and takes another drink. "I'm going to send you to Hever."

Hever is nowhere. The country. Far from Percy, who will change my life. Far from court and dance and music. Far from the king.

"You can't send me away." Desperation makes my voice wispy. Inconsequential.

"I can, and I will."

186

I look to Mary, whose eyes meet mine briefly and then focus elsewhere. She isn't going to stick up for me.

"What about the tournament? The visit from the king of Denmark?"

"What about them?" George sneers. "It's not like you're central to the success of either event."

"But I remember Isabeau from the Low Countries."

"You can't remember the Danish queen. You were seven years old."

I glare at my brother. He stares back, an insolent lift to his eyebrow and his eyes clearly reflecting his words. He doesn't believe me.

"I remember getting the highest apple from that tree," I tell him.

George clenches his jaw. He turns to the tray, refills his goblet, and takes a long drink. A drop of claret glistens on his chin until he wipes it on the back of his sleeve.

"You remember her. What difference should that make?"

"She was kind to me. I could make her visit here more comfortable. A familiar face."

"It's extremely unlikely that she'll remember you."

"I speak French!" I'm grasping at straws.

"Which is exactly why we're talking about this. Besides, her aunt, the queen of England, speaks French fluently. I think Queen Isabeau will be fine without you."

His snide, sarcastic calm boils inside me. I can't let him win.

"You can't make me go," I say, the words tumbling over each other. "I'm going to be a countess!"

George laughs.

"Of *Ormond*. Not exactly the highest rank in the world. And even that isn't guaranteed. Not if I have anything to do with it."

"You can have your piddling little birthright," I hiss at him. "Because I'm going to be the Countess of Northumberland."

Everything in the room stops. Mary is frozen in place, hesitating between us, unsure which side to support. George can't quite seem to alter his expression from one of contempt to one of surprise.

My insides twist, lurch, and plunge. I've just broken Henry Percy's very first "rule."

"How's that?" George asks finally.

"Nothing."

"Henry Percy?"

George is cleverer than he lets on. Latin, he never understood. But politics and manipulation come naturally to him.

I say nothing.

He takes a step closer to me. He reaches up to my face, and I try not to flinch away.

But he strokes my cheek. Places a hand on each shoulder. Leans in close.

"Little Henry Percy?"

Percy is taller than George. George means "little" in the sense that George has a bigger personality. A larger circle of friends. More self-confidence.

I say nothing.

"Are you telling me you have an understanding with Lord

Percy? Future earl of one of the oldest earldoms in England? A family that came over with William the Conqueror?"

Percy's voice is screaming at me to stop. But I can't. It's the first time since we were little children that George has shown anything like admiration toward me.

"Not an understanding," I say. "Exactly."

George's expression dissolves into distrust.

"Well then what, *exactly*, is it?"

His voice is low and rumbling, like the purr of some great cat.

"An . . . interest."

"An interest." The contempt is back. "Like Henry Norris's interest? Like Thomas Wyatt's? That's not the kind of interest that makes you a countess, Sister." He leers.

"It's not like that."

But George sees that he has regained the upper hand.

"And Wyatt's not really interested, anyway. To him, you're more of a . . . challenge."

A piece of truth tears away from my heart, and I feel my resolve begin to break.

"Henry Percy seems like an honorable man," Mary interjects. "If Nan thinks he intends to marry her, then perhaps he does."

Mary has sunk her teeth into the depths of the issue.

"And we should stand by her," she adds. "Because family is blood. And so much more important than these tentative and fleeting connections made here."

"Blood spills easily."

"Not ours, George. Not Boleyn blood."

George looks at me, and for an instant, I see his face across from mine at the dinner table, rigid with pain and determination. Because he blamed himself as much as my father did.

"I will keep Father at bay," he says quietly. "Mary will sweeten the king."

He strides back to the door, suddenly purposeful. He stops, one hand on the latch, and turns.

"And you, Anne, make sure this interest of Percy's becomes enthusiasm. Whatever it takes."

29

I DON'T TELL WYATT ABOUT MY CONVERSATION WITH THE KING. I can't face his criticism as well. We have just started speaking again. So as we walk up Greenwich's apple orchard, I pretend that all is well.

"How many have asked you for a favor to carry in the joust?" he asks, twirling an apple leaf between his fingers.

"Checking up on my progress?"

"I have to know how my protégée fares."

He is all nonchalance and superficial concern. *Protégée.* George's words walk with me—that Wyatt sees me as a challenge. Not a person. Just a girl.

"Henry Norris has asked," I snap. "And my father. Pleased?"

"Your father? Why? He won't even be here."

A shout and the sound of splintering come from the tiltyard beyond the towers and viewing platform. Practice for the tournament has reached a peak of fervid anticipation. Pestilential war games.

"Because he thinks so highly of his youngest daughter that he declared his intention in letter by courier, assuming no one else would offer. Couldn't bear to be embarrassed long-distance."

"Your father's largesse knows no bounds."

"My father's largesse is notoriously negligible."

"You sound bitter."

"Do I?" I want to strangle him. "Why, that was never my intent."

Wyatt stops me and holds my gaze. Will not let me go. I'm itching to slap him. Spit at him. Dare him to criticize me one more time.

"Your father is a commoner. He comes from trade. But you, my dear, are descended from royalty."

"Flattery from Thomas Wyatt?" I ask, my bitterness encompassing everything. "I suppose I should consider myself honored."

"Not flattery. Truth. You're clever. You have poise and beauty and therefore bright prospects. You just have to help your father realize it."

I think of the time I tried to correct my father's French when he was ambassador to the French court. And how he didn't speak to me again until I washed up on England's shores, bedraggled and alone, two years later.

"You don't know my father very well, do you?"

"I know that he has more ambition than the rest of us put together. And that any attachment you make that will bring you closer to the peerage will get his attention."

"So I should just tell him that I'm bound for greatness and that he'd better get out of my way."

Wyatt laughs. "Even I wouldn't tell my father that I'll be better known than he will be. That my name will go down in history, and he will be long forgotten. He would slap me senseless and send me back to Kent, and then where would I be?"

"Kent."

Wyatt throws his head back in that delighted roll of laughter that makes me want to spin with joy. But he grabs me around the waist and does it for me.

"Of course, you're right." He stops, nearly breathless. "But what I mean is that you can know the truth and not tell it. I will be famous. My father will not."

"You certainly think a lot of yourself."

"I have to. No one else will. Certainly not my father. And you are in the same position."

He says it so blithely. Points out with supreme indifference what broke my heart when I was seven. My father abandoned me as soon as he realized Mary was pretty and I never would be.

"So Henry Percy hasn't asked for your favor for the joust?" Wyatt sounds almost too casual.

"No." I keep my voice purposefully neutral.

"And that disappoints you."

It isn't a question.

"It does a bit." I hate to admit it. Especially to Wyatt.

"Your paramour doesn't wish to be connected to you."

"Don't be rude." I'm stung by how close he is to the truth.

"It's true, though. He sits next to you in the queen's chambers, but is never seen with you elsewhere. He doesn't buy you trinkets or ask you for any. He barely looks at you at banquets and dances, when the other men at the court are falling over themselves to accompany you."

My anger layers over itself. At his nerve. At how devastatingly he points out the truth.

"It's not him," I hiss, my voice tight. "It's his father. It's the court. Gossip. He just wants to avoid it."

"There's nothing wrong with having a mistress."

"I don't want to be a mistress! A whore. I don't want to share a bed and not a life."

"And have any of these men asked that of you? Has Percy?" Wyatt's eyes look like a falcon's. Hooded. Unflinching.

"Percy's been nothing but noble. But Norris has made insinuations. And some others."

"And have you said yes to any of them?"

"No!"

"For a favor in the joust," he says, leaning close to my ear. "Not for your maidenhead." The scent of sugared almonds encompasses me. I lick my lips.

"No."

"Good. You shall grant it to me."

"My maidenhead?" I look at him from the corner of my eye, like a teasing flirtation. Two can play at this game.

"God forbid," Wyatt replies tightly.

I suddenly feel like I should cover myself and take a step back.

"Thanks for the compliment."

"My pleasure," he says, his body at ease again. "Your favor is all I ask, my sweet."

"What sort of thing are you looking for?" I think of a colored handkerchief, tied to a jousting lance, fluttering like a helpless maiden.

"This."

Lazily, Wyatt raises the index finger of his right hand and lets it come to rest on the gold *A* that hangs between my collarbones. He leaves his finger there, as if feeling for my pulse, and stares directly into my eyes. His own, glass-blue, reflect the sky.

We are so close. It's unnerving. If I took a step forward, his hand would be flat on my chest, directly over the breakneck rhythm of my heart.

I struggle to move my mouth—to smile or flirt or speak—never letting my eyes waver from his.

"My lady Marguerite of Alençon gave me this before I left France," I manage.

"Perfect." He traces the letter with his finger and then strokes the pearl that hangs from it, never once touching my skin. "Meaningful."

I reach for the knotted ribbon, but Wyatt stops me. There, in the garden, with anyone and everyone watching, Wyatt reaches, his arms encircling me, so close we almost touch. Almost, but not quite. His chin is the same height as the crown of my hood. I suppress the urge to raise my face to his.

His fingers are deft—as if used to managing unseen knots. I picture him unpinning his lover's hood. Untying the sleeves of her gown, the stays of her bodice. Something feral claws inside me.

He pulls the ribbon from around my neck and ties it quickly around his own, the *A* peeking out of his collar. He raises it to his lips with two fingers of his right hand, kisses it.

"Wyatt . . ." I want to ask him to stop. Stop flirting with me.

I want to ask him for more.

"Perhaps it's time you started calling me Thomas."

Yes, I think. *More.*

"Everyone else calls you Wyatt."

"All the men call me Wyatt, Anne. You are supposed to be my lover."

Supposed to be.

"No, *Thomas*, I am the white-assed roe deer you pursue. There's a difference."

"A distinct one."

Silence wraps around us like the summer sunlight—hot and smothering. Another crash from the tiltyard steps me backward, and the spell is broken.

"What will you be wearing?" Wyatt—I cannot call him Thomas because I am not his lover, I am nothing to him—asks, turning to walk me back through the orchard. "To the joust."

"Blue."

"No."

"Now you wish to dictate my clothing choices to me? You tell me where to go, how to walk, to whom I may speak and grant my favors. And now you restrict my choice in gowns?"

"It's for your own good, Anne. The queen will be wearing blue. To match the king. You'd do better to stand out. Wear yellow."

"And it's as easy as that, is it? You can tell me what to wear just like all the rest of them? Like my father, who insists I limit my use of velvet because it is too dear. Like my brother, who tells me I look like a slut in a French hood. Like the Duchess of

Suffolk, who tries to make me up like a halfpenny whore. Like my sister, who claims I should lower the neckline of my bodice to display my assets." Like Henry Percy, who asks that I disappear into the background as he does.

"Well, there's not really that much to display."

"You are full of honeyed words today, aren't you? Just the observations to make a girl feel good about herself."

"My job isn't to make you feel good about the things that are wrong. My job is to ensure you get noticed for the things that are right."

"Your job?" I cry. "You see me as a debt? You claim to be my friend. And I thought you were. Probably the only person who truly knows me. Who knows what I'm afraid of. Who knows what I want, who I am. But you only see me as a challenge."

"No, Anne."

"You may carry my favor, Thomas Wyatt," I say, and walk away from him. Away from the smell of apples. Of almonds. "And I'll wear the yellow gown. But I won't speak to you."

"You'll have to if I win the joust."

I'm forced turn around to look at him because he hasn't followed me. He's grinning. I want to rid him of the grin. Erase the dimples. I want to hurt him.

"Then I shall simply have to hope you lose."

"Only witchcraft can make me lose, Anne."

"That confident, are you?"

"I have to be confident about myself, Anne. No one else is going to do it for me."

"It could earn you the reputation of a braggart." I still want to hurt him. But he deflects all my weapons.

"It seems you're in serious danger of earning a reputation as one who breaks her promises."

A sudden panic overtakes me.

"What do you mean?"

"Well, you swore never to speak to me again," he says with a flourishing bow. "And here you are."

I open my mouth to speak, but he steps close to me, obscuring the sun, and places an ink-stained finger on my lips.

"I listen to every word you say, Anne. You may think no one hears you. You may think no one listens. That you can toss off sentences and condemnations, promises and speeches that will fly into the wind and will never be remembered. But I remember, Anne."

"Because it's your job?" The feel of his touch on my lips nearly takes my breath away.

His hand drops back down to his side. My chest tightens, but my weapons are already unsheathed.

"Because it's a challenge?" I pursue.

For a moment, I think my words have pierced his armor. His eyes flash and flicker over my face.

And he steps back.

"Because someone has to remind you of your promises, my dear."

30

THE MORNING OF THE JOUST DAWNS GRAY AND MURKY, THE SKY reflected in the turmoil of the Thames at the incoming tide, as if swirls of sediment fill the very air we breathe.

The queen dons her gown—a deep grayish-blue silk with heavier velvet oversleeves the color of steel reflecting the sky. The bodice is decorated in swirls of seed pearls like wisps of wind, but the whole ensemble makes her look a little dumpy—like a fat cloud on a winter's day.

Nevertheless, the ladies of her chamber—from my step-grandmother, Agnes, the Duchess of Norfolk, all the way down to little Joan Champernowne, who has her sights set on the thin-faced Anthony Denny—all wear similar hues. The entire household is a sea of blue with the occasional flash of green or magenta. The entire flock of sheep obsequiously trying to blend together.

In my yellow gown, I stand out among them. The black sheep. I squared the neckline of my bodice using an ingenious stitch that secures the corners to the lining and fits the bodice flat and smooth. I added chevrons of russet velvet—small enough not to break my father's taut purse strings. Cream-colored sleeves hang to just below the tips of my fingers. And the skirt boasts a train slightly too short so I can move easily and dance quickly at the banquet following the joust.

Each of the alterations on their own would have caused a kerfuffle amongst the ladies. But the combination of all, plus the color of the gown, has created a veritable cacophony of whispers. The French hood I had fashioned from yellow velvet is seeded at the crown with pearls and embroidered with silk of azure blue—my one nod to the monochromatic nature of the other dresses. It sits far enough back on my head to contrast with the black of my hair, but close enough to my face to offset my "sallow" skin.

I feel very, very visible.

Suddenly, all the noise in the rooms ceases. The queen is looking at me, her bright eyes questioning. And a little hurt. I've broken the tacit agreement to prove to our visitors that we are all alike and all agree.

Just before she speaks, a herald comes to the door, ready to announce her at the tiltyard tower. The fun can now begin.

The ladies sigh in disappointment. For now they've been deprived of the fun that had already commenced.

I am free to go, yellow gown, exposed hair, square neckline, and all. For once, fate is with me.

I follow the other ladies from the queen's chambers down the great stair and into the hall. It is already decorated with swags of colored silk, as the lists will be. The forest green of the Tudors, accented with white and gold.

And alternating with swags of blue.

Jane falls back to join me as the ladies make their way to the

viewing towers. The duchess casts one scathing look back at her, and I wonder that Jane doesn't combust on the spot.

"Are you sure you want to be seen with me?" I ask. "I'm certainly persona non grata today."

"I'm through with the Duchess of Suffolk and her crowd. I want to be like the Boleyns."

"And what are the Boleyns like?" I ask. We are opinionated. Ambitious. Jealous.

"Different. Exciting."

"No one wants to be a Boleyn."

She looks into my eyes, and the strength of the passion behind hers surprises me.

"I do. More than anything."

We are interrupted by a cheer from the tiltyard. The competitors bow as the queen moves toward the towers, then return to slapping backs and play-wrestling. They know they are being watched. They know they have to show off their strength one way or another.

Percy is not among them.

He is already in the stands, sitting up straight and purposeful. I expect my heart to melt at the sight of him. To feel that pulse of recognition. But there is nothing.

When he sees me, his eyes widen, not with desire, but with shock. I must truly stand out in the sea of blue. Whereas he blends in, a Percy amongst the royal elite.

Queen Isabeau of Denmark enters the stands and curtsies to her aunt, head bowed, deferential. She wears a simple white coif with a short black veil that looks almost like a nun's

wimple. She is nothing like the girl I remember from my time with the Archduchess of Austria.

The Isabeau I knew sported bright colors and gaudy embroidery. This one wears gray. The girl I knew fell in love with a portrait, with the idea of being in love. She insisted on marrying this great love of hers at the age of fourteen.

King Christian—on horseback, but not riding in the lists—utterly ignores her.

This girl is pale and meek in her white kerchief and dark furs. Queen Katherine takes both her hands and speaks to her, and Isabeau stands beside her. Two drab sparrows. Fitted tidily into place by rank and preference and then forgotten.

By contrast, the field seethes with a corruption of color and sound. Men and horses are decked in silk and metal. Everywhere, gold braid and silver tissue gleam against the beams of light that shift from the clouds like the fingers of God himself. Gilded metal flashes reflections of the sky, and velvets flutter in the stands in fountains of color.

The horses, dressed in armor that shines like the skins of beetles, stamp with an impatience matched only by that of the men who will ride them. They look like the very devil come to tempt the unlucky into Hades.

The queen moves to a velvet-cushioned chair, shaded by a canopy of state with her initial entwined with the king's as it always has been—almost since my birth. *H* and *K*. Her pomegranate emblem, embroidered in blood-red silks, competes with the white and red of the Tudor rose.

The queen lays her hands primly in her lap, her eyes hid-

den beneath the gable of her hood. I can just see her chin and jowls. Though I stand some distance from her, amidst the unwashed and unwanted on a hastily constructed viewing platform.

Jane stands with me, squeezing my hand.

"You shouldn't be here," I remind her. "Your family has more status. You should be closer to the queen."

She squeezes my hand again.

"I like the view from here."

She nods to the field. George sits astride his charger, which dances sideways, wild-eyed and ready to run.

George raises an armored fist in salute and spurs his horse toward us.

I think my fingers might break in Jane's grip.

"Sister," George calls, and Jane's hand releases mine. "I have come to ask for a token to bring me luck in the joust."

Father. George does this grudgingly. I can tell by the way his eyes don't rest on me; they scan the crowd.

"I have already given one to another," I call, and his gaze snaps back to me.

"Then perhaps"—his grin is just the right side of contempt— "I must yield to one more exalted than I."

He nods and then turns to the crowd. And raises his fist to Percy in salute.

I can't look.

"Brother," I call. My voice cracks, and I clear my throat. "Mistress Parker needs a competitor to champion her. I can think of no one more suited to the task than yourself."

I sense George's desire to scowl, but he flashes one of his disarming Boleyn grins.

"It would be my honor."

I think a little of Jane's soul escapes in her sigh.

George raises his lance, and I help Jane to tie her pale-blue kerchief to it. She bites her lip, face somewhere between tears and ecstasy. I notice she keeps her hands away from her face.

A roar rises from the crowd. The men on the field roar back, shining in the spurs of sunlight. Nearly all of them, like the queen's ladies, are dressed in blue. The Duke of Suffolk wears the same deep velvet as the duchess and sports his crest of the unicorn against the sun in splendor. Norris is in black with blue slashings in his sleeves.

Even the king, his horse caparisoned in cloth of gold and Tudor green, wears a color like the sea in sunlight. On his chest is embroidered a cluster of forget-me-nots, all in gold. I remember seeing my sister sewing it. I think of her fingers, so close to the skin of his chest. And cough.

"Are you all right, Anne?"

"I was just thinking, Jane." I pause. I shouldn't go on. "Don't you think the king is . . . irresistible?"

"What do you mean?" Jane turns from George to look at me.

"I mean he's . . . luscious."

"Anne Boleyn!" I can tell Jane hasn't fabricated her shock. "It never occurred to me. He's . . . well, he's anointed."

A sense of wickedness makes me blurt, "That doesn't mean he isn't . . . beddable."

Jane turns an unbecoming shade of scarlet and giggles vio-lently into her hand. My gaze lingers on the king as he rides once around the lists, applause following him like a wave. He stops before the queen and lowers his lance. She kisses her fingertips.

As the king rides away, he touches his fingers to the forget-me-nots embroidered over his heart. And casts a sideways glance at my sister.

"Oh," Jane says, the sound like a broken breath. "Oh, my."

I turn quickly. Did she see that? Did everyone? But Jane is staring at the other end of the field.

At Thomas Wyatt.

Wyatt doesn't wear blue. He doesn't wear the red and gold of the Wyatt family. He is wearing yellow. His doublet glows like sunshine, like a beacon, pointing directly at me. The noise of the crowd dips nearly to silence then rises again.

Jane flickers her gaze between us.

"Well." She raises an eyebrow, but a trumpet blast prevents any further remark, and the tournament begins.

George is in the first joust. He charges toward his opponent, who shies away from the oncoming lance and almost unseats himself. The crowd roars with laughter. I cannot see George's face behind his visor, but I can imagine the bitterness in it. As he turns his horse, the kerchief flutters from his lance. Jane bites her fingers when the horse tramples it into the mud. Forgotten.

The king and Duke of Suffolk joust next, and the crowd falls into silence. The men lower their visors, and the horses

thunder toward each other—towers of steel and muscle. It takes three passes before the duke is bested, but both are dented and winded when they meet again in the center to shake hands.

Wyatt rides forward on his roan charger. Jane nudges me with her shoulder and giggles. I catch several other ladies glancing at me.

Wyatt rides once around the lists, as the king did, in and out of the patches of sunlight that escape the clouds. He takes his position at the far end of the lists, finds me with his eyes. He bows, deliberately and showily.

In the tower below the queen, Percy stands as though pinned to the wall by his shoulders, his deep-blue doublet and gray sleeves a counterpoint to the queen's costume. He watches Wyatt with an expression of loathing and disbelief.

I hold my breath. Wyatt looks once to the tower, to request permission from the queen, who nods. But his gaze lingers a moment too long on Percy. Then he lifts my gold *A* on its ribbon from beneath his collar. It flashes once when he kisses it. And then he raises his hand to salute me.

Without a backward glance and with barely a show of deference to the queen, Percy leaves the tower entirely. He doesn't look at me at all.

I am left to watch the sickening play at war, gripping Jane's hands so that neither of us shows our reaction to the crack of the lances and the fall of the bodies.

31

The banquet hall adjacent to the tiltyard is lit with countless candles, the shimmer reflecting off the gold plate in the buffet against the far wall. It gleams on the silver goblets on the table—gold is too good for a deposed monarch who tried to rid his country of the nobility.

As everyone is seated, there is a minor confusion at the end of the room. King Henry and Queen Katherine sit at the head on a dais, seen together for the first time in ages. King Christian sits to King Henry's right. But then Mary, Duchess of Suffolk, is given precedence over Isabeau. The duchess, who was once married to the king of France, is seated higher than the queen of Denmark. Isabeau takes a step back from the table, causing a minor blockage in the flow of food and wine being carried from the kitchens. But she doesn't say a word. She melts into her place like a farmer's wife.

The Duchess of Suffolk preens, arranging her black velvet hood—of the French style, I notice—decorated in rubies and pearls. Her gown contains all the colors of a peacock, and seems quite fitting.

"Mutton dressed as lamb," I mutter.

"Watch your tongue, Anne."

I turn to see George beside me. Goblet in hand.

"As well as you watch your lance?" I ask him. "Jane was gutted when you trampled her kerchief."

"She'll recover." George takes a drink and doesn't look at me.

"She fancies you, George."

"All she does is watch and judge. She sees everything and does nothing. It's like being beneath the very gaze of God himself."

"I don't honestly think Jane has the ability to judge you quite so ferociously."

"Oh, you don't know what the judgment of girls can do to a man. You should talk to Wyatt."

The Danish envoy stands to give a speech. His accent is lilting and somewhat soothing. I try to give him my attention. Try to ignore my brother.

"I think it's the reason he moves so quickly from one girl to another." George slings himself up off the wall and practically stands on my toes, leaning into me. "Why they say he is so experimental with his sexual appetites."

Bile rises in my throat, but I keep my eyes fixed on the Danish envoy. Pretend I don't hear. Pretend I don't care.

"So unlike the boring, bland Henry Percy."

George always knows what will hurt most. Like lashing a fresh wound.

"Not everyone can be like you, George. I wouldn't want Percy to be."

"What? Charming, well-dressed, and personable?"

"No. Drunken, womanizing, and rude."

"Oh, Anne, you wound me."

"Not deeply enough, it would seem."

George is quiet for a moment. Takes another drink. Bends his head close to mine, his hair tickling my temples. And whispers.

"Father is coming home tomorrow."

The tension plays out between us like a single, sustained note. The Danish envoy continues to drone on as the noise level rises around him. No one is listening.

No one will notice us.

George takes another drink from his goblet. Refills it from a leather flask he carries in his other hand.

"You'll have to give them up, you know," George says. "Your paramours. Norris."

He pauses.

"Wyatt."

Droplets of wine stand out on the fuzz on his upper lip. He slides his tongue over it to lick them off.

"But that will be a shame. Just when things were progressing so well."

I glare at him. "What do you mean?"

"He knows how to keep you in line."

"Keep me in line?" I barely manage to keep my voice below the volume of the droning Danish emissary.

"Oh, settle down, Anne. Rein yourself in."

"No, I will not settle down. And don't treat me as if I'm a dog or a horse. You have no right to speak to me that way."

"I do if you're a bitch or a nag." George drains his goblet again, the laughter apparent in his eyes.

"You watch yourself, George Boleyn."

"Or you'll do what, Anne? Needlepoint me to death?"

"You're drunk."

"And you're an outspoken harpy."

"How dare you?"

"Father is away."

My fists clench. "So that makes you brave?"

George pales, though I'm sure it's more from anger than from fear. His voice drops a notch.

"It's my job as the man of the family to make sure all the women act as they should."

Another voice cuts in from behind me. "It appears to me you're making her act just the opposite, George."

The banquet returns to my consciousness with a flash, and George's anger and surprise are quickly replaced by a laugh.

"Thank God you're here, Wyatt. See if you can talk some sense into my sister."

I can't even look at Wyatt for thinking about his sexual appetites.

"See if you can put down your goblet for a minute and get yourself something to eat." Wyatt tries to take it away from him.

George shakes him off, splashing wine on the floor and the skirts of the Danish waiting woman next to him. She huffs and moves away, catching my eye. I see something I understand

there: a wish to be far, far away, back where she feels most comfortable. She's been exiled from her home because of the political insanity of the men around her.

"Get off me, Wyatt." George stumbles back, nearly knocking me down.

"I'm thinking of your own good."

"I know what you're thinking of," George counters with a sneer. "And it's certainly not my good. More like my arse."

"Don't, George."

"Well, you don't seem to be interested in women anymore. It's the only logical conclusion. You can't sweet-talk me or bully me or inveigle me like you do my sister. Though I have to say that whatever it is you're doing with her finally seems to be working."

Wyatt casts a quick look at me, his eyes wide with shock.

"He's not doing anything with me!"

I step away from them both. Away from George's insinuations and Wyatt's sexual appetites.

"Oh, I don't expect he's *sleeping* with you." George shudders obviously.

"Then what do you expect?"

"George—" Wyatt doesn't move. His eyes are on me. Ashamed. He doesn't want me. No matter what he says.

"I expect a little more deference from my baby sister." George pushes me hard enough that I fall into Wyatt, who wraps his arms around me to keep me upright. The smell of night air and almonds engulfs me.

"Try a little harder, Wyatt."

George turns away with a stumble, narrowly avoiding spilling the entire contents of his goblet over the poor Danish woman, who looks ready to scream or kill him. Or both.

"Excuse me, madam," George says, doffing an invisible cap and bowing gracelessly over his shoes, his wine decorating her hem. She doesn't move, frozen in horror. He raises his face and peers at her closely, only inches away from her nose. Her eyes grow more round and she leans backward, barely able to keep her feet below her.

"Yes," George mutters. "Yes, a female. Despite the mustache. You nearly had me fooled."

He clucks his tongue as if she's been naughty and showily grabs her hand for a kiss. Then, with a flourish that nearly unbalances him, he staggers out the door. The woman sags with relief and wipes her hand furiously on her skirts. I pray she doesn't understand English.

"Don't listen to him," Wyatt murmurs. His arms still encircle me. I want to lean back and rest my head against his chest. Breathe him in.

Instead, I release myself and speak without looking at him.

"He's drunk. And he's my brother. I never listen to him."

"Probably for the best."

I wish I could see his face. Something George said chafes the corner of my mind.

Wyatt takes my elbow and steers me away from the crowd. "He does speak the truth about one thing," he whispers.

"What's that?"

I hold my breath and look at him, his face so close to mine. He's going to tell me his sexual appetites do lean toward men. He's going to tell me I need reining in. He's going to tell me—

"That woman does have quite a mustache."

32

WYATT HUMS A TUNE—HIS VOICE DRAMATICALLY OFF-KEY—AS WE approach the donjon through the middle courtyard. He's looking very pleased with himself. I'm still nauseated over George's insinuations. And something else. Something that has lodged itself deep in my chest.

"Well, that was certainly a success." Wyatt's cockeyed grin tells me he has another plan up his sleeve.

"That, Thomas Wyatt, was a dismal failure." I stop moving. I don't have the energy to face any more.

"Forget George. He'll feel better tomorrow."

"Father's coming home tomorrow. None of us will feel better."

Wyatt hesitates. He takes a deep breath and attempts to guide me to the stairwell. To the queen's rooms.

"No," I say. "No more."

"It's the place to be seen."

"I'm not sure I want to be seen."

"You do, Anne. You can't back out now. Even the king talked about you."

Whatever has settled in my chest flutters a little. Like a living creature stirred by longing.

"What did he say?"

"Just that you had the darkest eyes he'd ever seen. He couldn't keep his own off the little jewel you gave me."

He fingers the black ribbon. My *A* is hidden beneath his collar. Against his skin. I want to touch it. I want to ask for it back. So I say nothing.

"Neither could Percy." Wyatt's voice is wary, and his stillness unnerving. As if he hopes to contradict any expression of joy on my part. Or take the opportunity to point out again that Percy could never love me.

"Oh." I won't give him the satisfaction.

"Did we make him jealous?"

"I don't know. I haven't seen him."

Wyatt doesn't say anything. I can't meet his eyes, his criticism. So I continue talking.

"He walked away. Left the tiltyard. I haven't seen him since."

"It sounds like he's jealous."

"Or maybe he just hates me, Wyatt!" I finally look up at him. "Maybe he just thinks I'm a whore like all the rest do."

Wyatt holds his breath, growing even more still, then says with a sigh, "Jealousy can make a man act in baffling ways, Anne."

"Well, I'm baffled."

"That's why we started this in the first place, is it not? To make the others jealous? To make them want what is between us?"

"There is nothing between us." My throat constricts. I look down to where my hands are pressed against my skirts.

"Of course. All I am is the flag on your ass." The bitterness in his voice may be my imagination.

I take a deep breath.

"Maybe this deer is ready to be caught."

Wyatt turns away and walks farther into the darkness of the courtyard.

"A deer ready to be caught is a deer resigned to the slaughter."

I shudder at the thought.

"Don't be morbid, Wyatt."

He stops, the bare specter of a silhouette. "You know how I feel about Percy."

"My father is coming home tomorrow." I catch up to him. I hate the pleading in my voice. "I don't have time to wait. Percy is my best chance. My only choice."

"You do have another choice, Anne."

Wyatt's voice has pitched to that rolling bass he gets when he's trying to be seductive. He lowers his face just inches from mine, one corner of his mouth curved into a dimple.

"Don't say it again, Wyatt," I tell him. He doesn't mean it. All my defenses collapse, and I shrug away from him. "Just don't."

"Fine." He straightens, raises both hands, empty, as if to show he has no hold on me. "You don't need me? You're on your own." He turns and walks away. Leaving me. Letting me go. Abandoning me.

I wait until he's gone. Until I can no longer hear the echo of his footsteps or the dolorous reverberation of my own heart. Only then do I enter the palace, which has become suffocatingly crowded. People are crammed into every corner, Danish

courtiers piled into guest quarters and the English relegated to houses and inns round about.

Everyone has eaten too much and had too much wine and lies about, lazy with gluttony and self-satisfaction and war. The tapestries in the queen's rooms are sagging with the moisture of a thousand breaths. The place is full of ladies in heavy gowns and men in padded doublets, throwing dice and fumbling with cards slick with sweat.

I sit down, uncomfortably, next to Jane. Her cerulean gown that looked so vibrant in daylight now matches the shadows beneath her eyes. George has thankfully fallen asleep in the corner, head lolled back against the wall, and she gazes at him, her face full of pain and tenderness. Wyatt sits down to cards with Henry Norris and two Danish men. I don't watch them.

The queen arrives, agitated. Not her usual serene self. After acknowledging everyone's deference, she sits. Fidgeting. She's like Jane. Without her sewing in her lap, she doesn't know what to do with her hands.

She catches my eye and an idea appears in her face.

"Mistress Anne," she calls, over the lolling bodies and lazy voices. "I hear you play the lute and sing."

I don't know who could have told her. Not my sister, certainly.

I wonder, suddenly, if it was the king. And I feel a hum. All the way from his privy chamber where he talks politics and war with the Danish king.

"A little, Your Majesty."

George has woken up and leers at me. Wyatt doesn't even glance my way.

"Will you?"

I move to the foot of the dais on which the queen sits. I pick up a lute and caress the smooth ebony veneer of the neck. I try to get away with just fiddling with the strings and plucking out harmonies that blend into each other. None of the sots listens. None of them matters.

"A tune we recognize, if you will, Mistress Boleyn."

I hear rustling from the duchess's confederacy.

The only song that comes to mind is in French. I hesitate. Surely the court cannot deny the art of the country, even while they are lusting for the blood of its inhabitants.

And this song is perfect.

It reminds me of what Wyatt said. That I am destined to be like the heroine of a ballad.

I sing the first verse. The meeting. Boy. Girl. Love at first sight. It's obvious these two will never be together. I pause and catch Wyatt watching me. I roll my eyes at the ridiculous premise, and he looks away.

The next verse; the girl tells the boy that she is already promised to someone else. The boy tries to convince her to run away. He says how much he loves her—the way she smells and the color of her eyes.

I risk a glance from the strings, and my eyes go to the card table. Wyatt is studying me. Sadly. I look away and see, by the door, Henry Percy. I get the sense he's been watching me the entire time. Ever since I started to sing.

He's wearing a russet doublet and deep-blue sleeves matched in color by the lozenges of lapis lazuli in his heavy double collar. His cap is the same russet velvet, but edged with gold braid. His cheeks look almost hollow in contrast to his sharp cheekbones and raw-edged jaw.

My fingers fumble the first note of the bridge and I feel a compression of panic. I look down at the lute. It isn't mine. I don't recognize it.

I come to the verse in which the heroine of the story tells the boy she will always remain his, and then drowns herself so that her spirit can do so. Then comes the repeating line, *à toi pour toujours*—"yours forever"—the sound trilled like ripples of water on the lowest notes of the lute.

I waver on the high notes, my voice out of practice. Hardly Orpheus. I glance again at Wyatt, afraid he'll be laughing at me, ready to criticize. My gaze meets his like a lock tumbling into place, and there is no laughter in his eyes. I realize I'm singing the song he was humming earlier.

My fingers stumble again, and I look to the door in time to see Percy disappear through it.

I stop, unable to finish the last verse.

"Thank you, Mistress Boleyn," the queen says. There is a hard note of irony in her voice. "That's quite enough."

I hear laughter on the far side of the room. The Duchess of Suffolk has her hand diagonally across her mouth, and her eyes are viciously merry.

George appears to be laughing with her. Wyatt will not look at me.

"Shall I play something on the virginal, Your Majesty?" Jane asks. She has risen and stands next to me, her fingers splayed to keep from biting them.

"Yes, Mistress Parker. Perhaps you can find us something more cheerful."

Jane bites her lip and nods. She grabs my hand, giving it a quick squeeze.

"I'm sorry," she whispers.

I look at the empty doorway.

"Me, too."

I don't rival Orpheus at all. I am unable to recall even the living.

33

I DON'T NEED A WHITE FLAG. THIS TIME, THE DEER SHALL DO THE pursuing. I put the lute beside the dais and make my obeisance to the queen, who nods sleepily. Every line of her age and tiredness shows.

I hear the voices from the card table as I pass by on my way out. The crack and slap of cards. The mutters. It sounds like Wyatt is winning. I don't look.

James Butler steps in front of me.

"Where are you going?"

His grip is surprisingly gentle on my arm. I barely look at his face as I pull away.

"Air."

I step from the room into the crowded stairwell, down through the hall and into a sea of courtiers. I scan the swells of velvet and silk for the russet and gold braid of Percy's cap.

He's leaving.

I follow him out into the night and through the middle court to the lodgings. The noise recedes the farther we get from the hall, and darkness encloses us. It seems everyone is packed into one end of the palace, not wanting to miss anything. Not wanting to miss the chance to shine.

And I am here, walking through the empty rooms and galleries behind Percy. Alone. Dust settles on the floors and tapestries, illuminated by the rising moonlight that shines in fractured pieces through the leaded windows.

"Percy." My voice barely stirs the air. I gather my strength. "Lord Percy!"

He turns, and his eyes are as dark and empty as the gallery. Cold. He takes two steps, and is so close upon me that I can't think to move. I just stand and stare.

His lips barely move when he speaks. "You need to tell me what's happening between you and Wyatt."

Not a question. An order.

"Nothing."

"Nothing?" His voice is quiet and low. And as dark as his eyes. "He seems to think it's something. He's wearing your colors."

Henry Percy flicks the yellow sleeve of my gown. The embroidery on my hood. The collar of my bodice. The movements are quick enough to be violent, to make me flinch, but not hard enough to hurt.

"He carries your favor."

He lays his finger on the spot between my collarbones, where the *A* once rested. His finger feels cold, smooth. Like marble.

"We're friends."

My words—my *excuse*—sound feeble, even to my own ears.

He makes a sound that could be a bark. It could be a laugh—though a forced one.

"It's nothing." I can't face his silence. "It means nothing. He's

Thomas *Wyatt* for pity's sake. The man's soul is made of sugar paste and poetry. You can't believe a thing he says. Or does."

Guilt. Remorse. Sharp as a blade between my ribs.

"It's because he's Thomas Wyatt that people will believe it's true," Percy says. "He's a known rake. A scoundrel. It's assumed that any girl associated with him must also be in his bed."

"I haven't been in *anyone's* bed," I say defiantly. "Ever."

"But you lived in the French court," Percy stutters. "They say no one . . ."

"They say no girl leaves there with her virginity intact," I finish for him.

"And the way you spoke to me . . . The way you flirt . . ."

"It's a game," I tell him, thinking of Wyatt's words to James Butler the first day we met: only the witless and sanctimonious believe the game is real.

"If I . . ." Percy can't seem to keep his thoughts straight. He shakes his head. A rumble of laughter from the courtyard drifts across the darkened cobbles, blurred by the windows.

"Come here," Percy says. He reaches out to catch my hand, but then draws his own back to his chest. Afraid of getting burned.

He dodges suddenly to the right, through a doorway, into an empty room. This one doesn't connect to any others. It has the one door, opposite two tall, narrow leaded windows. These don't allow the rays of moonlight in, but face, instead, the shadow of the lodgings. And the orchards deep in darkness all the way to Duke Humphrey's hill.

Henry Percy steps toward me, and I think for a sudden, ter-

rified moment that he might wrap his arms around me. Tell me he loves me. But he doesn't. He dodges to the right to close the door behind me.

I hear the lock turn.

He faces me. Doesn't touch me. The space between us is like a bulwark.

"If I . . ." He begins again. "If we . . . form a union, you cannot play this . . . game. I won't have you seen with the likes of Thomas Wyatt. I have to know that you're mine."

Union. He will make me a countess. Part of the circle. Elevated. Accepted. At the head of the table. Closer to the king.

But one word rings hollow. *Mine.* I muffle it and push it from my mind.

Percy waits.

"If we form a union," I whisper, taking a step closer. Measured. Choreographed. I see the scene playing out in my head. All a performance. I'm an actor—a dancer—playing a part. "I will be yours."

I tilt my chin up. He is shorter than Wyatt, so I would have to stretch my neck only a little to reach his lips. To press mine to his. Or for him to press his to mine.

He doesn't move.

I do. My body touches his. I smell lavender and smoke. The scent of moonlight infuses his clothes. I lift my lips to his ear.

"Everything will be yours."

Henry Percy steps back and clears his throat. Finally looks at me. The planes of his face are mere shadows amongst the shadows, his pale eyes hidden in darkness.

"I—" The sound catches on something high-pitched and sharp. He clears his throat again.

"I don't want Mary Talbot." Now he is whispering, too. "I want you."

He wants me. He wants me, Anne Boleyn. I know what I'm expected to say. It doesn't have to be rehearsed.

"I want you, too."

"My father is always telling me that a promise is as good as a contract," he says. "That because he promised I would marry Talbot's daughter when we were infants, we are as good as married."

I nod, iron bands around my chest. He wants me to be nothing but a mistress. To be nothing.

"But it is a promise I never made. It was made for me. I have never spoken it. And it has never been . . . consummated."

He coughs. Even in the cold, somber light, I can tell his cheeks are flaming.

I hold my breath and don't speak, daring him to ask for real what Wyatt did in jest. Hoping that he doesn't.

He reaches for my hands, spasmodically, and grips them too tightly.

"If we make a promise, Anne—to each other—and if we bind that promise, no one can break it. Not even the Earl of Northumberland and the Earl of Shrewsbury. You will be mine."

There it is again. That word. I stifle my reluctance to embrace it and turn instead to his other words.

A promise. A promise is as good as a contract.

Because there are no promises in adultery. Henry Percy is asking for more.

He moves a step closer, and I finally see the light in his eyes. The intensity behind them is devastating.

He bows his head, his forehead close to mine. "That is what I will tell my father."

A legitimate vow made through words and actions. A promise. And a consummation.

I will no longer have to face James Butler. I will no longer be held in contempt by my brother. I will no longer be nothing.

"Do you agree?"

He has not said he loves me. I know I cannot say it to him.

"We have to keep it a secret," Percy says. "At least until my father announces it. It must be official."

"The announcement."

"Yes." He nods emphatically. "That has to be done properly. When my father sees there is no way out."

He makes it sound like marriage to me is a trap. I have to clench my jaw to prevent myself from saying this.

"And you must stop any flirting with the other men of the court. I can't have your name associated with any of them. Bryan, Norris, Wyatt. Especially Wyatt. It all has to stop. It will ruin us."

His father is powerful and has powerful friends. If they decide I'm unfit to join the family, they will find some way to get rid of me. Legally, or not.

Surely Wyatt will understand.

"Do you agree?" Percy asks again. "This will break any nego-

tiations made with Butler as well. You will be a countess. You will be mine, forever and always, and no one can deny it."

I will be someone. Belong somewhere. *To someone.*

All I have to do is say yes.

"Yes." And then, to make it more like a marriage, more like we've conducted this in the usual manner, I add, "I do. I will."

Marry you. Be with you.

Be yours.

"Good."

He reaches up and unpins my hood. My hair, set free from the snood, falls loose down to my waist. With his right hand, he smooths it aside, then lowers his mouth to mine and kisses me.

His lips are hard, close to his teeth. He puts one hand on the back of my head, pressing us together. My mind runs wildly. I think of the king's kiss, how it tuned a note deep within me. I think of the taste of sugared almonds.

Percy breaks away to pluck one of my hairs from his mouth. He takes off his cloak and lays it on the bare floor.

He means to do this now.

I want this, I think, as he pulls me down beside him. *I want this.* He kisses me again, and this time I put my arms around his neck. The kiss lengthens and deepens, and he pushes me. Lowers me backward onto the cloak, onto the floor.

It is so dark in the shadows below the windows. I can't see his face anymore. I feel his mouth. His weight. He doesn't speak. Hardly makes a sound.

Before I can move, before I can even think, my skirts are up

around my waist, his hose removed, his face above mine, invisible, his breath heavy as sea mist. One hand pushes my left thigh and I feel a sudden dragging, stretching, tearing lurch and a bright, hot stab deep within me.

With a groan, his entire body goes rigid, sending a renewed surge of pain through me. He drops his forehead to my chest, then abruptly lifts it again and pushes my hair away, spitting it out of his mouth. He turns his face away from mine and covers me with his entire weight, my spine pressed hard into the scrubbed wooden floor. Then nothing.

Nothing.

The quiet steals in from the corners of the room.

What have I done?

34

THE COURT TAKES ON A HUSH—WHICH COULD BE CONFUSED with expectancy, but probably has more to do with inebriation—the morning after.

I feel like I am holding my own breath. Waiting. For Father to return. For Percy to acknowledge me.

Except for a dense, aching feeling and a bit of blood, I am not physically different. I am treated no differently. I can act no differently.

But I am different. I am better.

And somehow, I am worse.

Early in the afternoon, Wolsey gathers his cardinal's robes, his papers and seals, and his hangers-on and returns to York Place.

Percy goes with them. My husband.

I watch them leave from one of the towers overlooking the river. I can smell the sweet herbs burning in the barge, but they do little to dispel the stink of the Thames. At least not from where I stand. The choppy tide knocks the men together like tenpins as they step from bridge to boat, and I see Percy look up to the palace. If he sees me, he does not acknowledge it.

I leave the galleries and confining rooms of the donjon and

go into the orchards. The trees are covered in ripening cherries, the thin hips of growing apples, the promise of apricots.

I suddenly want to climb one of the trees. I want to sit on one of the branches, eating unripe fruit the way I used to do with George when we hid from Father. From his disappointment. We claimed we would stay in the trees until we were forgotten. But George always ate too much, stuffing the hard bitter fruits into his mouth until he was sick. Mary would find us hiding in the grass, surrounded by the reeking evidence of our degeneracy. And then George would lean on me as we walked back to the cold and heartless house of our childhood, Mary clucking all the way.

"Worrying about your father's arrival?"

Wyatt is walking toward me. Weaving between the trees as if dancing with them. In and out of sunlight. In and out of shadow.

"You know me too well," I say. My voice catches a little. He's the only one who knows me. And I have to sever that.

"I know you well enough to see that your father's hold on you can't prevent you from achieving greatness."

"Such flattery."

I know him, but I no longer know how to talk to him.

"It's true!" he cries, twirling me straight into an espaliered apple against the garden wall and holding me there. "Look. This tree is bound, pinioned to the wall, but still bears fruit. It still strives for the sun. Can you not do the same?"

My hands are over my head—held in place by his right arm,

his left still around my waist—my senses, like strings, pulled taut to him.

"Dare I not reach and ask for more?" His voice is barely more than a sigh.

The moment spins between us like blossoms on the air. He neither moves away nor kisses me, and I find I want him to do both with equal measure. Until I remember.

"But don't you see?" I slip out from beneath his arm, the summer breeze suddenly chilling. "As a man, you can do what you like. And all the court will admire you. It will not matter if you sleep with your wife or a hundred others. It will be forgiven. For me, it is not the same. Court gossip is a tarnish that cannot be wiped away."

"No, Anne," he says, reaching for my hands. "You will be great, too. Your life will be poetry, the very way you live it. And they will all forgive you because it will be beautiful."

"You have a sugared tongue, Wyatt, and a knack for poetry and flattery. I think you will go far."

"And you, my dear."

"Yes." My throat constricts. "I will be a countess."

He drops my hands.

"What happened?"

I want to tell him everything. About Father. George. How Percy's mouth is so unlike his. My stomach squirms at the thought of telling him about last night.

"He asked me to marry him."

"And he has his papa's approval?"

"Don't be snide."

"I don't have to be, Anne. That whipped puppy can't take a piss without his master's permission."

"He can!" Somewhere in me Wyatt's words strike a chord of truth. I silence it. "He does. And he has."

He waits. Stares.

"Anne," he says hoarsely. "What have you done?"

I hold his gaze, willing him to understand. I can say nothing. There is nothing I can say.

"Jesus." He covers his face in his hands and rubs vigorously. "Shit."

"It's done." My tone is flat. "No one can change it."

He turns and strides up the hill toward Duke Humphrey's Tower. The angle of the morning light sets him ablaze.

"Northumberland can change it," he calls over his shoulder.

"Not even God can change it, Wyatt," I cry as I struggle to catch him up. "Don't you understand?"

"I understand all too well." He stops again, and I nearly run into him. We stand an inch apart, and yet the gap between us feels unbridgeable. "If the earl didn't endorse it, it never happened. A match not made in the circle of power is no match at all."

"It's a love match," I say. "Even the king would honor it. He loved Queen Katherine." Once. "He married her even though his father had broken off the engagement."

Wyatt doesn't speak for a moment, his disbelief carved into the hard lines of his face.

"How can it be a love match if you don't love him?"

I don't want his doubt, and I don't want his pity, so I square up to him, stick out my chin, and let my eyes blaze with challenge.

"Maybe I do."

He looks at me for a moment.

"Then say it."

But I can't. Say it. I'm not even sure I can feel it. I spread my hands on my skirts.

Wyatt watches pointedly and then continues.

"You're just like your father. Scheming and manipulating to get a place as close to the center as you can. All head and no heart."

I will not let him see how much that hurts.

"So which is worse?" I ask. "Being the head that gets to the center? Or being the hand that gets others there?"

"You're a fool."

"No. I'm not foolish. I have chosen my husband. I have made a difference in my life."

"You've traded one tyrant for another—your father for a boy who isn't half the man, despite his lands and titles."

"At least I didn't allow myself to be whipped into a wretched marriage. At least I made my own decision. Not like you."

I spit the last words out and watch them land like poisoned barbs on his face.

"True," he says. So quietly I almost can't hear him over the sough of the trees and the plaintive call of a hawk in the mews.

"Not like me. But because of my own situation, Anne, I know you will never be happy. Not with him."

"Not happy? I'm ecstatic. This is what I'm made for. To be a countess. To escape my family and their limited vision. To be *here*." I stamp my foot on the ground of Greenwich.

"You will not be happy because you don't love him. And he doesn't love you."

"And love is so important?"

Wyatt doesn't hesitate.

"Yes."

"So maybe it can be learned," I say quickly, and look away to where St. Paul's points accusingly at the sky. "And you don't know. Maybe he does. Love me."

I think about Percy's kiss. About how quickly it was all over. Surely that meant something. Surely it meant he at least desired me.

"Love and sex are different things, and should not be confused."

As if he knows what I'm thinking. He always knows what I'm thinking.

"What do you know? You've said yourself that you never loved your wife."

"That's how I know. I have a son with her, but I do not love her and never have. Nor she me. But that doesn't mean I have never loved."

His words grind a hole in my heart so deep I feel I will never again see the sun. So I try to claw my way out.

"Well, I've never had that luxury. My family doesn't beget

love, no matter what they pretend. And I don't know how to love in return. Your concern is misplaced."

I can't stand the pity in his eyes, so I turn away.

"You lost the bet, Wyatt. Your services are no longer needed."

I leave him there. High on the hill, with nothing but the desolate cry of a hawk for company.

35

My father returns. He goes to see the king, the Privy Council. Days go by.

He doesn't ask for me.

He goes to York Place to debrief Wolsey. Matters of state are more important. The war with France is more important. Wolsey is more important.

I am woken in the darkness of predawn. A rough shake. A stumble over a discarded slipper in the maids' chamber. A curse.

"George?" I whisper. I feel Jane stir beside me, feel her arm move. I reach for her hand and hold it down beneath the covers. "George, you can't be in here."

"It's not like I haven't been before," he mutters. Jane stiffens.

"Go away, George. I'll see you in the morning."

"No, Anne." I feel his face near mine, see the almost imperceptible glitter of his eyes. "You'll see me now. And Father's wrath."

"Father? Did he ask for me?"

I release Jane's hand and swing my feet out of the bed. The floor is cold and dusty beneath them. Desolate.

"His very words were, 'Go and get your slut of a sister and bring her to me this instant.'"

Something cold runs up the back of my neck.

"So you came for me?"

"First. I came for you first, Anne. We must go and get Mary, too."

"He doesn't want me."

But I fear he does.

"Please, Anne." The voice is soft and green. "Don't make me go alone."

We creep through the quiet rooms and galleries of the palace, relieved to find only Mary in her room. Then the three of us make our way beyond the palace walls to Father's lodgings at an inn. The Palace is too full to house him. I expect he will somehow add that insult to our perceived transgressions.

As the bleary-eyed innkeeper leads us up the stairs, I number each one in my mind, repeating the refrain, *countess, countess, countess*. I will be a countess, I remind myself. The Countess of Northumberland. Wyatt's words echo back: *no heart, no heart, no heart*.

The three of us stand together but separate as we wait for Father to allow us into his rooms. I do not hold George's hand as I used to do when we were children. But our shoulders touch. Mary takes an audible breath when we hear a voice from within.

"Come."

A single, devastating word.

We enter.

Father is sitting at a little desk. He is still dressed in his court clothes: a doublet that sports more velvet than all my

gowns put together; padded shoulders; jeweled cap. His hair is still a bit shaggy from weeks on the road and in war camps.

He doesn't speak.

He waits. Waits for us to stand still, for the door to latch. Waits just long enough for the sweat to stick my linen shift to my skin.

"How could you let this happen?" His voice is like the hiss and rumble of distant thunder, low and menacing. It's inaudible to the innkeeper on the other side of the door, but we hear and understand every word.

He stands up abruptly in one swinging motion, and I'm reminded that my father has always excelled at the joust and the lists, at hunting and hawking and tennis. At war. Despite his age, my father moves like a young man. Like a predator.

We do not move or speak.

Father stops in front of George.

"One of my children creates a false engagement?" he hisses. "Without consent?" A cataract of shame and terror flashes through me. George looks neither left nor right, but straight ahead. Unseeing. Unfeeling.

"Did you know?"

George opens his mouth. No sound comes out.

"Don't." Father and George are face-to-face, and I see how much George has grown. Yet he is diminished by the flare of Father's wrath. George closes his mouth again—the lips a firm, thin line—and lowers his eyes.

Father gaze never wavers. "How could it become known before it was sealed?"

Father doesn't know that I did seal it.

"I didn't—" I start, but Father raises a hand. Not to strike, but I flinch anyway.

"Do. Not. Speak," he hisses.

George is unmoving beside me. I feel his tension run through the room like a whirlpool.

"I return from Spain to find all of York Place in an uproar." Father returns to his chair. He leaves us standing side by side. Not touching. "The cardinal was in the gallery with only his chamber servants but could be heard from every corner, including the door of the council chamber."

So of course Father stopped to listen.

"The cardinal's voice was audible from every corner of the inner courtyard. 'How dare you defile your good name!'" Father shouts in a good imitation of the cardinal's tenor.

"'I marvel at your peevish folly!'" Father continues. "'And to tangle yourself to that foolish girl in the court. You are due to inherit the greatest earldom in England and yet you ally yourself with the daughter of merchants. Of little wealth and no name. One of the king's minions.'"

George sucks in a breath, and Father glares at him.

"So I listen. Wondering who this boy is and with whom he has entangled himself."

Wondering whom he can use the gossip as leverage against.

"'I am a man,' says Henry Percy." Father slams his fist into

the desk, making the inkpot jump. "Heir to Northumberland. Sounding like a mouse. 'I am old enough to choose a wife as my fancy serves me best. I cannot go back on my word. My conscience will not allow it. I have committed myself'"—Father pauses, a dramatic master equal to Thomas Wyatt—"'to Anne Boleyn.'"

Father lets the final two words drop into the room like cannonballs. Heavy and indefensible.

I feel as if I am floating. Percy stood up for me. Percy will honor our union. Father's anger comes only from not knowing first.

"You're married, Nan?" Mary whispers. She has turned away from Father and is looking at me. "Betrothed?"

I nod, and she smiles at me. A little tentatively. Unsure.

"No." Father answers for me.

Mary's smile drops, and we turn again to Father. His hands are laid out before him on the desk, gripping the curl of it on the far side.

"No, she is not. Even if some kind of *agreement* was made"—Father manages to make the word sound salacious, indecent—"the boy's father will disown him if he goes through with it." Father looks at George as if he wishes he had a similar excuse. "Wolsey will throw him out. Even the king commands that he never see her again if he intends to avoid the full wrath of his majesty."

The room settles into silence, asphyxiated by Father's vented spleen.

Father glares at George again, and it is as if they are the only two in the room. In the universe.

"This is your fault. She was your responsibility. And now she is a scandal."

He will not look at me. Neither of them will.

"She is not married."

He won't even say my name.

"She is nothing."

36

None of us speaks on the return to the palace. The muddy streets of Greenwich glimmer, illuminated by a day just beginning to break; then the shine is snuffed by the clouds.

"You did it," George finally mutters as we enter the courtyard through the gate.

I can't even nod. I'm strangled by the knowledge that Percy will be married off to Mary Talbot. And I will be sent—alone—to Hever.

I am devastated by the thought that the king knows what I've done.

"Congratulations—you managed to be more of a disappointment even than I am." George's hair has fallen over one eye. The corner of his mouth is raised.

"She made a mistake," Mary says quietly.

"There are no mistakes in Father's world. There is only failure."

George leaves us on the cold cobblestones, squaring his shoulders before he enters the donjon to go and serve the king.

"If Lord Percy made a promise"—Mary turns to me—"he must honor it. He will have to defy his father."

I wonder if Percy will choose me and disinheritance. I like the idea of a man who would change his life, his status—his whole world—for me. A nobody.

But if he lost everything, I'd still be a nobody. Exiled. Unwanted. Silenced. Besides, no one does that. That's fodder for fairy tales and romantic ballads.

"Would George defy ours?" I ask.

Mary pales a little. No one defies our father.

Then her face softens, and I think I see tears in her eyes.

"Do you love him?"

"I don't think the Boleyns know how to love."

The tears threaten to spill over.

"We love each other."

"Do we, Mary? We don't show it."

"There are different ways to show love. Forgiveness."

Mary doesn't look away, challenging me to contradict her.

"Loyalty is a form of love," she says. "Even in the face of betrayal. And taking the punishment for someone else's mistakes."

"Failure, Mary," I whisper. "There are no mistakes."

"If you love each other, it's not a failure."

I can't reply. Mary studies me. Silently.

"I'm sorry, Anne." She wraps me tightly in her arms and I want to stay there forever. Protected. Safe. Her hair and neck are still scented by sleep. But then I catch the scent of cloves. The king.

I push her away. "Don't feel sorry for me."

My body feels rigid. Solid, but on the verge of splintering.

"Maybe he'll convince his father," she says. "Maybe he'll come for you."

"Maybe Tottenham will turn French," I mutter, so I'm not fooled into believing the fairy tale. "Maybe we'll all become Lutherans. Maybe Father will decide he loves us and let us marry whom we like and we can all live happily to the end of our days."

Mary looks as though she might speak again, so I turn on my heel and go back to the real world. Alone.

I pack. I pay my respects to the queen. I listen for gossip—anything that will give me hope or tear it from me. Father makes arrangements for a few rooms at Hever to be opened and aired, but I hear all this through servants. He will not speak to me and will not suffer me to speak to him.

I haven't seen George. Or Wyatt. Even my sister avoids me.

I want to hope, but Percy never comes.

Instead, the day before my exile begins, I get a visit from a short and spotty youth of imperious demeanor and dubious hygiene.

"Good day to you, Mistress Boleyn," he says, sitting beside me and leaning close. His breath smells like the Thames at low tide.

I edge away.

His face appears as if he were afflicted with the pox, and his eyes do not light on anything for more than an instant. Like flies.

"I am James Melton, and I bring word from a mutual friend."

"Friend?"

I claw through my memories to discover who might be a friend of Melton's. I'm not sure I have any myself.

"A certain lord with whom I believe you are close," he says, angling toward me. He's practically sitting on my lap. My stomach roils.

"Please keep your distance, sir."

"But this is information of a very delicate nature," he breathes. "Something only you should hear."

I turn my head away, as if listening to music. More to avoid the reek of his words than to save my reputation. My reputation is already stained irrevocably.

"It concerns a certain young lord in my lord cardinal's household."

I glance at him quickly, knowing that only one young lord could be sending me word through this cretin. Knowing what it means.

"His father has made an emergency visit to London," Melton continues. "He arrived at York Place and immediately requested an audience with both the young lord in question and the cardinal himself. He spent well nigh an hour berating the young lord, calling him a 'waster' and comparing him to his brothers. Not kindly, mind you. The father threatened to disinherit him."

I bite my lip.

"You see the problem," Melton says, and allows himself a snaggletoothed smile.

I nod curtly, barely inclining my head.

"So the young lord will return to the family lands," Melton says quickly. "The marriage arranged for him is going ahead. He will not lose his inheritance. He will not lose his honor."

All of this is said as if to make me feel better. As if I don't matter. My feelings. My desires. My honor.

Percy left without me to keep his father's promise. To keep his inheritance.

"Thank you for letting me know," I manage.

"But there is more," he says eagerly, his shoulder nudging mine. "The information about the father's visit you could get from anyone. I'm surprised you have not heard the gossip already. No, mistress, I have a private message for you from the young lord himself."

He will escape. He will wait for me. He will convince his father of my suitability.

"He bid me to beg of you," Melton says, and I hold my breath as his words graze my cheek, "that you remember and honor your promise. Which none can break but God himself."

He looks at me meaningfully.

My promise. *My* promise.

I shudder. I cannot believe that Percy has told Melton what occurred between us. After exhorting me never to tell anyone. After making me give up my closest friend for our farce. He has told Melton, who ogles me as if he could be the next in line.

I can't believe that Percy bids of me that I remain unmar-

ried, a spinster, a *widow* to him. Remain his property. While he goes off and marries the Earl of Shrewsbury's daughter. Has children. Becomes an earl. Has a *life*.

He wishes me to be faithful? To a hurriedly whispered oath in a back room in the dark? To a painful, pathetic excuse of a consummation?

He wishes to have my humiliation known by this ridiculous waste of space, who could tell anyone. Could tell everything. Could ruin me. But nothing can touch the future Earl of Northumberland. The English aristocracy will circle their pikes around their own, shutting me out entirely. I could proclaim my virtue before an entire courtroom full of lords, and they wouldn't believe a word I say.

Effervescent wrath sings in my blood and it is all I can do to keep my hands still. "Get out."

"Pardon?" Melton asks, head tilted, an unsure and obsequious smile on his face.

"You know nothing," I say, standing abruptly. "Whatever the 'young lord' told you is a complete fallacy. The vicious lies of a jealous suitor."

He gapes. Unbecomingly. I long to slam his jaw closed.

"Leave," I command. "I never wish to see you again. Or him. I will never speak to him more. *That* is a promise you can tell him I will keep."

Henry Percy has no idea who he's dealing with.

Melton stands reluctantly, looking bewildered. Like a dog whose bone has been stolen by a fox.

He shoulders past James Butler on the way out. But Butler doesn't acknowledge him. Butler is staring at me. Not with the angry, belligerent glare he used when he caught me with Wyatt or Percy or even George. No, Butler is smiling, and it freezes my anger and my blood with it.

Then he blows me a kiss and turns away.

Hever Castle
1523

37

My father calls Hever a castle, and long ago, it was. These days, it is just a fortified and moated house with small windows and freckled walls of golden stone and a garden picturesque in its tidy forms. All of it perfectly represents the Boleyns—the outward show of opulence and strength, the simple lines and calm exterior. Not a hint of what lies inside.

It is hell. Worse, it is purgatory. At least in hell you have something to do. In purgatory, all you do is wait.

Summer fades, and the blue sky is clotted with clouds that change shape like witches from old stories, one moment, a face, and the next, a dragon.

The fruit ripens in the orchard. I avoid going out. Too many memories associated with the scent of apples.

I find myself on long afternoons just staring through the window of the little sitting room. The blue sky crossed with threads of black lead. I let the sky and the lead go in and out of focus, blurring between freedom and prison.

Father's steward makes me jump by entering the room with a bang. He's short and skinny with thin strips of hair stretched across his skull and a permanently sour expression on his pallid lips. A jug of ale totters on his tray and he scowls at it.

"Visitor."

Thomas Wyatt stands at the door like a ray of sunlight too early for spring.

"Well, don't you look pasty," he says, his Kentish drawl like a salve.

"Wyatt!" I leap up and run to him, to throw my arms around him. But the immediate fear in his eyes stops me short. We are no longer on the same footing we once were. And I must tread carefully.

"It is so good to see you."

He's wearing a forest-green doublet that intensifies the color of his eyes. But they flicker around the room. He's purposefully not looking at me.

We stand, unable to speak, for what feels like an eternity. Until the steward coughs and I realize he's still in the room.

"Thank you. You may set it on that table. And tell the cook that Master Wyatt is staying for supper."

The steward scowls again and exits with barely a bow.

"You want me to stay?"

Wyatt sounds forlorn. Again we face a wall of silence.

"I—" I start to speak, but he interrupts me.

"Don't."

I bite my lower lip. "Don't what?"

"Apologize. Isn't that one of the first things I taught you?"

He looks me in the eye and the dimple appears. Finally.

Relief runs through me like a zephyr—a gentle wash from head to foot.

"Thank you."

"Don't thank me, either, Anne. There is little to thank me for."

"Well," I say, bustling to serve us. Trying to hide my confusion in busyness. "I can certainly thank you for coming today. For breaking my boredom. Tell me, what news of court?"

His face falls again, and I rush to continue.

"I hear nothing here. Not even the servants speak to me. I have a maid and a part-time cook. And Father's steward, of course."

I cut my eyes to the closed door and raise my voice.

"Who I think was only returned here to spy on me."

Wyatt grins again. Two dimples. I'm so delighted, I could kiss them.

"I believe," Wyatt says, leaning closer to me, "that I can hear him holding his breath."

I pause for a moment to savor the scent of almonds.

"Show me the house," Wyatt says, stepping back. "Surely he can't spy on you everywhere."

We pass the scowling steward on the way to the entrance hall. He doesn't follow.

"Father had this hall built when he came here," I say. "To make it seem less like a fort and more like a home." I hesitate. "He wasn't very successful."

Wyatt listens as I explain everything. Display everything. In every room. I'm afraid to stop talking. I feel as though only my constant prattle will prevent us from falling back into the inability to speak. To *not* talking about why we're not talking.

"Father had a gallery built upstairs." I point to the ceiling in the dining hall.

Then I stop. The chill of the room overwhelms me.

"I don't eat here," I finally manage.

Wyatt stands close to me. The only warmth in the room.

"Why?"

"The table reeks of broken promises and disappointment."

"Then we shall go." Wyatt offers me an arm. Warm. Solid. I finish the tour. The upstairs gallery. The bedrooms.

"This is the guest room," I tell him, showing off the Boleyn bull over the fireplace, the velvet curtains, the bed.

"It has a real feather mattress." I find myself speaking faster. "No straw ticking for our guests." I pause, smothered in silence. "I think sometimes the feathers give me nightmares."

"But you sleep here anyway."

"Shhh," I whisper through a laugh. "It's my one act of rebellion."

"Well, you can notch up another one now. Not only are you sleeping here, but you've invited a man in as well." He steps so close his breath tickles my ear. "And a married man at that."

"You will be the ruin of me, Thomas Wyatt."

Silence washes over us. Because Thomas Wyatt is not the bringer of my ruin. I am.

Without speaking, we return to the sitting room and I order supper. It's simple: cold meats and plain bread. But it had been intended only for me.

"I wasn't expecting company," I say to sidestep apology. "You'll have to warn me next time. And I'll cause more scandal by ordering one of Father's finest wines."

Wyatt glances at me sharply.

"You want me to come back?"

I lean forward to make my point. "You are welcome at any time. I will be offended if you don't visit every time you are at Allington."

He frowns. Swallows.

"My wife is at Allington."

The painful gaps in our conversation are starting to make me tearful. I've been alone too long.

I clear the lump from my throat.

"What news at court?"

Wyatt tells me the gossip. Norris's latest paramour. Wolsey's latest political conquest. I watch him as he speaks, the taut-ness of his expression dissolving into familiarity, the tension in his body dissipating into that lissome nonchalance. Until he pauses.

"Suffolk has left for France. With fourteen thousand men."

I sag back into my chair.

"He's really doing it, then."

I had thought better of King Henry. And some little part of me—the childish, infatuated girl in me—still thought that we were mystically connected. That he would listen to me, and reconsider. That I meant something. That my words had power.

Wyatt nods soberly. "The duchess has already set herself up as a martyr to the cause."

"I just bet she has."

"And your sister . . ." He hesitates.

"What?" I ask. "What about Mary?"

"You haven't heard? From your family?"

I shake my head.

"My family has cut me off. Now that I'm worthless."

Wyatt looks at me for a moment long enough to become uncomfortable. "You're not worthless, Anne."

I smile wryly. "I am to my family. Now, please, tell me about Mary."

"She's pregnant."

"Oh."

There is no room in our conversation for me to ask the identity of the father.

"I believe she is hoping for a girl."

"If it is a girl," I say slowly, "he won't claim her." I can't say his name. Because of family pride? Or jealousy? "An illegitimate girl is more useless than a legitimate one."

Wyatt nods, his eyes on my hands in my lap. No. His eyes are on my belly.

"The other news at court," he says, and each word sounds as if it is hammered on a forge, constructed with great effort. "The other news is the upcoming union between Shrewsbury and Northumberland."

Percy.

This is why he's watching me. Perhaps this is even why he's come here from court. To find out if I, too, am pregnant.

I stand and turn away from him.

"You are very cruel to remind me of the man who broke my heart."

"He never broke your heart, Anne."

"He broke my ambition, then," I revise. "Because of him I am exiled. So in a sense, my heart is broken."

"You never loved him."

"He didn't love me, either. No one loves me." I cannot get by without pinching the softest parts of my own pain. "Love doesn't matter."

"It does matter, Anne," Wyatt says. He moves to stand beside me. Close enough to touch, but not touching. He looks me steadily in the eyes and repeats himself. "It does matter."

"Maybe for a poet it matters," I tell him bitterly. "Maybe even for a man of some significance, like the king. But for the rest of us, love has no place in our lives. Especially women. If I want to break out of the prison of my birth, I need to have the right person at my side. Whether I love him or not."

"That's awfully cold, Anne."

"It's easy for you; you're a *man*. You can make your own way. Befriend the king, be accepted into his circle." Jealousy stabs me again, and my words crowd my mouth in a bid to escape before I combust. "You can leave your wife and come here and still have friends and lovers. You can still write your poetry and play cards and joust in the tournaments. *You* can have a life."

Wyatt takes a step back, as if he's been slapped. Lightning strikes of anger flash across his expression.

"You know what your trouble is, Anne?"

"That the man who fucked me is marrying someone else?"

The muscles along Wyatt's jaw spasm.

"No."

We are plunged again into a hole of silence that we ourselves excavated.

"What then?" I step toward him, lifting my chin. "What is my trouble, Wyatt? What kind of criticism do you have to offer now?"

We stare at each other, unflinching. Then his jaw relaxes and I see something like sadness—or pity—in his eyes.

"You've never been in love."

"And I'm not likely to be, either," I say, sitting down again. I find I can no longer take my own weight. "It seems a criminal waste of time."

"You sound just like your brother." Wyatt sits on the stool beside me, our shoulders touching.

"That hurts."

Because it is true. It is exactly something my brother would say.

I lay my head on his shoulder, and for the first time that evening, our mutual silence is comfortable. We listen to the chatter of the fire and the shuffling of the steward outside the door.

"I'm not pregnant," I whisper.

"I know."

I raise my head a little to look at him, my lips inches from his.

"How?"

"Because I know you as well as I know myself, remember?"

"Then tell me this." I lay my head back down on his shoulder. "Do you think I am capable of love? Are any of the Boleyns? We're certainly not capable of saying it."

"I think everyone is capable of both." His words stir the hair that escapes from my hood.

"You've been in love, haven't you, Wyatt? Is it really all that wonderful?"

"Yes, Anne," he murmurs. "And yes. It is."

Hever Castle
1524

38

I START TO LOSE THE BATTLE TO RETAIN MY SANITY. SOME DAYS I sit still as stone, unmoved by cold or hunger, and I think I would not flinch if someone were to set me on fire.

Other days, I fling myself at whatever pastime or obstacle I come across—working my tapestry needle until my eyes ache, practicing dance steps until I stumble from exhaustion, or screaming at my maid until she cries.

And all days I wait for Wyatt to return, berating myself for every moment I spend thinking of him. Depending on him. He visits sporadically and always without warning, and my mind and heart are clear for days after.

The summer gave up its fight against the onslaught of the cold English winter. Ash trees gilded the hills, the fields ran rampant with ripe wheat, and I could almost believe I was back in France, so beautiful was the waning light. Then winter arrived on gray, heavy feet. I was not invited back to court for the Christmas celebrations and got little from my family for the New Year. Though Mary sent a book of hours—handwritten and beautifully illuminated and obviously very expensive—with a note that says she misses me.

I find that I miss her, too. I could use a mothering influence, since our own mother has been visiting Howard relatives, despite my residence here. Conspicuously absent. Conspicuously silent.

On Twelfth Night, I get a note from Wyatt saying that he will visit the next day, that he has something important to tell me.

I order manchet bread and meats and spiced wafers for his arrival. I insist that a jar of preserved strawberries be brought from the cool recesses of the buttery and that one of Father's best wines be opened.

After all, I promised. I don't want to earn a reputation as one who breaks her promises.

"I have to send a request to your father," the steward informs me when I tell him about the wine.

"It's for tomorrow," I snap. "You must take the order from me."

"It is my duty to address any unusual requests to Sir Thomas directly."

"This is not an unusual request, but a common one." I stop, considering the true intent behind his words. "You don't take orders from me?"

He offers a thin-lipped grimace.

"No, mistress."

Of course not. Why would Father have the household placed under the command of a disgraced youngest daughter? Who knows what kind of trouble I could get myself into if given too much power?

"Fine. The usual wine will have to suffice."

The steward doesn't even attempt to hide his triumphant grin.

When all is ready, I have the maid bank up the fire and send her away. I sit alone, embroidering a falcon on my yellow bodice. The light fades from the window, gray and lackluster.

As all grows dark outside, the steward enters. Smirking.

"Wine and supper for one, mistress?"

I nod. Wyatt is not coming. The steward has one more piece of news to report to my father.

I take a goblet of the wine to the fire and drink it quickly. The sour tang of it reminds me of George. I drink it all. And then another.

A brisk knock, and the steward reenters. Scowling.

"I'm not finished yet," I say to my goblet. "Go away."

"But I just got here."

"Wyatt." I turn. I want to wrap my arms around him. Keep him here forever. "You're late."

He nods. Cagey. Doesn't leave the doorway.

"You must stay the night."

The steward sucks a breath through his teeth.

"It is far too *dark* to return to Allington on icy roads," I say more loudly, and then turn to speak to the steward. "Food for Master Wyatt, please. And more wine."

He slides past Wyatt, who still stands at the door.

"Come in!" I say finally. "Get warm. Sit down. You're making me nervous."

I pour more wine as he enters. Drink as he sits on the edge of a stool.

The steward brings the food, and when I excuse him for the evening he leaves grudgingly. My father will hear all about this, and I find I don't care.

"Your note said you have something to tell me."

He takes a deep breath.

"I've left Elizabeth."

His wife.

"It's hardly news, Wyatt."

"No. I've said so. It's known in the court. I'm afraid I've upset everyone."

"Well, you didn't have to announce it publicly! You could just go on as you have been."

"I didn't want to."

"So you chose to live outside the norm. Risk being exiled." Like me.

"The king will forgive me."

"Why?" I ask.

"He always does. He finds me charming."

"More fool him," I tease, and realize it's something else the king and I have in common. "However, my question is, why are you leaving her?"

"We are nothing alike."

Like me and Percy.

"But you have a son." I find the words difficult to say. "Surely that means you must have . . . wanted her. Once."

I take another gulp of wine.

Wyatt clears his throat and crumbles his bread between his fingers. The silence in the room rises like heat, stifling.

"Never mind," I say, my words brittle as fallen leaves. More wine.

"No," Wyatt says. "There was a time. I wanted . . ." Again the grinding in his throat. "Everyone. Anyone. I tried hard to be faithful. Elizabeth, she . . . she threw it back at me. Laughed at me. She would get all painted up, like a doll . . . and go and sleep with someone else."

"And you were . . . jealous?"

"No. Humiliated. I never loved her. I think that made her hate me. So we both just . . . lived without regard. Ignored each other. Slept with whomever we wished." He looks away. "Last week she used my bed. With the steward."

I finish another goblet. The room is so warm. Wyatt stares into the fire and his eyes seem consumed by it.

"And when I . . . when the duchess painted me in her ceruse, it reminded you of that humiliation?" I don't want to say it, remembering his anger. But my tongue—which is never tame at the best of times—has been loosened by the wine.

"I reacted badly."

A single statement. No explanation.

"You did," I say lightly. "But our friendship survived."

Wyatt looks at me. Looks like he wants to say more, say something important, but remains mute. I take another gulp of wine.

"You know"—I break the silence—"George says men and women can't be friends."

"You know," Wyatt replies in the same tone, "George doesn't always tell the truth."

I laugh, and Wyatt raises his goblet to me in a toast. I watch him over the rim of mine as I drink, and he does the same. I pause, holding the goblet just level with my lips; the feral creature deep behind my ribs expands and stretches, bringing me to the verge of tears. And laughter.

Wyatt lowers his goblet, leans toward me, ready to speak.

But I jump forward. Spill my wine. Ignore it.

"I need a friend, Wyatt," I say, perching on the edge of my stool. "A true friend. I think so many people wish me ill. So many want me gone."

"We'll stay away from them," Wyatt says quietly. "It will just be you and me. We don't need the court. We don't need your brother or your family or the king. We'll conquer them all. Just the two of us. Together."

"If I see only you"—my voice cracks—"I'll never be married, Wyatt."

"Maybe marriage isn't the pinnacle of success."

I think of Percy in that tiny, dark back room. And I think of Wyatt. Here. Now.

"I'm inclined to believe you're right."

He looks at me for a moment. We are on the verge of something. I feel it like a precipice before me in the dark.

"Why?" Wyatt's voice comes from the other side of that crevasse. I know that if I bridge it, our friendship will never be the same.

I cannot make that leap.

"Well, let me tell you," I say, pulling back from the brink, and begin counting on my fingers. "It makes a woman boring and unattainable, to begin with. No one really flirts with a married woman. Especially one married to a powerful man. Not fun at all."

Wyatt laughs and sits back. His eyes are half closed.

"It's far too much work." I take a swig of wine. I'm beginning to see why George drinks so much. It makes life easier. It makes talking easier. "Not only must a wife run the household and raise the children, but she must also tend to all the needs of her husband."

"Such as?"

Wyatt's eyes are now almost fully closed. But I sense he is watching me.

"Planning his favorite meals, enduring his odious friends." John Melton comes to mind. "Sewing endless hems on endless shirts."

"Don't forget nightly entertainment," Wyatt adds lazily.

I ignore the implication.

"Not only all of that, but marriage completely destroys the equilibrium in the court, taking away all the eligible and interesting men."

"Oh?" His eyes are open now. Guarded. Thinking of Percy. I take another drink and crash on, trying to be humorous.

"Francis Bryan," I begin my list.

"Your cousin from hell," Wyatt snorts.

"Henry Norris."

"You keep going on about him, but I don't think you're really interested."

"Shows how well you know me then!"

He leans forward, over his empty plate.

"I know you better than I know myself, Anne. Henry Norris is not your type."

"Well, he is already taken, anyway," I quip, not ready to give up the banter. "And then there's George."

"He's not married."

"Yet. But poor Jane Parker is ready and willing."

Wyatt makes an appropriately concerned face for her.

"The king."

Wyatt laughs his great burbling roar, more intoxicating than the wine.

"The king belongs to a completely different circle, Anne."

I almost don't say it. But it spews out of me. "And you, taken from the flirting pool long before your prime."

Wyatt coughs on his wine.

"Doesn't seem to have stopped you."

"Nothing can stop me, Wyatt," I say dizzily. "You said it yourself."

"I did," he says, entirely too thoughtfully. Too thoughtful by half for the deliriousness of the wine.

"You must stay the night with me." I stand too quickly and have to grab the table for support. Just one more sip of wine to steady me. I barely taste it. My lips are numb. I press the rim of the goblet to my mouth, awed by the absence of feeling.

Wyatt takes the goblet away. When did he stand, too? He's so close. So close to me. I can taste the velvet of his doublet. Breathe the blue of his eyes.

"Where?" he asks, his voice rough on the skin of my cheek. His mouth so close to mine.

My lips want to kiss him.

"In the guest room," I say, the words troubled on my tongue.

He hesitates. Pauses in the spinning of the room.

"But quiet." I lay one finger on his lips to silence him. Almost like a kiss. "My room is just down the gallery."

"I won't breathe a word." He speaks with a sigh.

"It would ruin your reputation if you did," I scold, shaking the finger under his nose. And I laugh. I try to step away from the table, but my train and skirts turn against me, and I stumble.

"Come, Anne." Wyatt puts an arm around my waist. "Time for bed."

"I bet you say that to all the girls."

I lean into him, my feet happy to be relieved of weight and responsibility. Up the stairs and down the gallery, my hip bumping his, the length of him against me. We stop just inside the door of my great, empty bedroom, and the numbness rolls down my body in a wave, followed by a crash and thunder of sensation. I can feel every point where our bodies touch.

I lift my face to his, sure that he feels it too.

"Undress me," I whisper.

I feel his entire body groan as he takes a step backward, catches me by the shoulders before I fall.

"You're drunk, Anne."

Is that regret I hear I his voice? Or pity?

"My maid," I mumble. "I sent her away. I can't reach my laces."

I turn around and fumble with the knots to demonstrate. Bow my head to hide my face.

I feel his sigh on the back of my neck, his fingers light and quick, unbinding the leather and buckram that hold me together.

"Thank you," I say to the floor. I cannot look at him again.

He turns me around, and I clutch the gaping bodice to my chest. Gently, he pulls the pins from my hood and slides it off. He smooths back my hair, running his fingers through the length of it.

And kisses me.

On the forehead.

He steps out into the gallery and closes the door behind him. I am alone. The moment is lost. I step out of my skirt, drop my bodice to the floor, wrenching the laces out of the last few eyelets. I shed all my layers of protection and crawl beneath the soft, worn counterpane. I press my fingers to my lips. Imagining.

Before succumbing to oblivion.

39

I DREAM OF THE COURT. IT CRACKLES WITH COLOR AND LIGHT, each gown and doublet more vibrant than the last and my head rings with the cacophony of hues. Faces mash and blur and I recognize no one, am recognized by no one. The howl and call of their voices welcome and repulse me.

I dream that the queen has recalled me for a special event. She wants me to play the lute and to sing. I am given a tiny room of my own at the back of the palace, north-facing windows letting in little sunlight but all the smells of the river at low tide. I am told to change my clothes. But I can't find my green damask gown. I can't find the white sleeves shot with gold silk. I can't find my French hood. Everything available for me to wear is red. The color of claret. The color of blood.

Red gown. Red kirtle. Red sleeves. Red hood, gabled so steeply I fear it will block out all light.

And for jewelry, nothing but a string of pearls.

I dress carefully. All in red. Somehow, my fingers manage the laces all on my own. I follow the sounds of laughter and dice down to the queen's rooms, where the men play at cards and the women whisper gossip.

I pick up the lute and stare at the strings. The lute is like an instrument I've never seen before. It feels utterly foreign. I remember the last time I played. *À toi pour toujours.* The look on Percy's face. The look on Wyatt's.

I can't play.

I can't sing.

I don't know how. Silence descends as everyone turns to stare. The string of pearls tightens, like a garrote, and I wake with a start to the pale darkness before dawn. Cold, the air heavy with moisture. My chest heavy with tears. The black bars of the window barely visible against the dark sky.

Then a shadow moves across it.

"Who's there?" I sit up, clutching counterpane and pearls, terror lodged in my throat.

"Anne?"

I recognize his voice. His shape. His weight when he comes to the bed to sit beside me. His breath on the bare skin of my back.

"I had a nightmare."

"I know."

"I was lost," I say. "Dressed in blood. I couldn't remember how to play. I couldn't remember how to sing. They watched me. And I couldn't. I couldn't even sing."

"But you can sing, Anne."

"I wasn't me. I was someone else. Dressed and silenced."

I forgot to remove my pearl necklace before I went to sleep. I fumble to unclasp it and feel Wyatt's warm fingers on mine. Inhale the metallic smell of ink. The pearls cascade from around my neck, and he brushes my hair.

I am painfully aware of my bare skin, like a lute string ready to play music at a single stroke.

"Lie down."

I do.

Wyatt lies down beside me. I freeze, every fiber of my body taut. Remembering how much I wanted his touch outside the door. Remembering the feel of Percy's skin against mine.

"Shhhh," he says. "I promise to stay right here." He tucks the counterpane between us, and I relax. Wyatt is not Percy. He has not come to take anything from me. Even if I want him to.

His weight pulls me into him, the center of the mattress dipping beneath us. His knees are behind mine, his chest against my back. One arm wraps around me, folded over my own, his hand still holding the pearls. He twines his fingers through mine, pearls sliding on my skin.

I close my eyes.

"You still haven't won the bet," I murmur, my words slurred with sleep and the dregs of the wine.

Wyatt tenses. His arm tightens around me.

"Bet?"

"That I'd want you in my bed."

He lies still for a moment.

"I'll go if you wish." Almost a whisper.

"No. Stay. Please." I reach out from under the counterpane to pull his arm closer to me. Don't hesitate at the touch of skin on skin, the warmth of his on my wrist and forearm, cool night air breathing across my shoulder. I retwine my fingers with his. "You win."

I feel his heart beating rapid against me. It slows until my own heart matches the rhythm, and I can no longer decipher whose heart is whose. Whether I can really feel his or just imagine it in my own.

Wyatt moves closer, resting his face against the back of my neck. He doesn't brush my hair away, doesn't push it down as Percy had, trying to tame it. Wyatt buries himself in it, breathing deeply.

I'm closer to sleep than wakefulness when I hear him whisper something, but I can't make out his meaning. His lips brush words over the skin on my neck. I feel them skim across my cheek and down my jaw. They smell of almonds.

When I wake in the morning, head aching and tongue dry from wine, he is already gone.

Back to Allington.

40

He doesn't return.

I want to write to him, but cannot send a letter. Not only could it be opened and read by his wife, by my father, by anyone, but I don't know what to say.

I miss you?

I'm sorry?

I'm jealous that you are at court and I am not. I'm jealous that the court gets you and I do not. I miss his company. Having someone to talk to. Having a friend.

Just a friend.

On a troubled day in early April, one that spits with rain then trembles with a cold north wind, a clatter in the courtyard wakes me from my lonely stupor. I look out of the leaded window and see a big bay horse. A flash of green.

I am suddenly embarrassed by my old gray gown, the high neckline, the simple coif that covers my hair. I am completely unadorned and unbeautiful, and I am suddenly afraid to see him.

"Master Wyatt."

The steward, barely gracious, leaves the room abruptly.

I just stand and stare, tugging at my gown as if I could make it fit better with a pull in the right direction.

"Wyatt."

I flame with embarrassment at how drunk I got the last time he visited. How I practically threw myself at him. How I drove him away with my brazenness and childish fears.

"Anne."

His voice is rough, unused. He is so uncomfortable. We are so uncomfortable.

"Why are you here?" I blurt, and bite my tongue. "I mean . . . welcome."

He doesn't move. I've offended him and yet I can't apologize. I can't face his criticism or his censure. Nor can I face his expression—a combination of fear and sorrow.

"I have news."

"From court?" My voice sounds small—pathetic—even to my own ears.

"Yes. Your sister. She has a daughter. Catherine."

Another Boleyn girl.

"Thank you for bringing such good news." We don't move. He's still at the door, ready to bolt.

"There is more. Not so good. Our mortality is so close to the surface, Anne. It takes only a fleeting event to break the skin of it."

"Is it Mary?" I finally manage to whisper. Images flood my mind. Mary making me a crown of daisy chains. Crying when she left me in France. Wrapping her arms around me like a mother.

"No!" Wyatt takes one step toward me, hand outstretched. "The king . . . it's the king."

My extremities tingle. As if with cold. As if with too much wine. I fall back against the paneling.

"What?"

Wyatt is not the messenger of death. I would have known. I would have felt it. But he is disheveled. Agitated.

"You haven't heard?"

I shake my head, unable to speak.

"There was a tournament. He was . . . showing off."

"What happened?" I croak, my lips barely able to form the words.

"The Duke of Suffolk. His lance struck the king."

Wyatt is visibly shaken. A little wild. He's staring right into my eyes as if his very gaze could keep me from flying apart.

"Unhorsed him?"

"Yes." Wyatt sinks to a bench. "His visor was up."

"It struck him in the face?"

No one could survive that. Not even the king. I start to shake, and clench my skirts to still my trembling hands.

"No." Wyatt has not moved, but somehow seems more distant. "The chest. He fell, heavily. But the lance shattered—splintered in his face."

"He's . . ." I can't say the words. Disfigured? Blinded?

"He's fine. He got up and rode again. More fool him." The last is a whisper. It is treason to speak against the king.

"He had to prove he was well." My words and my small voice cannot encompass the relief I feel. "He has his country to think of. He had to show his strength."

"Our strength comes not from our ability to cheat mortal-

ity, Anne, but from our capacity to love. If I were so close to death, I would run. Even if I were called a coward. Run to the one I love and find life there. Life and truth."

He stares at me. Into me. I think of his arms around me, safe in the dark. *Life and truth.* What is he telling me?

"And the king didn't do that," I say quietly.

"No."

I think of Mary and her new baby girl. A familiar twinge of jealousy followed by shame. I'm ashamed of my own relief that he didn't go to her.

Everything I feel is tight in my chest—packed in cotton wool and doused in gunpowder—ready to explode at a single spark.

I rub my hands on my skirts and say the first thing that comes into my head.

"I'm glad the king is well."

Wyatt nods. Stares at his hands. Runs one across his face. Stands quickly.

"I brought something more tangible than news." He retraces his steps to the door. From behind the frame, he retrieves a lute. Its back is a beautiful blond wood that fairly glows, and the rose is carved with intricate knots.

My chest aches.

"Oh," I say. "Oh, Wyatt. It's beautiful."

He hands it to me. Carefully. As if I might bite. The lute has nine courses, and when I pluck at each of the seventeen strings, they're already tuned. He must have done it himself before coming inside.

I can't stop the tears that spring to my eyes.

"Oh, Wyatt. It's the most thoughtful gift anyone has ever given me."

"Perhaps now you can call me Thomas."

"I don't know if I can," I tease. I look up from the lute.

"Try."

"Thomas." The name feels odd on my tongue. Precious. Decadent.

His gaze is so concentrated I have to look away. I pick out a tune, slowly. The notes don't resonate beneath my fingers. The music I make is dull and timorous.

"I haven't played since . . ." I can't tell him. I haven't played since I gambled away my virginity to Henry Percy. "Since the night of the joust."

"I see."

I want to be able to play it. I want to play it for him.

"I think my dream is coming true," I blurt, my fingers stumbling.

"You just need the right music."

He takes the lute from me, plucks a note. He is not an accomplished lutenist. But he makes music. Something I haven't heard in many months.

> *"Lucks, my fair falcon, and your fellows all,*
> *How well pleasant it were your liberty!*
> *Ye not forsake me that fair might ye befall.*
> *But they that sometime liked my company,*

Like lice away from dead bodies they crawl.
Lo, what a proof in light adversity!
But ye, my birds, I swear by all your bells,
Ye be my friends, and so be but few else."

"The story of my life," I say. "None but the birds as my friends."

"I thought you'd like it."

"And you, of course. You are my friend, no matter what George says."

Thomas nods and hands me back the lute. Our fingers touch on the neck of it, and a chord strikes bright and perfect beneath my skin.

He lets go. Pulls away. Walks back toward the fire.

"I'm going to be given the clerkship of the jewels," he says. "My father is vacating the position specifically so I can take it on. Some responsibility."

"Not exactly poetic. Inventory and valuation."

"No. And it means I have less freedom."

"Ah. Your father sounds like mine. The less freedom, the better. And no room for music and poetry when there are numbers to be reckoned."

"The king seems eager to keep me at court, as well. To keep me close."

"That's a good thing," I say, more to remind myself than to remind him. I swallow my jealousy. And my disappointment.

"Isn't it?" I add lamely.

I want him to disagree. But he nods, slowly.

"Yes. Our fathers would agree on that."

I stare at the lute so he can't see my tears. I run my fingers along the knots of the rose, keeping my eyes wide so the tears don't fall.

Thomas kneels in front of me and lifts my chin. He strokes my cheekbone with his thumb, taking a tear with it.

"You *can* sing, Anne. No matter how he tries to silence you."

I nod, and he sits back on his heels.

"Try," he says again.

I pick out a tune. My fingers are unsure and unpracticed. The notes throb against me like an age-old bruise, feeling good and painful all at once.

The tune is one the king wrote, a combination of chords and individually plucked strings. I remember him playing it one night in the queen's chambers. He called it "If Love Now Reigned."

The more I play, the more the music feels a part of me.

"You play like he does."

The thought warms me, warms my fingers. I bend deeper into the notes, forgetting myself, forgetting Hever, living a memory of music and the scent of cloves.

"I'll leave you to it."

Lost in thought and melody, I hardly hear him. But one word spikes through my reverie.

"You're leaving? You just got here."

He stands and strides to the door.

"I must go back to court. Responsibilities."

"Thank you," I call, uncertainty wavering my voice. "For the lute. And for the song."

"I wanted to visit." He turns, but doesn't smile. "I can't come back."

He leaves behind an empty hole of doubt. I fill it with the weight of all my words and play the lute until my fingers bleed. And still the pain doesn't match that of my loneliness.

41

THE SUMMER LOSES SWAY TO THE DESOLATION OF THE COMING winter. The days, such as they are, get shorter. I consider leaving, taking a horse to the wilds of the north and becoming an outlaw. Finding passage back to France, regardless of the war. Running away with the stable boy—the steward's thirteen-year-old nephew, who looks at me like I'm a goddess and laughs at even my blackest jokes.

But all I really want is at the English court. I maintain the fruitless hope that one day I'll return. I am always looking over my shoulder for a pardon without apology.

Then one evening, just after the equinox, Father and George ride in through the portcullis gate at Hever on black horses, looking for all the world like Famine and Conquest having left the other two horsemen behind.

When they dismount, the servants scurry about them like mice, tending their needs and responding with obsequious bows to Father's barked orders. I stand in the doorway of the entrance hall and watch. Waiting.

"You're going back," my father says, with no preamble, and pushes past me.

For a single, shining instant, I feel a cascade of relief, like the rush of water at the breaking of a dam.

"You will need to do exactly as I say and not set a foot out of line."

The stopper goes back in the bottle. I am silenced.

"You should stop talking altogether." George pauses beside me and kisses my temple.

"Heed your own advice, George," Father mutters.

George's smugness at delivering criticism disintegrates. His face, still handsome, is becalmed and wary of Father's contempt.

"Sounds like prison," I blurt.

George cuts me a look that begs me not to speak.

"It will be a prison of your choosing," Father says. "Here or there."

"Or marriage to James Butler."

"That possibility is no longer. You ruined that chance."

"So you need me at court to marry me off to someone else."

"Don't turn this around. I do not need anything, Anne. It is you who needs a husband. You who needs this opportunity. I will not pay forever for you to spend your days here sewing and playing your little melodies."

He turns and walks into the desolate dining hall, engaging the steward immediately in conversation. Leaving me with George.

"You'd do better not to vex him," he says quietly. He is protecting me, like when we were children.

"I can't help it."

"You have to, Anne. Father never should have allowed you an education. It made you think. Thinking makes you speak—something you really shouldn't do."

The memory of our friendship dies, and all I remember is what has happened since. I forget that he protected me from our father's chilling disappointment. And all I see is his.

"Jesus, George, aren't you opinionated today?"

"I'm opinionated every day, little sister. It's the right of an educated man."

"But not an educated woman."

George levels his gaze. "You are clever. You always were."

He leans forward with the grace of a cat, his eyes becoming keen like those of an animal identifying its prey.

"Your cleverness is your greatest defect." Emotions ride across his face like soldiers in retreat. I watch in wonder, because at court, George wears only an expression of amused sarcasm or begrudging sycophancy.

"Father is negotiating for a wife for me," he says quietly.

George is confiding in me. George is asking me to listen. George is here to keep me company.

"Who is it?"

"Jane Parker."

"She might be good for you."

"She's a ninny. A dullard. A skinny, staring, mutton-faced mare. Sleeping with her would be like bedding a sheep."

"You are cruel, George! You don't even know her and yet you judge her." I ball my hands into fists. When we were children, we used to fistfight when we disagreed. I landed a couple of

decent blows to his head one day before Father pulled me off him, swinging and snarling like a cat.

It was the only time Father ever slapped me. One of the few times that I was the one who provoked the silence at the dinner table.

George watches me, his gaze flicking to my hands, the tension in my shoulders, my distance from him.

"I don't think you could best me now, Anne, despite your vicious temper."

He takes a step forward that is stunningly swift, and I flinch away from a blow that never comes.

"I didn't come here to fight with you, Anne."

When I look up, his hands hang limp at his sides.

"You could have fooled me."

"You need to curb your temper, Anne. You don't have Wyatt here to discipline you now."

"Leave Thomas out of this."

"Oooh." His voice glides up and down like someone trailing fingers over the keyboard of the virginal. "It's Thomas now, is it?"

I bite my lip, thinking of the warmth of Thomas's breath and heartbeat sending me to sleep.

"Forgive me—I would hate to interfere with your perfect romance," George spits.

"There is no romance." I wonder what he knows of Thomas's visits. I wonder if I'm lying.

"You got one thing right, then."

"What do you mean?"

"Exactly what I say. Thomas Wyatt was never interested in you, Anne. And never will be. You're not his type."

"He doesn't like clever women?" I ask, unable to prevent a trace of bitterness.

"I wouldn't know about that," George sneers. "All I know is that when he visits the stews, he likes the ones that are blonde and busty." He leans closer to whisper in my ear. "The ones that scream with passion. I don't believe cleverness has anything to do with it."

I feel sick.

"Are all men the same?" I ask weakly.

He studies me, and I think I see a trace of contrition or perhaps compassion. Until he speaks again.

"Not, apparently, squirrelly Percy."

He has taken all the fight out of me. Just as he used to when we were children, when he'd describe Father's wrath until the words were more frightening than the reality.

"I'll go pack my things," I say, and my voice is dull and tuneless even to my own ears, "and write a note of thanks to the queen."

"The queen didn't ask for you."

I pause.

"Did Father find me a position?"

"No." George sniffs. "Hardly so. In fact, he tried to place you somewhere else entirely."

"Then why? Why am I to be recalled?"

"It isn't Father or the queen who wants you back," George says. "Mary does."

Windsor Castle
1524

42

A DEEP BREATH IS ALL IT TAKES TO ENTER A ROOM.

This time, I do not pause. I do not wait outside the door, avoiding eye contact with the guard. I have kept my head up and my hands steady as I made my way through the thick battlement gates, across the expanse of the upper ward, the ancient layers that protect the heart of the royal court.

This time, I walk through the door into the queen's presence chamber, allowing my sleeves to cover my fingertips, my too-short train barely skimming the floor behind me. I don't even adjust my hood or smooth the broad expanse of hair it exposes.

It is more than a year since I left. More than a year since the Duke of Suffolk charged his way across the Channel to Calais to wreak havoc on the French. More than a year since I let Henry Percy take from me the only thing that was truly mine to give.

This time, I won't let the whispers get to me.

This time, I have something I didn't have before.

I have Thomas Wyatt.

He is the first person I see when I walk back into the queen's watching chamber. I am drawn to him as if he is a lodestone.

My anchor. When he looks up, a single, perfect note stretches between us. Audible. Visible.

A hiss of whispers ripples through the room, replete with knowing nods and well-timed glances in my direction.

"She's back."

"Again."

"What is she wearing?"

The single note transcends the whispers. I will not let the gossip or the lies deter or defame me. I make my obeisance to Queen Katherine, who smiles tightly and sends me away.

"Anne!"

Jane Parker leaps up from a stool by the window and weaves her way between courtiers and ladies. They watch her, whispering, but she doesn't seem to care, her eyes focused just on me.

There is something different about Jane. The past year has treated her well. She isn't taller, but seems somehow *more*. Better dressed, in a gown of aqua-blue damask split to show a kirtle of pale-blue silk. More vibrant. More beautiful. Her smile lights up her face.

Jane Parker is happier.

"Jane!"

When she hugs me, her arms feel like a steel vise, holding me together.

"You've changed," I murmur.

Jane pulls away, and her gaze flickers over my face.

"So have you." Cautious. Her voice steady.

"You are prettier than ever," I tell her, and slip my arm

through hers. We walk slowly toward the window, knowing that the angle of afternoon light brightens the tawny orange of my gown until I glow like a flame. It sets off the darkness of my eyes and the black of my hair, and only the blind and the stupid will be able to take their eyes off me.

I resist the urge to find out if Thomas is watching.

But Jane clutches my elbow rigidly against the hard edge of her bodice and slows her pace.

"Look." Her voice is strangled.

So I look.

Thomas's eyes are on his cards, and I feel a river of disappointment. But next to him, George is staring, the expression on his face indefinable. As though he can't decide if he's happy to see me or wishes me gone. Probably the latter.

I glance at Jane, who is smiling tentatively, her eyes fixed on George. And I realize that this is one of those situations where she can't tell which of us he's focused on. She thinks he's gazing at her.

When I study George again, I can't really tell, either. He seems to be staring right between us. His expression is unreadable—but . . . yearning.

"Is he looking at me?" Jane whispers, her voice just slightly too loud. I know the tables nearby are listening, the clack of dice not enough to drown her out. I steer her away from him.

I lean my head toward hers, hoping to make the conversation more private. I take in the lavender scent of her sleeves, the point of her gable nudging my own hood farther back on my head.

Out of the corner of my eye, I see George still watching. Now Thomas is, too, and his fierce scrutiny makes me suddenly want to run.

"Because he could be looking at you," Jane continues, doubt creeping into her voice. "But why would he be looking at you like that?"

Like what? I long to ask her. But don't. Whatever Jane saw is not what I saw. I push her quickly out of the chamber and into the next, away from George, away from Thomas.

"Can you keep a secret?" Jane asks. She stops in the middle of the room and glances over each shoulder. Subtle. "I have a secret."

"You, Jane? The most transparent girl in the entire court? You have a secret? It can't be."

"I'm learning to be discreet. I'm learning to be the perfect courtier. No one knows my thoughts anymore."

I imagine even George knows Jane's thoughts.

"I'm sure it will serve you well," I say. "What is your secret? I've been known to hold a few."

Jane lowers her eyes, and a blush tilts up her cheeks.

"My father is talking with your father."

Just as George told me. George was looking at Jane.

"They're discussing a dowry."

What was in George's eye? The same thing I saw in Thomas's?

"We're to be sisters. I'm to marry your brother." Jane lifts up on her toes and bounces.

"Your father agreed?"

She nods and sticks the index finger of her right hand into her mouth and delicately nibbles her cuticle.

"I'm so glad we will be sisters." That, at least, I can say with complete honesty.

"Thank you." She hugs me, limply.

Then she nibbles the cuticle of her little finger.

"Do you think he likes me?"

I consider the truth. How George belittled her. How he has never considered her for one of his conquests.

"George likes all women," I say. I realize how that sounds, so I edit myself. "He must like you. If he has agreed."

"You lack conviction, Anne."

This is the trouble with Jane. The time she has spent studying the people of the court without speaking makes her a keener judge of expression—both facial and vocal. She reads people like some read books.

"One doesn't need affection for marriage." I'm thinking of what happened between Thomas and his wife. But that has not gone well.

"Yes, but one wishes it." Jane's voice is small and ragged. She knows.

I try to look her in the eye. The weak light from the window throws her face into silhouette, her bobbed nose arced upward.

"Affection can grow," I tell her.

"You knew you could never love James Butler."

"That's true. But who could?"

She laughs a little and turns toward me.

"George is nothing like James Butler. But you must know his mind. The two of you are so close. It's like you're more than brother and sister. It's like you're one and the same. The male and female sides of a coin.

"I'm not worried about loving your brother, Anne. He is lithe and funny and handsome and chivalrous. I think . . ." Jane's gaze slides away, and she blushes again. "I think I've loved him from the moment I first saw him."

"What does it feel like, Jane? Love?"

The question comes out before I can stop it.

Jane looks up at the ceiling. Her eyes unfocus as her thoughts turn inward, and a smile like sunrise appears on her face.

"Like music only plays when you're together. Like the very air tastes of strawberries. Like one touch—one look—could send you whirling like a seed on the wind."

Oh, God. My palms begin to sweat and I itch to wipe them on my skirts. My heart feels like a levee about to burst, and my mind is full of green and gold and poetry.

"I hope love is worth the trouble it causes, Jane," I say finally. "For all of us."

43

I CAN'T BE IN LOVE WITH THOMAS WYATT.

I make excuses to Jane. Fatigue. Headache.

"You do look shaky," she says. "Do you want me to go with you?"

She glances once over her shoulder. To the watching chamber. To George.

I shake my head.

I have to be alone.

I practically run down the gallery, skirts swishing around my ankles, and into the hall beyond. It is full of the king's courtiers and Wolsey's men. I walk close to the wall, for once not eager to be seen. In fact, desiring the opposite.

I reach the tower—mercifully empty—and breathe my relief. When the door bangs behind me, I turn to see James Butler. My knees threaten to collapse.

I don't have the energy to face him.

"Truth? Or rumor?" His tone is accusatory.

"That I have returned?" I ask. "What do your eyes tell you?"

"My eyes may lie," he says, stepping forward to block my access to the outer door. To the upper ward. To fresh air and freedom.

"My eyes saw you leave the banquet at Greenwich with Henry Percy. You didn't come back. Then he married Mary Talbot. And yet, here you are."

He pauses. "Surely my eyes deceive me."

He looks to where my hands are pressed against my stomacher to still them. "You were gone for nine months. And more."

"If your eyes do not deceive you, your presumption certainly does."

I step sideways to get around him, but he's fast for someone so large. He presses me against the doorframe.

"Did I deceive Wolsey then? Because I only told him what my eyes told me."

"What are you saying? That you told Wolsey what you *think* you saw? It was you?"

Butler presses further. "It was Percy."

"Your eyes aren't the only parts of you that lie." I slip beneath his arm and out the door. My face feels as if it's been slapped, and I welcome the cooling, rain-drenched air. I gulp it, as if to drown.

"He was spouting poetry." Butler follows me. "You like poetry, don't you, Anne?

"I prayed her heartily that she would come to bed.
She said she was content to do me pleasure."

I round on him. "Everyone knows that poem! That poem is about a dream!"

"I kissed her,"

he sings.

"I bussed her out of all measure."

"You know nothing, James Butler." I step toward him. To show him that I'm not afraid. That I'm not guilty.

"Oh?" His granite features creak and his teeth appear between flattened lips—a leering grimace.

"He told you nothing," I say quickly. "You have nothing."

"No. *You* have nothing. You are nothing. You will never be a countess."

"That, at least, gives me comfort," I spit at him.

"You could have been," he whispers in my ear, the meatiness of his breath making me want to gag. "You could have been mine, Anne Boleyn. You could have had a man. Not a hasty boy on the floor of some back room."

I do gag, and Butler takes a quick step back.

I square my shoulders and look him in the eye. Swallow.

"One day, I will," I tell him, and remember the feel of Thomas's arm around me. "I will have a man who doesn't think he owns me. A man who tells the truth and doesn't gossip like a laundry maid."

A man who loves me.

Shaking, I turn and leave him.

44

I creep through the rooms of the palace lodgings to my sister's door, fear and shame twisting inside me until they spatter like hot oil.

She sits by the fire with her baby on her lap.

"Nan," she says, quiet and meek. "You're back."

Little Catherine has a head full of honey-brown hair and brown eyes like Mary. She looks nothing like either of her possible fathers.

"I have you to thank for it," I say. "I guess the Boleyns do stick together."

"Right." Mary's not wearing a hood. Her hair hangs in strands around her face. She looks like a serving girl, not like the wife of a courtier, or the mistress of a king. But with Catherine in her lap, she looks content.

"I guess it's all over court," I blurt.

"What is?" She finally looks up at me.

"You know what, Mary. Me. Percy."

"The Earl of Northumberland will silence it. And Wolsey. The power of the elite is remarkable. They don't want his name tarnished."

They don't care about mine.

"I suppose that's true." I pause, unsure of how to continue. "I haven't heard anything about . . . about Catherine."

Mary is playing a finger game with the baby. Catherine's eyes follow the finger with avidity, and she burbles with laughter when Mary taps her nose. But Mary's face is grave.

"I don't know," she mumbles.

"You don't know what?"

"I don't know if she's his."

I don't have to ask whose.

"Don't tell me that, Mary."

"But it's true." She closes her eyes.

"If you tell him, he will love her," I say quietly. "He showers affection on little Henry Fitzroy."

"He's looking for another heir. Little Fitzroy is his only son to survive infancy. It doesn't matter who the mother is."

"And your baby is a girl, so it doesn't matter who her father is."

"William will raise her."

"Well, goody for William. He sounds like a real prince. He'll raise her to be passive and browbeaten."

"He may not have the type of personality that you think is the best . . ."

"He has no personality at all!" I cry. "When he leaves the room, I can't even remember what he looks like!"

Mary turns away.

"You shouldn't say such things."

"Well, can you? Can you remember what he looks like with any degree of accuracy? Now, any one of us could describe the

king. His visage is burned onto our eyelids. We could recognize his voice at the end of a pitch-black hall."

I recognized Thomas simply by the weight of his body in my bed.

"Are you trying to pick a fight with me, Nan?"

I stop.

"No. But don't you want more for her? More than boring mediocrity?"

"I certainly don't wish for her to be the butt of jokes," Mary snaps, her face splashed with color. "I don't wish for her to be followed by gossip like dogs after the meat wagon. I don't wish for her to be called a whore." Catherine starts to cry. "Or the daughter of one."

"If he loves you, he should take responsibility. And if you love him, don't you want her to know?"

Mary laughs. Bitterly.

"Oh, Nan, don't be such a child."

"Stop calling me that!"

"Childish? You are a child. For asking such questions." Mary looks up from the crying baby. "I do not love the king. And he does not love me."

"You love William?" I can't keep the derision out of my voice.

"I love my daughter."

"But daughters are worthless," I blurt.

"No, Nan. That's where you're wrong. Daughters are everything. I'll make sure she knows that. No matter who her father is. Or her husband."

She strokes the hair from Catherine's forehead and kisses her there.

I look at Mary and see her probably for the first time. Past her fair skin and beautiful hair. Because of her sex, all she has to give is herself. And she gives it freely. So she is labeled a whore. A concubine. No one else can see past that. Not even our father.

I, too, would want my daughter to feel she was worth more than that.

"The Boleyns always stick together," Mary says, looking directly into my eyes as if she wants to *will* me to agree with her. "Shouldn't the Boleyn girls do the same?"

"I don't know."

She looks at me questioningly, so I continue. "We never have before. When King Louis died and Mary Tudor scampered off back to England with her ill-gotten husband, you left me. Abandoned me. And when you got here, you took it all. You took a place at court. You got a husband. You got the king." I pause, almost unable to continue. "You took Father's love."

"You think I wanted that?" The pain is evident in Mary's voice. "You think I did that on purpose? That I left you on purpose?"

"Maybe you didn't, but Father did. Father sent me to the Low Countries to get a good education. And then to France to cultivate sophistication. Anything to compensate for the fact that I was the ugly one in the family."

"You're not ugly."

"Don't lie to me. Do you see beautiful English skin here? And lovely blonde locks? And pale, limpid eyes that reflect whatever a man wishes? No. You see sallow, swarthy skin. You see the black hair of a witch. You see a girl who should be grateful to get the attention of a waster like James Butler. Or Henry Percy."

"Believe what you like, Nan."

"It's not belief, Mary. It's the truth. I don't have to believe it. I see it every day."

"You don't know what goes on in other people's heads," she mutters. "Nobody knows."

"I can guess."

"Can you?" she asks the wall. "Can you guess that I've been told in confidence that you stir a man so greatly that he hardly dares to breathe around you? Can you guess that he will not tell you so because your opinion is so great and so fixed that he is too terrified of your rapier wit and your unguarded tongue to mention it to you?"

She turns back to me and levels her gaze.

"Can you guess that he would leave his wife for you? If only he could get a word, a look, a touch that would indicate you might feel the same way."

"Who?" And I barely manage to guard my tongue enough not to blurt out, *Thomas?*

A gust of fear pales her cheeks, and she doesn't answer.

"A man is afraid of me?" *Is it Thomas?*

"Most men are. You do tend to speak your mind."

"And they've told you this?"

"No one has to. I've observed their fear of your tongue. I've felt it myself."

A hot needle of regret runs through me, pulling behind it a thread of shame.

"I can speak indiscriminately," I admit, on the verge of apology.

"Yes, you can. But I love you anyway."

"Is it love?" I ask, attempting a tease, but wanting an answer. "Or is it loyalty?"

Mary turns away. "Call it what you will, Anne. It's what holds us together and keeps us here at court. Whether we like it or not."

45

I AVOID WYATT. I CAN'T TALK TO HIM. I CAN HARDLY THINK ABOUT him. But he watches me. I feel it. Guilt sits like a demon on my chest. Because I shut him out for Percy. And even though Percy couldn't kill our friendship, love surely could.

I ponder Mary's revelations. Butler's gossip. George's reluctance for marriage. Jane's belief in love.

I throw my emotions into my music. Only now, I find that people listen. I feel exposed. Naked. As if people are listening to my girlish fancies for the king, my weary disgust of the ongoing war with France, my frustrated affection for my family.

My feelings for the man I can't have.

I seek out quiet places, empty places. Except when Wolsey and his men are visiting. I never want to be alone with James Butler again.

One night, the queen's ladies present a musical entertainment in the king's apartments and Wolsey brings his choir to sing. The bright stars of the court attend in all their glittering sycophancy. I sit in the queen's chambers with the left-behind, the second class, and play for myself.

Quietly.

Norris sits down beside me. He has been standoffish since

my return. Now he sits stiffly. Too close, but not touching me.

"Mistress Boleyn."

"Sir Henry."

I pause.

"Are you not going to the entertainment tonight?"

"I just came from there," he tells me. "Mistress Carew was butchering a song on the virginal. I came in search of someone to distract me while I listen so my ears don't begin to bleed."

I laugh.

"A shared burden is a lesser burden?"

"True enough. Though someone should show Mistress Carew that she needn't mash the keys like a baker's boy kneading dough."

"I'm sure her enthusiasm does her credit." I attempt diplomacy. Elizabeth Carew is, after all, a distant cousin.

"I wonder at the rumors about her."

I angle my chin toward him. "Rumors?"

"That she was the king's mistress."

I arch an eyebrow. "And how does this correlate with her musical ability?" Elizabeth is prettier than I. Paler. Blonder. Kinder.

"I'd hate to think she treated him the same way she treats that instrument."

A vision of Elizabeth's fingers on flesh rather than wood and bone brings a flash of jealousy that settles quickly into a slow burn deep beneath my ribs. I raise a finger to my lips.

Norris grins.

"Will you join me, Mistress Boleyn?" He stands and holds out an arm that I can't begin to refuse.

The king's withdrawing room is crowded and smoky, the windows closed against the gathering cold of the oncoming winter. The noise is great—a bellow of gossip and whispers beating against the glass.

Norris directs me toward the back of the room, while Elizabeth Carew finishes.

"Merciful timing," he whispers, and I feel a shiver of delight. Norris is fun to flirt with. Maybe that's a good thing. Easy. Noncommittal. Not the falconlike swoops and dives of flirting with Thomas. Or the dizzy, escalating vibration of conversing with the king.

The choir launches into an old carol that has been arranged into a sweet harmony. There are twelve boys, and the music they produce is like the voices of the angels. The tallest boy— one who appears to be about to crack, his voice dismissing him from his position—sings with the most passion, as if the music itself has possessed him.

"Who is that?" I ask, pointing to the boy with the neck of my lute.

"Mark Smeaton," Norris says. "He is one of Wolsey's boys. Flemish, I think. He plays the lute, too."

I hope he plays the lute as well as he sings, because he may need it soon. I can see the strain on his face as he pushes his voice to the very edge of its capacity, the knowledge etched across his visage that soon his voice will change, and his life as well.

"I should like to hear him play," I say quietly.

"Then you shall. Come with me." He takes my hand and leads me to the front of the room, where the king sits on a little elevated platform.

"Your Majesty."

Norris bows deeply and I curtsy.

"Norris. Mistress Boleyn."

The two men exchange a look loaded with meaning.

"Mistress Boleyn would like to hear the boy Smeaton play the lute, Your Majesty."

"Have you heard of his prowess, mistress?"

"His voice is extraordinary."

"Let's hope it continues to be so after it breaks."

"Yes, Your Majesty. Even so, I had hoped he had another talent."

"I'm sure he does." Norris winks lasciviously at me over the king's shoulder.

"Sit here." I do as the king commands and I sit just below the dais. A servant brings a goblet of wine, and the king claps his hands, interrupting the choir.

"We should like to hear young Smeaton play," he says. And all the world scurries to do his bidding.

Smeaton pales just slightly—the skin stark against his dark curls—but takes the offered lute with a bow. And I see on his face a glimmer of triumph.

Wolsey stands from his chair on the other side of the king, throws me a look saturated with venom, and moves to re-arrange the choirboys, clouting one on the ear. The boy—the

youngest by the looks of him—visibly struggles not to cry.

Then Smeaton begins to play. His fingers move so quickly over the strings that they appear to be vibrating themselves. The music resounds throughout the silent room as the world holds its breath, willing him never to stop. When he does, the audience rises to its feet in unanimous admiration.

"What do you think, mistress?" the king asks.

I feel light-headed, as if I have just looked over the edge of a great height. "I wish I could play half as well as he. I wish I could create such beauty."

He turns to me and smiles, his eyes merry with mischief.

"Perhaps you already have."

"I think you flatter me, Your Majesty, and it doesn't suit you."

"Mistress Boleyn"—the king angles his body to face me, and everything around us disappears—"in all our lives, we hope to come across the beauty of someone who will truly change the world just by being in it. Flattery is superficial. Beauty runs deeper."

I forget all my words and wit and arguments and I look the king in the eye and say nothing. Nothing at all. I don't need to. Because crouching within the recesses of my mind—deep behind the disbelief—is the knowledge that the king is interested. In me.

"A poem!"

The room reappears with the shout, and the king turns back to the musicians with a frown. But it is not the musicians who have interrupted us.

It is Thomas. He takes the lute from Smeaton's uncertain hands and strums a handful of notes that are not a chord. Nor harmonious.

He sweeps a bow to the king and throws a quick smile in my direction. He's wearing a black doublet and sleeves, slashed with green, and he looks diabolical in the torchlight, his narrow chin and arced eyebrows adding to the illusion.

> *"Blame not my lute! For he must sound*
> *Of this or that as liketh me;*
> *For lack of wit the lute is bound*
> *To give such tunes as pleaseth me;*
> *Though my songs be somewhat strange,*
> *And speak such words as touch thy change,*
> > *Blame not my lute."*

"Somewhat strange, indeed," the king murmurs. His expression is a cross between a question and petulance. "What means this?"

> *"My lute, alas, doth not offend,*
> *Though that perforce he must agree*
> *To sound such tunes as I intend,*
> *To sing to them that heareth me—"*

Thomas turns to the entire audience, including everyone in his little oratory, but only one in his little joke.

"Then though my songs be somewhat plain,
And toucheth some that use to feign—"

Thomas pauses, his eyes fixed on me as if I am the only person in the room.

"Blame not my lute."

Thomas bows and hands the lute back to Smeaton, then exits the room.

"I do believe you are blushing, Mistress Boleyn." The coyness in Norris's voice suddenly makes me want to vomit.

I feel the king turn to look at me, feel the smile leave his face, feel the vibration that runs through me lose its hum. I feel the loss keenly.

"Please excuse me, Your Majesty," I whisper, not daring to look him in the eye. "I believe the heat in the room conspires to make me ill."

"Go, mistress."

The voice is cold, no longer flirtatious. All interest withered and gone. I curtsy and stumble from the room.

46

THE NEXT ROOM—FILLED WITH THE HANGERS-ON WHO WISHED to be invited but instead clamor for attention separately and alone—is even more stifling. I push through the crowd, through the rooms and down the stairs, out of the donjon and into the upper ward. The yard leads to the lodgings of the court. Courtiers make secret pacts and gossip by the doors. The cobbles clatter with moonlight. At the far end of the yard, I see the flash of gold hair, the lightlessness of black velvet.

The moon has risen high and full, casting silver and shadow over the trees of the great park. I follow Thomas through the gate and down to the river walk. I gulp at air that smells like the end of summer, the fall of leaves, and the river taking the heat from the land.

"What was that?" I call to him.

Thomas turns, the glow of moonlight flashing on his face.

"A poem," he says soberly, walking backward like a player in a highly choreographed masque. "A trifle. It means nothing. It says nothing."

"Your poems always mean something, Thomas." I pursue him, my haste and confusion making my words sharper than I intended. "You think I don't hear you? Or are you trying to hint that what we once pretended—what we *feigned* to be—is now real?"

He stops. Only moonlight between us.

"There is so much you don't know, Anne," he murmurs, his voice low and mellow like wine. I feel my heart beat again, as if his is speaking directly to it.

I pause. I could tease him. I could flirt. I could challenge him. But I can't.

"Then tell me."

I speak seriously. Quietly. I ask for him to spill his greatest secrets. I want to hear them. I want to tell my own.

He searches my face as if he could read there my meaning, my intention. As if he could read the future and see my reaction to whatever he might say next. I step forward, ready.

"You're heading into dangerous territory, Anne."

I watch his eyes for a hint of teasing, or a flirtatious wink. There is none.

"I told you to stay away from that family. They can't be trusted."

This I didn't expect. I expected this string—this song—between us to crescendo. But I guess he doesn't hear it, or hears another song entirely.

"What family?" I ask. But I know. He told me to stay away from the duchess. And her *brother*. Not her husband, as I originally thought.

"He holds all the cards, Anne. Cards of life and death. He will have whatever he wants, and you . . ." He stops. As if in agony. "He's your sister's lover."

The song within me ends abruptly with a discordant crash.

"Since when have you become my moral compass, Thomas Wyatt? When did you set yourself up to be my confessor? My father?"

"I'd like to offer some advice."

"No!" My voice pitches higher. "I think you've offered enough. I'm sick of your infuriating rules."

Tears prick at the corners of my eyes. My year at Hever has made me maudlin.

"I'm sick of you," I lie.

Thomas steps between me and the castle gate and any who watch through it, blocking their view of me. Blocking my voice from them, always aware of the ears and eyes of the court.

"You're making a show of yourself," he whispers, his breath quieter than the breeze on my hair.

"I'm always being criticized, Thomas. By you and everyone else. Told who I can or can't speak to. Be with. What I should look like. I need to be more like everyone else. I need to be seen but not heard. I need to marry a man of my father's choosing and disappear into oblivion."

"No!"

Thomas grabs my wrists and squeezes until I look him in the eye. He's staring at me so intensely that the moon appears to be peering out of him.

"No, Anne. You are better than that. You are not meant to be shackled to a man who binds you into his own perfect image. You don't want to be known throughout your days as Anne

Percy. Or Anne Butler. Or Anne the king's concubine. You are Anne! Anne Boleyn."

"I won't be when I marry."

"Then don't."

I laugh then.

"Don't be ridiculous, Thomas. My family won't take care of me forever—no matter how closely the Boleyns stick together. My father looks forward to the day he can foist my expenses off on a rich and profitable husband. Someone who will give back what I've taken for so many years. He'd never pay a living for a single woman forever."

"You can't live your life being somebody else."

"But that's exactly what you asked of me. To do only as you say."

"I thought I had your best interests at heart." He steps closer. "But now I see that I really only followed my own interests."

Still not a tease. Nor a flirtation. This is truth.

"What are your interests, Thomas?"

He doesn't speak, and it's as if we're frozen, our breath stoppered by moonlight. The strand of melody between us singing silently.

"I will not blame your lute," I finally whisper. "I hear the tune, but I do not know the words."

His eyes flicker back and forth between mine. Searching. My hands are still wrapped in his, pressed between us.

One step closer, and our bodies will touch. One word, and I will be his.

"What do you want, Thomas?"

"Money."

Thomas drops my hands and steps away. We both look to see my brother venture out of the shadows.

"George."

There is warning in Thomas's voice. And something else. Something that almost sounds like fear.

George walks toward us, and I can see how hard he concentrates on walking a straight line.

"Why are you here, George?" I ask.

"To stop you from causing more of a scene than you already have, Sister. Flirting with the king. Leaving in a rush after a . . . a . . . *poet*." The mocking twist to his mouth has returned. The look that says he has found a way to triumph. To disburden himself of Father's disappointment because someone else can carry that mantle.

"Thomas is my friend."

But Thomas has taken another step back. The distance feels farther than that between Hever and Allington. Between England and France.

"That's not possible, Anne. I think you know that. Thomas Wyatt is not your friend. He never was."

"When I returned to court, everyone ignored me, even you, George. You claimed I did nothing but embarrass you. Father was away and Mary was otherwise occupied. Thomas was the only one who helped me. He steadied me. Kept me sane. Got me noticed."

"Yes." George nods. "Got you noticed. That was the point."

His wide mouth has grown even wider. The grin bares all of his teeth, like a snarl.

"The point?" I glance at Thomas. His face is closed. I turn back to George, who snarls again. "The point of what?"

"The point of the bet."

The earth falls away beneath me, and the trees along the river close in, looming black and heavy against the sky, spinning like a night full of wine. My lips go numb.

"What bet?"

"George." Thomas speaks in barely a whisper. As if he hasn't the strength to protest.

"The one I made with Wyatt. I said over cards one night that no one could ever make a lady out of my awkward little outspoken sister. Wyatt said he could. So I set him a challenge."

"What kind of a challenge?"

I ask this of Thomas, who seems to be rendered immobile. And speechless, for once.

"That he could make you the court darling," George says. "That men would want to pay you suit."

And he laughs. He's enjoying this.

I have to struggle to make myself heard over the roaring in my ears. "How much did you bet?"

I step closer to Thomas, look him directly in the eye. I cannot read what he's thinking. My heart no longer feels the beat of his.

"And what did you do with the money?"

"He never got it," George scoffs. As if just the two of us are having this discussion. As if Thomas isn't even here.

"Why not?" I don't turn away from Thomas's eyes. I already know the answer.

"Because he didn't win."

47

I AM UNFETTERED. UNBOUND. FLASH-DIVING TOWARD THE earth, which reaches for me with the greedy talons of nightmare. I sway and stop myself against a tree. Even George is quiet. The night is a held breath.

Thomas's expression is creeping off his face, leaving him blank and flat as water beneath the fog, his eyes importunate. Confirming everything.

"Anne . . ."

"No." I straighten and move away from both of them. "No. Neither of you has the right to speak to me. Neither of you has the right to say another word."

I turn and walk down toward the river, blind in the darkness, stumbling over the lifting of roots and stones. Grasses tangle my skirts, and branches tear at my hair. I will sleep in the reeds. I will sleep on the grass of the hillside and drink in the moonlight, be given magical powers to destroy my enemies.

I will lose myself.

I will lose them.

George's laughter follows me. I taste its bitterness on my tongue.

So I turn back. I will not run away. I am not in the wrong. I will not let either of them win.

George stumbles to the courtyard gate, abandoning me. But Thomas watches me. Sees me turn. He strides down the hill toward me. I do not slow down but rush up the hill to meet him.

"Please, Anne. Please let me explain."

I am downslope of him, looking even farther than usual up into his face. But my wrath makes me a giantess. Fearsome.

"There is nothing to explain, Thomas. And nothing you can say that I will believe. Your words are no more meaningful than a castle manufactured from sugar paste. It may look beautiful, it may taste sweet, but in the end, it crumbles and melts and becomes nothing. It cannot sustain a person, and only serves to blacken the teeth and coat the tongue."

"You deserve better."

"*Yes*, I deserve better, Thomas! To you, I am nothing. I am a fabrication. I am nothing but a filthy gamble. And I deserve to be more than that."

"You are more. I didn't know you then, Anne. All I knew was that you had returned from France. You were opinionated and clever and impolitic and different. George wanted you to listen and follow and be discreet and fit in. I thought I could do that. I thought I could . . ."

"You thought to win money off my brother and my virginity off of me. You thought it would be fun."

"Yes."

"You would get me my place at court. You would introduce

319

me to the most influential men. You would take me to bed. You would move on. Dispose of me like so much refuse."

"Yes. That's what I thought."

"But Percy beat you to it." I fight hard against the tears that threaten to engulf me. "You humiliated me. Made a project of me. A failed project."

"I am sorry."

The apology makes me stutter to a halt. Because I almost think he means it. Because it doesn't make me feel superior to him, not like he said. It makes me feel small and trapped, like a frightened animal.

"It's too late."

He should have told me before. If he truly was my friend, we could have won the bet together. But he is not. I want to throw his apology back in his face, to see if he really means it.

I watch him carefully. "I think you're just sorry that you didn't win."

"I'm sorry for so much more."

"Such as?"

He's holding something back. He's still lying.

"I care about you, Anne."

He won't even look at me. His eyes are raised to the sky and his lips are pushed together in a flat line.

"And you're sorry for that? Thank you, Thomas. That makes me feel better."

"You're making this harder!"

"Good!" I shout, not caring who hears or who looks or who

writes down every bloody word. "I hope I make your life a fraction of the misery mine is. I hope you feel the frustration and the anger and the agony, Wyatt!"

My voice catches and I gulp back a sob. I will not let him win. I straighten my shoulders and take a deep breath.

"I thought you were my friend."

The words come without my bidding them. Stupid. I can't let him think I care. I need him far, far away. It hurts too much.

"I can't be your friend, Anne."

Thomas's voice is barely a whisper. Perhaps I've confused it with the murmur of the wind in the grass.

"What?" I ask, not wanting to know, not wanting to hear. "What did you say?"

"I said I can't be your friend."

He still won't look me in the eye.

"Why? Because you believe, as George does, that men and women can't be friends? That I will try to control you? That I'll make you into some kind of effeminate fool who can't carry a lance or drink himself under the table?"

He doesn't answer.

"Or is it because you desire me?" I pursue angrily. "Because that's the other reason George gives. He says a man and woman can't really be friends because the man will forever be wondering what she's like in bed. Imagining her naked."

Thomas groans.

"The man will become overwrought with jealousy when the woman marries. But you, Wyatt. No. You don't feel that way.

You flirt with one half of the queen's maids and fuck the other half, but you only ever saw me as a project. A means to an end. An object. A prize."

"That's not true, Anne."

"Then what am I, Thomas? What am I to you? I'm nothing. So you get nothing from me. No favor to carry into your ridiculous mock battles. No fodder for your overwrought poetry. And certainly no friendship, Thomas. Because I think I finally agree with my brother. It's impossible."

"What can I do, Anne?"

"Just go away."

"I don't want to lose you." The words are ensnared in his doublet as he hangs his head.

"You already have."

He bites his lip. "Anne." His gaze lifts from the grass and roots beneath our feet and he looks right at me. Eyes the color of the sea at sunrise, the color of what used to be friendship.

Thomas squares his shoulders. Straightens his spine. Takes a deep breath. Just like my father taught me. When he exhales, his breath is a silver tissue of brume in air just beginning to frost.

He looks at me steadily. Doesn't say a word. Waits a beat. He is a master of timing. I know it. He taught it to me.

I don't want to wait for what he has to say for himself, what he thinks will make a difference between us. But I can't move.

"I love you."

My heart lurches forward as if reaching for him through my rib cage. I take a step back to prevent it from doing so. For

once, the words that form of their own accord and spill from me without thought will not be uttered.

I shake my head.

Thomas closes the gap between us and kisses me. Hard. This is not wet and sloppy like his playful kisses. Or dry and desperate like Percy's. Or teasing like the king's.

No. This kiss is eloquent and alive and speaks directly to my soul. My heart ruptures, and the splinters freeze and tumble all around us with the musical sound of broken glass.

I place my hands on his chest, feeling the pulse of his heart beneath my fingertips.

And I push.

Thomas stumbles back, off-balance.

"Don't," I gasp.

I turn.

And run.

48

THE ENTIRE COURT TAKES ON A HUE OF UNREALITY: THE WOMEN in their gaudy dresses with their strident voices and overly exaggerated gestures, the men with their dizzying doublets and straight, stuffy gaits. Everything is too clear, too sharp, the movements too jerky.

And it is all so suffocatingly close.

Everything within me pulls in different directions. It's like I'm a piece of linen, washed, boiled, beaten, stretched. Everything happening at once, and everything fighting against itself, threatening to kill me by degrees.

He lied to me.

He loves me.

Mercifully alone, I writhe in my bed from the pain of it all, like some unmade creature shedding its skin. My life is nothing but a game. I am nothing but a single, low-ranked card. Played and spent. A . . . nothing.

I have been defined by others. By my father and his cold disappointment. By my brother and his wily manipulation. By France. By Thomas Wyatt.

Thomas built me in his image. I want to strip away the paint and gilt and discover what is underneath. If anything.

I slide from my bed and stand on shaky legs, a fawn newly born. A fledgling.

I kneel in my room and make a pledge to myself never again to let anyone tell me what to do. Anyone. Not my fiancé. Not my husband. Not my father or my brother. Not society. I will rule myself.

I pull out my book of hours, the book Mary gave me for Christmas. I am more like Mary than I ever thought possible, pleasing others at the expense of being myself. The book's beautiful illuminations glow faintly in the candlelight. I turn the page to the miniature of the Last Judgment.

I will no longer be judged by the standards of others. I will judge myself. I will not live by someone else's rules. I will make my own.

I pick up my quill and write *Le temps viendra*. The time will come.

I sit back on my heels.

"I am not nothing," I say to the empty room. "And I refuse to be nothing. I will become someone, Thomas Wyatt. Without you. I will be more than you. You will not shape me. Because I have a shape of my own."

I pick up the quill again, dip it in the ink. Hesitate. Then I bring it back to the paper.

Je—

I stop.

What am I? I cast my mind into the future. Seeking light. Enlightenment.

I sketch an astrolabe, a tool used predict the movement of

the moon and stars. To predict the future. And I know. I want to be heard. I want to be seen. I want to be remembered. As me.

Anne Boleyn.

The ink seeps into the page. Permanent.

I am me.

I own me.

I will not be held to earth by someone else's tether.

I will let go of the past.

And I will start with Thomas Wyatt.

49

I CANNOT LIVE IN THE SAME HOUSE WITH HIM. EVEN ONE THE size of Windsor Castle. I cannot bear to see him or hear his voice.

I cannot stand the treacherous, feeble thing within me that suffers from his presence. I have to make him go away.

So with a half-formed plan in mind, and a heart full of caustic bitterness, I go to the one person I know who has enough power and enough cunning to do it for me. A person who has no qualms about manipulating the lives of others.

"Father."

Father doesn't look up from his papers. As usual.

One day, I will escape his disappointment. I will find a way for him to respect me—a girl—even if it kills me.

"Father."

"I know you're there, Anne. Allow me to finish."

One day, I will keep him waiting.

"Father."

"Anne!" he barks. "You obviously do not realize how much work goes into being a diplomat during times of war. It actually requires effort. Not sitting around singing and playing cards like a maid-in-waiting. No, being an ambassador means

I have to concentrate and write letters and make decisions. Something you wouldn't understand because you simply follow your whims without regard to the consequences."

He is right. I act and speak before thinking. But I do regard the consequences, because I have to live with them. And I know exactly what it means to be a diplomat in times of war. I am at war within the court itself. A war of attrition.

He throws his quill into the inkpot with a vicious thrust.

"Now. What requires my attention so badly? A new gown? The loss of a slipper? Lute strings?"

I glare at him, but he's too busy shuffling papers to see me.

"All my family ever does is ask for more money," he mutters.

"Father"—I manage to keep my voice calm—"I have no need for extra allowance."

"That's good because I have no extra to share. My family has depleted my treasury. All of my funds. I send money to your mother for gowns and baubles and gifts though it serves no purpose. I never see her. And you! I maintain two households so you can fritter away your time in the country. Your brother spends a fortune on women and wine and is nothing but a joke in the king's service. Worthless. The way you all live is prodigal, even for court. Why, when I first married your mother, we lived on fifty pounds a year. A *year*. And she brought another mouth to feed every six months."

His voice slows down over the course of this speech, and I see that he isn't even thinking about what he's saying, much less conscious of my presence in front of him.

"That's physically impossible, Father."

The words are out before I can stop them. I don't care. I know for a fact there were two years between each of us, including the two baby boys memorialized in the churches at Hever and Penshurst.

"Nine, then." He taps his index finger to a passage on the letter he's reading, his focus fully occupied by it. He doesn't listen even when I point out he's a fool.

I see how I can turn his complaining into a weapon against him. I see the perfect opportunity to present my scheme to him, before the idea fully takes shape.

"Father, I'm concerned about your workload. I wondered if someone else might help carry that burden."

"Are you thinking of becoming a diplomat?" he asks with a curl to his lip. He studies me slowly, taking in my long sleeves and my French hood, then cocks his head to the side with a knowing look. "You have to conform to be a diplomat. Blend in."

"Thank you, Father, for thinking I'm capable enough that only my attire bars me from a post," I say, trying to keep the ice from my voice. "It is not myself I wish to put forward, but a friend." Not a friend. I cross my fingers against the lie.

"Oh?"

"Do you not think our old neighbor, Thomas Wyatt, would make a good diplomat? He definitely knows how to blend in. He speaks excellent French. Everyone likes him." Except me.

Father looks at me. I cross the fingers of my other hand.

"You're right, of course," he says with a nod. "You always were a perceptive girl."

A compliment. Fancy that.

"Thank you, Father."

I offer a little curtsy.

"I shall mention it to the king."

"You know Sir Henry Wyatt, as well. He can be very persua-sive." In a harsh, critical, demanding sort of way.

"I shall mention it to Sir Henry, as well," Father says deci-sively, as if it is his idea. Simple.

"Thomas mentioned he always wanted to go abroad."

I squeeze my fingers so tightly I stop the blood. Thomas loves England.

"Did he now?"

"And he admires you so." I can't feel my fingertips.

Father preens.

It is so simple. Which must be why I feel I am diving off a cliff. Simple—and dangerous.

"I'll see what I can do," Father says.

Father can be very persuasive as well. Thomas Wyatt is as good as gone.

And Thomas certainly won't make Father's life easier.

Two birds. One small stone. But the one time my father hears my words is the one time I wish I could take them back.

I turn to leave, certain that my father has forgotten about me entirely. But his voice cuts the air just as I start through the doorway.

"I know what you're doing."

I almost trip because I stop midstride.

"Seeking preferment for your lovers is commonplace at

court, Anne," he says. I don't turn, but I can hear that he speaks to his papers. He doesn't raise his head. "You just don't want it to ruin you. It's the best thing for you that Thomas Wyatt leave court. That he no longer drag your name through his own muck. That's why I will do this, Anne. Not to lighten my workload."

I don't even attempt to tell him that Thomas is not my lover and never will be. My father believes what he will.

"Just don't mourn his absence." One last piece of fatherly advice.

"I won't." This lie is the hardest to tell.

Because I already am.

Greenwich Palace
1524

50

THE CHRISTMAS SEASON HURTLES TOWARD US WITH PLANS FOR another of King Henry's lavish entertainments. *The Castle of Loyalty—The Château Blanc.* There will be a pageant on the tiltyard. Chivalric oratory and romantic ballads. There will be a tournament of jousting and swordplay and feats of archery. And there will be a great battle over the Château Blanc itself.

In a court obsessed with symbolism, the Château Blanc can stand for many things: Loyalty. Integrity. Trust. Devotion to king and country. Purity.

Virginity.

Unexpectedly, I am one of the four maidens chosen to occupy it. We are given the keeping of the castle, but in reality, we are just ornamentation.

Something over which the men can fight.

The good news is that if I'm meant to represent virginity, perhaps Butler isn't spreading his vicious gossip. Or no one believes him.

The bad news is that Thomas Wyatt is among the men chosen to safeguard the castle. No one else seems to recognize the irony that the man who is rumored to have stolen many a maiden's virginity now rushes to its defense.

And when Henry Percy is selected for the assault, I begin to think I am the butt of an elaborate joke. I would blame George, but he is too busy making merry to conceal his disappointment at not being picked for either side.

I try to console myself with the honor of being chosen at all. And I am determined not to repeat my personal disaster from *The Château Vert*.

The men of the court throw themselves tirelessly into the tactics and technical details of this false war because the real war—the war against the French—has to be suspended due to winter weather.

The king will lead the challengers—symbolically putting to the test the loyalty and integrity of his men. He spends countless hours designing ingenious siege engines that will breach the castle defenses, mechanisms to vault the fifteen-foot ditches and elude the great rollers at every entrance that can unbalance an attacker at the slightest touch.

The strategy and avidity applied to this game only serve to make me hope more fervently that they are never applied against the French.

Even so, I, too, feel the hunger for battle. I wish I could pick up a sword and descend with all my fury into the breach. Wyatt. Percy. George. Father. All of them would feel the power of my wrath.

But no. I sit and sew. While Wyatt helps to oversee the construction of a wooden castle out on the tiltyard, I embroider a thousand tiny gold stitches to create the ridiculous emblems on the pageant banners. The castle could probably withstand an actual assault. I feel my defenses weakening every day, every time I see him.

While he is fitted for new armor, I sew dozens of seed pearls onto a pale-blue bodice. Pearls are a symbol of the feminine, of women. And women are the ones considered to be fragile and mercurial. Weak. But pearls are also a symbol of the never-ending cycle and so represent unending loyalty. The cycle I see in the court is not one of loyalty, but one of distortion. Manipulation. Self-obsession.

I guess I fit in well.

The slippery smoothness of the pearls reminds me of the night Thomas came to my bedchamber in Hever. How his hand held mine, interlaced with pearls. How he soothed away my dream. How I felt that I belonged there.

I think I knew then that he loved me. I just didn't know he had already betrayed me.

The pageant begins on Saint Thomas's Day, a day swamped in symbolism. Thomas the doubter, who would not believe in the resurrection until given physical proof. His saint's day is the shortest of the year, the day that night engulfs the earth.

Countless candles and torches are lit in the great hall to dispel the darkness, belching soot and vapors to the ceiling, the dragons of the court circling below. A clamor of trumpets and the bellow of canon fire from outside announce the commencement of the festivities. A herald enters, carrying a placard painted with the symbols and colors of the castle and its defenders.

I stand to one side, shoulder to shoulder with Jane.

The king is up on a dais, sitting in an intricately carved chair with gilded armrests and a velvet cushion. The cloth of state is canopied over him, gold embroidered with Tudor roses.

Energy radiates off of him like a cataract. He is insatiable. Unstoppable. No effort has been spared in this production. It's like he has something to prove, something to win.

He leans forward slightly, ready to pounce.

He is looking at me.

I reach for Jane's hand, and she squeezes mine.

Before the herald can issue the challenge, the king stands and strides to the edge of the dais. He towers over the throng, and the herald—who is young and visibly intimidated—is rendered speechless.

He is supposed to announce us—the four maidens—so the king can challenge the defenders. It will be a contest over who will be our champions. But if there is no announcement, there is no contest.

I step forward, tugging Jane with me. A rustling murmur rises around us, lapping to the far corners of the room.

"Impudent."

"Presumptuous."

"Brazen."

I ignore the whispers, propelled forward by the eagerness in the king's countenance.

"Before you stand four maidens," I begin.

The herald shudders and steps in front of me. I fight the urge to kick him.

"Before you stand four virgins," he squeaks. Behind the king, Henry Percy looks like he has swallowed a toad.

Jane squeezes my hand. "The king hasn't taken his eyes off of you," she whispers as the herald lays out all the details of the challenge. "What did you call him? Delicious? It looks like he could say the same thing about you."

I raise my eyes back to the king's, and all of my bones vibrate with the hum coming off of him. His expression is volatile. Covetous. Hungry.

"Who defends these maidens?" he asks, glancing at the herald and then about the room. "Their integrity? Their purity?"

He looks back at me. "Their beauty?"

He raises his voice, and it echoes in the silent room. "Who defends the Château Blanc?"

Fifteen men step forward. All of them are young, in their teens or barely out of them. These men—these *boys*—have never been to war. They have never faced a siege. But I can see in their faces that they are ready to. Ready to protect. Ready to prove themselves. Ready to go to war in one way or another.

Thomas strides to the forefront, cutting off Leonard Grey, the captain of their phalanx. I grip Jane's hand to prevent myself from running.

"We will defend the castle and these maidens," Thomas says, and glances once between me and the king.

He pauses. Takes a deep breath.

"And we defend against all comers."

51

THE KING IS LIVID. FOLLOWING THE PAGEANT'S ANNOUNCEMENT, it is discovered that the siege engines he designed have been constructed incompetently. His martial fervor has been quashed by the ineptitude of English carpenters. Everything he hoped for has fallen apart. The carpenters flee before his wrath, and courtiers scramble to fill the void. Jesters. Musical entertainments. Gifts.

Christmas Day is celebrated beneath this cloud—a fog of waiting and desperation.

And then it is announced that the tournament is to go ahead as planned. On the day of another Saint Thomas: December 29, when Thomas Becket was murdered by the knights of a different King Henry for defying royal wishes. The siege of the castle will be postponed.

The morning dawns bright and cold. Frost tinges the trees and runs up the hill all the way to Duke Humphrey's Tower. The cold makes the outlines of everything stark and hard-edged but subdues the colors to a wash—like silks left too long in the rain.

The castle stands to one side. Its walls of wood and fabric and the crenellated battlements, braced and whitewashed, are a simulation of invulnerability. But for today, that conception will remain unchallenged.

George sidles up to me shoulder to shoulder, looking in the same direction. I have not spoken to him. I will not speak to him.

"Ah, the imagery," George sighs. "The Castle of Loyalty cannot be broken by any of the king's devisings."

I keep my silence.

"And the maidens it protects remain unspoiled."

"I wonder, though," he says, quietly enough that only I will hear. And I am lost in the wary darkness of his eyes. "Do its defenders realize the extent of the pretense? For virginity lost needs no protection."

I turn on him, ready to do battle myself. I don't care if the whole court watches. He sees my movement. His eyes go wide, and he takes a swift step back onto Jane.

"Ow!"

George spins and catches Jane before she falls. His grace is barely marred by his early-morning inebriation, and he manages to keep his balance and hers. Her fingers clench on the muscles of his arms and then she goes a little limp.

"I'm sorry," she says, breathless.

"No, forgive me, fair damsel," he says, tugs her upright, and braces her before stepping away.

Jane giggles.

He spins on his toe, back to us, ramrod straight.

"I go to survey your lodgings. Inspect your Castle of Virginity."

Jane presses both hands across her mouth to disguise her giggles as shock.

He waves a dismissive hand at me and walks away. Jane watches every move he makes.

"He's very charming."

"He's maddening."

Jane studies George from beneath the gable of her hood. She looks the very model of the ingenue courtier, the virginal maid-in-waiting watching her knight on the field of battle, just like in a romantic ballad.

I take a deep breath, square my shoulders, and stand next to her. I suppress an inward curl of pain, knowing she loves him, that the marriage agreement is signed. That she is consigned to her romantic fate that cannot—will not—end well. My brother is a lost cause. She says nothing. I say nothing. And we watch, shoulder to shoulder.

Suddenly the field goes silent. The men stop shouting. The women stop gossiping. Even the horses stop clanking their armor. All we can hear is the snap of the banners in the breeze.

The queen enters the viewing tower, and we bow as she makes her way to her gilded chair. She seems even more tired than usual. Stooped. Sad.

A cannon fires and the defenders enter the field fully armed, six of them charging across the drawbridge of the counterfeit castle. The crowd roars its approval. I know which one is Thomas by the way he rides, the way his body moves. I grip the rail of the viewing platform with both hands, caught in the still point between running toward him and running away.

Jane catches my eye, but says nothing.

A sudden silence from the audience turns me back to the field. The defenders have adjourned to one end of the lists. And at the other end, two ladies enter on horseback—ladies I've never met or even seen. Veils hide their faces. Their hair is perfectly coiffed beneath French hoods. They look awkward on their palfreys, shifting in their skirts and sidesaddles.

They lead chargers carrying two old men whose silver hair and beards shine in the shifting light. The men's robes are purple damask. The vibration starts deep in my chest. Even grizzled and disguised, I know him. He is a head taller than the rest of the men at court, his shoulders so broad that even when stooped, he looks majestic.

The queen narrows her eyes.

The two ladies ride directly to the queen and bow as best they can. One nearly topples, and some of the men in the stands laugh. Then the tallest lady hands a rolled parchment up to the queen's usher. As the man unrolls it, I watch the lady. She sits back on her saddle. Scratches under one arm.

That is no lady.

It's Mark Smeaton.

"'Youth has left these ancient knights,'" the usher reads. "'And yet courage and goodwill are with them, obliging them to break spears, if the queen is pleased to give them license.'"

The taller of the "ancient" knights scans the crowd. I follow his gaze as he examines each face quickly and then moves on. He's looking for someone. I straighten my spine, take a deep

breath, and wait. When he finds me, I don't look away, nor do I curtsy.

I am not being disrespectful. For the sake of the sham, we both have to pretend he is nothing but an old man. The brim of his shapeless cap dips low over his gray eyes.

But they remain on me.

"You look too old and infirm to challenge the young men of the court." The queen sounds weary, as if she is tired of the games and the pageantry, the disguises and the trickery that can go on behind them. "I should hate to send you to your destruction and humiliation."

"We shall do our best to avoid that, Your Majesty." The knight sounds irritable as he turns and bows to her.

"I praise your courage, sir," the queen says carefully, "and I grant you the right to challenge any and all in the competitions today. May luck be with you."

"Thank you, Your Majesty." The knight pulls away the silver beard. He throws off his robe. Beneath it he wears a gorgeous doublet of white silk and cloth of silver that turns his chest into a broad, shining expanse, upon which shines a gold-embroidered heart, bisected.

The other knight removes his disguise to reveal Charles Brandon, Duke of Suffolk. The duchess rolls her eyes, but raises two fingers, kisses them, and extends them toward him.

Cheers erupt from the stands and the air reverberates with the stamping of feet and pounding of fists. The men already on the field quickly rush to welcome the newcomers.

Wyatt grins and clasps hands with the king—a gesture

of goodwill before the hostilities begin. Eye to eye with the greatest man in the kingdom—possibly in the world—Thomas appears perfectly at ease. I think about his arm around me, about the kiss of his words on my neck.

As if he can hear me thinking about him, Thomas looks up and offers a smile that dives straight to my heart and plucks it from me.

I press my thoughts deep beneath my ribs and pull out the ragged memories of his duplicity. Of every time he hinted seduction. Of every compliment he ever paid me. Lies and betrayal to win a bet.

Then I see the emblem emblazoned on his chest. A heart bisected.

I turn away and lean with my back against the partition. It's like he's still trying to win. But is he trying to win the bet? Or me?

Jane looks me full in the face—her expression an exposed question.

"They wear the same emblem," she murmurs. "The king and Thomas Wyatt. An open heart."

I close my eyes.

"An open heart," I repeat. "Or a broken one."

52

THE KING AND DUKE FIGHT SAVAGELY, AS IF THEY ARE TRULY AT war, and their very lives depend on their winning. During the tourney, the king attacks Anthony Browne with such determination that I'm afraid he'll take Browne's head off.

Needless to say, the defenders of Loyalty don't stand a chance.

After the tournament, the entire court moves indoors, where the ladies must provide the entertainment. The mass of sweaty men and overly perfumed women fills the great hall of the palace with strangling odors and a miasma of smoke and steam rising from damp doublets. The men cannot let go of their bellicosity, and the atmosphere is one of frenzied carousal and blistering self-importance.

The herald enters, leading the defeated defenders, the crowd parting before them, cheering and jeering and making ribald remarks about loyalty, virginity, and sexual prowess.

But when the king is announced, all banter ceases. The men always bridle their vulgarity when he's around. The room sinks to its knees as he walks to the dais and turns to face us.

"Let the defenders of the Château Blanc—the defenders of Loyalty—approach."

The defenders kneel before him. All part of the pageant.

"What say you?" the king asks. "Do you have a spokesman?"

The men hang their heads and glance at one another from the corners of their eyes.

"Thomas Wyatt?"

There is an edge to the king's voice. He is less jovial.

A hush follows. Thomas raises his head, and the two look at each other for a long moment.

"Rise."

Thomas stands, his stillness counterpoint to the king's undeniable energy.

"What say you?" the king asks. "In your defense of Loyalty? Of the maidens?"

"The maidens survived the day with the purity of their characters and persons intact," Thomas says, his eyes never leaving the king's, his expression grave.

The king smiles. Just a little. "Thanks to the decency and rectitude of the challengers."

"As you say, Your Majesty." Thomas pauses. "But the Castle of Loyalty survives intact, undisturbed by any assault. The maidens in question remain ours to defend."

It's a direct challenge, faulting the king for being unable to attack the castle. The king seethes.

Thomas waits a moment more, eyes never leaving the king's face.

"The maidens remain ours to entertain."

I can see the king's jaw working, the spark of ferocity in his eyes. The court holds its breath, waiting for the ax to fall.

"That will remain a subject for debate," the king says tightly. Then he relaxes visibly, as if by great internal effort. "However, as a show of goodwill, I submit that you shall start the dance, Master Wyatt. Whom do you wish to partner?"

Thomas doesn't hesitate.

"Your Majesty, I wish to dance with Mistress Anne Boleyn."

The king stills, just for a moment, then nods his assent.

Thomas turns, his movements loose and graceful. But I can see the calculation in them, the tension in his shoulders, the hesitation in his stride. He's afraid I'll run away. Make fools of us both.

But I can't run away. My body senses his—as if his is the note that will complete a chord, and mine waits for that note to be struck.

The rest of the court melts away. For once, I have no idea what other people are thinking. Whether they see me. If they comment on the fact that I cannot break away from Thomas's gaze.

Behind those eyes, I know a mind is working. I know he is planning, calculating. I know he chooses his words carefully. I know his mind runs to poetry.

And poetry can't be trusted.

"Are you still not speaking to me?"

I find I cannot speak. My mind and heart and body are all at odds. All I can do is shake my head.

His hand touches mine and sends a cascade of sensation all the way down my arm. And I don't know if the music comes from the musicians or from us. But we move to it. With it.

Through it. As if we were formed as two, matched, and became one.

I don't want this. This feeling of completion.

We turn in the dance, my back to him. He takes one step too close, and I feel the length of him against me, like when we were in Hever.

"A man could get lost in you, Anne Boleyn," he whispers, and we are separated by the dance.

I feel as if I have taken flight, as if my body is not my own, as if I have no past. The music pours through me. I want this. This moment. This man.

When we return to each other, palm pressed to palm, he says, "The king is watching you."

It sends me crashing back to earth. And I hear a vivid, reverberating hum shimmer through me. Undeniable. I want that, too.

I look up into Thomas's eyes and see all air and ocean there.

"So are you," I tell him.

The words slip out. A flirtation.

Triumph shines in his two-dimpled smile. I spoke to him. What am I doing? He lied to me. What guarantee do I have that he'll not lie to me again? The only certainty is that we can never be together because even though he left his wife, he's still married. With Thomas Wyatt, all I can ever be is a mistress. Disposable.

But he makes me feel indispensible when he looks at me. When he speaks to me. "Then he's watching both of us."

I have to turn. To look.

The king stands on his dais, looking out over the crush of people. In the dim and smoky light of the hall, his gray eyes are dark and piercing. Directed at me.

His very stillness vibrates.

I break away from Thomas, bow my head, and curtsy.

Thomas's hand slides down my arm and grips my fingers. The king's eyes flicker once to our hands, once to Thomas, and back to me.

The room grows so hot the very walls could melt. Outside, the wind rages, the ice breaks upon the Thames, the beasts cower in their forest lairs, and people die from cold and starvation. But inside Greenwich, men grow fat and red in the face, the ladies grow light-headed, and the music plays on.

"You should go."

Thomas's voice is toneless.

"If you disappear, he'll want you more."

"The king? That's ridiculous." But something tugs at the corner of my mind. The king flirted with me. The king looked for me, challenged the defenders of my castle. His symbol is an open heart.

"Not so ridiculous, Anne," Thomas says soberly. "After all, that was the plan. It's the way the game works. When a deer is spotted, the hunters follow."

"And you're the white flag on my tail."

"I used to be quite crude."

"You are quite crude. No need for past tense."

"Don't tease me, Anne. There is so much I did wrong. The worst was to underestimate you."

I want his words to be enough for me to forgive him. I'm just not sure they are.

"So what next, Thomas?" I ask. "You set yourself up to rival the king? Another challenge? Don't you see how ludicrous that is?"

Even if he is interested, it's impossible. He's married. And I need a friend, not a hunter. Not a man I can't have.

"Why? Because he always wins? Not this time, Anne."

He takes one step closer.

"You love me," he says, so quietly I feel he is lodged within my soul. "I know you do."

"You certainly think a lot of yourself, Thomas Wyatt."

"I know you better than I know myself." He looks up, his expression wary. "He's coming. Go now."

I squeeze Thomas's hand once and let go.

"No."

Because the time has come. Not the time to follow his direction, but for Anne Boleyn to decide her own actions.

53

THE EXPRESSION ON THE KING'S FACE ALMOST SHATTERS MY resolve. I see reflected there my own desires—my childish longings from when I first saw him. In him I see a beginning. Possibility.

Thomas bows beside me and I sink into a curtsy.

"Loyalty has taken a beating this evening," the king says. The edge is there in his voice, his words directed at Thomas.

"Metaphorically speaking, Your Majesty," I say. "The loyalty of your people will never falter."

"Even those who are called more French than the French?"

Looking at him is like trying to look at the sun. Blinding me to everything else in the room. I can't even hear the music anymore. There is nothing but him.

"I appreciate French culture, Your Majesty." I falter, unable to think of anything clever to say.

"As do I, Mistress Boleyn. Grace, beauty, art, and music. I steal as much as I can. Because it's wasted on the French."

He moves closer, bending slightly, immersing me in sensation. The glitter of gold, the scent of cloves, the memory of his lips pressed to mine. The taste of his tongue.

"Beauty, especially, is wasted on them," he murmurs.

"And what makes you say that?" I tilt my chin. The best angle for him to kiss me if he wishes.

"If they appreciated it, they would never have let you go."

For the first time in my life, I feel that I am beautiful. The warmth that cascades through me is not a blush. Guiltily, I recognize it as not embarrassment but a rush of sudden desire.

"Will you dance with me?"

"Of course, Your Majesty."

The distance between us creates a cushion, one that allows me to breathe, to think. Of Mary. Of wounding her yet again. And of Thomas.

But then the king takes my hand in his, and all thought is lost. As we dance, each touch is like a miniature lightning strike, every parting a vacuum.

I hear George start singing in the corner, leading a group of men in an off-key rendition of "Anguished Grief," Gilles Binchois's singularly memorable tune marred only by the joyless lyrics of the Christine de Pisan poem. George stumbles about in mock torment, giddy from laughing at love.

"Interesting that your paramour is not with your brother. For Thomas Wyatt would normally be at the forefront of such a crowd. Perhaps the dart of love has actually pierced his heart."

"I'm not sure anything can pierce his heart." But as I say it, a sliver of doubt pierces mine. And guilt.

The king laughs—a sound like bells. And all else is erased. We turn away from each other in the dance, and when we come back together, the king pulls me just a little bit closer. His touch is so sure, his gaze mesmerizing.

I wonder wildly what perception his fingers could incite on the skin of my back or along the hollows of my ribs. Then shame, in the image of Mary, crashes through me, followed swiftly by jealousy that she has already experienced that touch.

"A woman such as yourself deserves more than a man like Thomas Wyatt."

Another blow of contrition, and a glimmer of anger. My family has never acknowledged that I'm anything more than a child. Not my father, nor my brother. Certainly not Mary. And Thomas treated all our interactions as a game, though not a childish one.

"I shall just have to keep looking, then."

The intensity of his gaze flares, the heat of it reflected beneath my ribs like fire on glass.

"You may not have to look far."

I stumble, and he catches me easily with one hand, pulls me into the crook of his arm.

"No need to be afraid of me, Nan."

I take a deep breath.

"I'm not afraid, Your Majesty."

I look at him directly. Douse the intoxicating heat. Tell myself it's impossible. Remind myself that the Boleyns stick together.

"And no one but my sister calls me Nan."

He stops abruptly—a jolt of surprise and choler.

My breath catches and I look away. I've gone too far, let my words fail me yet again.

"Then I shall have to think of something else to call you."

He swings me back into the dance, but his voice is intimate. "Something private. Just for me. For us."

The flare returns, and I am grateful that the dance requires us to part. I keep my eyes lowered as I execute a turn that bells my skirts around me.

I look up to meet the king's eye as I come out of the turn, and there, behind him, is Thomas. His face is anguished, agonized, like the song. But I only see him for an instant. For as soon as the king returns to his proper position, he blocks everything else from my vision.

The music stops, and the king raises my hand to his lips. Kisses the solitary pearl-studded band that adorns my finger.

Smiles.

"I shall call you Anna."

Greenwich Palace
1525

54

My dance with the king leaves me feeling drunk, and as the year lurches to a close, I suffer the aftereffects. Not headache and nausea, but guilt and jealousy in equal measure.

All I did was dance.

And want.

The new year rides in like the tide, and the court shifts and moves like a house built on the Lambeth marsh. Tottering. Unstable. No one really knows where anyone else is going. No one knows what might happen next. And as the tide retreats toward spring, it leaves everything exposed.

It feels as if everyone is watching me. I am no longer invisible. I hear that some are placing bets on who will share the king's bed next, that the odds are on me. But the men at court will bet on anything.

We relocate, moving from Greenwich to Eltham, Eltham to Bridewell, and Bridewell back to Greenwich like a pack of stray dogs. There is no stability, no promise.

The king watches me. I can feel it. The entire court watches him watching. I no longer know how to act or what to say. I'm not even sure what I want.

And the person I have always asked for advice has disappeared into the columns and tabulations of the clerkship of the jewels. Into his poetry.

I cannot face Mary. I remember too well her desperate heartbreak when King François moved on. She claims she doesn't love King Henry. But surely this betrayal will shatter her.

George is lost in his gambling and drinking. George is lost to me, full stop.

And Jane.

Jane comes to me in tears. The hollows of her cheeks are gray, and her wide, catlike eyes are dull and unseeing.

"I can't marry him," she sobs, and throws her arms around my neck. We are in the queen's watching chamber, surrounded by courtiers. All of them watching.

"Why?" I wrap my arms around her, too. Hide her face in my hood and guide her from the chamber and down the stairs to the Middle Court. Here, people can see us as they rush to perform their duties, but at least they do not pause to listen.

"What has he done?" I whisper.

She gasps, shocked, and pulls away to look at me.

"George? He's done nothing. It's my father. He doesn't have the ready cash to pay the dowry."

And my father will never let him get away with anything less than what was originally negotiated.

"But the agreement was signed." I cannot follow my own thoughts, for they move too quickly.

"There are ways around that." Jane's voice is dripping with contempt.

"Maybe it was never meant to be."

"No, Anne! I love him!"

"You don't really even know him."

She sobs again and falls back on my shoulder.

"Without him I will die unmarried!" she sobs afresh.

"Jesus, Jane." I push her away and hold her at arm's length. "You're young and desirable and very pretty. Your father is Lord Morley. You have time."

"No, Anne! I grow old and withered and I will never marry if I don't marry now!"

She's becoming hysterical. I pat her back awkwardly, wondering what I can do for her. What I can do with her.

"Is it someone else, Anne?" Jane asks.

The question startles me, and I'm happy to be able to answer truthfully. "Not that I know of."

Jane's face turns to steel and she clenches her jaw.

"I know he doesn't really want to marry me," she says, "And I know men can't really change, but I'm afraid I'll be a very jealous wife. I'm even jealous of you."

"Of me?"

"Well, not only are you beautiful—"

I cough through my nose.

"You are, Anne. Everyone remarks on it."

Only because Thomas told them so, and they believed the lies of a poet.

"But you also have George's love. He protects you. He advises you. He is the one who told me you're beautiful before I realized it myself. You are so lucky."

"Lucky?" I can't hold it in any longer. "You don't know him,

Jane. You know what he looks like on the outside, but not who he is on the inside. He made a bet." I choke on the truth. "A *bet* with someone that I would *not* be accepted at court no matter what endless sculpting the other man employed. He thinks a woman's worth is only what's between her legs. Not her mind or her virtue or her thoughts or her words. To him, the only thing a woman is good for is as a plaything."

"George isn't like that!"

"He is, Jane. And you need to face it sooner rather than later. You'd be better off not marrying him. Marry someone else. Marry Francis Weston or some other pliable young fool who will think you're clever and feel lucky to have you."

"So only a fool would want me, is that what you're saying?" Jane's tears are frozen on her cheeks. "George wants a clever girl, a pretty girl with a keen mind who he can talk to. Who can make him laugh. A girl like you, is that it? Do you love him yourself, Anne? Do you want him? Is that why you're not married? Is that why Butler won't have you? Why Henry Percy ran away? Is that why you're jealous? Do you think your brother is the only one good enough for you?"

"Jane!" I cry. "That's an evil thing to say!"

"It's an evil thing to do, Anne. But evil doesn't always stop people."

Her words fall on me like a hail of blows. She juts out her chin as if daring me to punch it, and part of me wants to. But I'm terrified that any defense will be seen as acceptance of guilt.

We stand for an eternity. I watch as the color drains from Jane's face, taking the anger with it. Her eyes fill with tears and

beg forgiveness, but she says not a word as she turns and walks away.

The perfect courtier, sleek and sinuous in her thinking, cutting in her remarks about others.

Someone who doesn't apologize.

"Walk with me."

I startle at the buttery voice at my elbow. I quickly drop into a curtsy at the king's feet, berating myself for being so unaware.

"Rise, Mistress Boleyn," he says, "and do as I ask."

Walk with him.

We pass through the door and into the long gallery, where all the courtiers and ladies sink before us. It is like watching a multicolored sea dip into the troughs of waves, heads bowed and eyes averted.

As we pass, I hear murmurs and a few singular shouts for attention, but the king merely waves a finger and they are silenced behind him. I catch looks of surprise and suggestive significance as people see my face before they lower their gaze. I hear murmurs of gossip behind me like the sough of a wave on graveled sand.

People are not avoiding me because I'm an embarrassment. They are deferring to me because I am elevated. This is what it feels like to be inside the royal circle, that bubble of protection, the ring of acceptance.

We walk out into the newly manicured gardens, a dozen or so attendants following at an obsequious distance. I can smell the river and see Duke Humphrey's Tower high on the hill beyond, reminding me of the day I incurred the king's wrath.

I look quickly away to the man beside me. His hands are still, his gait even, but I sense his restlessness, his mind working, his eyes roving.

"I wanted to be the first to tell you, mistress. King François was captured at Pavia. The French have lost the war."

With this, the hum of his energy rises a notch. A half step.

"The French have surrendered?" I ask, stunned.

"Soon."

I risk a glance at him. He smiles patronizingly.

"You think his mother and sister will simply hand over the country to you." I can't avoid saying the words.

The king stops and holds my gaze.

"They are women."

I will him not to look away, terrified that I have his attention, that I stand so close to him and cannot touch him. Even more terrified that I am about to argue with him again.

"Women can be formidable when aroused."

A wall of shock crashes down between us, and I take a step back.

"Opposed," I correct myself. "Women can be formidable when opposed."

The king bites his bottom lip and I remember the touch of it on my own. The horror of my verbal flux washes me afresh.

"They can." The king closes the gap I created with my retreat. I am stunned into paralysis by his gaze, like a deer ready for slaughter.

"It appears that you and Mistress Parker had a disagreement."

"You saw that? You heard?" Oh, God. What if he believes it?

"Saw from a distance. Heard nothing."

Relief floods through me.

"You and Mistress Parker have always appeared to be cordial. What was the cause of your disagreement?"

"It wasn't so much of a disagreement." I falter. "She is upset because the plans for her to marry my brother may not come to fruition."

"She loves him?"

I nod, unable to say so in words.

"And you want her to be happy."

"She's my friend." Was.

"I shall speak with Lord Morley," he says abruptly.

"Oh, no!"

I immediately throw my hand over my mouth. I should die. Now. Instantaneously.

He narrows his eyes for a fraction of a moment, then bursts into a full, rolling laugh. I hear a couple of the attendants chuckling sycophantically behind us. They can't help themselves.

I smile weakly.

"Don't do anything on my account, Your Majesty," I say, and sink into a curtsy. I don't want Jane to marry George. I don't want it to be my fault.

"No, Mistress Anna." He offers a hand to lift me up, the vibration buzzing through my fingers, igniting every nerve. "I do it for young Jane. Leave it with me, and I will ensure it comes to fruition. Jane is a sweet girl and deserves to be happy."

"Yes. She does."

I can't tell the king that George may never make Jane happy. I may never speak again, made mute by wanting what I can't have.

"As do you, Mistress Anna."

I stare at his hand, afraid to look in his face. The rings on his fingers have made ridges on his palm. His nails are slightly ragged, as if he chews them. The imperfections only serve to make me want him more.

"You deserve to be happy. The most happy."

I hold my breath and look up. His face is shy. Boyish. As if all the confidence has fled him.

As all of mine has fled me.

The man I fell in love with at the age of thirteen is holding my hand. A man nearly twice my age. But still so handsome it hurts the eyes. And he is looking at me. Really looking. I feel the hum begin to fill me.

He is my sister's lover.

He is married.

And I'm in love with someone else.

The thought hits me like a storm at sea crashing, thundering, blow upon blow. It rocks me over then buoys me up only to plummet me into the next trough. I shake my head to clear it.

"You think you don't deserve happiness?" he asks, mistaking my action. "What would make you happy?"

He looks at me earnestly. As if I can answer that question easily. I would be happy if Thomas wasn't married. If he had never taken that bet. I would be happy if I had never left France. If I weren't tangled in a sticky mess of choices and innuendos and the desires of other people. If I were holding someone else's hand.

"Love."

The word answers for me.

The king smiles. Gorgeously. Dazzlingly. It singes me.

"Perhaps that can be arranged."

As he takes his hands from mine, he slips the ring from my finger, the plain gold band with the single pearl.

"I should like to keep this," he says, and kisses it before sliding it onto his smallest finger. The only one that was bare.

55

THE FIRST RULE OF THE HUNT IS NEVER TO LOOK BACK AT THE hunter.

When I leave the king, my feet take me through the gardens. I don't check behind me to see if he's watching. I pass through the gate, looking ahead into the orchard.

I see a figure dressed in green, conjured from my thoughts and wishes. Vivid. Solid. More. I cannot stop myself from going to him.

"Looking for me?" He cocks his head and grins at me, but his body is still. Stiff. There is tension behind his words.

"No." *Yes.*

"For him." His jaw tightens, and I see the hope diminish.

"What? No!"

"Don't lie to me, Anne," Thomas says, his voice laced with sadness. "I saw you. How you looked at him. How you reacted to him. I know you as well as I know myself. Remember?"

I remember. And say nothing.

"You want the court to fall at your feet."

"I did," I admit. *I do.*

"You want the king, Anne?" His voice cracks. "Is that why you agreed to go along with all of it?"

I did want the king. From the first moment I saw him—gilded and brilliant on the Field of Cloth of Gold. I wanted him more after that foolish, teasing kiss in my sister's room. The one that meant nothing to him and yet everything to me.

Now I don't know what I want.

"Don't be stupid," I croak. "It's ridiculous." *Isn't it?* "A childish fancy. A fairy tale. The influence of too many chivalric ballads."

"The ones that always end badly."

I shiver.

"You should know, Thomas Wyatt. None of your love poems end well."

"I deserve that."

"You do. And more."

"I certainly don't deserve you."

"But you can't have me. Not as a wife. Not as a mistress. Don't you see? This is a chance for me to be heard."

"You want to be heard," he pursues. "But do you know what you want to say?"

"Does it matter as long as someone's listening? I want to say what I think and be taken seriously. I don't want to be nothing. If I have the king's ear," I say, my words slowing upon themselves, "I can be anything."

"It's not his ear he follows you with."

Thomas's voice is low and dangerous. I think of what that implies, and I shiver again.

"I don't want to be the next Mary." I speak without thinking. What I should have said was, *I wouldn't do that to Mary*.

The angles and contours of his face blur beneath the scudding shadows of an early spring sky. His cheekbones stand out against the stubble of his beard, and his eyebrows curve gently above it all like the sharp lines of bare trees.

"Then be with me. Not as a wife . . ." Thomas clears his throat. "Nor as a mistress. Not even as a friend." He smiles warily. "But as the girl I love."

The words stifle him and he doesn't say any more, but his eyes keep asking.

I have no answer.

He reaches out a tentative hand, the fingers a little too knobby, the knuckled bones standing out, the tips blunt, stained with ink. He hesitates, but I don't move away.

His hand catches the side of my face and I lean into it, breathing in the scents of ink and paper, of almonds, of warmth. I close my eyes. There are no words for what I'm feeling. Or perhaps there are too many.

I feel the skim of his breath on my face, the brush of it against my lips.

And he kisses me.

So softly at first, I'm not quite sure he's touching me. The fog of breath. The scent of almonds. The faint roughness of his beard, the flicker of skin on skin.

I lean forward, pressing my lips to his, and it breaks me open. His hand leaves my face and traces notes up my arms, strikes chords on my throat and up into my hair. His mouth forms lyrics that expose my soul.

This kiss is like a song played only once. And forever.

And then I remember that Thomas Wyatt has had lots of practice. He knows what he's doing when he kisses a girl. When he touches her.

No wonder it feels so good.

"I can't."

I pull away. My mind is filled with reasons. I open my eyes and look into his. I have the queerest feeling that he's been watching me the entire time.

"Can't what? Kiss me? I think you just did. And rather well, I might add."

A ghost of fear hides behind his eyes. He can't cover it with a joke or bravado, or a single-dimpled smile.

That ghost shadows all my defenses. Because he has lowered his.

"I will never make you do anything you don't want to, Anne," he says.

I think of Percy, how I could want something and not want it all at once. Want it for the wrong reasons. How do I know what are the right reasons?

"I want you to kiss me again," I say without thinking. Always without thinking. Perhaps it's only when I don't think that I say what I really mean.

He traces my hairline with his fingers, following my jaw until he holds my face in his hands, and kisses me again, as if drinking me in. But this kiss is different from the first. It has no melody, just percussion.

I listen to his breath, to his heart. I listen to the words he doesn't say. The three words he said before.

And I believe him.

56

SPRING COMES IN ON A COLD NORTH WIND, FLUTTERING THE sprouts of new leaves while the heads of daffodils plunge beneath it. Narcissus bowing before his own reflection.

Thomas is kept even busier. I see him less, now that I want to see him more. And the king . . . keeps watching.

I finally work up the courage to visit my sister. To apologize, no matter what Thomas told me. To tell her . . . what? That nothing happened? Nothing has. But I know that doesn't mean it never will.

I make my way past the courtiers preening in the new sunlight, their feathers and silks bannering in the wind. Pick my way through the crowded lodgings to her door. Take a deep breath. Square my shoulders, as Father taught. And enter.

"Nan!"

Mary doesn't sound angry. If anything, she sounds delighted. She jumps up and holds me at arm's length.

"Nan, are you all right?"

Mary loops her arm through mine and leans close. I can smell her hair—the lavender she uses to rinse it. Her cheeks are slightly flushed, and the skin of her hand is so smooth.

"Do you love him?" I blurt.

She doesn't have to ask who.

"Yes and no. I love Catherine more than anything. More than I ever imagined was possible. So I love whoever gave her to me."

Mary doesn't know who Catherine's father is. It might not be the king. And perhaps, just perhaps, the king's waning interest will not break Mary's heart. I succor myself with that thought, but it's like trying to fill an empty stomach with cherry comfits.

"You look pale, Nan. Like you've seen a ghost."

"I'm fine."

She pulls me through the door and sits me down by the fire. She moves so smoothly. She is so serene.

"Will you play?" she asks. My lute—Thomas's lute—is in the corner.

"I don't think so."

"You're not my Nan." Mary smiles gently. "Give up an opportunity to play? What have you done with my sister?"

She no longer knows me. She knows nothing of what is happening at court. My sister inhabits her own world, and no one can puncture the bubble of it and intrude.

"I'm *nobody's* Nan," I say, and pinch my lip between my teeth to prevent the tears that threaten. "I belong to no one, Mary."

"You will marry soon enough," she soothes, still not understanding. "The Butler marriage would never have made you happy. Shall I ask Father to find someone for you?" She pauses. "Or perhaps the king?"

She says this in a small voice, unsure.

"I think you have asked enough favors of the king."

"Or perhaps given too many."

"I didn't say that, Mary." I stop short of actually asking for forgiveness.

"No, you didn't have to."

"I'm not bemoaning the lack of a husband. I want to belong to myself."

"You do already. Don't you see, Nan? That's why he wants to possess you."

Men only want what they can't have.

Mary knows. We hold the moment, caught tight in the stillness at the center of a storm. I am incapable of apology. And she is incapable of censure. Neither of us is willing to talk about it openly.

"I wish I were more like you." She says it so simply. A statement of fact.

"No one wants to be like me. At least, no one should." Lost. Alone. Hunted.

Broken.

"No, you're wrong, Nan," Mary says softly. "You're strong. You're so sure. You know what you want, and you're not afraid to make it happen. You don't let anyone walk on you or take anything from you."

But I do. I did. Percy took from me.

And Thomas could take everything.

Her eyes slide away from mine. Mary has always had what I wanted. Beauty. Charm. Kindness. The king.

"I'm afraid."

I don't realize the words have come from me until I see Mary's reaction to them. Her eyes widen, and she presses her lips together.

"You?" she asks. "Nan, what are you afraid of?"

This.

I'm afraid I was wrong. Wrong about Mary, who never wanted to be better than anyone else; she just wanted to be herself. Never meant to mother me, just wanted to be a mother. Wrong about Jane, because she never deserved my pity. Wrong about George, who maybe never was my friend, no matter how I remember it. Wrong about Thomas.

I'm afraid all the things I've said and done will hunt me down and haunt me. Because the thing I'm afraid of is the same thing I told the king would make me happy. The thing I've been pursuing through the forest of my own life.

"Love."

57

THREE DAYS BEFORE HIS WEDDING, GEORGE DISAPPEARS. JUST vanishes from the court.

Someone says he saw George on a horse. Someone else says George has taken a hawk and walked out over the hill behind Duke Humphrey's Tower. Another says George clambered aboard a dinghy and headed downstream to London.

Most likely to the stews.

That is the rumor the court believes.

Jane doesn't say a word, and her face betrays no emotion in public.

But when she finally comes to talk to me—trapping me in our little corner of the maids' chamber—all of her fear and love and desperation show.

"Where is he?" she demands.

"I don't know."

I don't need to make it worse.

"Why isn't he here?"

She wrings her hands, and I see that every fingertip is bitten to the quick, the cuticles ragged, one finger freely bleeding.

"I don't know," I say again, and reach out to put a hand over hers in an effort to still them, but she flinches away from me.

"Of *course* you know!" she screeches. "The two of you are like *this*." She shows me two fingers intertwined, a dark scab standing out against the white of her twisted knuckle.

"I tried to tell you," I say. "George and I are not that close."

"Everyone at court knows that's not true. That you and George have been inseparable since birth."

I struggle not to roll my eyes.

"Except for the seven years I spent in France."

"He *pined* for you, Anne. He told me so himself." She says this with such intensity I have to believe her. I don't doubt that Jane remembers with absolute clarity every word she has ever heard George utter.

"What else did he tell you?"

"That he stole apples from the orchard for you when you had a cold."

He did. And ate half of them himself.

"He said he taught you your first word in Latin."

"Shame it was a word that earned me punishment"—the dinnertime disappointment from Father.

Jane stops trembling. Sits down on the bed. Gazes out the far window at the clouds scudding across the sky.

"I thought if I got close to you, I'd get close to him. I thought you'd help me win him."

I feel her confession like a punch in the chest. It knocks me back. The edge of the next bed catches me behind my knees and I collapse onto it.

"You lied to me." Like Wyatt. Like George. Like Father.

I'm a fool.

Jane hangs her head, letting it nod twice.

"I thought you were my friend," I whisper. Feeble. "You fought for me. With James Butler."

She turns to me, her eyes glazed and slightly manic.

"It wasn't you," she says. "He said . . ."

She hesitates as if what she has to say is painful to her.

"He said George was in your bedchamber. He implied . . ."

Oh, God. She was defending George. Not me. I got it all wrong from the beginning. I got everything wrong.

I stumble to my feet. I have to get out.

"Anne." She reaches for me, grabs my hand in hers. I try to shake her off, but her grip is like a vise. I pull again, yank, ready to scream.

"Stop!" she cries. "Wait! That's the day it all changed!"

I stop. My arms drop to my sides. I don't look at her.

"I have loved your brother since the moment I set foot in this court."

I see her hands from the corner of my eye, the nails of the left tearing the skin of the right.

"But the best thing that love brought me is you, Anne. You *are* my friend. It was I who had all the wrong reasons. After what the duchess did to me, perhaps I didn't know what friendship was."

She pauses.

"Butler said those things. And I hated him. I thought it was for George. But then I hurt you. And I couldn't bear it. I realized I . . . I loved you, too. That made me want George even more, so you could be my sister."

Silence envelops us, gently loosening the iron bands around my heart.

"You know, before I told my father about George, he was talking about marrying me to someone else. Some old, fat man with bad breath and a worse temper. Someone who isn't even at court."

"Really?" I ask. "You didn't tell me."

"You didn't give me a chance! You started saying all those bad things about George, trying to make me hate him. But I couldn't face the alternative. I was the one who mentioned George to my father. I was the one who suggested it. Before he could promise me to . . . to . . ." She shudders.

"You changed your own destiny."

"I'm sorry." She winces and puts a finger in her mouth.

I unwind the string of pearls from around my neck and place it over her head. I take her hand and put it to her throat, to feel the rolling beads. They clack gently like the distant chatter of gossips.

"Whenever you want to bite your nails," I tell her. "Whenever you want to hurt yourself, hold on to these. Like rosary beads. Listen to their music, Jane, and let it calm you."

"I can't take these," Jane says. She strokes them with the ragged fingers of one hand. The other hand is still, for once.

"Yes, you can." I press my hand again onto hers. "George will come back. He'll come back to court. He'll come back to you. And then you'll be a Boleyn, and the Boleyns always stick together."

She hugs me.

"I'll be a good Boleyn, Anne."

"I know you will." I hug her back. "Better than the rest of us."

"When I first loved him, Anne, I thought it would just be another infatuation, like all the others that go on here. Something that might be passed along as gossip and then just disappear. Like yours with the king or Norris or Thomas Wyatt."

I flinch at the mention of his name.

Jane stops her soliloquy to study me. And I remember what George once said about her. That she sees everything.

"You love him," she says slowly. "Thomas Wyatt."

I don't have to tell her it's true. She knows.

58

It's not unusual for the king to attend the wedding of one of his courtiers. George is a gentleman of the Privy Chamber, and Father is treasurer of the household.

But I don't believe the king is here for George, or for Father.

I believe he is here to see me.

And so is Thomas.

My emotions pull taut between them, twanging every time either one moves or speaks. I feel visible, exposed. And thoroughly grateful when Jane appears.

She is elegant in pale pink trimmed with coiled crimson satin. Her father is fluffed and preening in the presence of the king. Mine is stuffed with pride. Mary is beside him, quiet, humbled.

George arrives five minutes late. His hair is a mussy nest of spikes and whorls. He looks younger than his twenty years, like a child just out of bed, being dragged unwilling to church.

Jane is smooth and poised, every hair in place. Her smile, clear and bright, breaks my heart. She's marrying the man she loves.

The wedding party moves on to a lavish banquet—Father

for once not caring about the expense, or trying to appear not to care. There is venison and brawn, pigeon and sparrow, lamb and rabbit. The bridecake is demolished and devoured. I linger over strawberries soaked in wine.

I feel Thomas circling. But he doesn't approach.

When everyone has had their fill and the men begin to argue over the bones, the king orders the tables to be taken away and requests music.

The lutenist tunes his instrument, humming over the strings. He wears an expression of detached arrogance. I realize, with a shock, that it's Mark Smeaton, from Wolsey's household. The king has poached him—or his voice has finally changed.

Smeaton knows he's good. He knows he can do this. He feels superior. He smiles, gazes about the room to see who is watching, doesn't watch his own fingers.

And strums.

The noise that vibrates through the room is not the sound he expected. It is discordant and jarring, his fingering all wrong. The look on his face is priceless.

I giggle to myself and then stop. Because the king is looking at me. He is laughing, too. The room is small. He is so very close.

Smeaton recovers himself and dives into a complicated melody that the rest of the musicians do their best to follow. The king and I stare at each other as the music rains down and encapsulates us.

Until Mary brushes by me when she leaves the room, and the king follows her with his eyes. The bubble bursts and I don't look at him again.

The party goes on until nearly dawn, the musicians almost falling asleep over their instruments. The king regales everyone with war stories; my father competes with tales of his diplomatic missions.

George stays awake and away from his chambers, something noticed by all but remarked on by none, until the musicians finally stop.

"I think it's time to bed the bride and groom!" Norris cries.

"One more drink." George's words are nearly unintelligible already. Jane flushes hot by the fireside, one hand gripping the pearls at her throat.

"Nothing more to drink!" Norris declares. "We will carry you bodily to your chamber and listen through the curtains!"

"And don't forget we will check the sheets in the morning," Bryan chimes in.

"It's already morning," George mutters, but allows himself to be removed from his wine and pulled into a mob of backslapping and bawdy remarks.

Jane hides behind her veil and I catch her just before she peels the healing skin from her index finger. I squeeze her hand silently and she squeezes back before she allows herself to be swept through the door by the rowdy throng.

"Come with me." Thomas grabs my hand amid the chaos. He's pulling me back toward the middle court. Away. I glance at the ebb of activity in the room. The king is looking elsewhere.

We cross the court quickly, the May rain saturating us, the castle walls, the chapel and chimneys. Turning the world into a long, wet wash all the way to the Thames.

Thomas plucks at my sleeve and melts into the shadows of a stairwell. I follow him silently, my slippers making no sound on the stone steps.

The clouds hide the moon, and the sun is too afraid to rise.

I kiss him before he speaks. I want to shut it all out. Jane and George. My father. Mary. The rain. The king. I stand on my toes to reach him and twine my fingers in his hair. He tries to hold me back at first. He wants so badly to say what he thinks he needs to say. I silence him with my mouth, steal the words from his tongue.

For a moment, we are lost. His fingers move over the pins and stays in my hood, pulling off the black velvet coronet, dropping the snood to the ground behind me. He tugs my hair from its plait and it falls to my waist. He lifts it with both hands and buries his face in it.

"It smells just like you." He turns to me, and a shy look steals through his expression. "You must think I'm perverted."

"No," I say quickly, thinking again of how Percy treated my hair as a nuisance. And me, too, in the end. "No, it's quite charming."

"Quite charming," he mocks.

"Endearing."

"Would we say endearing?" he asks. "Try enchanting."

Thomas smiles wickedly and pushes me back up against the wall, one arm cradling my neck from the rough, cold brick, the other wrapped tight around my waist. He breathes into my ear.

"Tell me I'm enchanting."

"You're resplendent," I tell him. "Heroic. Majestic."

I tilt my chin for a kiss that doesn't come.

"Ah. There you're wrong, my dear." He takes a step away.

I am unmoored.

"Majestic I am not. And I cannot compete with it, either."

His expression begs me to disagree.

"There's no need to compete."

"Everything at this court is a competition. Especially with the king. Did you think the Castle of Loyalty was just a game?"

Youth versus experience.

Thomas against the king.

He is so far away from me. Watching me. Gauging me. What can I say? My tongue cannot form the three words he needs to hear. No matter how strongly I feel them.

"I am not a prize, Thomas."

"Don't I know it." The tease has a bitter aftertaste. "You are a gamble, Anne Boleyn. One that I won't risk losing."

His words rankle and I move away. Just a little.

"We both know which Boleyn girl he prefers," I argue, the words dusty in my throat.

"We both know that interest is fading." Thomas reaches out a tentative hand to stroke my hair. "I also think he can't help himself."

"From what?"

"From falling in love with you."

382

The moment freezes, and I with it.

"I don't think the king falls in love," I say finally, awash in the guilty hope that I'm wrong.

"I think he falls in love every day," Thomas replies. "And that's what I'm worried about."

59

THE RAIN HAS DAMPENED THE CHANCE OF ANY SPORT. No tilting, for the mud in the yard is as thick as paste. No hunting, for the season has yet to start. A move to Windsor is discussed for the use of the opulent tennis court alone. As it is, here in Greenwich, the men are irritable and peevish, as if itchy in their own skins.

When it stops raining, I search out Jane and drag her to the orchard with me.

"My hem will get wet," she moans.

"But no one will be able to hear us. And I want to hear everything."

Jane burns red. I can feel the heat from her face.

"Don't be disgusting, Anne. He's your brother." The pearls click beneath her fingers.

"I only meant . . ." I have no explanation. "Are you happy?"

"He doesn't love me."

She says it simply and with no trace of emotion.

"Maybe love can be learned."

A shout from the tiltyard gallery interrupts Jane's response.

"George," she breathes. Plucks at my sleeve, drawing me to the watching towers.

The men have converted the gallery into a bowling alley. A gaggle of them hover at one end, shaking hands and drinking wine. And betting. I am not surprised to see George amongst them.

At the other end of the improvised rink, nearest to us, are the players. The king. And Thomas Wyatt. I step back into the shadows of the tower and pull Jane with me.

They have obviously already played several ends, because the men betting are getting louder and more belligerent. The game must be close.

They did not expect an audience. Thomas has removed his cap and, as I watch, the king sheds his doublet.

"I really must have an alley built here at Greenwich," the king says, stretching, the fabric of his shirt tight across his shoulders. "This gallery is far too small."

"And a tennis court!" Henry Norris calls.

"Perhaps I will." The king laughs. "And a new mews for the falcons while I'm at it. Come, Wyatt. Let me best you."

A fleeting frown crosses Thomas's face, but it vanishes before he clasps the king's hand. He's playing the game. The jack is thrown, going a fair distance down the rink, coming to rest almost at center. The men cheer and drink and bet again.

The king rolls first, and his shot goes wide. He toes the ground in disapproval and turns away—clenching and unclenching his fists. Thomas rubs his hand over his mouth and chin to hide a smile.

I want to grab his hand and drag him away somewhere. Silly

men. Silly competitions. The betting continues, heating up. George is handling the book. Of course.

Thomas takes his shot, which comes much closer to the jack, the bias of the wood making it curve out and then in again in an elegant arc, coming to rest not two feet from the jack.

There is silence. Then a rattle from the onlookers, the exchange of coins.

This goes on until both men have thrown all four woods, a cluster of bowls at the far end, crouched menacingly around the little jack.

"The king's shot is closest!" shouts Norris from the boundary. Another cheer. More drinking. The clink of coins as the winnings are counted.

The king gives a little nod. He reaches for Thomas's hand.

Then Bryan shouts, "I beg to differ, Norris, but Wyatt's first shot lies closer."

Silence.

The king and Thomas exchange a look, and without speaking—like a dance, choreographed—they turn together to stride down to the end of the gallery. I cannot hear their banter, but I see a strange look on Thomas's face. His normal complacency is missing. The casual, assured courtliness has been replaced by rivalry.

They stand for a moment over the jack, the only sound the hiss of rain as it starts up again. The king shines gold, his hair fiery in the dim light. Thomas rubs his hand across the back of his neck, twining in the curls of hair there, his apple-green sleeves fluttering.

He looks up, shoulders set for a challenge.

"I believe Bryan is right, Your Majesty," he says. "Mine is closer."

Time stops.

Everything is a competition at this court, Thomas said. *Especially with the king.*

But the game keeps changing.

The king smiles. A heart-stopping, mischievous smile.

He lifts his right hand, glittering with rings, his eyes never leaving Thomas's face. He points to the cluster of bowls using his smallest finger.

"I tell you, Wyatt," he says. "I am closer than you think."

On his finger is a ring. My ring. One I have obviously worn throughout my time at court. The one he kissed so extravagantly when we danced after the Castle of Loyalty tournament. The one he took from me as "payment" for getting Jane her dowry.

He caresses it. To make his point.

I feel sick. I reach a hand behind me to steady myself on the wall and take a step farther into the shadows. I need to escape.

Thomas stares at the ring for half a moment. Then he straightens, looks the king directly in the eye.

With his right hand, he reaches down inside his blue-green doublet and extracts a worn ribbon.

"If you will allow me, Your Majesty, I should like to measure it," he says; his words carry over the entire rink, where all have frozen silent.

Thomas stretches the ribbon out between the king's bowl and the jack. Then between the jack and his own.

His wood is indeed closer.

With a carefully timed flourish, he opens his hand and something heavy drops to the end of the ribbon and sways there. A golden *A*, a teardrop pearl flashing beneath it.

"I believe that it is mine." Thomas sits back on his heels and flashes a look of triumph at the king. I could kill him.

The king approaches him. There is no sound but the rain. The bettors huddle in the corner as if trying to render themselves invisible.

"It may be so." In the silence the king's voice sounds loud—violent—though he speaks quietly. "Perhaps I am deceived."

He stands facing Thomas, only inches away. The king is taller, broader. Thomas, with his slight build, appears as a willow before an oak.

The king nudges the jack out of place and picks it up to hold between them.

"Perhaps," the king says, "the call is not ours to make."

He spins and strides back the length of the gallery, calling out, "No more games."

He sweeps into the rain-ravaged tiltyard, followed by Norris. The other men swiftly exchange their coins, no longer up for argument, and hasten after their monarch. Except for George, who spreads the coins in his palm, his face conflicted between a frown and a grin.

Thomas watches them go, and then kicks the king's wood, sending it careening after them.

60

I PULL JANE BEHIND ME INTO THE GALLERY, PICKING UP THE still rolling bowl along the way. I hurl it at Thomas, but it is too heavy for me and thunders to the floor. Thomas turns, his smile flickering when he sees me.

"Why did you do that?" I shout.

"Did you see? Fun, wasn't it?" Thomas pauses. "I won."

"It was a stupid, foolish, childish competition! I am not something to be won, Thomas Wyatt. I am not a prize. An object. A possession."

"Now who's being foolish?" Thomas cocks his head, feigning blamelessness. "Nothing was said about you, Anne. It was just a game."

"Nothing is just a game in this court."

George pushes himself between us, and Jane takes a step back. George ignores her and hands Thomas a goblet of wine.

"It looks like I owe you five pounds, Wyatt."

Thomas flicks a glance at me.

"You owe him nothing, George," I say.

"But he did it, Anne. He's made you the queen of the court." George pauses. "Figuratively speaking, of course. Unless circumstances change."

"I don't want your money, Boleyn." Thomas looks at me now. Steadily. "The bet was forfeit a long time ago."

"Excellent news, my friend, because I don't have it." George laughs and pockets his coins with a clatter. "Though it appears my luck may be changing."

"Always looking to your own advantage, George, aren't you?" I bite across his laughter. "Always looking to sell your sisters to the highest bidder." Bought. Sold. Won. Lost. A prize. A jewel. A possession.

"When my sisters attract the highest bidder of all," George crows, dancing around me, "I don't see why not. I don't know how you did it, Wyatt, but you did. You are definitely my hero.

"And you, Anne, you're the rising star. The flying falcon. I wouldn't have thought it possible three years ago, but you've gone higher than any of us would ever have dreamed. You just need to carry the rest of us with you."

He turns back to Thomas. "Right, Wyatt? Surely there's something you want from my sister. You can't let all your hard work go to waste."

Thomas swallows visibly. George is too caught up in his own tide to notice or care that no one else is speaking.

"I need you to work your witchy magic, Anne," he says. "Cardinal Wolsey is planning to purge the king's chambers of anyone unnecessary or undesirable. Heads will roll. And there's a rumor afoot that I've been pilfering the king's wine. I need you, dear sister"—he pokes a bony finger at the center of my stomacher—"to convince our potentate that I am indispensable."

A look of desperation crosses his face at my lack of an answer, and he hurls a genial arm around my shoulder.

"I cannot be thrown from court, Anne. I'm afraid it would kill me."

"No, George," I say quietly. "Your words and the wine will be what kill you."

George loses his bonhomie, his handsome face hard as stone.

"So you just throw me to the wolves, now, is that it? You've surpassed us all, and the rest of us can hang? You've got what you wanted: the king's dick in your pocket. No one else matters."

Thomas coughs and extends an arm to Jane.

"Come, Mistress Par—Boleyn. Let us leave these siblings to their rivalry."

"No." George seizes Jane's wrist. "Stay. You should know what we're really like."

"George—" Jane starts to say, but he silences her with a glance.

"You always wanted everything, Anne. Everything I had. You had to do everything I did."

"I just wanted to be like you!"

"You just wanted to be better than me. You had to be the best. The best at French. Get the best apple. Have the highest reach. And you let me fall and catch all of Father's wrath."

I let him vent and spit. He cannot rouse me. Not like when we were young, and two words would raise my fists to him.

"You know what he said?" George leans in, a gobbet of

spittle on his lips. "The day you broke your finger getting that exasperating apple? He said, 'Your sister is clever and brave, George. More than you'll ever be.'"

"Father said lots of things."

"He *said*," George shouts over me. "He said, 'I wish she was my boy. I wish Anne was my son. I would give her everything. You don't deserve it.'"

George's face is stripped of guile, excoriated, every raw thought and pulsing emotion bleeding and sore.

"But you came back from France and you were nothing. Nothing you did was right. So I made Wyatt here take you on."

I glance once at Thomas, who is watching George with bleak intensity. I level my gaze at my brother.

"Hoping he'd tarnish me beyond redemption."

George chokes and Jane reaches for him, but doesn't touch him. Bites her lip. The rattle of the pearls beneath her fingers is the only sound she makes.

"Hoping he'd win," George whispers.

"Father never . . . " I start, but can't finish.

"He never cared about Mary and me. Just you. He loved only you, his clever, impish princess."

"He didn't love me—"

"He did!" George shouts again, and steps closer, ready to strike. Thomas tries to pull him back, but George yanks away from him. "It was you he loved. I was the failure. The disappointment. When you left, he was only cold. Dead."

"He never loved me!" I scream, everything in me finally tearing loose. "He *left* me!"

George is silent. Stunned.

"He took me. Put me on that horrible little boat that shuddered at the hint of a wave. Took me to that gaudy, glittering Habsburg tomb in the Low Countries. A child, George. A child beneath the weight of all that gilt."

I gasp. My words squeeze the breath from me.

"When he took me to meet the duchess, I grabbed his hand and said, 'I love you, Da.' And do you know what he did? He shook me off. Wiped his hand on his doublet, the look on his face like I'd handed him excrement. He said, 'You're sweating, Anne. It's unbecoming.' He left me there."

My gaze briefly meets Thomas's.

"It's the last time I said those words. And now they choke me. Because nothing I did, none of the letters I wrote or the songs I sang or my perfect bloody French, convinced him to bring me home. To love me back. Maybe if I'd failed at my lessons like you did, maybe if I'd fucked King François and half the French court like Mary, maybe then he would have brought me home. Maybe then I would have been more than nothing. But no, my reward was just more punishment."

The world breathes around us, but George and I are no longer breathing. It's the silent moment before armies charge. Or declare a truce.

George takes a deep breath. Squares his shoulders. "You're a Boleyn, Anne. There's no escaping it."

The specter of his cockeyed grin lodges in his expression.

"And the Boleyns always stick together," I say. "There's no escaping that, either."

I want to be like we used to be, when love was simple. When we would sit back to back in the apple orchard, before I climbed to the highest branch to pick the best one. While George sat with the pile in his lap, ready to consume the lot, even if it made him sick. I want to say to him now, *Slow down. Not so much.* I want to make him stop.

"You don't need me to keep you here, George. The only way to stop the rumor that you steal the king's wine is to stop drinking."

"It makes my life tolerable."

I feel more than see Jane stiffen, and reach for her hand, cold and still ragged. George looks from me to Jane and back again, the realization of what he's said etched across his face.

"There is more to life than wine, George. It will be your undoing."

"No, Anne." He sighs. "You will be my undoing."

He takes Jane's hand from me and I see him squeeze it.

It is not a truce. But at least it is not a war.

61

I look past Thomas to where the rain slithers from the roof tiles and into the deep, wet mud of the tiltyard. George has left, Jane following. I don't know if they'll find a middle ground in their marriage, a compromise between love and ambivalence. I don't know how Jane can face being a Boleyn after what she saw today.

I'm waiting. For Thomas to say something. Do something. Make it right. Kiss me. But he just stares at the bowl—his wood, the one that was closest—as he rolls it in circles beneath his foot.

"I didn't mean to antagonize him," he says.

"Yes, you did."

"You're right, I did."

He isn't joking. The fierceness in his eyes punctures me.

"He has your ring."

"I didn't give it freely."

"He's married, Anne."

I almost laugh.

"So are you."

He looks away, up the steep hill to Duke Humphrey's Tower. He gasps. And when I look, there, in the distant shadows, stands a deer, shrouded in a curtain of rain. It is poised on the impossible points of its narrow legs, eyes wide and dark, still bearing the dappled marks of its youth.

"One of the king's," he murmurs. "Makes me hope I never see it in the chase."

And the deer, as if hearing him, picks its way into the darkness, disappearing like a ghost.

"You're not going to apologize, are you?" I ask him.

"Should I?" He turns to me, his expression an open challenge. "For what?" He pauses. "And to whom?"

"*To me*. For . . ." Confusing me with a thing to be won. For not wanting a doll, but making me into one. "For being married."

Thomas folds himself around me like the wings of a falcon, pressing me into him. I feel the laughter in his chest.

"I can't make things any different from the way they are," he says. "All I can do is love you."

And he kisses me with the deep desperation of a drowning man. This kiss is a song of longing. A ballad that doesn't end well.

I cling to him, digging my fingers into the back of his neck, suddenly, acutely jealous of any girl who has had the chance to know him. To touch his skin. To taste it. Hating his wife, and any future mistress.

"I love you," I whisper into his mouth and into his hair when he kisses my throat.

I cannot say it loud enough for him to hear.

62

THE KING MOVES TO WESTMINSTER AND ON TO WINDSOR, completely caught up in politics and hunting, leaving the queen and her quiet life in Greenwich. He takes a group of favorites with him. And Thomas. He will not leave Thomas behind.

I swallow my guilty conscience and go to see Mary.

Three ladies stand by the door of Mary's private room, huddled like witches over a cauldron.

This does not bode well. My steps slow, and I dread whatever is in that room.

I cough. Once. Then again, louder. The ladies look up and scuttle away like cockroaches in a sudden light, leaving me alone at the door. I knock.

"Mary?"

The only response is a cross between a sob and a moan.

And a splash.

I curse under my breath. All those vexing women flocking to Mary but refusing her any help or solace whatsoever. I curse again.

Another splash. A sudden fear that she might be drowning herself propels me through the door.

The heavy velvet curtains are drawn. The only light comes

through the door. This room is shrouded in darkness and smoke from a single candle. The bed is rumpled, the counterpane flung onto the rush-mat floor.

In the far corner, away from any light, sits a little bath on a stool. Next to it, completely naked, sits my sister.

She has taken a piece of rough linen and is scraping at her body with long, deliberate strokes. The skin of her arms and shoulders and breasts and belly glow red in the dim light.

"Mary?"

She attacks her legs, using both hands to rub the linen down her thigh, the muscles in her shoulders knotting beneath the skin, her head bowed, the hair falling around her face in wet, curling curtains.

I creep up behind her, afraid. She gives no indication that she sees or hears me. She concentrates fully on the long, red marks on her skin.

"Stop."

I put a hand on her shoulder, and she twitches me off. Moves to the other thigh. Determined, purposeful strokes down the thin, sensitive skin on the inside.

"Mary, you'll hurt yourself."

"You think I'm not already hurt?" She rounds on me. A twist of hair is stuck to her cheek, filtering over her upper lip and into her mouth.

"Mary," I say, and a twinge of panic cuts me off. Silence descends until I finally regain my voice.

"What happened?"

"I happened, Nan. Stupid, lazy, selfish me. Ignorant girl

who can't tell the difference between love and sex. Foolishly imagining that if I sell myself, I'll be worth having."

"Mary, you're not—"

"I am. I'm a whore. Everyone says it. You've said it."

"No, Mary!"

But I did. And the guilt of it sends me to my knees. She looks down on me while continuing to ravage her raw skin.

"Never be a mistress, Nan. A mistress is no one. Dispensable. Trash. Dirty."

"Mary, stop!"

"I can't get him off me!" she cries, scraping again at her arms, tears churning down her face. "I can't get rid of him! I can't make him go away."

"Who?" I whisper, knowing the answer.

"The king. My lover."

"But I thought you wanted . . ."

"That's what everyone thought. Because I was getting what everyone else wanted. Father wanted prestige and position for the family. He got that. George wanted a place at court and manor holdings and money. He got those. Even my husband wanted a quiet life, the ability to make a difference in the Privy Chamber, and money. It all comes down to money. And that's what makes me a whore. Selling sex for money and preferment."

I'm shocked by the bitterness in Mary's words. Mary, who has never done anything but agree and look pretty.

"But the king loves you."

Mary laughs. A harsh sound, like gulls crying.

"He never loved me. He doesn't even love his wife anymore."

"He was with you for three years."

She stops, finally. Looks at me. Rests her hands with the twisted and ruined piece of linen on her knees.

"Three years? You speak as if that's a lifetime."

"It's as long as I've been in England," I say. It feels like a lifetime.

"It hardly matters now. He's found someone else."

We stare at each other for a long, slow stretch of time. We have to talk about it now.

"I thought he was just teasing," I finally manage to whisper, knowing it's a lie, after what I saw in the tiltyard gallery.

"That's how it starts."

"I didn't mean for it to happen." Not a lie. "I didn't mean to hurt you. I didn't mean to hurt anyone."

Mary sighs. She picks up the counterpane from the floor and wraps herself in it tightly, despite the heat.

"I know." She sounds weary.

She doesn't look at me. Then she sighs again.

"He was the one who had you recalled, Nan. From Hever."

"The king wanted me back at court?" I can scarcely wrap my mind around it.

"He said he missed your clever repartee." I wonder if Mary makes her voice sound deliberately dull with this sentence. Still she doesn't look at me. She's picking at the threads of her counterpane.

"He missed . . . talking to me?"

"I don't think there are many women who talk to him like you do. I mean, we never talked. For what it's worth, Nan,

I think he likes you. Intellectually. Not just . . . physically."

And it feels like a betrayal to Thomas, but her words send a little thrill through me. This man, this unattainable, golden god of a man, is actually interested in me. Anne Boleyn. In my words.

"Is he . . ." I don't want to ask. I don't want to cause Mary any more pain. But I have to. "Is he the man you said was interested? The one who is afraid of me?"

Mary barks a little laugh. "The king is afraid of no one, Nan."

"Oh."

"No." Mary turns and finally looks at me. "That was Thomas Wyatt."

I sink the rest of the way to the floor, and my skirts belly out around me. Mary rests a hand on my head and strokes my hair. I lower my head onto the folds of velvet covering her.

"I've made such a mess, Mary. It's all such a mess."

Again a little sad bark. "Not as much as I have, Nan."

I tilt my head and look at her. "But now your life can go back to normal."

"Normal? My life has never been normal, Nan. For the past three years, it's like I've been married to two men. Or not really married at all. I don't know my husband. I don't know the father of my child."

"Catherine is well taken care of. You love her. That's what matters."

"I'm having another," she whispers.

I sit farther back.

"Is it his?"

"Wouldn't that be what Father and George want?" she asks. "Wouldn't that just be the making of the Boleyn family? A royal son?"

"Do you know?"

My own treacherous thoughts race to calculate when the king first expressed interest in me. And my calculations tell me an unsavory truth.

"No, Nan. I don't know. I don't remember."

Her voice is hollow, completely empty of emotion. But I think maybe she does know. She just isn't going to say.

"It would be the making of William, too," she says quietly. "He's so far into debt, he can't even see the surface. Right now, it's only me who is keeping us in clothes and candles." She pats my knee. "And I won't be for long."

"I won't let it happen to me, Mary. I won't be his mistress. I won't be easily discarded."

"Don't be anyone's mistress, Nan." She looks at me sadly, and I know what she's saying. *Not even Thomas Wyatt's.*

"Make sure you know what you want," she finishes. "If anyone can achieve it, you will."

"What do *you* want, Mary?"

Her eyes are almost as red as her skin.

"You know, you're the first person to ask me that. Everyone else just thinks I'll do whatever is asked of me. I've spent my entire life being what everyone else wants. An object to be passed around."

"Do you know what you want?" I whisper.

"I want to be loved, Anne."

Mary finally uses my name. My real name. It sounds awkward and makes me strangely sad. She turns, and my arm drops from her shoulders.

"I want to be somebody to someone."

She pauses and gazes at the thin bead of light perched on the edge of the velvet curtain over the window.

"And I want everyone else to leave me alone."

63

THE RAIN TURNS TO SUNLIGHT AND THE SUN SITS UPON THE earth like a blacksmith's anvil, pounding everything to the consistency of iron. There doesn't seem to be a drop of moisture in the air, the sky gleams without a cloud, and even the grass begins to crumble beneath our feet.

The women shed their heavy velvets like snakeskins, opting for silks and damasks, but we still sweat through the light-colored fabrics, chemise, petticoat, kirtle, bodice, gown, and sleeves weighing us down.

I receive a summons.

To see my father.

I try to move serenely through the donjon and down the stairs into the hall. The palace is stiflingly hot and the galleries are haunted by the smell from the river, suffocating and steamy. I may never complain about the rain again.

The palace is quiet and uncrowded, so Father has claimed a double room, with bed, closet, and outer chamber—the latter perfect for meeting with recalcitrant children.

I curtsy when I enter, reminding myself of Thomas's words. *I am clever. I am more. I am loved.*

The last thought helps me smile as I rise to look at him.

"Daughter."

"Father."

"You come to me at a very busy time. Very busy. I suppose you want money. What do you need, girl?"

With that one word—*girl*—he used to be able to render me small and useless. But I am worth more than that now.

"Father, you summoned me."

I no longer want to control my verbal flux. I want to beat him with it.

Father glares at me from under the ridge of his brow, barely taking the time to look up from his correspondence.

"If that's the way you want to play this, Anne, that's the way we'll play. I know what's going on. I know about your activities."

"From George?"

"From everyone."

The silence grows and fills the room.

"Speak!" he barks. "I have other things to worry about. The king is quarrelsome and petulant about the money I'm to collect for his war. Your brother is making a name for himself as a rake. Your sister is about as much use as a decrepit breeding mare. And you"—he points at me—"have yet to earn your keep."

I don't say, *One day you will have to earn yours*. I don't say, *One day you will be a decrepit old warhorse*. I hold my tongue. One day I will say these things, and more. One day, my words will matter. Even to him.

"What say you?"

"Maybe you should have married me off when you could."

Father stops shuffling his papers. I have never spoken to him so directly. None of us has. He stands and walks slowly toward me, leonine. It takes everything I am not to run away.

"That would have cost me not only a dowry but also the earldom of Ormond. Don't be disingenuous, Anne. It doesn't suit you."

I press my lips together and stay silent. My father is playing with me. And I'm still learning the rules of the game.

"However, you have somehow managed to become the delight of the court. At least certain members of it."

"How do you know that?" I ask, my voice rising again and my color with it.

"So it's true, then."

He didn't know. It was a bluff. It's all a game to him. A risky one. One with high stakes. But a game nonetheless. My feelings, desires, and words count nothing to him.

"Your silence is encouraging," he breathes. I feel it on my face. The words smell like pewter. "Well done."

And then my father smiles at me. A smile I haven't seen since I was six years old and began speaking French better than George. A fist of pain clenches in my chest when I smile back. His minimal praise warms something long-concealed inside me. I still *want* to be the one he admires. The one he loves. The one to whom he wants to give everything.

And I hate myself for it.

He turns away abruptly, back to his desk. Lays just the fingers of his left hand upon it and looks over his shoulder to me.

"Did you know I'm to be made a viscount?"

I shake my head. Another elevation. My sister's efforts made him a baron.

"Congratulations."

"The king assures me it is because of my *continued* service to the crown."

I don't like the way he stresses the word *continued*. His first elevation to the peerage was a payment for the prostitution of his oldest daughter. Is this new one because of me? Is the quality of loyalty and service dependent on pandering?

"The Ormond earldom is also likely to be restored to its rightful inheritors."

The Boleyns. I begin to feel I am fetching a high price. I'm not sure I want that on my head.

"The king asked that you attend the creation ceremony at Bridewell next month," Father continues. "He would like to see you there.

"I have already ordered a new gown for you. Slashed with cloth of gold, as befits your status as the daughter of a viscount."

For my father, the deal is already done. Signed, sealed, and delivered in a cloth-of-gold gift wrap.

Father shuffles his papers and brings out a little wooden box, decorated with the Boleyn bull, edged in gilt.

"For you, Daughter," he says, and gives it to me. "Make me proud." He strokes the newly acquired ermine collar of his doublet.

My hands shake as I open it. It is lined with crimson velvet.

With one finger, he pushes aside the folds of velvet to reveal a string of pearls—much like the one I gave to Jane. But this

string carries a pendant. A gold *B* from which hang suspended three teardrop pearls.

"So you don't forget where you came from."

He walks back behind his desk, then turns to me with something almost like affection in his eyes.

"My clever girl."

I look at the box and the jewel it contains, the fresh gleam of the gold. For once, I'm the prized possession of Thomas Boleyn. But my rise in value is dependent on the depreciation of my siblings.

"I may be clever, Father," I tell him coldly, "but I am not yours."

I curtsy and leave him there. I will make my own choice, whether or not it elevates my father.

Still, I fasten the chain around my neck. Because the Boleyns will stick together. I can never forget where I came from, whatever choice I make.

Bridewell Palace
1525

64

THE COURT RECONVENES AT THE CONFLUENCE OF THE THAMES and the Fleet beneath the hottest sky I believe I've ever seen. It is white with the height of summer, not even a trace of blue above us. The many-paned windows glitter against the gaudy red and white of the palace façade and fill the rooms with the blanching bright light until the curtains are drawn and the entire palace is cast into manufactured gloom.

I escape to the little hemmed garden between the palace and the wall of Whitefriars. The heat of the sun has flattened everything, pounding the golden grass to the earth, the blossoms from the trees, and the river Fleet to dead, miasmic lifelessness. The sun feels close, heavy. My shadow doesn't appear before me. It's stuck tight to my slippers. I have no advance notice, no rearguard. Only me.

I see him before he sees me. He is a man with direction and purpose. With reason. With choice. I can do nothing but stare as he approaches.

I'm in love with the curls in his hair, with the way he walks. I thrill at the sound of his voice and the thought of how his body moves. I want to know him, touch him, see him, devour him.

As always, Thomas knows my mind as well as I do. He takes

the last three steps to me like a comet drawn to earth. I feel like I did the day Jane knocked the breath from me. He kisses me to the point of collapse, and then follows me down to the long grass at the base of a gnarled apple tree.

I can't let kisses make the choice for me.

"Listen to me." I open my eyes to the grass, the tree, the sky. To him.

"I am," he murmurs, trailing kisses down my throat. "Every move is music." He follows the neck of my bodice to where the skin is so sensitive I forget what I'm thinking.

Almost.

"Stop." I push him away and he sits back, irritable.

"I can't." I can't look at him when I say it. "You're married."

"I've left her."

"It doesn't change the fact."

"Don't be intractable, Anne," he says, desperation graveling his words. "There are plenty of men at court who are in love with women who aren't their wives. Look at my father. Look at your uncle Norfolk. Look at . . ."

I feel the tears burning and itchy against my lashes.

"Look at the king? That's the point, Thomas. I don't want to be Mary."

I don't want to end up weeping on the floor. I don't want to hate myself for my choices. Or my love.

"No, Anne," he says harshly. "Look at me. I'm not him. Don't you see? Can't you see me?"

I see him. I also see the future with him. Hiding away from the eyes and gossip of the court, from whispers. Being with

him. My body aches with wanting it. I see the months and years curl away like smoke, my words and possibilities with them. Because no one would speak to me. No one would listen. Not even my family.

"I don't want to be a mistress to anyone."

I feel a tear traverse the sunburned patch of my cheek. And Thomas catches it.

"The king wants to send me away," he says. "Away from England. He thinks I would make an excellent diplomat." He flashes a sardonic smile. "I think what he really wants is to get me away from you."

I stare straight ahead of me, unseeing. The weight of the B around my neck presses the breath from me.

"Apparently your father put the idea forward. And my father thought it was a good one." He sighs. "Good riddance, more like."

I force myself to choke out the words. "I'm sorry."

I'm sorry for being the craftsman of that path. I'm sorry I can't tell him I love him. I'm sorry I want so much. I'm sorry I'm me.

He pulls me to him so my head rests over his heart.

"Never apologize. I thought I taught you that long ago."

"But it's my fault. I'm the one who started it. I was so angry with you and I wanted you gone."

"You could do penance, then, and come with me," he says, stroking the path of my hair where it twists beneath my hood. "We could travel the world together. You've always wanted to leave."

"And you've never wanted to."

"It wouldn't matter if I were with you."

I lift my head to look at him. His face is so close to mine, I can see the chips of flint within the blue of his eyes.

"The life of a diplomat is no life for a girl," I say, repeating the words I heard so often from my father. But I know they are true. Long, grueling hours on the road. Rough, primitive sleeping conditions. War camps. The girls who travel with them are not mistresses, but worse.

"What would you do if I asked you to come to Allington? If I could hide you away there? Forever?"

"What are you asking me?"

"To give up the admiration of a thousand people for the love of just one."

We stare at each other for a breath. For a lifetime.

"What would you do, Anne? If I asked you for that?"

"I would . . ."

Love you.

"Would you go if I asked?"

Something about his question rings untrue. I sit up.

"If?" I can hardly speak through the constriction in my throat. Through the doubt and hope. "If you asked? Because right now you're not really asking me that, are you?"

Thomas stops. He is right next to me, but he is so far away.

"The castle belongs to my father."

"And he would never condone such a sordid use of it."

"It wouldn't be sordid to me, Anne. It would be sacred."

He tries to pull me back down, but I resist.

"And Elizabeth—*your wife*—lives there."

"I'll throw her out." He looks at me hopefully.

"Even you wouldn't be so heartless, Thomas Wyatt."

He turns his attention to the grass by his knee. I watch him slide his fingers along one blade at a time. The tips of his fingers are stained with ink and he wears no rings. He plays the lute with little talent and none of the feeling he expresses in his poetry. And yet those fingers make me sing beneath his touch.

"He asked about you and me."

I don't have to ask who *he* is. It is now as if this hum encapsulates the three of us. Like a bubble. Like a web. Emotions crash through me. Delight. Fear. Anticipation. Guilt.

"What did you tell him?"

I ask it casually.

"That we were neighbors. That we share a love of words." Thomas pulls up a strand of grass and examines it. "He laughed at that."

Tension coils like an iron band across his shoulders. He stares at the blade of grass, as if pulling his thoughts from it. He's holding something back.

"What else?"

"He asked . . . he asked about our relationship."

His words are almost lost in the shadows. His fingers pick at another blade of grass, peeling one at a time from the earth.

"And?"

He finally looks at me.

"I told him the truth."

"Which is?" Even I don't know the truth.

"That I'm in love with you."

I wonder if this is my reprieve. There will be no choice. It will be made for me. The king believes in love. The king will let me go. There is a certain amount of serenity in this thought.

"What did he say?"

"He laughed again."

Thomas returns to his study of the grass, wrenching larger clumps out by their roots. The sound is like the shredding of dreams.

"And then he asked if you felt the same."

I remember Jane's words: *Like music only plays when you're together. Like the air tastes of strawberries. Like one touch—one look— could send you whirling like a seed on the wind.*

"I told him I didn't know." Thomas examines the green that stains his fingers. "That you had never told me so."

"Oh."

Terror strikes hot in my chest. I'm going to have to say it. I wipe my hands on my skirts.

"I—"

"He asked," Thomas interrupts, "if I'd ever shared your bed."

My mouth goes dry.

"What did you say?"

"Yes."

"But that's a lie!"

I push him roughly and scramble to my feet. Push him again when he tries to get up. He cowers. Doesn't defend himself. His actions are defenseless. And he doesn't apologize.

"Why would you say that?"

416

"Because it's the truth; don't you remember?"

The night at Hever. Of course I remember. That night was magical. That night should have been left untarnished.

"Or were you too drunk? Always trying to outdo George."

The accusation flings me backward, and I stagger against the orchard wall.

"That night was mine," I gasp, feeling again that he's knocked the wind out of me. "It wasn't yours to tell."

Thomas sees the damage he has done. Recognizes it. He leaps up, all grace gone. He cannot land on his feet this time.

"I love you, Anne," he says desperately, reaching for me, but I stumble out of reach. "It makes me crazy. Insanely jealous.

"He made me kneel before him. Like a supplicant. We've been friends for ten years, and he made me do that. Treated me like no one. Like nothing. I wanted to hurt him. To stop him from wanting you. Because *I* want you. All of you. All for myself."

I feel like this should make me happy. He loves me that much. But I don't want him to have all of me. I don't want to give that to anyone.

And I don't want all of him. Not the jealousy. Not the possessiveness, the willingness to see me as a gamble, as a prize.

What was it the king said over that game of bowls?

"Perhaps the call is not yours to make."

Even beneath the radiant sky, his eyes have lost their airy lightness and have become dark and deep and vivid.

"So you don't want me," he murmurs.

I want him so badly I feel like glass on the verge of shattering.

"Do you want him, Anne?"

"I don't . . ."

But I do. Or I did. Contrition and despair stanch the flow of words. The time to answer expires, and we are silent.

"You don't what? Want him? Or you don't know?"

Whatever I say, I can't take back. Wherever the next moments take me, I will not be able to alter the course of my life once they are past.

"I don't want to be nobody," I say finally, "locked away in the country while you travel the world in service to your king. You say you want all of me, but how can I give up my family, my friends, my position at court? My self?"

The words come out without me thinking about them. As usual.

"Thomas, if I were to leave—this court, this life—don't you see? I would always wonder what would have happened if I stayed."

I can't abandon the life I was meant to live.

"I don't want to be forgotten."

"But you will not be forgotten, my dear. Remember?" A dash of his bravado returns. "I will make you famous in my poetry. Your name will go down through the ages, rolling from the tongues of strangers."

"I don't want to be remembered because of you, Thomas," I choke. "I want to be remembered because of me."

Thomas wraps his arms around me. Kisses my forehead. I can't move.

"For what it's worth, I don't think he believed me. I must

have looked like I was lying, because what I implied bore no relation to the truth of what I felt."

"Your grip on the truth is tenuous, Thomas."

I feel his smile on my temple. And we stand there in an embrace that isn't.

"He told me never to speak of it again," he says quietly. "He made me promise."

Thomas releases me and rubs his hands over his face. Stares up into the heat of the sky.

"Do you want to be chased all your life, Anne? To run always, trying to stay ahead of the pack?"

"No, Thomas, I don't want to run." I look him straight in the eye, daring my heart to break. "I want to lead."

He closes his eyes, his face twisted like someone recovering from a blow. When he opens them again, they are hollow.

"Then you win, Anne. You win the bet. I will not pursue you."

He stops. Swallows. "But I will follow you anywhere."

He takes my hand and turns it over. Strokes it open. I feel the kiss on my palm all the way up through my arm and into my heart.

Which snaps into ragged halves.

65

BRIDEWELL IS TO BE THE VENUE FOR THE CREATION CEREMONY in which my father will become a viscount. And Henry Fitzroy, the king's six-year-old illegitimate son, will become an earl and a duke in a single day. The men of the court simmer and sweat as some of them strive for elevation and others remain stagnant. It is like living in a stewpot.

The day before the ceremony, I seek out coolness and quiet, my lute newly strung. Instead of playing, I sit and stare at my hands on the strings. They are very pale, nails smooth and short. Calluses on the tips from the lute strings. A single ring. One crooked finger.

I think of Thomas's poem, the one he spoke when I played Atalanta. The riddle over my name—the same backward and forward or even split in two. Anna. I pluck two notes. An-na. Two halves. Incomplete.

An usher approaches me and bows.

"The king requests your company."

A personal request. From the king. For me. All the notes fly from me, my fingers like startled birds. I barely manage to control my tongue.

"I should love to see His Majesty."

"Good. Then he expects you at eight of the clock."

I stand, still and anticipatory in the quiet that follows.

Was that a request? I wonder. *Or an order?*

When I sit, I discover that I can no longer find the music within me.

As the hour approaches, an usher comes to escort me through the guard and presence chambers, the last of the sunlight slanting through the towering expanse of glass on the south wall, the gardens and the Thames splayed out below.

We pass through the closet and into the Privy Chamber, where King Henry stands, alone. The usher bows low, and I kneel into a curtsy.

"Leave us," the king says, and the usher beside me scuttles away. And I am entirely alone with the king. I wonder if he will keep me kneeling, ask the same questions he asked of Thomas.

I can feel his presence in the room, his restless energy. The inaudible hum as though from a constantly vibrating lute string.

"Rise, Mistress Boleyn." He breaks the silence. "There is wine, if you would like some."

I look up, surprised. The king is offering to serve me?

But no. Two glasses have already been poured. Every need anticipated.

"And strawberries."

A dish of them. Red and round and glittering like jewels.

"I saw how much you liked them at George's wedding."

He looks shy. Wanting to please.

"Thank you."

421

The color of the claret and strawberries reminds me of the dream I had months ago. A dream of red and blood and the inability to sing.

"No, thank you for answering my request. You didn't have to come."

"Didn't I?" I blurt the words, and stutter the next through my hand. "Your Majesty, my greatest fault is my inability to stop my thoughts from becoming spoken words."

The king laughs. He throws his head back, the wash of red-gold hair flashing against the last of the sun's rays. His wine sloshes in the goblet, sending drops scattering across the wooden floorboards like fallen beads.

"Then your greatest fault is one of the things about you that I find most charming." He cocks his head and squints at me a little. "But are you so used to following orders?"

"The men in my family expect subservience."

"I doubt you give it to them."

His gray eyes are childlike despite the fan of sun-worn creases just beginning to show around them.

"I believe," I begin, and look at him again. His posture invites intimacy. "I believe people should have the right to make their own choices. Even women."

"In life? Or in love?"

He studies me, waiting. We are talking around the very issue I want to avoid. I do want a choice. My choice. I just wish it were easier.

"Both."

"Did you choose young Lord Percy yourself?"

422

He asks this so conversationally. As if speaking to an acquaintance, a friend. Not to a subject. Not to the girl whose very choice was thwarted by the machinations of his own chief minister.

I nod. I chose Percy. More fool me.

"He would never have made you happy, Anna."

I nod again. I won't make that mistake twice.

"Now I have no prospects at all," I say. If the king truly was part of the plot to end the match, to get Percy married to Talbot's daughter, let him feel a little remorse.

"None?"

"Because of the Percy scandal, the man to whom I was betrothed now shuns me. And no one else is interested."

"The poet Wyatt seems to be."

There is nothing childlike in his face now.

"He's married."

"That's hardly an impediment to true affection."

"It seems to me," I say pointedly, "that the outcome is always the same. At the end, the woman is left with a tattered reputation, no self-esteem, and the label of a whore."

He frowns and inspects the contents of his goblet. I stare at his lowered brow, holding my breath.

"You certainly speak your mind. I wonder"—he looks up at me again, and I see shame on his face—"what is your opinion of me?"

"You certainly ask direct questions."

"I wish to know the answer, Anna. I see no reason to beat around the bush. You are the only person who has ever spoken

to me as if I am a man as well as a king. Flawed, but by things that can be rectified. I cherish your words even when they run counter to my own thoughts. And I love to hear your voice." He takes a step toward me, and all the air is sucked from the room.

I see the man—my body makes this embarrassingly clear. But I am also painfully aware of the power embodied in him.

"I think you are a great king," I stammer. "A humanist and a patron of the arts."

"Enough flattery." He fixes his gaze on mine. "What do you really think?"

I take a deep breath that fills me with elation and terror in equal measure. He's given me license to speak my mind. Without censure.

"I think you treated my sister as if she were disposable. As if she didn't have feelings of her own. I think you rushed to war with the French over a flimsy excuse, to prove your might and masculinity. I think you wield the fear people have of you like a sword. And that you are blind to the feelings of those around you."

King Henry's face darkens. His eyes narrow. The vibrations of his energy increase in speed as if tuned to a higher pitch. A long, sharp note.

I have gone too far.

He twists a ring on his right hand. My ring. I stare at it, sure he'll take it off. Throw it at me. Send me back to the beginning. To where I came from. To Father. To nothing.

Then he sighs.

"I regret any pain I caused your sister. She is a sweet girl, and

beautiful. But not someone who is truly my match. I thought it better to cut our bonds now, rather than extend the pain later."

I say nothing, pegged still by his nearness, by his response, by his confession.

"I have no remorse over my war with the French, for they are a constant threat. But I can tell you now that you were right: women can make formidable foes. And I have ceased my crusade against them."

He looks at me, his gaze clear and direct.

He said I was right. My words made an impact. Or at least an impression. He has stopped the war. Just as I suggested so long ago.

My words have power. My opinions were correct.

"So it was not God's will."

I will push him to the brink of detonation. He doesn't speak, so I press on. If this is the man I am to choose over Thomas Wyatt, he has to know who I am. My heartbreak has made me reckless.

"It was a waste."

His gaze will not let me go.

"This sword of fear you say I wield," he says. "It does not seem to affect you."

I am afraid. Only my tongue is not.

"I have but a little neck," I tell the king. "It will not hurt if the blow comes clean."

He suddenly crosses the distance between us in two strides. His movement makes my heart flutter in panic. His nearness turns it to liquid ready to boil.

425

The scent of cloves and orange water fills my senses. And something else. Earthy and animal, like ambergris. Wild. I have to lay my hand on the table to steady myself. Everything I ever wanted is right here before me. Everything but one thing.

"I believe I am blind to nothing," he murmurs, the words fragrant and honeyed. "Especially not the feelings of others."

He takes one more step forward and moves to kiss me.

"You already have a wife," I say as fast as I can before his lips touch mine and everything is lost. "And I will not be your mistress."

"You are very sure about that."

He is close. Too close. He doesn't move away. I can almost taste his lips from here.

"All my life I have been shipped and trundled and bought and sold by my father. I want to be mine. I don't want to be a mistress, Your Majesty, because a mistress is not a person, but a thing. Worse than that. Nothing. I don't want to be nothing."

I watch him for a long, slow moment, and he studies me. Cautiously.

"You are not a possession, Anna. Not a *thing*. And you could never be nothing."

"Exactly, Your Majesty," I say. Soaring, untethered by the knowledge that he understands. "I will never be anyone's mistress. Ever."

"Then there is no hope for Thomas Wyatt, is there?"

The sound of his name makes me want to sink to the floor

in defeat. But I manage to keep my limbs stable, to keep my feet under me. I look the king directly in the eye. And shake my head.

"Good." The king erupts into that devastating smile that first caught me at the age of thirteen and refused to let go. "I will ever live in hope, Mistress Boleyn. Hope that you will never be a mistress. But a partner. A friend."

"My brother says that men and women can't be friends."

"Well, let's see if we can prove him wrong, shall we?"

He extends his hand, to escort me back to the door.

"What seems impossible is not always so, I have found," he says slowly. "The sun can turn dark in the sky. The flat earth is actually round." He stops. Turns to me. "A commoner may marry a king." He pauses. "My grandmother was the daughter of a 'new man.'"

A tingling buzz spreads up my arms and into my scalp, sending my thoughts scattering like wisps on the wind. I catch hold of one. "Your grandmother was related to the courts of Europe."

He chuckles. "Distantly. My grandfather married her for love, not connections."

"What are you saying?" I manage to whisper through the howl of my thoughts. I can't take my eyes off of him.

"Only that there are more ways than one around a problem. And that there is always hope."

My mind retraces all the steps of the conversation, lurching from one point to the next, throwing each one down so I don't expect too much. I tell myself all the lies I need to hear. He's

flirting with me. Pursuing me. Just like Wyatt used to with his offers to make me his mistress.

The king's eyes are once more like a child's. Buoyant. He's offering friendship. Nothing else.

"A kiss, Anna?" he asks. "Just this once."

I lift my chin, tilt my cheek to offer it. But he kisses me full on the mouth, warm and strong and sweet.

And wild.

It is not a friendly kiss at all.

And I like it.

66

ON THE MORNING OF THE CREATION CEREMONY, THE SUN RISES quickly into the white of the sky and the world is drenched in lemon. The flavor of the air changes the higher the sun rises, from citrus to rose to claret, and the sultriness submerges us as the court makes its way to the king's chambers.

My father has had me dressed head to foot in finery— my gown, my sleeves, my hood decked with jewels and gold embroidery. And my *B* strung from its chain of pearls. *B* for *belonging*.

I want this. The elevation. The ceremony. The belonging.

The king.

The sun comes hot through the windows, the room awash in gold and silk. I am surrounded by the press and stench of perfume, the musk of ambition.

"Make way!"

Three ushers abreast, arms interlinked, push their way through the crowd. I am stuffed beside Lady Kildare and Lady Arundel. Pushed back against the men behind us, solid as a wall. I step on a wide-toed boot and turn to its owner.

Henry Percy. My skin threatens to crawl off my bones to escape even the possibility of touch, my spine prickling with revulsion. For him. For myself. One wrong choice. I press down the fear that I might make another.

His face betrays nothing.

A blast of trumpets signals the beginning of the ceremony. The Earl of Northumberland, swathed in superiority and ceremony, enters, carrying a sword before him. A herald bears the new coat of arms. And next comes a little boy, flanked by the earls of Arundel and Oxford, shining like a newly minted coin, cast in the mold of his father.

The Countess of Arundel mutters, "Two earls and a bastard."

I hold myself still. Tell myself I won't react. Won't respond. Won't say a word.

Then I take a deep breath and turn on Lady Arundel.

"Two earls and a *prince*, your ladyship."

She purses her already thin lips until they disappear. "And what right have you to an opinion, *Mistress* Boleyn? What right have you even to be here?"

I look at her, knowing I shouldn't say what I'm about to.

"I received a personal invitation from the king."

The words are just too sweet.

I look to the dais, where he sits. Where the little boy shines, the king is positively radiant. Dressed in red and gold, he is my memory made manifest, the embodiment of all I ever wished for. And I am here at his request.

The cardinal, Wolsey, stands on his right, the two dukes on his left. But he dwarfs them all. For the rest of the ceremony, its parade of pomp and cloth of gold, I can't take my eyes off him.

Little Fitzroy is granted the title of his grandfather, Duke of

Richmond, and the title of the Duke of Somerset, the earldom of which had belonged to the boy's great-great-grandfather, himself the illegitimate son of royalty. Fitzroy's grandfather became Henry VII. I'm sure the entire world wonders if this little boy will become Henry IX. Princess Mary is the king's only legitimate child and therefore his heir. But these men don't want a girl on the throne. Rumor has it that Queen Katherine has gone through the change and will now never have sons. So the court—and the king– may be seeking other options.

He needs a legitimate son. She can no longer have children. He has good reason to wish to replace the queen. *A commoner may marry a king.* I tell myself it's impossible, but his words beat against the back of my mind like the tide: *what seems impossible is not always so.*

The list of elevations grows long, and the number of peers increases. The king honors each new peer with a word, a glance, a smile. Each man takes a turn as the center of attention, the heart around which the world revolves.

I allow myself to imagine, for a moment, what it might be like to be that heart forever.

Finally, my father stands before the king, kneels, and is given a blessing. Raised from nothing. The Boleyns, sons of merchants and mayors, commoners, but not common.

The king looks out at the crowd over my father's head and finds me immediately, following the line of tension between us. It resonates through me. I cannot look away.

When the ceremony is over, the crowd spills out into the garden and courtyards, finally able to move and breathe. I find

myself in the outer court, baking and breathless beneath the midday sun.

Face to face with the Duchess of Suffolk.

"You're here," she says, looking me up and down over the bridge of her nose. She knows. Somehow, she knows.

She holds a tiny boy by the hand. Her three-year-old son has been made the Earl of Lincoln today.

"Well?" she snaps. "Do you not honor the new earl?"

I curtsy to the little boy, who looks about to cry.

When I rise, I match the duchess's level gaze.

"Only an earl, Your Grace?" I ask, delirious with the pleasure of watching her pout.

She flounces away, dragging the boy behind her, his thumb in his mouth.

The king and his son enter the courtyard. They greet the new peers one at a time, following courtly rules, following precedence. After each greeting, the king scans the crowd and finds me. Every time. Acknowledging me. Wanting me.

Fitzroy is starting to droop, his face flushed, his eyes heavy. But he maintains an air of strength and control, despite his age, despite the heat.

He might actually make a good king.

"Mistress Boleyn," the king says, as his son arrives at my skirts. "May I introduce the Duke of Richmond and Somerset."

I curtsy deeply, my head almost at the height of the boy himself.

"Your Grace," I murmur, look into his face, and wink.

Little Henry Fitzroy grins back, and squinches up his face in an attempt to wink as well. Then we both giggle.

"Will you be attending the banquet and dancing later this evening?" the boy asks, standing to his full height, which is still just level with my midriff.

"Yes, Your Grace."

"Will you do me the honor of a dance?"

I like this boy. Almost as much as his father.

"Yes, of course, Your Grace."

He bows and I curtsy again. When I rise, I risk a glance at the king's face. His smile creases deep into his cheeks, his eyes alive with it. The hum starts to throb within me, and I take a deep breath, catching a whiff of cloves.

"Dare I exploit your generosity by requesting a dance, as well?" the king asks. He watches my every move.

"It would be an honor, Your Majesty."

He leans over his son so he can whisper to me out of the boy's hearing. "The honor to touch you will be all mine."

I am submersed in a premonition of that touch sparking like fireworks on my skin. I fall into a curtsy to hide my expression or to hide from his. I rise when he moves on to show off his son to yet another group of courtiers. He turns once to look over his shoulder at me.

And to wink.

"You've done it, Anne." George takes my arm, squeezes it, and swiftly kisses my cheek. "You are the clever one."

I look at him over my shoulder. I don't smell wine on his breath.

"Aren't you lucky to be related to me, then?"

He grins, but there is sadness in the corners of his eyes.

"I always have been, Sister."

"As have I."

The white flags are raised. For now.

"I have something for you."

"A gift?"

"Yes, but not from me. Even I don't change that quickly."

He presses a little package into my hand.

"It's from Wyatt."

I look away, across the courtyard to where the glass shines flat like eyes.

"I almost didn't give it to you."

When I turn back to him, George seems vulnerable, beseeching.

"I hope I did the right thing."

I nod, but cannot answer.

I find a corner beneath the all-seeing windows and open the parchment. Inside is my jewel, the bright golden *A*, the single pearl. The ribbon is gone. Instead, around it is a poem:

> *Whoso list to hunt? I know where is an hind!*
> *But as for me, alas! I may no more.*
> *The vain travail hath wearied me so sore;*
> *I am of them that furthest come behind.*
> *Yet may I by no means my wearied mind*
> *Draw from the deer; but as she fleeth afore*
> *Fainting I follow. I leave off therefore*

Since in a net I seek to hold the wind.
Who list her hunt, I put him out of doubt
As well as I, may spend his time in vain.
And graven with diamonds in letters plain,
There is written, her fair neck round about:
"Noli me tangere; for Caesar's I am,
And wild for to hold, though I seem tame."

I look for him, to tell him I am no one's but mine. Not his. Not Caesar's. I look to argue with him. To kiss him. To run away with him.

But he's nowhere to be seen.

He left me. My palms begin to sweat and I have to grip the paper between my fingers to keep them still.

No.

I fold the poem deliberately, paying careful attention to every crease until my heart resumes a steady beat.

He let me go.

A trumpet blasts. The king stands at the bottom of the processional stair, his son beside him. The entire court descends into a hot, heavy hush.

"Please accompany me into the great hall," he says. "We will celebrate this day with feasting." His eyes find me. "And dancing."

The crowd murmurs, a sound heavier than the buzzing of bees in the roses.

He extends his hand to the queen but watches me all the while.

Queen Katherine cannot begin to smile. She refuses to look the little duke in the eye when she passes him. She is here under duress.

Owned.

By him.

I hesitate, watching the guests scramble to queue according to precedence. None of them notices when the king winks at me again.

"Come, Sister." George is at my side, offering his hand. "Shall we embark on the future?" In his face, I see a glimmer of my childhood familiar. The one who challenged me to climb the highest, because he knew I could.

I look once more around the emptying courtyard. The shadows from the palace walls have just begun to nip at our feet. I step away from them and slip the poem and my jewel into the little pocket at my waist.

"Together," I say.

Hand in hand, we climb the processional stair, rising in the celebratory uproar of a capricious court. As we enter the palace, we are blinded by the ascent from sunshine into darkness.

Author's Note

A considerable amount of research goes into any work of historical fiction, and I am indebted to the writings of the multitude of historians who devote their time and their passion to discovering the truths of history and making the past come alive in the retelling. Particular thanks are due here to Julia Fox, Antonia Fraser, Eric Ives, David Loades, Claire Ridgway, Nicola Shulman, David Starkey, Simon Thurley, Retha Warnicke, Alison Weir, and Josephine Wilkinson.

The facts about Anne Boleyn's early life are sketchy at best. There isn't consensus among historians even about the year of her birth. Strong evidence presented by Hugh Paget in 1981 suggests that she was born in 1500 or 1501. Most modern historians accept this date. However, a marginal comment in a seventeenth-century biography of Anne's daughter, Elizabeth I, suggests Anne was born in 1507. This theory is supported in detail by Retha Warnicke in her biography *The Rise and Fall of Anne Boleyn*. Because I wanted to write a book about a teenage girl who returns to a "home" that is patently not her own, I

chose the latter date. I don't necessarily think it is more likely, but it serves my purpose best. I am, after all, a writer of fiction. Though I am committed to historical accuracy in my novels, to me, the story matters most, and I will leave the debate to the experts.

We know that Anne participated in the pageant of *The Château Vert* at Shrovetide in 1522, performing the part of Perseverance—a name that ultimately describes her well. I suggest that Anne is sent to Hever in disgrace after the pageant, but because she disappears from the accurately dated historical record for a while, there is no evidence to support or contradict this.

There is evidence that Anne formed an attachment to Henry Percy, the eldest son of the Earl of Northumberland, during the spring of 1523. In fact, Percy was interrogated twice about this relationship—it would have been an impediment to Henry and Anne's marriage, but it also might have provided grounds for divorce when things went sour. Both times, Percy swore upon the Bible that there had been no precontract, no betrothal, no attachment. Do we believe him?

During the reign of Katherine of Aragon's daughter, Mary I (who temporarily was made illegitimate when Henry declared his marriage to Katherine invalid and subsequently married Anne), several stories were written defaming Anne Boleyn as promiscuous and possibly a poisoner. One story involved Thomas Wyatt and a visit to Hever during which he spent the night in her bedroom. Another tells how Henry interrogated Wyatt, who admitted to a relationship with Anne, which the king told him to keep quiet. These stories could be hearsay—invented by Mary's supporters, who would naturally want to depict Anne and her daughter, Elizabeth, negatively. I have my doubts about the truth of these stories—their intention was slander—but found the concept interesting.

Anne's detractors also made much of any perceived physical imperfections. Though I don't believe the myth that Anne had a sixth finger, I give a basis for the invention of one by creating a minor deformity caused by a childhood accident.

Thomas Wyatt's grandson George wrote a biography of Anne Boleyn as a rebuttal of her detractors. In it, he describes an argument between the king and Wyatt over a game of bowls during which both men produced little trinkets belonging to Anne Boleyn. George Wyatt's tale was written decades after Anne's death and, again, the accuracy is questionable—it was probably passed to him verbally by Thomas himself. If my version is slightly different from his, couldn't it be because a poet would want to present himself in the best possible light—and his rival in the worst?

No one knows the exact timing of the beginning of Henry's interest in Anne. Some place it as early as *The Château Vert* in 1522. Others speculate that Henry's displaying the motto "Declare I Dare Not" at a joust in 1526, proves that was the beginning. And still others trace it to 1527, when they think they can date his first love letters to her. David Starkey, in *Six Wives: The Queens of Henry VIII*, suggested *The Castle of Loyalty* and Christmas 1524, and I have gone with that. I shortened the time line and slightly altered the chronicle of the pageant

Thank you. To Bret Ballou, for well-timed texts and e-mails and for being the closer. To Donna Cooner for seeing the point and offering distraction. To Veronica Rossi for a fabulous title and late-night chats, and for saying you love my "wicked words." To Talia Vance for loving Thomas Wyatt as much as I did, even before there were kissing scenes. And to the rest of my honored and trusted confederacy of beta readers: Jackie Garlick, Kristen Held, and Beth Hull. And thank you to the Class of 2k12 for picking me up when I fell down and for creative curse words that made me wish I wrote contemporary novels so I could use them in my work.

Like people, every book has a family. *Tarnish* wouldn't exist without my agent, Catherine Drayton, who asked if I could write more than one novel set in the court of Henry VIII and then made it happen. Thank you, as well, to Lyndsey Blessing, for taking my books abroad and to Lizzy Kremer for being their advocate in the UK.

From day one, the team at Viking and Penguin Young Readers have been enthusiastic champions of my work. Special thanks go to Joanna Cardenas for perceptive comments at a crucial time, to Theresa Evangelista for a stunning cover and Kate Renner for an equally gorgeous interior. I must thank Janet Pascal and Kathryn Hinds a thousand times for checking my continuity and accuracy and for correcting my punctuation—a vexatious job, I'm sure, but I am ever so grateful. And to Marisa Russell and all of the Penguin marketing and publicity family, thank you for holding *Tarnish* up to catch the light.

Writing a book is a solitary endeavor, but revising it is a team effort. You can't always see how a sibling helps shape your life, but I can see on every page of this book how my editor's gentle touch and keen eye added structure, emotion, and depth. Thank you, Kendra Levin, for everything.

And finally—but most importantly—thank *you*. A novel needs a family of readers to have life, so thank you for being a part of Anne's.